IMPOSTOR
IN CHIEF

To Helen,

..May thanks for your support

All the wishes

Freddie P. Peters x

Also by Freddie P. Peters:

In the HENRY CROWNE PAYING THE PRICE series
INSURGENT
COLLAP$E
BREAKING PO!NT
NO TURNING BACK
SPY SHADOWS
HENRY CROWNE PAYING THE PRICE BOOKS 1-3

In the NANCY WU CRIME THRILLER series
BLOOD DRAGON

Dear Reader,

I'm thrilled you've chosen IMPOSTER IN CHIEF, Book 5 in the
HENRY CROWNE PAYING THE PRICE series.

Think about getting access for FREE to the exclusive Prequel to the
HENRY CROWNE PAYING THE PRICE series: INSURGENT.

Go to freddieppeters.com/impostor-in-chief

IMPOSTOR IN CHIEF

FREDDIE P. PETERS

HENRY CROWNE PAYING THE PRICE BOOK 5

Chapter One

There was no cry. Just the sound of an object falling through the air and the distinct crushing noise that a body makes upon impact.

Henry jerked his head up from his newspaper, witnessing the latter part of the fall. The body bounced once and didn't move after that. The calm inside the atrium that Henry had settled in whilst waiting for his Washington DC contact was ripped apart by the shockwave.

Two women who had just walked in screamed; one of them dropped the large milkshake she was holding. The young man who was manning the Benugo coffee shop inside the reception area rushed towards the body lying on the floor.

Henry stood up. His contact was nowhere to be seen and he couldn't wait any longer. Soon, the place would be teeming with police.

He had seen too many dead bodies during his last assignment to be shocked by the sight of one corpse. And yet, in the middle of Washington, inside this pristine office building, death felt more shocking than he cared to admit.

Henry dropped the paper on the large coffee table in front of him and made his way to where the body had landed. Bystanders had gathered around it, both drawn and repelled by the sight.

He moved behind the two women who had first noticed the fallen man. One of them had started to cry softly, her shoulders moving up in small jumps. The other was on her mobile calling emergency 911.

The man had fallen from a height backwards, it seemed. One of his legs was folded in an unnatural position underneath his body, no doubt broken by the impact. The dark pool of blood that was collecting

1

at the back of his head looked ominous. There was no chance the man was still alive.

The dead man was facing the other way. Henry could only see his chestnut hair – a little too long perhaps. The body was tall, with an athletic build. The man on the floor looked familiar to him. Henry took a step back, then stepped in again, forcing himself to look for clues without checking the man's face.

The man's tie that had followed him down was now draped over the side of his neck and his left shoulder. Part of the navy-blue tie with a light pink stripe was already soaked in blood and Henry froze. These were the unmistakable colours of one of the Cambridge colleges, Churchill College.

His jaw clenched. He had to be sure.

Henry slowly circled the group of people who had gathered around and glanced briefly at the dead man's face. His blue eyes were still open. A lifeless stare had replaced the calm expression Henry had learnt to appreciate.

Rush Huckerby, his CIA contact in DC, could no longer tell him why he'd wanted Henry to meet him so urgently.

Henry's stomach churned. He swallowed down the bile he felt rising up. He stepped back from the scene and slowly moved towards the large sliding doors.

The shrieks from an ambulance outside burst into the atrium as the automatic doors opened to let Henry out. Two paramedics had already stepped out from the vehicle and were running towards the opened doors. Henry moved sideways to let them through.

There was no point in waiting to hear the outcome. Rush Huckerby was dead and someone had pushed him to his death.

Henry stepped out onto D St NW and turned the corner onto 6th. A couple of police cars had arrived, and the buzz of the officers' radios crackled in the air. Henry kept going without looking back.

The wind had picked up along the streets Henry had become familiar with, but the weather was still pleasant enough that he didn't need his coat. He accelerated his pace, his winter coat across his arm, as the gusts turned rapidly colder. The image of Rush's lifeless face kept flashing in front of his eyes.

Henry's last MI6 assignment in the Middle East had exposed him to unimaginable violence and gruesome death. He would never forget the moment he first entered the city of Mosul in Iraq...

Henry shook his head to dispel the frightful memory.

But he also reminded himself of the positive results his assignment had yielded – a targeted operation, code name SHADER. The systematic bombing campaign of Islamic State positions and oil production sites in Syria and Iraq had shaken IS's hold. IS was finally losing money and territory in these countries.

Henry hailed a cab and made his way back to his apartment. His meeting with Huckerby had been planned for the end of the working day. They had agreed to a drink in exchange for an important Human Intelligence download, the content of which Huckerby had refused to speak about over the phone. But instead, Huckerby would now be finishing the day on an autopsy slab.

He had the cab stop before it reached Logan Circle – part of a trailing countermeasure habit he followed wherever he went. Today was certainly no exception, and of utmost importance that he followed it on his way home.

Out of the cab, Henry retraced his steps, moving back in the original direction the cab had come from. He crossed the street against incoming traffic, turned right and right again, until he arrived back on the same street, only a block away from his starting point.

Henry stopped at a grocery store to pick up a few essentials. From there, he used a back exit that few people knew about but that the owner did not seem to mind him using. Satisfied he had not been followed, he made his way to 1308A Rhode Island Avenue.

Henry reached a red brick building a few moments later and climbed a set of white stone steps. The main door and its glass surround were guarded by two Corinthian half-colonnades either side, painted black. The glass made it easy for him to see who was standing in the hallway.

Remembering something he'd noticed when he'd first moved in, Henry took his keys out and got inside quickly. He looked back at the glass of the entrance door he knew to be bulletproof.

He walked straight to the lift, got in and exited on the second floor. He dropped his bag of groceries to the floor outside his apartment door and turned the key slowly. The piece of paper he'd stuck inside the door frame when he'd left that morning fluttered to the floor – an old-fashioned but effective trick of the spy trade. He was sure at least of one thing: no one had entered through the door.

Still, he proceeded with caution, opening the door gently and listening out for signs of trouble. Everything was quiet in the apartment. He waited a moment, walked in, and shut the door behind him.

Henry moved to the large open-plan kitchen. He chucked his coat next on the counter and moved through the rest of the apartment – two bedrooms and bathrooms – alert and methodically.

The place was secure, and Henry relaxed a little.

He moved back to the lounge, shifted the coffee table to one side, rolled back the large, silk rug he had bought on his travels in Europe and started pressing on the floorboards. He pushed harder on two of the large boards; they gave way with a mechanical click.

A panel opened, and when Henry placed his right palm over it, the panel asked for a sequence of numbers and characters. Henry entered the 17-digit passcode. A different panel opened with barely a sound to reveal a safe. He retrieved a laptop from it and carried it to the kitchen. There, he began the lengthy process of logging in.

Henry filled the kettle and switched it on. After what he'd just seen, he needed a good cup of tea – a remedy for all ills, according to the British. His Northern Irish father would have preferred something harder, but Henry had yet to locate a place that served decent Guinness. Tea would have to do.

He smiled sadly at the thought. His old life in London felt so far away.

* * *

Harris got out of bed as soon as his mobile vibrated. He had joined his wife, the most patient Sarah, shortly after midnight and kissed her shoulder gently to avoid waking her up. Harris had fallen asleep almost instantly.

Now, he moved quietly to the corridor to avoid waking her.

"What's up?" Harris stifled a yawn.

"Huckerby is dead." Henry Crowne's voice was low and tense.

"You mean...?" Harris mumbled, still emerging from the fog of sleep.

"Which part of dead don't you understand, Harris? No longer alive, deceased."

"I get it," Harris said. "It's after midnight in London. What happened?"

"He fell from the top floor of his office block, landed in the atrium... and I don't believe it was suicide."

"Why were you meeting him so soon? I thought the next meet was scheduled for a week's time."

"He sent me an urgent request this morning through the emergency channel."

"Did you see him fall?" Harris asked calmly.

"I was sitting in the reception area at the time."

"Shit..." Harris crept downstairs to the kitchen to make a cup of tea. "I'd be surprised if it was a coincidence that you were there at the time."

"You mean someone suspected Huckerby and wanted to give a message to whoever Huckerby was meeting?"

"Possibly... even probably... Listen, Henry, you follow his lead you go the same way." Harris squeezed his mobile between ear and shoulder, opening a series of cupboards to fetch the tea caddy and a mug. "I presume you checked you were not being followed?" he added.

"Really, Harris, who do you think I am? If I can survive infiltrating the Islamic State, I can survive this assignment too. And to answer your question, no, I was not followed."

"It doesn't mean you are in the clear though. You might have been followed in the few days prior."

Harris pushed his MI6 asset hard for a reason. True, Henry Crowne, former banker and financier to a terrorist organisation, had been an exceptional recruit, but complacency was dangerous in the opaque world of espionage.

"I use countermeasures every day, but I take your point. They, whoever they are, may have been better at it than me – as surprising as it sounds."

"Remember, unlike with the Middle Eastern operation, you're flying solo here. It pays to go the extra mile and assume the worst."

Harris poured tea into a large mug without making too much of a mess. He took a sip and grimaced... too hot. He added some more milk and stirred his tea.

"So, what now?" Crowne asked. "Huckerby was supposed to meet the target next week to organise my introduction as financial adviser and fixer."

"I'm aware..." Harris took another sip of tea and sighed – much better. "I need to think. Rush did well in promoting you as someone who could help the target in opaque situations. I'll contact you again before midnight East, your time."

Harris heard grumbling on the other end of the line and smiled. Crowne hated not being in control, but for once he would have to be patient.

He killed the call and opened his laptop. The protracted login process gave him time to finish his tea... he felt like a new man as he put his cup down.

The joint CIA-MI6 operation he was running looked like a standard identification and infiltration op when he'd proposed the idea to his friend and CIA counterpart, Jack Shield. Huckerby was to be used for the identification part, Crowne for the infiltration one. Steve and Jack were happy to co-head the op. It wasn't the first time they'd worked together sharing assets to achieve their goal.

Steve had gone on a hunch that was supported by more intelligence pouring into GCHQ in the UK. Russia appeared to be pushing hard to recruit, or at least ingratiate itself with several highly successful businessmen and politicians in the West. The Cold War had been over for almost 25 years, but relationships between the free world and the not-so-free world in the East had been deteriorating for some time.

Crowne had protested at the idea of being pulled from the Middle East to be placed in a much more secure location like the US. That meant he would have to work with the CIA. Henry Crowne preferred to do things his own way. The fewer people looking over his shoulder the better.

But Harris had promptly reminded Henry of the lethal tricks Russia was willing to use. The poisoning of Litvinenko in 2006, and more recently the invasion of Crimea in 2014, were stark reminders of how far they were prepared to push. The West was still struggling to respond to the annexation of parts of Ukraine by the Russian Federation, let alone find a way to restore Crimea to its rightful owner.

Harris's long-term involvement in operations in the Middle East as an MI6 intelligence officer had taught him a few things. One of them was that nothing was ever as it seemed. The West's efforts to crush terrorism had perhaps resulted in his scepticism. They had, he thought, focused far too long on the region.

The West was understandably focused on a real danger that risked lives in Europe. The desire to defeat terrorism in the UK and abroad was politically and humanly strong but it meant that other key world powers such as China or Russia had been let loose, or at least looser than they perhaps should have been.

Harris called up on screen the file he was looking for: Operation RUSSKY BEAR.

He had managed to get a small team together and agree a budget before the last MI6 chief, Sir John Sawers, had retired. The new incumbent seemed less interested in the operation, but since it was already happening, he was happy for Harris to carry on – within reason.

Harris was on his own for now, until he could find some meaty piece of intel to serve up to the new chief, and this is what he intended to do. But so far nothing of value had surfaced – that was until this morning. The sudden death of Huckerby, a valuable CIA asset, had just cast a long shadow on the operation, but it also vindicated the need for it.

Harris read the CV for Rush Huckerby that Jack Shield had sent over to him. Huckerby had worked for almost five years in a small but high-profile Washington DC boutique finance firm. Top Capital Partners LLC specialised in providing cash to businesses in countries that were not always able to attract large international banks, due to extensive fraud check requirements. Top Capital intermediated and offered advice on ways to present a more favourable dossier, greatly reducing the likelihood of rejection. Top Capital also had a lobbying department, and an impressive list of contacts on both sides of the political divide.

Harris kept browsing the file on Huckerby. There was nothing about his job that made him vulnerable, and nothing that turned him into a suspicious character. Perhaps, the young recruit had stumbled upon something a little too hot to handle.

Harris poured himself another cup of tea and dialled Jack Shield's number in Washington DC on a secure internet connection.

Jack's face appeared on the screen, a deep frown across his brow.

"What's up Stevie? It's almost 1am in London where you are."

"I've just spoken to my operative in DC... There's no easy way to say this." Harris cleared his throat. "Someone killed Rush Huckerby."

Henry watched the street below from his apartment's three giant windows that made up the rounded part of the building's facade. The trees that provided leafy coverage in the summer and autumn were now bare. Henry leaned to the left. He could almost see the end of the street that connected to Logan Circle.

The streetlamps were on, providing enough light to spot movement on his street and around his building. A few cars drove past. His neighbour in the apartment opposite his had just arrived home, dropped off by a cab that did not linger. Henry stayed at the windows for a while. He moved to the right window and leaned against the wall, still seeing nothing.

Satisfied he could not detect any immediate threat, Henry returned to the laptop he had used to call Harris in London. He sieved through his notes, reading some parts aloud, hoping the sound of his voice might bring some clarity to the situation.

The information was all very predictable. In a previous life, Henry had been a brilliant financier in charge of a high-profile team in London. He had conceived and delivered some of the largest deals ever put together in investment banking, and had happily collected the astronomical fees that went with these.

Nothing much impressed Henry in the world of finance anymore, and certainly not Top Capital Partners the outfit Rush Huckerby had been working for. It organised funding for companies, preferably large and desperate, that needed to clinch a deal in parts of the world where a deal went hand-in-hand with bribery.

Henry smiled at what young Huckerby had reported thus far. He'd been perhaps a little naive, or maybe he was simply being honest. Huckerby had reported on the regular use of Panama and other such tax havens to route cash that financed some of the deals Top Capital had put together. Henry had nodded and absorbed the information without comment.

He too knew a thing or two about Panama. Henry had been instrumental in setting up a complex fund structure through which the IRA had, for many years, laundered their dirty money.

Henry inhaled deeply. The memories of how his past life had sucked him to the bottom of a deep and murky pool were still raw.

He returned to the notes he'd taken after each meeting with

Huckerby, and wondered whether Top Capital's activities amounted to the same thing: money laundering for organised crime syndicates, or perhaps Narcos.

If Huckerby had threatened the processes put in place to shift money around the world, the syndicates would have dealt with him swiftly and mercilessly. Perhaps, Harris and Jack Shield were barking up the wrong tree by looking at Top Capital.

Despite his youth, Huckerby had been smart and thorough, and he'd known exactly what he'd been looking for at Top Capital – evidence Russia was on a recruitment spree.

It was past 9pm, and Henry was only halfway through his notes. He stretched and yawned. Time to rustle up something to eat.

Henry moved to the open-plan kitchen, with its stylish, long worktop made of black Marmo Grigio, supported by large wood panels that had been painted duck-egg blue.

Henry remembered he had left the grocery at the door when he had walked in his apartment a couple of hours ago. He was on his way to collect the bag of food when a faint noise attracted his attention.

A soft metallic sound was coming from the hallway.

Henry moved slowly towards the entrance and froze.

Someone was trying to get into his apartment

* * *

On screen, Jack's eyes closed for a moment. When he opened them again, his expression had lost all its usual amiability.

"I need to speak to you from another desk." Without waiting for a reply, Jack hung up.

Harris waited for a fresh call to come through. The call came through on his laptop and Jack's face appeared on screen again.

"How do you know?" Jack asked.

"Crowne was meeting him late afternoon, in DC. He saw him fall."

"Did he see anything else?"

"Sadly, no... but at least Crowne is back at his apartment, safe."

Jack shook his head. "I didn't see it coming, Steve."

"None of us did."

Jack fell silent. He crossed his hands and stuck his elbows on the desk. He rested his forehead on them for a moment.

"You know what this means." Jack looked up.

Harris heard the strain in his voice. It was always hard to keep going after a loss like this.

"Yes. Crowne is going to miss the appointment with the target, David Upstage."

"We only have a week to find a replacement for Huckerby..." Jack's voice trailed off.

Harris took over. "And embed someone good enough and credible enough who can impress Upstage." He understood what Jack was going through. The loss of a contact was a big deal.

"Top Capital will be looking to replace Huckerby as we speak. I very much doubt they waited for the gurney to leave the building before they called their head-hunters."

"Even if they have, it will still take a few weeks to find the right candidate." Jack exhaled slowly.

Harris thought of something. "Forget about trying to replace Huckerby though the official channels... Top Capital will only pick someone they know. I suggest we introduce them to a man who fits their requirements – a person who can impress their best and most formidable client but someone they won't need to recruit. It'll be much easier to use Crowne directly, even if they've lost Huckerby to intermediate between Crowne and Upstage."

"I get it... A financier who understands how to deal with dirty money and has proven he is better than anyone at shifting it." Jack stopped and almost managed a smile.

"Exactly right." Harris nodded "Henry Crowne has just been promoted to direct contact with our billionaire target, David Upstage, and his legend and cover-up are fully activated... Now enters Henry Newborn, financial terrorist with an exceptional reputation."

10

Chapter Two

The low rattling sound had stopped. Henry wondered if it had been his imagination playing tricks – it *had* been a shocking day. But then, the sound of metal on metal started again, more insistent this time.

Henry returned to his laptop. He called up one of the surveillance applications he had installed on his computer. It relayed live images captured on the infinitely small but highly effective camera Henry had placed above the door to his apartment.

The image came up on screen instantly. The young man who occupied the apartment below was trying to get into Henry's apartment. It was not the first time Henry had met him in the main entrance, reeking of alcohol and hardly able to walk. Hunched against the door frame, the young man was trying but failing to insert his key into the lock. Henry grumbled an insult. He stood up to open the door and give him a piece of his mind, but thought better of it. He waited for a short moment, observing the man's actions.

The fumbling stopped. The man's inebriated stance morphed into an unexpected alertness. His gestures became precise as he dumped the ineffective key into his trouser pocket and retrieved a small compact multi-tool kit.

"Little fucker..."

Henry moved to the hallway. The door's top lock had just been unscrewed and the man was now working on the central lock.

Henry looked around for a weapon. Harris had advised him against getting a gun, even though Henry had thought it ludicrous not to have one in a country that ranked number one for civilian-held firearms per capita. He might have to revisit the issue sooner rather than later.

Henry raced into the kitchen, grabbed one of the larger knives from the block on his kitchen counter and returned to the door. He held the knife the way he had been taught for hand-to-hand combat – weapon held diagonally, blade forward. The forward grip offered much better thrusting capability and was a favoured angle for a classic throat-cutting attack.

The main lock gave way just as Henry positioned himself behind the door.

The intruder pushed it half open cautiously, his fingers clutching the frame for balance. As soon as his head came through the door, Henry slammed it shut, catching the man in a swift and lethal notion. The intruder shrieked in pain.

Henry swooped in and grabbed his hair, dragging him into the apartment and smashing him into the door. He pressed the knife against his throat.

"You make a noise and I slice your throat open... You get me?"

The young man tried to nod, but Henry's hard grip was pulling his head back too far. The man whimpered instead.

Henry let go and moved in from behind, controlling the man with an arm lock, knife still against his neck.

"Move."

Henry shoved the intruder towards the lounge. He expected more resistance from a trained operative, or perhaps the attack would come any minute now. Henry wouldn't give him the chance.

As soon as they arrived in the middle of the room, Henry slammed the handle of the knife on the intruder's neck, just below the skull. The man fell to the ground, unconscious.

* * *

The privacy pod Jack had used to call Harris from was needed for an urgent call, but he allowed himself a few more minutes. He had not lost an asset for a very long time, and never on US soil.

His boss at Langley, Robert (Bob) Hunter III, had given Operation RUSSKY BEAR a lukewarm reception. His attention was still on the Middle East, and more recently it had turned to China. Ukraine's Crimea woes seemed to have been de-prioritised if not forgotten, much to Jack's annoyance. Russia's actions should never be taken lightly. The threat may no longer be communism, but Russia had become a kleptocracy, in Jack's view. Russia's leaders had been happy to use state resources to further their own success and that of the people who supported them. Perhaps the idea of Russians stealing from Russians was not alarming enough for Hunter to do anything about – as long as American interests did not suffer.

The death of Huckerby was bound to refocus Hunter's attention, and Jack guessed it would not be to the benefit of the project. If there was even a hint organised crime was involved in the murder, Hunter would shelve Operation RUSSKY BEAR, and dispatch the latest operative MI6 had sent to the US back to London.

Someone knocked insistently on the door of the pod. Jack emerged and apologised, then left the office.

Ordinarily, Jack would have avoided the Langley staff restaurant at this time of the evening. Staff working long hours or starting a night shift often congregated there to get food before the long night began. But he needed a coffee and a brisk walk.

Jack entered the busy building, joined the queue and waited to be served. He was glad there was no one he recognised.

Why had matters gone so wrong so quickly?

Huckerby had either taken too much risk in his information gathering spree or the people he was working for were much more involved with leaking data for money than Jack and Harris had suspected. Or Operation RUSSKY BEAR could be compromised.

Harris at MI6 was much more confident than Jack was about getting their respective bosses to see the merit of their op, but this was Harris through and through. He would find the evidence they needed come what may and he wouldn't be shy to involve his best assets.

Jack understood why Harris trusted Crowne not only to deliver and get closer to their target, David Upstage, but also to look after himself.

Henry Crowne had survived an infiltration of the headquarters of Islamic State and returned with enough information to scupper the terrorist group's finance. That was impressive. Still, the operators Crowne would be facing this time had been involved in data extraction for profit for a long time. These people were hard to pin down. This was his and Harris's best chance.

If the Russians were involved, as Jack and Harris suspected they might be, the entire machinery available to the GRU (also known as the Main Intelligence Directorate of the General Staff of the Armed Forces of the Russian Federation... a hell of a name) would be behind the information collection.

After the collapse of the Soviet Union the GRU had emerged from the ashes of the KGB. It used old KGB tactics and training, making the GRU the most powerful and secretive spy agency in Russia. It now ruled supreme with unfettered global reach and a mandate to go anywhere and everywhere that served Russia's interests.

Jack bought a black coffee and sat at a table next to one of the ceiling-to-floor bay windows. He dropped some sugar into his drink and stirred the liquid slowly.

The information Huckerby had collected so far pointed to one man: David Upstage.

Upstage, a billionaire with a savvy sense of knowing what people liked to hear, was running a portfolio of lucrative businesses: exclusive luxury hotels, top-end spas and fitness centres, and more recently, casinos. He had diversified just as the financial crisis hit, and purchased companies in distress in the fashion and luxury goods industry. If the words expensive, exclusive or luxury were not involved, Upstage was not interested.

Huckerby had made a fuss about David Upstage's status as influencer on social media, a man whose opinion mattered to a following of 20 million people. That number was still growing. He was not in the same league as some of the biggest pop stars, but he was commanding a large enough audience to be, in Huckerby's opinion, a person of interest to a foreign power seeking to control and deceive.

Jack took his mobile out of his jacket pocket. It was past 9pm in Langley and 2am in London. Jack laid the phone down on the table.

He knew Harris well enough to call at any time – day or night. No matter how late his call was, Harris would pick up. Jack finished his coffee and with impeccable timing... his mobile buzzed.

Only two words in Harris's text to Jack... *Call back.*

* * *

Henry used strong craft tape to secure the intruder's wrists behind his back. He propped him up against one of the lounge's sofas, fetched a glass of water from the kitchen and threw it in the unconscious young man's face.

The man jutted upright, eyes opening wide. He looked around.

"What happened..." He did not finish his sentence as he was met with Henry's brutal stare.

"You cry for help, I slice you open like an apple and will claim self-defence... Understood?"

The man nodded.

Henry placed a chair in front of his prisoner and sat in it in silence for a moment.

"You live in this building, right?"

The young man nodded.

"I want a yes or a no."

The man mumbled a weak yes.

"Why are you trying to enter my apartment? And don't think about using the 'I was drunk' card. It won't get you out of jail. You and I know you are stone cold sober."

The man looked around, desperate to find a way out.

"You have 10 seconds to answer, otherwise I call the cops."

The young man squirmed. "I can't help it!"

Henry raised an eyebrow and sat back. Of all the answers he was expecting this was not one of them.

"Are you kidding me? Do I have imbecile written on my forehead? Try again. Why were you trying to enter my property?" Henry stood up. "You know what, forget it... I'm calling in the Blues."

The young man shook his head. "Actually, the Blues is used in New York. In DC they're called Metro Police."

"OK then, Mr Smart Arse, let me call the Metro." Henry grabbed his phone.

"No... please! I didn't mean to upset you." The colour had drained from the young man's face.

"It's a bit late for that, don't you think?"

"I know, I'm sorry..." He wriggled. "It's true, I can't help it. Ask Mrs Bartlett, the ground floor neighbour, if you don't believe me."

"What? Are you telling me you get into her flat and rob her on a regular basis?" Henry bent forward, causing the young man to recoil.

"Yes, but I usually give everything back to her."

"Explain the usually and the give back?"

"She sometimes lets me keep something small. Something she may not need anymore." The earnest look in the young man's eyes was unexpected.

"So, what are you... a kleptomaniac with a puppy face? Or are you taking me for an idiot?"

"No, no please... I can't help it. Sometimes I just like to try to open something nobody can or should... Please, ask Mrs Bartlett downstairs."

The panic in his voice sounded genuine. If he was acting, he certainly deserved an Oscar.

Henry rolled his phone in his hand, pursing his lips.

Mrs Bartlett, an octogenarian who lived with an army of cats, had given him her phone number. She was always willing to take in a parcel for any of the building's inhabitants in exchange for a cup of tea and a chat. There was no harm in checking the intruder's crazy story.

The man was secure and not going anywhere. Yet, he hadn't tried to get free. Henry wondered if the man had loosened the ties around his wrists and was perhaps waiting to pounce.

Henry shifted his chair away, changed the knife's grip, so the blade was now pointing down. There was enough space between him and the intruder that Henry could defend himself.

"Stand up," he ordered.

Terror flashed in the young man's eyes. He didn't move. "What are you going to do?"

Henry raised his voice, menacingly. "I said, stand up."

The young man struggled to his feet.

Henry remained alert, ready to deliver a slashing move that would inflict real damage.

"Please, don't hurt me... I can't help it." The young man's face had grown even paler.

"Turn around."

The young man let out a sob, "Please..."

He turned slowly; the ties around his wrists were intact.

16

Satisfied, Henry called his neighbour. Mrs Bartlett answered after a few rings. "Oh, hello, Henry..." She was about to launch into a long monologue when he interrupted politely.

"I'm sorry to cut you short, Mrs Bartlett, but I have one of our neighbours here in my apartment."

Mrs Bartlett fell silent for a short moment. "Oh dear... has he been naughty again then?"

Henry suppressed a grin. "Well, I fear he might have been."

"He can't help it, you know."

"So, he says..."

"He gets in, takes a few knick-knacks... but he always tries to give them back."

"Right... and how often does this little charade take place then?"

"Once a month, but Nick has been really good of late. I haven't noticed anything missing in the past six weeks."

"A reformed character, then."

The old lady chuckled.

Henry promised to come for tea soon and terminated the call.

"Sit down again," he ordered Nick.

Nick turned around and slumped to the floor. He had been holding back tears and could hardly contain them now.

Henry wondered whether Mrs Bartlett and the young Nick were in cahoots together, but perhaps this was paranoia. Then again, it was paranoia that kept people like Henry in the spy business, alive. Still, he couldn't quite convince himself the pair was malevolent and ready to assassinate him.

Henry took one step towards Nick. The young man recoiled.

"I am going to let you go, Nick, but if I ever find you breaking into my apartment again, I won't hesitate to call the police."

Nick simply nodded. He stood up clumsily.

Henry hesitated for a few seconds, positioned himself behind Nick and, with a swift move of the knife, cut off the tape that had been restraining the young man.

Nick tripped, almost fell over. He froze, as though he wasn't sure whether he was free to go.

Henry waved the knife at the door. "Come on, hop to it, before I change my mind."

Nick moved backwards slowly, terror still etched on his face. He turned around after a few steps, and was about to run for the door when Henry thought of something.

"Hang on..."

Nick froze.

"What's your name?"

"Fox."

"Nick Fox..." Henry grinned. "How appropriate. So, what else are you good at, Nick Fox?"

He turned back to face Henry, perplexity replacing the fear on his face.

"I'm good at puzzles, riddles... that sort of thing."

"Words or numbers?"

"Both actually." Nick almost spoke with pride. Henry sized the young man up for a short moment.

"And would your interest in riddles and cracking enigmas take you into cyberspace by any chance?"

The same expression of fear as before spread over Nick's face. "Sometimes... Why?"

"Just good to know. What's your mobile number?"

"But..."

"No but. I need a number and don't think about fobbing me off. I know where you live."

Nick gave a string of numbers, looking unsure whether he was in the clear.

But Henry was done. He jerked his head at the door, and within seconds, Nick was gone.

∗ ∗ ∗

Harris's timing couldn't have been better. Henry was making a second attempt at preparing supper when he called.

He switched the loudspeaker of his mobile on. "What's up?"

"I had a chat with Jack at Langley."

"Glad to hear. What does he say?"

"There was no indication that Huckerby was being watched or followed."

"Great... The CIA is asleep at the wheel then." Henry took out a couple of eggs from the fridge, some onions, green peppers, and tomatoes, and started preparing the ingredients for a dish he had discovered on a trip to the Basque country in France.

"I wouldn't be so harsh."

"I would... I'm on the receiving end of this. The CIA screws up and I'm as done as Huckerby is."

"Except that you are a trained operative, Henry, and Huckerby was a kid."

"All that means is that I have the marginal advantage of being able to spot if someone is following me or trying to interfere with my place." Henry couldn't help but smile at Nick's recent intrusion.

"Don't be such a goddamn whiner. You dealt with the likes of IS in Syria, you'll be fine."

"Except that it was easy in Raqqa. Everyone I met there was a beardo and out for my skin. Not a lot of spook skills required there." Henry broke the eggs into a bowl.

He continued, beating the eggs. "If the CIA can't spot these guys, then Operation RUSSKY BEAR has suddenly become a lot more complicated."

"My thought exactly..." Harris sounded almost upbeat. "We need to replace this unfortunate lad with someone who has a bit more cred and training."

Henry stopped beating. "Hang on... the deal was that I was to provide Huckerby with the technical knowledge he lacked... only making an occasional appearance until we had more concrete evidence to warrant proper infiltration. The appropriateness of such infiltration to be assessed in view of my previous career in London."

"What – you're losing the stomach for a bigger job?" Harris's cocky voice bounced around Henry's apartment.

Henry grabbed the phone in irritation. He switched off the loudspeaker and put the phone to his ear.

"That's a shitty remark, Harris. It's got zip to do with confidence, and you know it. If I get involved in anything to do with finance, someone could recognise me and blow my cover, as well as my legend. I can only use my alias Henry Newborn credibly in DC if no one can identify me for who I used to be."

19

"Unlikely... You've done a very good job at changing your appearance in your previous assignment and you dealt with the big international banks only in New York when you worked in London, not the smaller boutique firms of Washington DC."

"What do you mean... of course, I dealt with the lobby firms in DC. I spent enough time with the CEO of GL Investments, Doug McCarthy, to meet my fair share of them. I made enough representations on behalf of GL. They would remember me."

"But that was many years ago, mate. People forget more than you think."

Henry refused to bite. "Still, I can't be the only asset you have that knows anything about banking and finance."

"No, but you are by far the best one, and you established yourself very credibly in DC before."

"I don't care about your compliments. I need to be convinced I can viably do the job." Henry didn't mind taking risks, but he had to be able to manage them. He didn't even mind meeting someone from his past, but he had to be prepared for it. It couldn't be a random event.

"Forget about your old City banking background. The reason why you can crack that nut is that you – surprisingly so, but still – never dealt with the Russians."

"I agree, surprising, considering how much fraud McCarthy was prepared to tolerate within the bank itself. But I'm prepared to accept that GL Investment Bank seldom dealt with Russian oligarchs."

"There you go! Your cover can't be blown because they don't know who you are."

"I'm not convinced about that, Harris... Why not get someone else involved on the US side? I thought you trusted Shield at the CIA."

"I don't have a problem with Jack. My problems are closer to home."

"What, your wife has finally decided to kick you out owing to your smooth personality?"

"Nah, my wife's a saint... I'm talking MI6 business."

Henry returned to his cooking, although perhaps less enthusiastically than before. "How about you level with me and then maybe I'll agree to help."

Harris waited for a moment. Henry busied himself with chopping the tomatoes he had taken out of the fridge.

20

"OK, I'm prepared to say this, MI6 in the UK and the CIA in the US have been focusing far too much on the Middle East... And before you protest and remind me of the horrors you've witnessed there, remember I've been there, too."

Henry popped a piece of tomato in his mouth and chewed thoughtfully.

"I suppose Russia has become part of the problem in the Middle East rather than the solution."

"Exactly right, they are supporting Bashar al Assad and Iran... and now the Yemen. Russia uses these states in a proxy war against the US. And they are doing rather well at the moment. I don't think Bashar al Assad in Syria is going anywhere. This has emboldened them."

"And you think Russia is seeking to extend its sphere of influence elsewhere – just like in the old days?"

"You got it in one, mate, and we're not paying enough attention. So what do you say?"

"Send me the entity file... I'll approach Top Capital in the morning and tell them I have a meeting with Huckerby. No one will dare contradict me."

Chapter Three

Part of the reception area in the atrium was still cordoned off. Henry made his way to a temporary desk that had been set up to welcome visitors, well away from the area where Huckerby's body had landed.

The young man's lifeless face flashed in front of Henry's eyes. He pushed the image away and moved with fake confidence towards one of the receptionists. The middle-aged woman gave him a professional smile.

"I am here to meet Rush Huckerby, please." Henry spoke with assurance and detachment, the tone of a man starting a long day of meetings. "My name is Henry Newborn."

The woman's face dropped a little. She paused and asked Henry to take a seat.

He moved to a set of comfortable armchairs and sofas, choosing a seat that gave him a view of the reception desk. He kept his demeanour cool, no eagerness or concern. Business as usual.

Henry picked up the *Wall Street Journal* from the coffee table and started reading, one eye trained on the receptionist. The receptionist was speaking with someone on the phone, glancing at Henry from time to time.

He would give her five minutes, then go back to her and make a scene. He'd never resorted to spoilt-brat tantrums when he'd been a banker, but today might be the day.

The receptionist left her desk. She moved towards Henry, body tense, hands clasped tight in front of her.

"Mr Newborn... I'm afraid Mr Huckerby is not available."

Henry stared coldly at her. The capacity that business had to avoid talking about a tragedy to preserve a potential client relationship always amazed him.

She added, "But Mr Hernandez will meet you."

Henry dropped the paper on the coffee table with discontent.

He remained seated. "And who is Mr Hernandez?"

"He is Mr Huckerby's boss."

Henry grunted and pushed himself out of the seat. "I was supposed to meet a couple of senior people... I presume he is one of them?"

She gave him her best smile. "I'm sure it has all been arranged."

Henry gave her a stiff nod. Any good receptionist would now call Hernandez back to apprise him of what Henry was expecting.

Henry walked to the lifts, preparing mentally for the meeting. Huckerby will not have died for nothing. Henry would build on the young man's work. He felt he owed it to him.

Hernandez was on his mobile when Henry arrived on the fourth floor of the building where Top Capital, Huckerby's company, was located. Hernandez was nodding, looking a little concerned. From inside the glass elevator, Henry observed the expression on his face and the small hand gestures that betrayed anxiety.

Hernandez switched off his mobile as soon as Henry stepped out of the lift. He extended a welcoming hand, and gave him an uncertain smile.

"Ron Hernandez... I am sorry Rush is not here to greet you."

"As long as this meeting is not a waste of time... no matter."

Henry gave Hernandez a firm grip. The other man responded with hesitation. Good, he was already on the back foot.

"Rush told me a lot about you and what your company has achieved when it comes to brokering deals. He thought your company would be superb at supporting the transactions we arrange for our clients," Hernandez said.

"Excellent. We can go straight to the crux of the matter then. I rarely respond to an offer of working with another firm unless I have met with senior management, but Rush is an exceptionally bright young man."

Hernandez nodded, and for the first time Henry detected some embarrassment. Hernandez switched to some idle chit-chat as they walked. He led him into a meeting room he had reserved.

But the room was not empty. A man in his mid-thirties, sporty and impeccably dressed, was waiting for them. He had not bothered to sit at the table but was leaning against the wall next to a large window that overlooked 6th St NW. The man didn't move when Henry and Hernandez entered, nor did he unfold the arms he had crossed over his chest.

Hernandez closed the door, moving swiftly around the table to introduce the stranger.

"Mr Newborn, please may I introduce you to Arthur McNamara Jr? Mr McNamara deals with some of our high-profile clients."

Henry dropped his expensive satchel into a chair and waited. If McNamara couldn't be bothered to greet him, he certainly wouldn't budge.

There was an awkward moment, but then McNamara left his place against the wall and presented Henry with an outstretched hand. This time the grip was solid, assured – perhaps a little too insistent.

"How do you do?" Henry gave the man a faint but knowing smile. He had just travelled back in time and was staring at his younger self, albeit American, and clearly from a dynasty family.

Hernandez pulled a chair out and sat down. "Now, I'm not sure Rush had time to debrief Mr McNamara, so perhaps we could recap on the main purpose of this meeting?"

A cart of drinks was at the back of the room. Henry helped himself to a cup of coffee before sitting next to his satchel.

"I'm sure Rush would have debriefed you, Mr Hernandez, about the aim of the meeting, so why not get straight to the point?"

McNamara shot Henry a dark look. He was no junior in the firm, and judging by his attitude, he was almost certainly more senior than Hernandez, despite the age difference. Why had Huckerby not mentioned him? Perhaps, he was the reason why Huckerby had wanted to meet urgently.

Hernandez's face lost some of its amiability. He looked to McNamara for a clue.

"Rush contacted me after we met at Davos last year," Henry said. Whether Huckerby had established Henry's credibility with Hernandez by referring to a Davos meeting at the World Economic Forum was not the point. Henry needed to placate McNamara.

It did the trick.

McNamara held back what was almost certainly a provocative comment. Davos was where top political figures met, including the President of the United States and the wealthiest businessmen on the planet. Jeff Bezos of Amazon, Mark Zuckerberg of Facebook and Elon Musk of Tesla all made regular appearances.

Huckerby would have been far too junior or unknown to take part in Davos had it not been for his father's own attendance. This had given the young man an edge when mentioning a fortuitous meeting with Henry. Rush returning from Davos with a senior contact in the bag had helped him to be selected to service senior clients like Upstage.

Henry savoured the moment. At Davos he would have been rubbing shoulders with might and money. By the looks on McNamara's and Hernandez's face, they had not come across so many of these almost mythical financiers before.

Henry drank some coffee before continuing. "We discussed a possible collaboration with Top Capital Partners. I understand that some of your platinum clientele is in need of business introductions and of course sizeable funding."

"What level of funding are you able to offer?" McNamara controlled his sulky mood. His eyes roamed over Henry, looking for a sign that might betray weakness.

"I won't be involving myself unless the ticket is worth $0.5bn." Henry pouted. His right-hand moved slowly towards his left wrist. He half uncovered a Vacheron-Constantin watch. Hernandez did not react, but McNamara did. At $200,000 a piece, it was serious watch-ware for a serious player.

Henry discreetly checked the time. The gesture made the point to both men.

"Now, gentleman, shall we discuss the purpose of my visit?" Henry did not wait for an answer. "I believe one of your clients, David Upstage, is encountering difficulty with the financing of his latest project."

Hernandez face dropped. It would not do to discuss a client's requirements with someone who had not been vetted by the firm, let alone to discuss said client's monetary problems.

Henry might have adopted a less brazen approach had Huckerby still been alive, but Huckerby was not and Henry needed a swift breakthrough.

"Rush and I discussed the facilitation of a loan or other form of funding for some of the more –" Henry hesitated "– challenging property projects Mr Upstage is working on."

Hernandez was about to answer when McNamara cut him short with a sudden hand movement.

"I represent the interests of Mr Upstage in this firm," said McNamara. "Any propositions to be made to my client will go through me."

Henry locked eyes with the younger man and smiled. "No. You will create an introduction. By all means attend the meeting. In fact I would encourage it, but my proposition will only be vetted by one person –David Upstage himself."

A slap in the face would not have rendered McNamara more speechless. Hernandez was frozen, unable to decide what to do next.

Henry continued. "You will no doubt want to check my credentials." He took a couple of business cards out of an old leather cardholder and placed them on the table. He did not bother to push them towards the two men.

"I'll send Rush a short presentation about my firm."

Henry stood up. McNamara and Hernandez followed suit.

"I'll find my own way out."

He left his two interlocutors behind, still looking bewildered by the boldness of his approach.

* * *

Henry left the offices of Top Capital Partners, without glancing at the place where Huckerby's body had landed less than 24 hours ago. He had not bothered with a coat that morning and was glad of it. Washington's weather was proving unseasonably warm for early December.

He jogged slowly across the road, eager to put some distance between him and Top Capital. He decided against taking a cab. A walk back to his office was what he needed. He walked at pace towards his own office building, leaving Penn and heading towards Rhode Island Avenue, about a mile away.

On the way, Henry found a large branded coffee shop that spread over two floors. He didn't like their coffee much, but at 10.30am the place should be almost empty. He placed an order, climbed the quirky staircase to the first floor and chose a discreet corner at the far end of the room.

Henry took his mobile out, hesitating for a moment. The agreement with Harris was that, as his MI6 minder, he would remain his prime contact. Harris had agreed Henry could contact Jack in case of emergency or if Harris was not available. Harris was several time zones away and Henry needed some answers now.

A pretty waitress brought Henry his order and he mumbled a "Thank you." Her eyes lingered a little too long after she heard the British accent, and Henry gave her an amused smile. Her face turned red, and she disappeared downstairs in a hurry.

"You do not want to get involved with me, young lady," Henry murmured. Still, it was pleasant to receive the attention of an attractive woman.

Henry looked around casually at his surroundings. There were a few loners working on their laptops. A couple of mothers with their babies.

No one new had turned up since his arrival and sitting down. He scrolled through the names on his phone's contact list, found the name he wanted and pressed the call button.

* * *

Tatiana checked the picture she had been sent on her smartphone. Henry Newborn had entered the building for Top Capital 35 minutes ago and was out already. He was in a hurry, as one might expect of the busy financier she'd been told he was.

The man who was employing her had instructed her to find out more – a lot more than what they had gleaned on the internet and from Huckerby. She had found his home address easily enough. His business address was on a business card Newborn had handed over to Rush, a few weeks ago.

She allowed her target to walk out and decide on which route he would be taking before firing up the engine of her motorbike. She pulled down the visor on her helmet and moved slowly out into the road, heading towards the traffic light that had just turned red.

Tatiana watched Newborn hesitate before continuing on foot towards the north of the city. He no longer looked in a rush, but intent to walk at his own pace. Tatiana made a mental note. Perhaps Henry Newborn had not been hurrying to his next meeting but rather keen to leave the offices of Top Capital Partners.

The lights changed. She waited for the traffic to flow and followed the cars ahead. Her quarry was moving now at a brisk pace. She saw him entering a branded coffee shop and pouted. She doubted a European, brought up in a well-to-do family as his profile described, would relish a coffee there. But the place was large enough for an undercover encounter or to make contact with someone.

She parked her bike again, checked the time and waited. Henry Newborn emerged after 14 minutes, too little time to do any work, too much for a simple drink. Call or contact – it had to be one of those.

Newborn kept going until he reached Massachusetts Avenue before turning left. He was headed to his office, she surmised. Tatiana fired up her motorbike, turned around and cut through some of the lateral streets to reach a section of Massachusetts Avenue that would put her in front of Henry. She parked her bike near a small coffee stall and bought herself a coffee, making idle chat with the young man who was running it.

Henry switched over to the opposite side of the road. He came to a stop in front of shops with large bay windows. Tatiana watched the pattern unfold from a distance. It was all very discreet and natural. The shops were relevant enough for a man with his taste – a jewellery shop selling expensive men's watches and an electronic store advertising the latest iPhone.

But there was something in her target's body language she couldn't yet place, a self-assurance that was more than the arrogance of a man well connected. He was alert to his environment whenever he took his bearings.

Tatiana had been watching him only for a day or so and yet she was already wondering: had Henry Newborn been trained, and if so by whom?

* * *

Jack Shield's phone buzzed. He pulled it out. Jack's boss, Richard Hunter III, Head of Special Ops, was sitting at his desk, finishing a call. Hunter cast a dark look at the phone in Jack's hand. Jack pocketed the item without looking at the caller's name.

Hunter terminated his own call with the CIA Security Director. He pointed to a chair and Jack sat down.

"I don't want to hear that there was no indication Rush Huckerby was at risk," Hunter said by way of welcome. "I want to know why we didn't spot it in time."

"So do I, sir." Jack shifted on the uncomfortable chair for the *chat* Hunter had suggested they needed.

"Glad to hear it. And if there is a whiff, even remote, that the whole affair is linked to organised crime, this goes straight to the Feds."

Jack shifted on his chair again. Hunter took it as hesitation on Jack's part. "This is not up for discussion... I need your analytical skills on things other than a vague story about Russian recruitment."

"It's understood, sir." There was no point arguing. Jack needed to buy Operation RUSSKY BEAR time.

"Russia is not our priority. We are still nowhere near defeating terror in the Middle East. Syria is a shambles, Afghanistan is a shambles, Iraq is only marginally better. I don't need to draw you a picture. And Iran is being unusually quiet, which worries me no end."

Jack wondered whether to remind Hunter that Russia had been at the forefront of the Obama administration's mind when Russia had invaded Crimea, a few months back.

"What about this guy Crowne?" Hunter asked. "How are you organising yourself with London, now that Rush..." Hunter trailed off.

"For the time being he should stay here in DC. He has made contact with Top Capital Partners, that's Huckerby's office, and his connection might help us find out more." Jack omitted to say that Crowne had only made contact that morning and that Jack had no idea how it had gone.

Hunter grunted. "In principle, I don't like having an operative from another agency working on US soil. I don't mind joined operations abroad but here, on our own doorstep... I'm not keen."

"He's a very impressive asset and with exactly the right financial background."

"So you say, but don't we have enough assets of our own to find someone?"

"Not any of the same calibre."

Hunter pushed his chair away from his desk and stood up. He walked over to the window and looked outside.

Jack doubted his boss was admiring the woods surrounding the Langley complex building. He had learnt that Head of Special Ops Hunter III took the short walk to his office's window whenever he needed to clear his head.

"You've got a week to come back to me with some credible HUMIT. Otherwise, we'll assume Huckerby's murder is linked to OC, and we hand it over to the FBI."

Jack opened his mouth to protest, but was silenced by Hunter's raised hand.

"One week, Jack. You work well under pressure."

Jack left Hunter's office with the same feeling as he often did, whenever he struggled to make his voice heard.

In his irritation he had almost forgotten his missed call. He made his way to the lifts. A few of his colleagues climbed in and the lift started its descent to the second floor.

Jack checked his mobile. It took him a second to recognise the caller's ID.

"Shit."

The doors opened on another floor. He moved past the people trying to get on and turned towards the stairwell. He opened the door and pushed the call-back button on his phone.

Jack moved down a few steps and stopped. He was alone.

"What took you so long?" Henry's very British voice sounded irritated yet untroubled.

"Is everything OK? This is the emergency number."

"Huckerby's death *is* an emergency." Jack could tell by the sound of cars driving past that Henry was outside on the street.

"I'm not disputing that."

"You and I need to meet. I know this will piss off Harris but let me handle him. I have just been presented with a much more complicated situation than we'd anticipated."

"In what way?"

"I'm not sure Huckerby realised how much competition there would be for our target's attention. I've just met some cocky little sod who is very keen to replace Rush and I'm pretty sure this guy had that in mind way before Rush's death. I'm also wondering whether he had access to all the information he needed to give us a true picture of the way we should approach Upstage."

"This is harsh on Huckerby, especially now that he can't defend himself," Jack shot back.

"I'm not saying he didn't do a good job at going as far as he could, but he was perhaps a little too junior to be let in on the inner workings of his office's politics." Henry continued before Jack could reply. "I know his father was well connected but that doesn't mean he was being given the access he needed. Someone else has just been parachuted into the target's relationship. That is of interest."

"Where is the emergency, then?"

"I'll need to look credible to get where I want to get, and I need a team with me."

Jack leaned against the window frame of the stairwell corner he had moved to. "This is unlikely to happen... not with CIA resources."

"Don't bullshit me. You guys can't all still be running around the Middle East..."

"It feels like that at the moment." Jack might as well be honest with Crowne. "And I've just been told that we have a week to show progress, otherwise..."

"An even better reason to get me the people I need."

Jack straightened up. "I might be able to find you someone in the analyst department, but that's about it." Jack's mind raced. The lovely Mandy, so helpful in the past, might say yes. Hunter would not be sanctioning anyone, so Mandy would have to volunteer to work on Jack's project.

"Jack... are you still there or have you already given up?"

"How about Harris in London? Can't he find someone?"

"That's not very convenient, is it? And then are you OK with more MI6 operatives running around Washington DC?"

"Use them from London."

"No, I need to build up momentum around the small office I've rented. The people I am about to meet are seasoned professionals. They will be looking for issues, anything to discredit me. I don't need to mention the distinct possibility that they won't like an amateur or a suspicious character getting too close to them. I don't want to end up like Huckerby if I can help it."

"That goes without saying, and I'm not trying to be difficult."

"But the CIA has other fish to fry than track down a suspected Russian plot."

"That's the sum of it. The days of the Cold War have long been forgotten."

"I find that rather staggering. Putin is a pure product of that era. KGB through and through, and he still surprised everyone with his intervention in Crimea."

"Perhaps, but there are people in the US that view Crimea as mainly Russian."

"Do these people even know where Ukraine and Crimea are to start with? Sorry, I shouldn't be flippant."

"Probably not, but that's not the point –"

"And what *is* the point?" The irritation in Henry's voice only reminded Jack that Crowne was right. It was a failure of NATO and the West to allow Russia to annex Crimea away from the Ukraine.

"The US is battle weary and ready to look inwards more. It does not bode well for the future of international diplomacy, I'm afraid," Jack said.

"Or democracy for that matter..." Henry fell silent for a moment. "If you can spare one of your team, then perhaps I can start with someone from the London office on that basis. I worked with another MI6 asset on my Middle Eastern assignment. He'll be game, I'm sure." Henry continued before Jack could reply. "And also on the basis that this London contact is allowed to join me in DC if things take off."

Jack frowned at the request, but Crowne was right. The right credibility in the next 24 hours would make or break Operation RUSSKY BEAR.

Chapter Four

A set of double glass doors slid open and Henry walked through. He greeted the receptionist with a nod and a courteous smile.

He rode the lift to the top floor of the new eight-floor building, housing a collection of tech start-ups and consultancy boutiques. The suite Henry had chosen had never been occupied before. He liked that he was the first to put his mark on the premises. It was easier to kit a new office with the equipment he deemed necessary. It was also much less likely the place had been bugged, although caution was essential.

Henry went through his daily routine. He took the surveillance detection equipment he had brought with him out of his satchel and methodically swept each of the four rooms he occupied. Satisfied all was clear, Henry relaxed.

He surveyed the space critically, like a new client might. Did it deliver the message it needed to, to a savvy visitor?

The reception area had a brand new large settee and two comfortable armchairs. A large painting by a contemporary artist Henry had spotted recently in DC hung on the wall. Together, they made the reception area look welcoming and expensive.

Henry's office opened out onto a roof terrace with a clear view of the White House. The residence of the most powerful man in the world was less than three quarters of a mile away, its view unobstructed by the low-rise city.

Henry could not quite reconcile the idea of such power existing without skyscrapers and glass and steel towers, like in New York, where large sums of money changed hands hourly. After what felt like a lifetime spent in investment banking, either in London or New York, he had become accustomed to the massive offices and ridiculously large buildings that housed thousands of employees. This city felt more discreet than those places, almost understated, with its smaller buildings and pleasant architecture.

Henry moved to the two meeting rooms that completed the four-room suite he was renting. Everything had been chosen carefully to look high end, from the furniture – deep carpets, leather chairs, chrome and glass tables and cabinets – to the top of the line computers.

Henry picked up his satchel and returned to his office. He dropped the satchel to the floor, and draped his suit jacket over the back of his executive leather chair. He was back to dressing for power, just like at GL Investments, but the mood he was trying to create had changed. The clothes he had chosen this morning were part of his new legend. They no longer represented the status symbol they once had when he used to dress from some of the most exclusive shops in London, and the change in attitude made Henry smile.

Henry Newborn, financier guru and deal fixer, had been born many years ago, at a time when Henry had become one of the key architects of a money laundering ring. Newborn had been resurrected a few months ago, but this time to serve a very different purpose.

Henry had used the Newborn name for years whilst organising money laundering for the IRA. Henry's downfall hadn't come from his illicit activity but from a savage war of influence during a protracted takeover that had almost cost him his sanity. He had worked through the credibility of his legend with Harris during the six months debriefing with MI6, after his last assignment to the Middle East.

Henry had appreciated the extra time Harris had granted him between jobs, so he could forget what he had witnessed in Iraq and Syria. Some nights, Henry still woke up in cold sweat, images of the torture fields of Mosul haunting his dreams.

He placed another scanning device on his desk, this one designed to catch any attempts to intercept his conversation. The sweeping routine that had felt laborious before Huckerby's death was a comfort now.

He switched on the brand new PC and four monitors sitting on his desk. It looked a little of an overkill, but this was the way a trader on the trading floor would be equipped and Henry knew exactly what it took to look the part.

Finally, Henry took his laptop out of his satchel and went through the lengthy process of connecting to a secure website over which he could reach Harris. As soon as the connection was live, Henry called his MI6 minder. He didn't check the time. Harris would make himself available.

Steve Harris's bulldog expression appeared on screen. "What? I'm late for a meeting."

"Do you want the latest on RUSSKY BEAR, or would you rather I simply pack up and return to London?"

"If you know what's good for you mate, you ain't going to come back to London for a little while... Remember you're still classified as one of the most wanted fugitives by Interpol. Being one of my assets doesn't automatically put you in the clear."

"And I'm sure Interpol would love to know that MI6 was behind my escape from Belmarsh prison."

Harris laughed. "Who's gonna believe that?" His expression grew serious. "What have you got for me that is so urgent then?"

"I no longer buy the fact that the RUSSKY BEAR op is mainly about soft corporate connections to Russia."

Harris arched one eyebrow. "And what makes you say that?"

"No one seems to give a hoot about Huckerby's death at his office. In fact, had I not seen him fall myself, I would have said we'd been misinformed."

"OK... What else?"

"Huckerby was replaced within 12 hours of his murder by someone senior. This person is making it pretty clear that the target, David Upstage, is off limits unless he first vets who gets to approach him."

"So what? That just means they're possessive about their client."

"Sorry, Harris, but I have been around that block before, or to use a more American expression, I'm not new to that rodeo. You don't piss off someone who can broker millions for a high-profile client by blocking their access to that client."

"You're just fucked off because they didn't massage your ego the right way."

"My ego doesn't need massaging, Harris, but the ego of my legend, a certain Henry Newborn, adviser to the great and the good, most definitely needs it. As I said, these people are rattled, and they are closing ranks on Upstage."

Harris sat back in his seat. He sucked on his lower lip a few times, a sign that meant he was considering options.

"All right then..." Harris leaned closer to the screen. "I don't have the full picture yet. I've just got a bit of a gut feel."

"Fine." Henry nodded. "I like a good gut feel. It's often the best indicator you'll get on a deal."

"By the way, one of our GCHQ operators spotted a strange data exchange on certain social media accounts being used by a number of high-profile UK and US businessmen."

"Are you delving into people's accounts? I thought that sort of spook work wasn't allowed?" Henry pouted.

"Not sure, and anyway don't care. I just need more information about what these data points mean."

"Can you share the data with me via our encrypted comms?"

"No can do. My contact at GCHQ is already taking a risk by communicating what she found to me."

Henry sat back. He fought the temptation to give Harris a piece of his mind; the data was crucial. But now was not the time. Henry would get to the information the UK Government Communication Headquarters – also known as GCHQ – had sent Harris. It would simply need a bit more graft.

"At least level with me on what GCHQ told you about our target, David Upstage."

"Fair enough." Harris pulled a face. "Upstage is using his Influencer Twitter account in ways that feel controlled. I'm not saying someone else has hijacked the account; it would be too obvious. But he has started to retweet messages of people who GCHQ can't track..."

"You mean..." Henry paused to get his head around Harris's implication. "People who do not exist or who are using aliases, pseudos, etcetera, to cover up who they are?"

"That's right." Harris nodded emphatically. "But the most worrying part of that story is not that he was too stupid to notice he was being conned into following a bunch of people whose identity is questionable. What my contact at GCHQ believes is that he is aware he is dealing with fake identities."

"Yes, but on the other hand, a lot of people don't use their real names on social media. They create personas that are more in keeping with who they want to be." Henry leaned back in his chair.

"You can find the real person behind these names if you keep digging... What you're not expecting to find is some strange organisation that is yet another smokescreen."

"Has GCHQ been able to dig deeper?"

"It's not a top priority at the moment. My contact is doing this in her spare time."

Henry grinned. "I didn't know the GCHQ guys or girls were doing a bit of moonlighting for you, Harris."

"Well, I've got my contacts... it's a bit of 'you scratch my back and I'll scratch yours'." Harris shrugged, surprisingly modest.

"Then, if you'd like me to help you resolve this little, or perhaps large, conundrum, I need more people in DC."

Harris's eyes narrowed and he gave Henry a side look. "What do you mean more people in DC?"

"Well, exactly what I said. The office I found is perfect, trendy, and in the right business quarter, but I can't have Top Capital people coming here with just me working here. I need someone to greet them."

"Something tells me you've already got a pretty good idea of who that someone is..."

"You know me too well... James Radlett." Harris had recruited him to work with Henry on his Middle Eastern assignment. "As you know, he was my right-hand man in GL Investments. And a now a new recruit... a guy called Nick Fox."

Harris frowned. "And who the hell is Nick Fox?"

"A guy who tried to break into my apartment but didn't quite succeed. He was pretty crafty about the whole thing. I have the feeling he is a resourceful guy."

Harris shook his head. "Sorry, mate, I'm not allowed to recruit on US soil. And I'm not sure some petty thief is such a bright idea, anyway."

"How about you make an exception about your recruitment policy? I'm sure you and Jack can agree something. And by the way, I didn't say Nick was a petty criminal. He is more of a hacker sort of guy with kleptomaniac tendencies. He just needs to find a way to express his talents constructively and his part-time job is not quite doing the trick. My downstairs neighbour was a mine of information about him and I like what I heard."

"Oh, well in that case..." Harris rolled his eyes. "Let's just offer him a job on the basis of your neighbour's say-so, shall we?"

"That's the spirit! And before I forget, I think I've found the right person to fit in when I need more bodies on the ground."

Harris eyebrows shot up to his receding hairline.

"Or rather Jack has. He's got someone in mind and she sounds perfect."

Harris's face turned red. "What the hell, Crowne? You spoke to Jack on the emergency number?"

"Well, it was an emergency. If I'm not mistaken, I should be receiving an email from a man called Arthur McNamara Jr very soon, requesting a meeting at my office, and this meeting will be a make-or-break moment."

Harris grumbled. "You're a pain in the arse."

"Yup, that's why you enjoy working with me."

Henry enjoyed rattling Harris. It did not happen often. Despite his gruff demeanour, his MI6 minder was too experienced and incomprehensibly unfazed to get worked up about anything, but occasionally Henry found the chink in his armour.

He checked the news briefing on his BBG Terminal. There was nothing remarkable being reported, apart from the usual nonsense concerning the US election campaigns. The Republicans were in a pickle and Hillary Clinton, the Democrats' candidate, looked well placed to enter the White House. Henry could not help but smile. The first woman ever to hold the highest office in the land would also be the leader of the free world.

A phone shrilled, dragging him out of his thoughts. Henry took a few seconds to look around, finally realising it was his desk phone. The landline had never rung before and he usually let it go to voice mail. Now, he was unsure whether he should respond.

He picked up. The friendly voice of one of the downstairs reception-ists came on.

"Good morning. This is Joyce at reception. I have a gentleman to see Mr Newborn –" Her voice became muffled as she asked the person his name "– Mr McNamara Jr. He doesn't have an appointment, but he doesn't mind waiting."

Henry froze, unsure if he had heard her correctly. McNamara was downstairs? He knew it would happen. He had said so to Harris only a few minutes ago. He simply did not expect it would be so soon.

Henry returned to her call. "I need to check availability, Joyce. I'll call you back in a moment."

He left his office in a few rapid steps and entered the suite reception area. The building office manager had suggested a regular delivery of fresh flowers and newspapers was necessary for any office. Henry had hesitated at the time, but was now grateful he'd accepted.

He shuffled through the pile of unread newspapers on the coffee table, stacked up in a pile. He removed some old ones, spread the most recent out, and ruffled the pages, to give them the look of having been read thoroughly.

He went to the water cooler and pulled a few plastic goblets from the dispenser. He threw the cups in the bin next to the machine, making it look as though he had had some visitors already.

Henry looked at the empty receptionist desk. This would not do. No serious office would allow reception to be unmanned. It was not even lunch time, so Henry could not use that excuse. Besides, whatever the time, a vacant desk would not impress a critical visitor.

"Shit."

Henry ran a hand through his hair. Calling Jack for help would be of no use. Henry needed someone right now. He returned to his office and picked up his mobile.

He dialled the office manager's number.

"Good morning Tony... I wonder whether you could help?"

"Of course, Mr Newborn. How can I be of service?"

"I need a receptionist to help me man the Platinum Suite reception area. The person I had in mind cannot start for a few days yet."

"Not a problem... I'm sure I can find someone to help. When would you like that person to start?"

"Now would be good." Henry kept calm. In the world of banking, this would not be an unusual request.

"I see..." The manager dragged out the words. Henry heard the question in his tone. How the heck did this guy think he was going to summon a receptionist in the next five minutes?

The man fell quiet for a moment, but Henry was already thinking about a Plan B.

He could tell McNamara he was in back-to-back meetings, but this would only give the man a reason to report that Henry was too busy, and therefore unable to service a valuable client. He could wait until lunch time and offer lunch instead of a meeting at the office... that might work.

The manager came back on. "I'm very sorry. I'm not sure I can produce someone at such short notice. I'll ask around the other offices."

"Much obliged." Henry tried to stay civil... this was no longer invest-ment banking after all.

Henry hung up and looked at his watch. It was only 11am. The lunch idea would not work.

He scrolled through the list of contacts on his phone and pressed the number for one of them.

The phone rang a few times before Nick picked up.

"Are you awake?" Henry said.

The voice at the other end of the line became alert.

"Yes."

"Good, and I presume dressed?" Henry moved to the bay window of his office.

"I am."

"Get changed into something smart-casual, black jeans will do, with a white shirt or dark polo neck, no bright colours."

Henry waited to hear what the choice was.

"That sounds suitable. Get to 1701 Rhode Island Avenue. It's only a few blocks away. When you get there give me a call, and bring a couple of coffees from the Big Bear Coffee shop with you. I take mine black, double shot, milk on the side. You've got 15 minutes, so get a move on." Henry was about to hang up when he remembered an important detail. "And Nick... I hope you've shaved this morning. Whatever the answer, you still only have 15 minutes to turn up."

Henry smiled upon terminating the call. The young man had been rattled enough last night to do as he was told. A male receptionist would make a nice change, and it would be helpful to have someone who could lift items Henry needed for his latest assignment.

Henry called downstairs reception back and told them he could see McNamara in 20 minutes' time. For someone who did not have an appointment it was a perfectly good offer – professional, yet not too keen.

Henry had little time to turn his quiet office into a busy one. He recalled seeing TV sets in each of the conference rooms. They could be used to make conference calls, but could also be plugged into any news channel.

Henry switched them on and selected two different channels reporting on business news. He turned the volume down low, until the stream of conversation became difficult to make out. This would give the impression that both rooms were occupied and busy. He did not intend to keep McNamara for long and doubted the man had anything serious to offer so early. It was a good old-fashioned recce on Top Capital Partners' side.

If needs be, Henry could always claim he had a lunch meeting. He had to make sure that McNamara was out before the business news ended and the commercial breaks came on at 12pm.

Henry's BlackBerry rang. Nick Fox's number flashed on the screen.

He answered. "Are you outside?"

"Yes, just as you said."

Henry checked his watch. 11.26am. Not bad for a debut into the world of full-time employment. Henry walked out of this office and onto the terrace, and peered over the railing. He could see the young man holding a tray with drinks.

"I'm about to call reception to let them know you've forgotten your pass."

Nick was already moving forward. "Which floor?"

"8th floor, the Platinum Suite." Henry placed his call to downstairs reception and walked to the suite's main door. He opened it and leaned against its frame, arms crossed over his chest.

Nick Fox emerged from the lift, dressed in a pair of black designer jeans, and a dark-grey cashmere turtleneck showing through his open winter leather coat.

Henry eyed him and smiled. There was no way Nick could have afforded such clothes on the meagre salary he earned as a part-time online sales operator. Nick stopped in front of Henry, holding the coffee tray carefully, unsure of what to do next.

"Come in." Henry moved back and, with a sweeping gesture of the hand, showed Nick in.

The young man stepped inside the suite, looking around at the office space in surprise.

Henry grinned. "You can use a phone, can't you?"

"Well... yeah." Nick shrugged.

Henry grew serious. "'Yes, I can' is the proper answer."

Nick's face paled a little. "I mean, yes I can, sir."

"That's much better." Henry nodded. "And I presume you know how to be civil with customers, even when they are being a pain in the butt?"

"Actually, I'm not bad at that."

"And you can lift someone's wallet easily and without getting caught too, I guess?"

Nick's face turned crimson. "I'm not sure I want... to talk... about that," he stammered.

"Never mind, you're hired. Drop my coffee on my desk and get settled at the receptionist desk. I hope you haven't got a problem with doing a job that's supposed to be filled by a woman – I'm pretty open-minded when it comes to these things."

Nick looked a little lost, but nodded.

"Chop chop. Our first client is waiting downstairs." Henry headed for his office, but stopped before he crossed the threshold.

"You know what will happen if you screw up, don't you?" Henry said over his shoulder.

* * *

McNamara had left the building in which he had had his meeting without precautions. He stood for a moment at the end of the driveway that welcomed official cars and diplomat vehicles, as well as taxis. He took out a piece of paper from his coat pocket and stared at it.

Tatiana sat on her bike almost opposite to where McNamara was standing. But he was too absorbed in his own thinking to notice her.

There was no one around and the bike was almost too obvious. He raised his head, and for a moment Tatiana thought she would be spotted.

Instead, McNamara walked in the opposite direction he had arrived from, towards Embassy Row.

Tatiana shook her head. "This cretin is gonna get a cab."

She fired the bike up and waited a couple more minutes before she followed.

He had already turned left and was about to arrive on Observatory Circle. A yellow cab had just deposited its customers in front of the Serbian Embassy. McNamara hailed it. A few minutes later he was in it, speeding away towards his next destination.

Tatiana swore between gritted teeth. This moron did not understand clear instructions. He clearly could not abide the idea of mixing on the underground with the likes of her.

Tough. She'd gladly report on this omission. McNamara was a hindrance to the way she liked to operate, but she had been asked to work with him. She wished he would listen to what he was asked to do rather than think he knew better.

She followed the cab without trouble. She made sure she'd left a couple of cars between them. It was not because McNamara was proving too arrogant that she should be the same. She had professional standards to uphold and had been recruited by her minder because of her relentless appetite for details.

Her thoughts drifted to the other man she had begun to follow. Henry Newborn was a much more interesting proposition. She smiled wickedly at the thought of him. For once the men she'd been asked to tail were both rather attractive, in their own different ways. McNamara was the typical American playboy she always hated crossing paths with. Newborn, on the other hand, had charm bestowed by a British accent and an unusual charisma she couldn't quite make out.

The traffic light ahead was turning red. The cab accelerated through the light and Tatiana cursed. She found herself having to throttle up so as not to lose her tail, and almost jumped a red light.

She chastised herself. *Keep your mind on the job.*

Chapter Five

Was it too early to meet Brett at the club? Almost certainly not. Allner-Smith never needed a reason to get a drink, no matter the time. Today should be no exception.

Harris took out a new burner phone in leather casing out of his desk. He pocketed the packet of cigarettes he had been trying to hide from sight all afternoon and moved out of his office. He had promised Sarah he'd stop smoking, but this was six months ago, and she'd stopped nagging. Still, he could perhaps report his consumption was down to less than a pack a day.

The rest of his team was busy on other assignments and they hardly noticed him leave. He took the lift to the 4th floor, and walked in the direction of the small coffee shop that stayed open 24/7, and most importantly had access to outside space.

Harris walked straight through, already fingering the cigarette he was about to light. The sliding doors opened. He was halfway across the roof terrace when he stopped abruptly.

"Bugger..." He searched his pockets. He had forgotten his lighter.

Harris looked around. There was only one person sitting at a table outside. In December, the terrace looking onto the banks of the River Thames was cold and humid. Not many people would choose to be outside unless they needed a nicotine kick.

The woman turned halfway around to face him. She must have sensed him looking at her. Harris brandished his cigarette and shrugged at her. She seemed to understand immediately and nodded.

She took out her lighter and stood up.

"I'm sorry to trouble you." Harris reached her. "But I badly need my fix."

She smiled, offering the much-desired item to Harris. "You're in luck. I'm the one who usually forgets to bring something too, including my cigarettes."

"You're a lifesaver." Harris flicked the spark wheel a few times until the flame ignited.

He drew on his lit cigarette and inhaled deep. He took out his packet of cigarettes and presented it to her. She smiled and shook her head.

"Where are my manners?" Harris put the packet away and stretched out a hand. "Steve Harris."

"Debbie Martin." Her grip was firm but friendly. Harris handed back the lighter with another thank you.

"Good luck with your op, whatever it is." She smiled again and moved back inside, leaning in when a fresh gust of wind blasted the terrace.

He moved to the edge of the terrace and sat on one of the benches. The wind blowing across the Thames strengthened and he shivered, instantly regretting having forgotten his jacket. The same one with his lighter safely tucked in one of the pockets, all warm and cosy.

No time to delay.

Harris took the burner phone out and called the only number he had stored in it. It kept ringing and Harris was about to hang up, when Brett answered.

"I thought I was done with you lot."

Harris smiled. Crowne may have rattled him earlier, but he could now do the same to one of his most aristocratic assets.

"And here I was thinking you missed me," Harris drawled.

"What could have possibly given you that idea?" Brett's pinched and somewhat nasal voice made Harris forget about the cold.

"The fact that you are still on the MI6 payroll and still claiming expenses should act as a good reminder. But of course, I can remedy that pretty quickly."

Brett groaned. "Do you need to be so coarse? This money business can be such a bore."

"Why? Because I deal in cash?" Harris dragged on his cigarette, the tip of which grew bright red. "Is it not what you do when you bargain with your Middle East terrorist contacts whilst purchasing a stolen art piece?"

"It's an act of preservation, as I explained to you numerous times, and let me remind you that my sources in the Middle East are *not* terrorists." *Brett sounded offended.*

Good.

"I need a small service." Harris inhaled deep, and the nicotine finally did its job.

"In my experience, whenever you ask for a service it is never small."

"Granted, Brett, last time things might have gotten a bit hairy... but this one should be right up your street."

He could hear Allner-Smith moving around. "That does not fill me with confidence either."

"How much business have you done with Russian oligarchs?"

Brett's movements stopped.

"What, a bunch of rabid terrorists wasn't enough for you? Now, you're throwing me into the deadly embrace of Russia's organised crime, with connections to the FSB and the GRU?"

"That's a tad dramatic, Brett. For a start, you've been very happy to do business with these so-called rabid terrorists and help them sell on their looted antiquities. I also seem to recall that the buyers, on quite a few occasions, were the very same Russian oligarchs I'm interested in."

"As I said, there is nothing wrong with relocating one of these artefacts to better homes... better than having them blown apart," Brett ranted.

"Silly me... this is a salvage operation for your precious artefacts." Harris finished his cigarette and crushed the butt into the small sandpit provided for smokers. The tray was almost full. Staff at MI6 were clearly having a tough day.

He continued. "Remind me, what have you done with the hundreds of thousands of pounds you earned in commission?"

"One needs to earn a living."

"Quite." Harris walked back to the entrance. "Why don't we meet at your club for a drink and a little chat in about an hour? I'm sure that interesting and relevant information will have popped into this great mind of yours by then." Harris hung up and made his way back to his office.

Time to get ready to meet his asset, but to do so, he first needed to use the Airlock for a much-needed transformation.

* * *

The Giorgio Armani wool and cashmere suit McNamara wore was impeccably restrained and his silk tie created an air of assured elegance. Arthur McNamara Jr was here to make a statement.

Henry had left the door of his office open. He did not yet trust his new receptionist, recruited less than 15 minutes ago.

But Nick surprised him by playing his part beautifully – pleasant but not obsequious.

Nick relieved McNamara of his coat that he carried folded over one arm. Henry hoped Nick might also relieve McNamara of a few more things that might prove helpful. Nick then led the way to Henry's office, showed the man in, and shut the door without a sound.

Henry closed a mail that had no importance just as McNamara walked in, playing with assurance the overworked businessman he was pretending to be.

He moved from behind his desk and extended a hand to his guest, greeting him without a jacket and with rolled up shirtsleeves. He smiled briefly as they shook hands and guided his visitor towards the corner of his office with a leather sofa and chairs.

Henry rolled down his sleeves, and fastened the cuffs with the set of discreet cufflinks he'd had Harris purchase for him from Jermyn Street in London. Harris had almost had a fit at the price – a quarter of his monthly salary.

Necessary tools of the trade, Henry had argued.

Henry sat opposite McNamara. "What can I do for you?"

"I thought it would be much easier to have a conversation *tête-à-tête*." McNamara looked discreetly around Henry's office, assessing and memorising no doubt. Henry leaned back into the sofa, and with a small gesture of his hand, indicated his guest should carry on.

"One of our most prestigious clients is raising finance for a high-profile acquisition. We have been led to believe that you might be interested in joining the small group of exclusive investors." McNamara leaned back in his armchair, confident, body relaxed, and with a sharpness in his gaze that spoke volumes.

McNamara had yet to mention Rush Huckerby. The young man might as well not have existed.

47

Henry extended an arm along the back of the sofa and feigned surprise. "I had understood the deal to be slightly different... Rush was of the view that David Upstage's high-profile deal, as you put it, had proven difficult to finance and that your client was in need of help."

McNamara's ploy in pretending the deal was for a client other than Upstage wouldn't work. Henry wouldn't get rumbled that easily.

McNamara's face darkened, but his voice was even. "Disregard what Rush told you. We have moved on since then."

"You mean since 24 hours ago?" Henry's voice lifted a little, showing off a hint of sarcasm.

"A lot can happen in 24 hours, as you and I both know, Mr Newborn." Hardness flared in McNamara's eyes. The cruelty disappeared as quickly as it had come, replaced then by the same unshaken confidence as before.

"If the quality of the transaction has somehow improved all the better. I'm happy to consider once more how I can contribute."

"I told you, my client is not interested in intermediaries. His instructions are very clear – he will only speak to people committed to becoming business partners in the deal, and who are willing to share risk and reward with him."

McNamara's speech was impeccable. Henry was suddenly grateful to have spent years in McNamara's position, hooking clients to join questionable deals that were often too complex for them to fully understand. Henry doubted he had ever peddled a deal as rotten as the one McNamara was giving him now.

Henry had to hand it to him. He was impressive. A more than competent financial player.

"Then, I'm sorry you have made the trip for nothing." Henry glanced at his watch.

It was 11.52am. The TV channels currently fooling his guest into believing the meeting rooms were occupied would soon switch to advertising. Time for McNamara to go.

But the man did not budge. Henry couldn't quite decide whether McNamara was considering changing his tune, or if he saw though Henry's bluff.

"A shame, but this transaction is not to everybody's taste." McNamara took his time to stand up. There was something hairy about his assurance. "But if you change your mind..." He dug a silver card holder engraved with his initials out of his jacket pocket and handed a business card to Henry.

Henry stood up, took the card and moved to his desk as slowly as he could. The clock on the wall now indicated 11.55am. He dumped the card on the desk. Henry gave McNamara a professional smile. "I doubt I will change my mind, but if I do, I know where to find you." Henry extended an arm towards the door of his office.

McNamara took his time in leaving. "Excellent offices. You were lucky to secure a suite here."

"Indeed. It took me a while to find what I was looking for." Henry was already halfway across reception and Nick was handing McNamara his coat.

A collection of clocks displaying times in different time zones ticked away on the reception wall. All Henry saw was 11.57am. Three minutes to get McNamara out of here.

McNamara stopped. "Where were you before DC?"

Henry opened the front door as casually as he could. "This is our first office in Washington. I usually do business with my US clients from Switzerland. I thought it was high time I opened a satellite office here though."

Henry walked into the corridor and to the lifts. To his relief, McNamara followed.

"You'll see the address of our offices in Geneva on the card I gave you this morning."

McNamara drew the card out of his pocket and started reading. Henry pressed the lift call button. The doors pinged open. McNamara put the card back in his pocket, and briefly shook hands with Henry. His face was unreadable.

As Henry was returning to his office suite, he heard the mingled sound of TV commercials flooding the reception area. He dashed forward, closed the main door behind him and turned off the TVs in both meeting rooms.

Nick Fox was standing by reception, not certain what he was meant to do next.

"Let's go to my office."

With a nod, Nick followed Henry into his space. His eyes lit up at the sight of the high-tech equipment that was on Henry's desk.

"Don't even think about it."

"I wouldn't..." Nick protested half-heartedly. "But it's top-notch equipment."

Henry did not respond. Instead, he inclined his head towards the place where McNamara had sat only a few minutes ago.

Nick sat down.

Henry grabbed the coffee Nick had bought for him earlier on. It was lukewarm, but Henry needed the sugar and the caffeine. He sat opposite Nick.

"Anything of interest in his coat pockets?"

Nick's face turned red and he blurted out something incomprehensible.

"Look, I don't care if you took me at my word and checked what he had in his pockets, as long as you tell me what you found." Henry took a sip and pulled a face at the taste. "And stop blushing every time I catch you red-handed."

Nick nodded and made an effort to steady himself. "Nothing very interesting. A packet of Kleenex, a bit of spare change – which I didn't take," Nick added immediately. "And a used underground ticket."

"Do you remember the destination?"

"Sure... it was a ticket to Woodley Park Zoo."

Henry ran a hand though his hair, pausing it there for a few seconds. "How old is the ticket?"

"This morning."

"Find out if there are any finance boutiques or lobbyist groups that have an office next to the underground station."

Nick nodded and left, closing the door behind him.

Henry let his head drop against the back of the sofa.

Arthur McNamara Jr was proving to be a worthy opponent. Time for Henry to play the game like McNamara. Dirty.

* * *

"What have you got for me that's so under the radar it's not even authorised?" Mandy, the analyst at Langley, placed her tray on the canteen table opposite Jack's.

"And what makes you say that?" Jack protested with a smile.

"You've got that look about you... Plus, you haven't asked me for anything remotely subversive for months."

"Subversive is a big word."

"I'm not complaining... I was getting worried Hunter III had finally got to you." Mandy smiled, picking up her cutlery, but not eating.

"He sure is trying very hard. I have a week to get results for RUSKY BEAR."

"But you're still going to follow your hunch, right?"

"It's more than a hunch but it's not a sexy hunch."

"Should you even be saying the word 'sexy' in front of a female colleague?" Mandy squeezed some chilli sauce onto the side of her plate.

"Almost certainly not, but that's just the way this project feels, and I'm speaking to you."

"Who, the only woman on the CIA campus who can take a bit of light banter?"

"And thank God for that... and don't tell me I can't use his name either, otherwise I'll assume that Hunter III has got to go for sure."

"No chance... I'm one of the few women of colour who made it to a reasonably senior rank. I'm his diversity mascot."

"OK then, how about doing a bit of fieldwork?" Jack briefly looked into her eyes.

Mandy held her fork in mid-air for a short moment. "You mean proper operative work?" She grinned. "Here or outside the US?"

"At least out of this office, but I'm afraid it's here in our own backyard."

"Heck, who cares. Anything to see the world and not be stuck inside Langley's four boring walls." Mandy picked up a piece of enchilada, dipped it into the chilli sauce, and ate. "Delicious... When do I start?"

"Hang on, you don't even know what it's all about."

Mandy took another bite, savouring the second one as much as the first. "Don't need to. RUSSKY BEAR. It's Russia, and no one wants to deal with it because they can't admit they are underestimating Putin, yet again."

Jack smiled again, amused. "You know me too well."

"That's why I'm saying when do I start. You always come up with the most implausible of scenarios, and guess what? You're right most of the time."

"I'm not working on my own on this one."

"Who's your contact abroad then?"

"Steve Harris."

"The little English Bulldog... I rather like him." Mandy chuckled. "You know that I have never met him in the flesh, but I reckon I'm as tall as he is short fused."

"Now, now... Let's not put a dent in that special relationship, please." Jack chuckled too. He couldn't help it.

"Who's the contact in DC? Harris is not a field op, so he must have an asset over here."

"Henry Crowne, operating under legend."

Mandy's eyes widened. "The former banker who was doing time for financial terrorism, and who infiltrated the Islamic State in Syria?"

"That's the one."

Mandy nodded. "He's a risk taker."

"Does that worry you?"

"Nope, I'm just making sure I'm remembering correctly what I read about him."

Her words caused Jack to stop eating. "If you think he is taking stupid risks, promise me you'll pull out."

"All we do is take risks! Shall I list the number of times you have been in a pickle and I've helped you?"

"Fair point, but I lost Huckerby and..." Jack's words stuck in his throat.

"I know, and I'd quite like to put the douchebags who did that behind bars."

"That's the job of the Feds."

"But we can help." Mandy finished her food and looked at her watch. "If you tell me what intel you need me to gather, I'll make sure I deliver as soon as poss."

"I'm speaking to Crowne later today."

"Sounds good. Tell him I'm in."

Mandy stood and dropped her tray on the conveyor belt, before walking out.

Maybe involving her wasn't such a good idea after all. He hadn't been able to protect Huckerby. Why did he think he could fare better with Mandy?

Chapter Six

His Rhode Island Avenue apartment was only four blocks away from the office. Henry left Nick to find more information about the places McNamara may have visited before he'd paid a visit to Henry.

Something or someone had prompted McNamara to act fast. Henry was certain of it. It had not been a typical business meeting that might result in both men agreeing to work on a project together.

It was a reconnaissance mission – a know-your-enemy sort of encounter. What Henry could not yet tell was if McNamara felt personally threatened by Henry's desire to work with his client. Or was it Top Capital Partners that didn't like Henry approaching David Upstage?

Henry arrived back at his apartment. He waited outside the door for a short moment. Sure nothing was amiss, he opened the door, locked it and went straight to the wardrobe in his bedroom.

He removed the shoe boxes, stacked on the bottom, to reveal a panel. He slid the wood panel back, and pulled out a few items of clothing that he'd gathered during his first week of moving into his apartment. A UPS delivery uniform, a jacket and cap – all items he hoped would be useful. He slid the hatch closed and restacked the shoe boxes. Henry changed from his Savile Row suit, cut from the best handwoven cloth, into a pair of inexpensive jeans and a T-shirt.

He moved to the bathroom, where he hesitated for a split second. His reflection in the mirror still startled him when he least expected it.

The mane of dark hair that had been turning a little grey at the temples was now replaced by a short haircut, with shaven sides, light brown in colour. Together with the close-cut beard, the change in appearance to what Henry considered his normal face was striking.

Henry collected a black rucksack from the set of drawers. He rolled the UPS jacket and cap up into a ball and pushed them into the bag.

From the same drawer, he selected a small lock-picking set, which he placed in the back pocket of his jeans. He probably wouldn't need to use it in broad daylight, but he might as well be equipped for his outing. He put on a black puffer jacket, slung the rucksack over his shoulder, picked up some cash, and left his apartment for his next destination.

Henry stopped across the road from the office building housing Top Capital Partners. He bought a coffee and a small sandwich, which he ate seated on the stone surround of a large flower bed.

He spotted a small alleyway alongside the building with a flow of traffic and people moving in and out – delivery men and vans.

Henry pulled the UPS jacket and cap from his rucksack. He put the jacket on over his puffer, making him look bulkier. He pulled the cap down low on his forehead, shading most of his face. He moved up the street, crossed at the next set of traffic lights and made his way to the side alley.

A large van entered the side street. Henry followed from a discreet distance. The man hopped out of the vehicle, opened the back doors and pulled a couple of large items out from inside. He almost lost his balance, before kicking the door shut.

Henry smiled. He was in luck.

He jogged towards the van. The doors had not been shut properly. He cast an eye at the entrance through which the man had disappeared. Henry picked up a medium-sized parcel and made his way inside the building.

No one stopped him when he walked towards the main lift. Other delivery people were moving around the place. The mail room was signposted to the left, a sign written in large letters with an arrow pointing the way – impossible to miss. The doors of the lift pinged open.

Henry hesitated for a moment.

Very few deliveries required a direct signature these days, and certainly none where there was a central office to dispatch mail.

He was about to retrace his steps, when the man from the van appeared at the end of the corridor. The service lift's doors had just

54

opened; a couple of cleaning ladies walked out. Henry raced for it and pressed the button for the 4th floor. Too late to change strategy now.

The doors opened on the 4th floor. An older man pushing a trolley laden with buckets, brush, pans, and detergent bottles was waiting for the lift. The strong smell of bleach coming from his cart made Henry gag. Henry walked out. The older man got in, ignoring him.

Henry looked around, noticing that the men's toilets were situated outside the security doors for the floor. He moved slowly towards the security doors.

They flung open suddenly. A man raced through them and disappeared into the men's lavatory. Henry lunged for the closing doors, getting a foot inside the door frame before it closed. He waited a short moment. No one had seen him.

He pressed on into the large corridor where the internal lifts were located, and walked towards the reception area for Top Capital Partners. The glass door to the area was frosted, giving him no way to peer into the space. Henry rang the external bell with a couple of short bursts. A few seconds later, a woman's voice inquired about the reason for the call.

Henry noted her tone; guarded, perhaps a little unfriendly.

"Parcel for delivery."

"Then, please use the mailroom on the first floor."

"But I'm already here." Henry persisted. "It's for Mr Huckerby."

The woman hesitated. A silhouette passed behind the opaque glass and the door opened.

"I wouldn't normally do this, but I'll make an exception?" she said. She tried to look severe, but her eyes told a different story. She looked concerned that someone might see her handling this parcel.

"Sorry, but it says I have to deliver to Mr Huckerby himself."

The woman took a moment to understand the request. "This is ridiculous... this *is* Mr Huckerby's office."

"I know." Henry nodded, trying to hide as much of his face below the cap. "But I've been told only him and this is one of my first jobs."

The receptionist exhaled and frowned. "Wait here."

She left the reception area and turned to the left, towards what appeared to be the bulk of the office space for Top Capital.

Henry craned his neck. He had never been inside Huckerby's office before. The young man had preferred to keep their meetings low-key until he felt he was ready to introduce Henry to Hernandez, and ultimately Upstage. He was alone at reception. He took several steps forward. The office space had been split into two distinct spaces – the left working area and the right meeting rooms.

A door opened and a burst of laughter came out of one of the meeting rooms. Two men appeared, still involved in an animated conversation.

The tall man who walked out first was immediately recognisable. Muscular build through relentless training, tanned, and displaying the usual Hollywood bleached smile, David Upstage walked out of the meeting room first. He was followed by an equally tall and bulky man. Henry couldn't quite hear what they were saying, but he could have sworn he detected an accent from the second man – Eastern European, or perhaps Russian.

Henry surveyed the reception area and beyond, trying to remember as much as he could before having to retreat. He had not expected to see Upstage there.

A stupid miscalculation...

His disguise would not hold for long if McNamara came out too. Henry returned to the security doors for the reception area. He looked around for the release button but couldn't find any.

From his new position he could no longer see Upstage, but could hear the two men's voices getting closer.

Stay calm, Henry.

There had to be a release button somewhere.

He thought fast and moved swiftly behind the receptionist desk. He ran his fingers underneath the top of the desk and found what he was looking for. He pressed it and the reception door released with a sigh.

Henry disappeared just as Upstage was turning the corner.

In a couple of long steps Henry reached the lifts. He pressed the call button frantically. One of the lifts was moving up too slowly to the 4th floor.

2, 3...

The lift doors opened at the same time as the security door for Top Capital Partners did.

56

"Wait!" The receptionist called after him.

But the lift doors closed. Henry pressed the button to the 3rd floor. He exited on that level, found the men's toilets and jumped into one of the cubicles. He removed the UPS jacket, stuffed it in his rucksack, and reversed the UPS cap, turning it into a NY Yankee black cap.

Henry walked down one flight of stairs. He used the same trick as before to access the bank of lifts without a proper pass. This time it was a young lady in a hurry who obliged him.

He entered the first lift that opened, joining a crowd of three men and two women on their way down to the first floor. He followed them closely as they walked towards the exit.

To an observer, he might just pass off as one of them.

* * *

It was after 2pm when Henry returned to his office. He had changed back into his Savile Row made-to-measure suit and his Hermès tie. He no longer got satisfaction from wearing these elegant clothes, the price tag of which he now found ludicrous. But it was part of his new legend. At least he had played the game before.

The reconnaissance mission had been a flop, to put it mildly. He had gathered little information and almost blown his cover. A few bits of information might still prove useful, but it was a meagre catch.

The security of the building was a little loose. Henry was surprised by how easy it had been to reach the 4th floor without being challenged.

The security at Top Capital Partners, however, was another matter altogether. It was without a doubt a high-grade set-up. Henry had spotted miniature cameras that wouldn't have been visible to the untrained eye. The image would be good enough to give any face recognition software the quality it needed.

The meeting room area set-up had felt odd, as though it didn't quite belong to the rest of the office space.

Henry knew why now.

The walls of the meeting rooms were not simple office partitions but thick, triple-glazed glass, the likes of which he'd only seen at the MI6 building in London.

It couldn't have been easy to find a manufacturer that produced that type of elaborate glass for such a conventional company. Whatever company Top Capital used, they were highly specialised, perhaps even working for the military.

Henry walked into his Rhode Island Avenue office suite in a foul mood, hoping Nick Fox had not walked away with his office equipment.

But no, Nick was at his desk, a half-eaten sandwich poking out of its wrapper, and two empty extra-large cups of coffee stacked up in the nearest dustbin – a testimony to his dedication.

He nodded when Henry entered. "I've got information for you."

"Let's hear it." Henry grunted. "I've had a bad lunch... Come into my office and let's talk."

"Actually, would you mind if I showed you at my computer?" Henry cast Nick a dark look, but the young man was already facing his screen, fingers coursing at speed over the keyboard.

Henry reached Nick's desk in a couple of strides. Nick turned the monitor towards him, and Arthur McNamara's frozen image appeared. He was looking preoccupied whilst exiting a rather plain-looking building.

Henry frowned. "Where did you get this picture from?"

"You told me to get creative... so I did." Nick shrugged.

"You mean... You hacked the CCTV system around the Woodley Park underground station?" Henry could not hide his surprise.

"It's not that complicated." Nick looked almost humble. "But what is really cool is the facial recognition software I've been using."

"Hang on a minute..." Henry was stuck between concern and amusement. Had he stumbled across a hacking genius who did not know his potential?

Nick stopped, his expression bemused. "I thought you wanted me to find information about where the underground ticket led this guy, McNamara."

"I did but I don't recall asking you to hack your way into the Metropolitan Police's surveillance system."

"Well, if you put it that way, I guess it sounds more complicated than it is... I got in there really easy."

"That's not the point..." Henry crossed his arms over his chest. "It's a criminal offence."

Nick raised a finger. "Only if I get caught."

"Something tells me it's not the first time you've done this."

"It's just a bit of fun."

"So you keep saying. What about the facial recognition software, then?"

"A lot of small tech companies offer good quality software. I'm friendly with a few developers who don't mind sharing."

"And that's also completely above board, of course." This time Henry did not suppress a grin.

"I do them a couple of favours in return... no big deal."

Henry wondered what the quid pro quo would be – a question for another day. They returned to the picture Nick had frozen on his screen.

Nick pointed at a map of DC on his screen. "Guess what that building is?"

"It's the Russian Embassy on Boris Nemtsov Plaza."

Nick's eyes widened. "How do you know that?"

"I've been in this job far longer than you, my friend."

Nick cocked his head. "Which job is that, then?"

Henry moved slowly towards his office. "How does joining MI6 sound to you?"

* * *

The gusts of wind blowing over the River Thames pushed against Harris. He raised the collar of his old winter jacket and persevered over Vauxhall Bridge. He had not expected a call from the chief of MI6 that afternoon.

The new chief had taken over from Sir John Sawers only a few months ago, but he was already making changes that were being felt throughout the organisation. Harris had been commended for his work in the Middle East. The coalition of armed forces between the US, the UK, and the other EU countries had finally agreed on a plan to deal with the growing might of the Islamic State.

Harris was pleased with the result, and with his gamble that Crowne would come through in the end. But Harris's focus was on something else now. Something that had been at the back of his mind for a while.

The Chief did not share Harris's views on an old foe: Russia. The conversation they'd had a few weeks back was replaying in Harris's mind, disquieting.

"An intelligence officer of your calibre should not be focusing on the old beast," the new Chief had said. "You're reading too many Le Carré novels."

"I'm not sure Ukraine would agree with you, sir," Harris had shot back. He regretted the comment as soon as he made it.

"This is a political issue, perhaps a military one, but not one for MI6," the Chief retorted stiffly. "Russia's sphere of influence is waning."

"All the more reason to be on our guard, sir." Harris sat upright in the chair in front of his boss's desk. "A wounded bear is far more dangerous than a healthy one."

"I don't utterly disagree with you, Steve, but the war on terror is far from over. Abu Bakr Al-Baghdadi is still all-powerful. It will take a concerted effort between the UK, the US, other members of the coalition forces, and even Russia, to get rid of this psycho."

Harris had nothing to say against that. He, too, wanted Al-Baghdadi dead, but he was not the only foe worthy of his team's attention.

"Look." The Chief sat back in his chair. "I don't want to hamper you in what you do best. You have been good at ferreting out danger that many of our colleagues had not seen coming, and you think laterally to find solutions. So, I'll let you get on with –" the Chief tapped on his keyboard to check "– Operation RUSSKY BEAR. But I don't want you pulling focus from your entire team."

Harris thanked the Chief. At least he was still open to running the op.

Harris arrived at his destination in Pimlico.

The building he stood outside had nondescript features – a construction that had been erected some 30 years ago. He pressed his badge to an electronic eye to gain access to the ground floor there. There was no receptionist and no security guard. He came across a second door where he went through a more stringent security check process: fingerprint, voice, and facial recognition.

Harris progressed to the second floor, entering one of the flats he used regularly to prepare for meetings with some of his assets. The

60

Airlock was available 24 hours a day, seven days a week to the MI6 officers who were running operatives in the field.

Harris swapped his tatty jeans and old winter jacket for a tailor-made suit. The absolute bare minimum look he needed if he were to be let into one of the most select gentlemen's clubs in St James.

The podgy doorman rushed Harris into the small, but cosy reception area of the club. An attendant took Harris's coat, placed it in the cloakroom, and led him through the rooms towards Brett's favourite area: the smoking room.

Brett had arrived early, as he often did, and was already nursing an excellent whisky. No doubt, an old single malt – Glenfiddich or Macallan.

Harris nodded at Brett's glass. "I'll have the same." The usher gave an appreciative smile.

"You're learning." Brett extended a long, knotty hand towards his glass. "No please and no thank you."

Harris grinned. "That's OK. I'll give him a large tip when I leave this place."

Brett sighed. "You commoners... Why do you insist on ruining it for the likes of me?"

"Because we like helping other commoners."

Harris dropped into the old leather armchair opposite Brett. He looked around briefly. It had been a while since Harris had set foot in here. But nothing had changed, the same dignified men waiting on the same entitled men.

Harris's drink arrived. He took a sip of Glenfiddich and waited for the drink to have the desired effect. It had been a long and frustrating day.

He nestled into the back of the chair, enjoying the warming effect of his drink. "What do you know about the Russian expat community?"

"Not so fast..." Brett reached for the elegant crystal tumbler on the small coffee table and brought the glass to his lips.

He took a few sips, then continued. "Why should I help you? We had a deal if I recollect."

"That is true." Harris nodded. "But with a recall clause, if I also recollect."

"Such recall..." Brett raised a contentious finger. "To be left to my sole discretion."

"Unless it is a matter of National Security." Harris took another sip, then balanced the tumbler on the arm of his chair.

"And is it? If I were to listen to you, Steve, everything would fall in that category."

"You've got that in one." Harris raised his drink.

"Then we'll simply have to agree to disagree. Your interpretation of National Security is not the same as mine."

Harris cast a dark look at his host.

"It would be such a shame if the old files I sent to archives were to resurface." Harris relaxed again. He still had a few cards up his sleeve.

"And it would be such a shame if the story about a certain Henry Crowne were to find its way onto the internet... anonymous leak, of course." Brett looked at his whisky with a forlorn expression. His glass was almost empty.

Harris gave a short exhale. "All right Brett... How much will it take?"

"You disappoint me, Steve. Everything is about money with you."

"It's just that I know my assets pretty well. Your bank account has been looking very sparse of late."

"There is a bit of a lull in my business, I agree, nothing to worry about."

"What? The business of looting artefacts in the Middle East has taken a plunge?" Harris raised an eyebrow in jest. "No wait, there's nothing left to steal, and whatever is left is guarded by the Americans."

Brett waved nonchalantly at the waiter and he came to collect his glass.

"Will that be all, sir?"

"No, the same." Brett tapped his fingers a few times on the armrest of his chair.

"How much?" Harris asked again as soon as the waiter had left.

"If by Russian expats you mean Russian oligarchs, forget it." Brett looked serious.

"I thought you did well selling your stuff to them?"

"I did, but I was incredibly lucky too. I deal with terrorists all the time and I know how to handle them."

62

The waiter returned and Brett stopped speaking. He served him his second drink and left.

Brett continued. "But the Russians... Organised crime, ex-KGB, or FSB with Putin at the very top... You need to know how to bargain with these people and money is not always what they want."

Chapter Seven

The list of new equipment Henry wanted was long, the latest in surveillance, either to be used in a static environment or on a moving target.

Nick didn't query the request for such specialist equipment. He assured Henry he knew where to find top quality devices. The realm of surveillance was no longer preserved for agencies like the CIA or MI6. Private individuals with enough wealth to rival small countries valued their security, and so did large multinational corporations.

Nick was perched on Henry's desk. "Top technology is no longer developed solely by companies that work with military states, you know."

"Why aren't you working for one of them? From what I saw this afternoon, you know your way around encryption and complex systems."

"I don't like to be tied down, and also…"

Nick hesitated, and his brown eyes shifted around in embarrassment.

"You don't want to be tempted by too many bags, lockers, and various other items in an office?" Henry rolled his chair away from his desk and stretched his long legs out in front of him.

"In a nutshell."

Nick hung his head for a moment, lost in thought.

He jumped off Henry's desk. "Let's get on with it. I'll come back to you if I can't find the best equipment money can buy."

"Good man." Henry jotted down a credit card number on a piece of paper and handed it to Nick. "Use this for the online purchases. The credit limit on the card is 20k per day. Let me know if you get close to reaching it."

"You know the card number by heart?"

"Yes, and that of all my other cards. It avoids me having to carry them with me."

"Wow, that's cool." Nick left Henry's office looking suitably impressed.

Henry stood up and closed the door of his office. Harris hadn't called back yet, and he was not prepared to wait for him.

The plan he was starting to formulate to get close to David Upstage needed bold intervention in the world of finance, and he knew exactly who he needed for the job. Henry had left a message for his contact in London after his return from Top Capital Partners' offices, bypassing Harris.

Nick was delivering on his promise to build a serious arsenal of surveillance equipment. Now that Henry understood Top Capital Partners' true capacity at shielding from prying eyes, he had decided he needed to ensure his office was protected just as well. Top Capital's power of investigation would almost certainly be just as good as their power to themselves. The rest of the time he wasn't helping Nick to choose the best devices Henry spent researching the extent of David Upstage's wealth. The picture that was emerging intrigued him more than he'd anticipated.

The billionaire's wealth was, perhaps, less secure than many believed, including Huckerby. Uncovering several well-hidden defaults on banking obligations had surprised him. Henry was certain, though, that the state of Upstage's business would not have escaped Top Capital Partners.

At 6.30pm Henry closed the office, deciding to call London from his apartment. Nick headed off to meet friends for a drink. Henry made his way back to his apartment alongside Rhode Island Avenue in the direction of Logan Circle.

He crossed the road several times and retraced his steps, whilst applying the countermeasures he had been taught to follow to spot a trail.

He hadn't identified anyone, but the streets were busy at that time of night. Henry stopped at the Shake Shack and ordered a takeaway. Once his order was placed, he walked through the restaurant, and left by a side door he had spotted a few weeks ago during one of his eating recces. Henry found himself on 14th St NW. From there he reached P St, carried on towards Logan Circle and once there, he approached his apartment from the top of Rhode Island Avenue.

The blow to the head came as a surprise.

A bike had stopped on the kerb and the passenger had jumped off without Henry spotting him. He was dressed in black leather, the visor of his helmet only reflecting the glare of the streetlamps, as the light of day was dimming.

Henry fell forward, hitting the pavement with force. Despite the pounding in his head he rolled sideways, managing to stand up, hands outstretched. The man dressed in leather delivered a high reverse kick which Henry barely avoided.

Henry's blurred vision cleared a little, enough for him to quickly look around for a weapon. There was nothing obvious he could use. A second punch came and he swung his arms wide.

The force of the missed punch destabilised the assailant for a moment. Henry retaliated with a powerful roundhouse kick that caught the man in the back. The attacker stumbled and stifled a scream, but he was not done.

He resumed an attack position, circling around Henry, trying to push him closer to his accomplice on the bike. The motorbike would no doubt inflict a lot of damage if launched at Henry from behind. Henry crouched down and swept his right leg in a circle, catching the man across the front of the knees.

The man's sick cry was muffled by his helmet. He hit the ground with a thud. Henry brought his heel down hard, aiming this time for the small of his back. The attacker managed a partial roll, but Henry's foot hit the man's kidneys. He arched up in pain.

Henry regained some calm. There was nothing these two punks could throw at him that he couldn't cope with. Six months of indoctrination in the training camps of Islamic State had taught him that much.

His opponent tried to stand up again. The man on the bike was looking around. This was taking too long.

Henry threw a high-leg strike at his opponent's back and a low leg scissor against the front of the man's knees. The assailant landed on the ground. His helmet cracked against the pavement and the man lost his bearings for an instant.

The biker mounted the pavement, interposing the front wheel between Henry and his accomplice. Henry's assailant scrambled up and climbed onto the back of the bike. Grabbing the jacket of his mate for balance, the pair disappeared as fast as they had materialised.

A few passersby stopped.

A young couple approached Henry to ask him whether he was OK.

"I'm fine..." Blood was trickling from his nose. Henry drew a packet of Kleenex from his coat pocket and wiped the blood away.

"Perhaps, you should go to hospital?" the young woman ventured.

"Thanks for your concern... I'm very close to home." Henry did not need a hospital visit, or worse, the Metro Police getting involved.

He thanked them again. The young woman handed him his rucksack. Henry hadn't noticed he'd dropped it.

He arrived at his apartment a few minutes later. He stood in front of the door for a couple of minutes, alert to any suspicious sounds or activity. All seemed calm. He unlocked the door as quietly as he could and pushed it open. He stood again on the threshold, attentive.

The small devices he had placed at the door and in the entrance, designed to let him know if someone had been in, had not been moved. Henry shut the door and switched on all the lights from a central command. He went through each room methodically, but nothing was amiss.

Certain his flat was clear, he bolted the main door.

The damage to his face was less extensive than he'd feared. There was a small cut on his left cheek, easily attributed to a razor, and a scratch on the side of his neck that he could conceal with a roll neck jumper. The real damage was at the back of his head. A sore bump Henry felt underneath his fingers told him as much. But it was nothing a pack of frozen peas wouldn't sort out.

He grabbed a slim towel from the bathroom, went to the freezer and found what he needed. He wrapped the pack of frozen vegetables in the towel and applied it to his head.

Henry moved from the kitchen to the lounge and retrieved the MI6 encrypted laptop from its secret vault underneath the floorboards.

Harris could no longer deny him the backup he needed. He had surprised his attackers by being more prepared than they'd expected. They would not make the same mistake the next time they came at him.

"I can't get hold of Harris, so I hope you don't mind me calling directly." Henry had already logged into his MI6 computer and tried Harris. His minder was otherwise engaged, and he had no time to lose. If his minder was a bit too slow to the take, he knew where he could get what he needed.

"I thought your new assignment in DC didn't need backup in the UK," James said as his image came on screen.

In London, James Radlett was still awake at midnight. His solid army training, followed by a successful swap into investment banking, had clearly formed long lasting habits. One of them was to operate on a short night's sleep.

"That was the plan, until my contact in DC jumped from the top floor of his office building. I say jumped, but I'm certain he was pushed, and because of it, things have become a lot more complicated."

"Speaking of jumping, you seem to have had a bit of a rough end to your day." James came closer to his screen to take a better look.

Henry pulled the makeshift ice pack from his neck and waved it in front of the screen. "Frozen veg... At least I know what I'm having for dinner."

James nodded. "I take it you need my help?"

"That would be ideal." Henry gave him a genuine smile. There was a lot of history between the two men, some of it unhappy, but James had helped him whilst in the Middle East, and Henry still felt indebted to him.

"I received the mail you sent today about Upstage and I've had a look into this guy's business. He may be a billionaire on paper, but he has stretched himself a lot, financially."

"I gathered as much from my DC contact. He is desperate for some refinancing. Or so I understood until this morning. A chap called Arthur McNamara Jr came to see me and his story was very different."

James lifted an eyebrow. "You mean that he found a fresh source of finance for Upstage? Some white knight has just strolled in and written a blank cheque to facilitate Upstage's latest property project?" His former deputy could also smell BS a mile away.

"I would normally treat that sort of posturing as complete crap, but something about McNamara tells me he's a serious player."

James frowned. "I suppose he could be... with the right connections."

"I said McNamara was a serious player. I didn't say he was an honest one."

James lifted a mug and took a sip; strong tea with a splash of milk, Henry suspected.

"So, who are the bad guys?" James asked. "Harris left a message saying he wanted a word. I presume it was to speak to me about this."

"The name of the operation is RUSSKY BEAR." Henry moved the frozen veg around and winced.

"What, Russian organised crime? Wouldn't that sort of thing be more suited for the Feds?"

"If it was OC related then yes, the Feds would get involved, but Harris thinks there is more to it, and I am inclined to agree. It's unusual for an ordinary office to be equipped with military-grade counter surveillance equipment."

James whistled. "Now we're talking. And I presume we're talking about the office of this McNamara guy?"

"Yep. I need to get past this McNamara guy to gain access to Upstage."

"If the investors McNamara has in mind were to withdraw, then he and Upstage would need a high-profile financial fixer to find new people."

"I like the way you've spotted the fickle nature of some of these bankers... promising a lot and not always delivering." Henry grinned.

"I learnt that from my most excellent boss." James teased.

Henry laughed. "I'm glad to hear it."

"Let me do some proper digging... I'll find out who is offering to finance Upstage."

"Excellent, then we'll see how solid the deal and its funding are. And if they're not, I'll find a way to scupper that deal."

"You'll have something to work on by the end of your morning." James held back a yawn. "It's like being back in investment banking all over again."

"No, it's much better. We might get to put a bullet in some of these bastards' heads and this one will be a real one. Someone I worked with recently deserves some justice."

His simple dinner of vegetables and fish tasted much better than he had anticipated. Henry moved back to his lounge where he'd left his laptop open. He resumed the laborious task he'd started the night before of going through his notes of conversation with Huckerby, but there was nothing in the rest of them that he did not remember.

Huckerby had sent Henry a large file containing newspapers and magazine articles about Upstage. Then there were a few video clips and some social media messages Upstage was famous for. Henry had also started reading the file the day before, but hadn't had time to finish before he was due to meet Huckerby.

He returned to the mass of documents and resumed reading with fresh eyes. Huckerby had gathered a surprisingly insightful amount of information; some short snippets of conversations, some more elaborate tales that were meant to help Henry build an understanding of who David Upstage was. Henry jotted down some notes on a pad.

He stopped an hour later and reread his observations. Huckerby had done an impressive job. The young man had only met David Upstage 18 months ago, but the information gathered was excellent.

Henry clenched a fist. He had enjoyed working with Rush Huckerby and now that the sagacity of his observation had shown though his work, Henry felt the immensity of his loss.

Henry returned to the rest of the information. The video clip was particularly revealing. Upstage was being interviewed by one of the most controversial TV channels in the US. He was sporting a navy-blue made-to-measure suit that Henry recognised as one of Upstage's own luxury labels. The white shirt and red tie gave him the look of a Wall Street banker.

His body language struck Henry the most: self-assured, leaning forward, as though he was about to move on the interviewer, and the use of distinct manners that indicated extensive public speaking coaching. The hand gestures, the recognisable way he spoke and the articulated words he used were all for show.

Henry froze the video, then rewound it to watch and listen a few times more. Henry wrote a few words down on his pad, the favourite ones Upstage like to repeat – tremendous, fabulous, dynamic, and very bad.

Henry moved to the kitchen to brew a cup of coffee, and to take a moment to formulate a clearer picture of the man he was targeting, the man Henry Newborn had to convince to let him into his deepest secrets.

70

The coffee machine beeped. He dropped a dash of milk and a sugar cube into the burning hot liquid and moved back to the lounge.

Henry read his notes again.

He had met many men resembling Upstage during his banker's career, men who would do anything to be at the top. People who never questioned right or wrong. It wasn't that they chose evil on purpose, but they simply had no moral compass and no capacity to stop themselves.

David Upstage was without a doubt one of them. He spoke about expropriation for the purpose of expanding the luxury resort he was building, without any consideration for the people he was throwing out of their homes. It was good for the economy, he said in one of his videos, and of course, good for his pocket. But that he would never mention.

Upstage's amorality served only his need for self-advancement. The newspaper articles were clear. He had no problem screwing anyone who did business with him, as long as it helped him. He had fallen out with the banks that had funded him and with most people he'd ever done business with, right down to the IRS. Henry was almost impressed with the sheer determination of the man; nothing in his way.

He had no fear of confronting anybody, and yet Henry wondered if, underneath his brazen personality, Upstage was hiding a secret.

What Henry was certain of was this: David Upstage needed a new 'friend', a 'financial fixer' who would, for a time, help him advance his personal agenda.

Henry stretched, wincing when the pain reminded him that, in his attempt to attract David Upstage's attention, the competition was merciless and could cost him his life.

Chapter Eight

The alarm rang at 5.30am. Henry pressed the off button with an unsteady hand and rolled over onto his back. He had gone to bed shortly before midnight, but he needed to make a number of early morning calls to London before starting his day in DC.

A few bruises had started to appear on his body, and his head ached whenever he turned it sideways. A warm shower did him good, and by 6am, he had logged into his encrypted MI6 computer again and was enjoying a cup of Irish breakfast tea.

Unsurprisingly, James had been busy and had delivered what he'd promised.

Henry went through a list of transactions that Upstage was either trying to conclude or was in the process of litigating. The last item looked promising. Upstage was suing a large European bank for the collapse of one of his businesses. When Wall Street had refused to raise Upstage's credit, following numerous corporate bankruptcies, DS Bank had agreed to lend him up to $1bn. Upstage was now suing the same DS Bank that had helped him years ago, for failing in their duty of care during the financial crisis.

Henry couldn't help but smile. Upstage had no scruples. People were to be used, abused, and eventually discarded after they had served their purpose.

Nothing two former investment bankers like Henry and James could not cope with.

James had anticipated what Henry wanted next: a list of banks or other financial institutions Upstage and the Top Capital team had approached.

The list was comprehensive, and Henry sensed desperation from the Upstage team. Not many banks, including lesser known outfits that may benefit from the kudos of lending to a popular figure like Upstage, were prepared to take the risk.

Upstage's history of bankruptcies, followed by litigation, did not make Upstage a viable partner.

And yet, McNamara had sounded brazenly confident that he had sourced finance for Upstage. Henry and James must have been missing something. Something that even Huckerby had not spotted until perhaps a few days ago. Henry was convinced he would not find out what it was unless he gained Upstage's confidence.

Henry topped up his cup of Irish breakfast tea and returned to the laptop. Time to call Harris in London.

Harris picked up after a few rings. He sounded out of breath.

"You've got to get to the gym, Steve."

"I'm doing enough running around as it is, looking after my assets." Harris seemed to be speaking through clenched teeth; his usual cockiness was missing.

"Delighted to hear your utter dedication to looking after me. So, you shouldn't mind that I secured what I need to get on with Operation RUSSKY BEAR."

"Is that a what or a who?" Harris was on the move, no doubt trying to find a more secluded space to have this uneasy conversation.

"You know me too well. It's a who." Henry let the information sink in, then added, "Times two."

"Are you out of your goddamn mind?" Harris must have found the right spot within the MI6 office to allow himself a minor blow-up.

"I am not, Steve. In fact, I've never been more certain about my next step."

Harris tried to interrupt him, but Henry kept talking.

"I need James Radlett in London to carry out all financial research, and for backup in DC whenever I have a key meeting. And I'm proposing to recruit this guy Nick Fox to hack into whatever I deem necessary."

"No bloody way!" Harris exploded. "I might... just *might* be able to free up James to help you. But I'm not pissing off the CIA with the recruitment of this guy Fox who is a US national on US territory. We have an agreement with the CIA and I'm not going against that. I told you before."

"Bit late. I already told him he was part of the team."

"Then tell him he's just been sacked." Harris's furious tone had no impact.

"That's not going to do much for MI6's reputation." Henry refused to back down. "And I wouldn't mind a bit of reinforcement, locally. I had two nasty little shits try to beat me into a pulp last night."

Harris held back. "Do you mean intimidation?"

"A good attempt at it, which did not work as well as they thought it would, since I'm at my apartment rather than in hospital. But I'd be surprised if they don't come back."

"So, we are getting closer..." Harris's tone changed instantly, at the prospect of real progress.

"It seems we are, and I haven't even had a meeting with the target yet."

"Ideas about how you're going to organise that?"

"I do, but unless I have the right people with me, it won't work. I need –"

Harris interrupted. "Yeah, yeah, I heard you. Radlett and this guy Fox."

"I might even say please." Henry failed to keep the tease out of his tone.

"I'll need a CV for this chap, Fox," Harris grumbled. "...complete with criminal convictions."

"I'll get him to send something to me by end of my morning. Shall I have him stick to significant convictions? I fear the list would be rather long otherwise."

"Explain..."

"Petty theft and other minor larceny. He can't help himself."

"Fine." Harris's exasperated tone brought a smile to Henry's face. "But if he so much as steals a paper clip, I'll make sure he regrets having ever met you."

"That's fair. But I think he got the gist from me."

"Glad to hear it. I'll send you an address in a few hours' time for his onboarding with MI6. Take him there and let me know when you're done."

Harris hung up before Henry could thank him.

Henry settled back and read over the notes that James had sent him. He fired off a short reply to James, asking him to be available in one hour's time. He logged off, closed the encrypted laptop and returned it to the secret compartment underneath the floorboards.

Time to check on his new teammate.

Henry climbed down one flight of stairs and rang Nick's doorbell twice in short, sharp bursts. Nobody stirred in the apartment.

Henry rang again, this time more insistently. Still no sign of life.

Had Nick gotten spooked and left? Or had he simply decamped to carry out his kleptomania habit somewhere else?

Henry rang the bell, again, keeping his finger pressed on the button for a long minute. He had begun banging on the door when it opened suddenly.

"What time do you call this?" Nick was in a T-shirt and old boxer shorts, hair stuck out in all directions, dark stubble shading his handsome face. "It's 7.30am. It's a weekday and it's time to get to the office. I'm expecting you to be there in 45 minutes."

Nick yawned. "OK, but it may be in, like, one hour."

"45 minutes." Henry checked his watch. "And get used to this. You no longer work for a third-rate online marketing company."

Nick took a few seconds to process the information. Henry turned and headed for the staircase.

Nick stepped barefoot into the corridor. "What... you mean every day?"

"Yup,," Henry nodded. "...including weekends if need be. Welcome to the world of high finance."

The office building was quiet when Henry reached it. The security guards were finishing their night shift and the receptionist was taking over. Henry rode the lift alone and reached the 8th floor. He arrived at the door for the Platinum Suite and stopped abruptly when he saw it.

Someone had taken a pickaxe to the door and tried to smash the pane of glass.

The force of the impact had created a small hole, from which a criss-cross of lines spread outwards towards the frame. It had been a good call to replace the standard double-glazed door with a reinforced version as soon as he'd arrived. He wondered how much of this was intimidation rather than an attempt to enter the premises?

He cupped the back of his head and winced. The wound there was still sore to the touch. Henry drew his phone out of his pocket and called the office manager. It went straight to voicemail. He left a quick message, making his voice sound choked and distressed.

He pocketed his phone, and looked up at the CCTV camera by the lift and the one he had installed himself above the entrance to the suite. He would review both tapes soon, but he suspected there would be little to glean, except for a man in a hoodie sheltering his face, whilst bringing down a pickaxe on the door.

Henry typed the pin number on the entrance keypad and pushed the door open. The office was quiet but Henry took no chances, going from room to room, prepared to rebuff an intruder. He then followed with his morning routine of scanning the place for surveillance devices.

It was clean.

Henry settled at his desk and logged into his computer. He unwrapped the cheese and smoked-salmon bagel he'd picked up on his way, removed the lid from his coffee cup and started his breakfast.

Operation RUSSKY BEAR was back on track. Henry would have felt satisfaction had Rush Huckerby not paid the ultimate price.

He inhaled deeply and released his breath slowly. Whether he succeeded or failed in this operation, he would find the man or woman who had ordered Huckerby's murder and then –

Henry's thoughts were interrupted by his buzzing phone. It was the office manager calling him back.

The manager was in a flap. I'm so very sorry; absolutely dreadful; must call the police; must replace the door asap.

Henry responded with real annoyance. Calling the police was not part of his plan. Having them crawl all over his business was exactly what he was trying to avoid. The spying community aligned itself very nicely with the murky world of anonymity... Having the torch lights of the police shining all over his business was exactly what he was trying to avoid.

The entrance door to the suite opened slowly. From his desk, Henry could see straight into the small reception area. Nick appeared. Henry glanced at his watch. 47 minutes. The boy was learning fast.

"What happened?" Nick's hair was wet, and he appeared to have cut himself shaving, but he had made it almost on time, as requested.

Henry nodded to Nick from his office. "Someone's not happy with my client onboarding policy."

"The damage is a bit overkill. The keypad's not that difficult to crack."

"That's not their purpose, at least not yet."

Nick entered Henry's office and sat in one of the chairs in front of his desk. He set his coffee cup down. "I noticed you have some surveillance equipment above the door."

"I do. Start looking through the footage. Perhaps you'll spot something."

"Sounds good." Nick stood up and grabbed his coffee.

Henry lifted a finger. "But before you start playing detective, the office manager has called the cops, so is there anything I need to know about you before they arrive and find you manning my reception desk?"

Nick lowered his gaze to the immaculate, beige rug and started kicking it softly with his shoe. "Well, they'll find my name on their records..."

"I gathered that already. What I want to know is how bad are your records gonna be?"

"What d'you mean?" Nick looked genuinely perplexed.

Henry sighed. "Apart from legging it with a couple of apples from the local greengrocer or taking off with some worthless antique from Mrs Bartlett's apartment, are they going to throw anything big at me? Like hacking the Pentagon, breaking into the trading system of the NY Stock Exchange, those sorts of niceties..."

Nick scratched his head. "Nothing major as you say."

Henry gave Nick a sideways look. "But...?"

"It's just that... so far I've never been caught."

Good enough for him.

Henry clapped his hands, making Nick jump. "Great stuff. Nothing to worry about then. Get on with it."

Chapter Nine

Henry closed the door of his office and sat at his desk. The police would be around soon, but he still had time to peruse the fresh batch of emails he'd received from London. James had been his usual prolific self, producing more information about Upstage's business.

It made good reading for those who enjoyed diving into the murkiness of an unscrupulous business. Henry had seen his fair share of it when he'd been an investment banker but Upstage seemed to have turned it into an art.

The acquisitions realised by his main investment vehicle Upstage Ultra Lux were there to bolster his ego; luxury brands in fashion, mega lux spas and sports clubs, luxury holiday resorts, including yacht marinas. The word marina attracted his attention.

Henry checked his watch. He still had time to delve a little more into the list of properties James had gathered for him. He scrolled down a few pages, finding what he was looking for. Henry pulled back from the screen, astonished. Here it was in bold letters, a jolt from the past: Barcadere Marina.

Unwanted memories flooded his mind. With the police on their way this was not the time to reminisce, but how could he not remember?

The gunshots ring out in quick succession, failing to mask that Henry recognises one of the voices. He jumps up, almost toppling the coffee table in front of him, as he sprints through the bar, to where the gunshots come from.

People scream, some run out of the bar and flee.

Juan the bartender is the first one on the scene. Henry is the only one brave enough to join him.

78

Someone is lying on the pavement, legs and arms spread out. The man is not moving, and the pool of dark liquid that starts seeping into the ground makes people whisper and recoil.

Henry also stops, but the sight of the young boy standing next to his dad, frozen as he clings to his father's large cardigan, pushes Henry on.

Juan kneels next to the man on the ground, placing two fingers on his neck, looking for a pulse. Henry moves next to the young lad and wraps an arm around his shoulders. He can feel him shaking, and the boy is crying softly.

Juan looks up at Henry and shakes his head, removing his fingers slowly from the man's neck.

Nothing.

The sound of sirens in the distance tells Henry that the police are on their way. It's time to go. But the tremors of the boy's silent tears have shaken him to his core.

When Juan stands up, the young lad turns to Henry and slips his arms around his waist. The cries break free, and he blurts "Daddy" between sobs.

Henry closes his arms around the boy's shoulders. He doesn't know his name, but he knows his pain; this is not what it looks like – a robbery turned sour. It is an execution. The blood seeping though the man's shirt indicates grouped gun shots to the heart. This man, whoever he is, never had a chance.

Flashing lights are illuminating the street now. In a few moments the police will step onto the scene. A thought tugs at Henry.

You should go... Now.

The buzzing sound of Henry's landline slapped him back to reality. His mouth had gone dry. He grabbed the water bottle sitting on his desk and gulped down a few mouthfuls before answering.

"Newborn..." Henry's voice returned to its attractive baritone self.

"The police have arrived." The office manager sounded tense.

"Send them up." Henry closed the email he was reading. Time to play hide and seek with the police.

The two policemen came and went. Henry had managed to sound suitably distraught, but the policemen had been a blasé about the incident. Nothing had been stolen. They asked for any CCTV footage to be sent to their station. Probably a failed attempt at stealing high-tech equipment was their conclusion. Henry did not contradict them. He did not need a second or third visit from them. Instead, he wanted to send a message to whoever had tried to intimidate him. He did not need the police to deal with the situation.

Nick had made himself almost invisible at reception. Henry was the person who had discovered the attempted break-in; there had been no need to get a statement from his staff.

Nick let out a long sigh of relief as soon as the police officers entered the lift.

Henry smiled. "You're in the clear it seems."

"Thanks for that." Nick moved his fingers at speed over the keyboard. "I've got something for you."

Henry moved to stand behind Nick. "Show me."

He watched a section of the CCTV footage. Nick was playing it in slow motion.

"The guy who did this was wearing the predictable hoodie... so it's very hard to see his face."

"Nothing surprising here."

"But a couple of things happened." Nick froze one of the film's frames. "When he raises his arm to take the first blow, the sleeve of his jacket comes up and..."

Nick zoomed into the part of the man's bare arm. "There is a distinct tat on the wrist and hand."

"That looks like a wristband and a rising sun with letters next to it."

"I can't enlarge the letters more because it becomes too fuzzy but I used software that can recognise signs and I got Престчпгение Опгачивает."

"That's Russian, isn't it?" Henry leaned in to read the letters better.

"It's Cyrillic. And it means Crime Pays."

"Well, well... Russian mafia, then." Henry rubbed his still sore head. "Or at least someone who is inspired by them."

Henry was about to pull back when Nick moved the CCTV footage on and froze another frame. "And the icing on the cake."

The man's face had momentarily slid out of his hoodie. "I think a shard of glass flung in his face. He pulls back suddenly, and the hoodie comes off."

Henry slapped Nick's shoulder. "Brilliant work."

"Shall I send that to the Metro Cops then?"

"Not before you make a few alterations to the tape."

Nick frowned.

"Remove the footage that shows the tattoos and the face. Once it's clean you can send it to them."

"But –"

Henry was already moving back to his office. "Just do it. We don't need the cops to ID this guy."

* * *

The list now only held three names:

Mikhail Rostov

Vladimir Gurdiev

Boris Brovensky

Harris returned to each name one more time. One of them, Brovensky, was a dissident intent on ousting the current Russian president, Vladimir Putin. The others were the expected oligarchs who had started making money during the Yeltsin area and kept going when Putin took over. Their wealth had been derived from the investments in the Russian financial sector and the property sector.

Brovensky's connection with Operation RUSSKY BEAR's target, David Upstage, was subtle. Harris could not quite figure out why the two had met repeatedly. Perhaps the contact had been initiated by Brovensky, in an attempt to re-enter the billionaire circle from which he had been ostracised. It had not ended well in any case. Brovensky had been found dead a few months ago. The police suggested suicide. His family had a different opinion.

When it came to the others the links made sense. The business Upstage was in required large finance deals, making a business link to Rostov useful. Like Rostov, Upstage also favoured spectacular investments, and had, for some time, coveted the idea of building a luxury hotel to compete with The Ritz in the centre of Moscow. Gurdiev had the ear of the central planning committee in Moscow, and more importantly that of Putin.

Harris rolled back in his chair. Finding information at the level needed to make any inroads into Upstage's dealings in Russia required a lot more resources than he could afford. He was running a couple of operations that were doing well, and his team had what they needed so far to cope with these. Still, on his own, he could not mount a realistic surveillance op, and certainly not trawl through the past of three men whose business it was to hide their questionable transactions.

The afternoon had barely started, but Harris was sure his contact at GCHQ would not mind too much being disturbed by a call she wasn't supposed to take. He looked around the room he was in. The only person in the office was busy with her own calls and otherwise preoccupied. Harris picked up a new burner phone he'd been charging all morning and dialled a number he knew by heart.

"Another favour, Steve?"

"Next you're going to tell me I only call when I need something."

"You do, and I don't mind." The person sounded friendly and amused.

"As ever, I'll owe you one."

"As long as I can keep tracking these bad boys from beyond the Iron Curtain, I'm fine with it."

"Tasha, the Iron Curtain came down in the early '90s," Harris teased.

"And it went back up with the election of Putin."

"Then you're in luck. I need some intel about two oligarchs: Mikhail Rostov and Vladimir Gurdiev."

"Sounds interesting. What do you need? Links to David Upstage?"

Harris was gobsmacked. "How did you…?"

"I've done some digging for you already. I spotted the link between these three, and I can run a check on whether we've intercepted more data flow and encrypted comms from the pair."

"That would be bloody good."

"What's the new chief's take on all of this?"

"Not completely convinced. I think he knows Russia is an issue, but the T word still occupies everybody's mind."

"Just as well people like you are on the ball, then. I sometimes wonder whether I should have joined MI6 rather than GCHQ, to drill the message into their brain – Russia is not turning into a democracy any time soon."

"And they would tell you you're biased."

"Why? Because my dad got shot for doing his job as a liberal academic, and that the case was closed before it was even opened in front of the courts in St Petersburg?"

"Bingo..." Harris softened his tone. "Sorry, I don't mean to be flippant."

"That's OK... I think you're right in any case. I'm doing good here, and at least I can track down these bastards without ending up with a bullet in my skull."

They fell into a comfortable silence, both considering what they needed to do next.

"Anything else whilst you're at it?"

"Perhaps." Harris narrowed his eyes. He considered his next request. It could be worth a shot.

"Don't go shy on me, Steve."

"Any recent comms between these Russian guys and a certain Brett Allner-Smith?"

"What am I looking for?"

"Art or antiquities theft. He has a knack for picking up some of the most expensive looted pieces arriving from the Middle East."

"Rostov has amassed a large collection of Sumerian and Assyrian artefacts. All above board I seem to remember. It doesn't mean he wouldn't be tempted by some exceptional piece."

Steve was impressed. "You sure know these oligarchs' lives inside and out."

"Of course, it helps when deciding what comms are important. I've read everything we've gathered on the Russians living in London. You need to find out about anything else, ask me."

"Swell." Harris checked on his colleague in the corner. She was about to finish her call. "I'd better go... When will you get –"

Natasha interrupted. "This evening. Might be late though."

She ended the call before Harris could thank her.

* * *

The map of The Barcadere Marina took up his entire computer screen. Henry allowed himself a short moment to recall the unorthodox meeting he'd had there. He had never met a Narcos lord before and not since. But the dreadful issue he'd vowed to resolve whilst he was in the Cayman Islands depended on it.

What he was sure of when he'd left the meeting, unarmed and with the answers he needed, was that Barcadere Marina was being used by the drug cartels of Mexico. Admittedly, this was over 10 years ago, but nothing he'd read in the papers or heard on the grapevine indicated this had changed.

Henry resisted the inner pull that was attempting to drag him back to the Caymans and the marina. After hesitating for a short moment, he closed the map and opened the list of investment holdings James had sent him.

Upstage Ultra Lux investment had been a shareholder in The Barcadere Marina for almost 12 years. It was inconceivable Upstage would not have known about the Narcos presence. Henry opened a new document and created a new list, recording the controversial clientele and holdings in Upstage's portfolio. The shady Barcadere Marina was the first on it, and he was certain it wouldn't be the last.

Henry moved the document to the shared drive James had created, and shot him an email asking him to begin recording his own findings alongside Henry's.

He then turned his attention to the next step in his plan.

McNamara would never allow an introduction to Upstage unless he felt he had no choice. Henry refreshed the Bloomberg screen to check the business news. Nothing much of interest. The presidential campaign was sluggish, with no decisive candidate emerging on the republican side.

Henry used the squawk box and called Nick. The young man appeared at his door immediately.

"I'm almost there with the alteration of the CCTV footage."

"Good stuff, but that's not why I want to speak to you." Henry gestured to one of the chairs in front of his desk. Nick sat down. "How about penetrating a company's IT system and planting a few bugs there?"

Nick shifted on his seat, thinking. "That depends on a few things. How protected is this system you're talking about?"

He had not even protested. Henry could see it in the young man's eyes. He was hooked, at last, able to use his skills without constraint or criticism.

"You can assume their IT system will be very well protected, assume NY Stock Exchange."

Nick pursed his lips. "OK... How careful are the staff there? I mean, do they get regular training about cyberattacks, etcetera?"

"Almost certainly."

"Hmm, interesting..." Nick half-closed his eyes in a way Henry had learnt meant focus. "Do you have the names of the people who work there, as well as their email addresses?"

"I do, why?"

"I can create an email address that closely mimics one of the staff's emails. For example, if the company is called, say Newborn Capital, and the domain is called newborncapital.com, I would create a fresh account called newborncapital.com with a double C. Very few people notice the difference because they expect to see it written in a certain way and the double C won't be spotted."

Henry nodded. "That sounds excellent. And I presume this trick works even better if the mail comes from someone they know, like another member of staff?"

Nick smiled broadly. "Hey... I'm the one who's supposed to be the hacker here."

Henry grinned back. "But deception is my trade. When you've finished with the CCTV camera footage, start the process of creating a domain to replicate the email of Top Capital Partners."

Henry handed McNamara's business card to Nick. The young man took the card cautiously, holding the card edges between index finger and thumb. He mouthed the name silently and nodded.

"I'll use a double I inside the word capital... That should work well."

He got up and headed back to reception, closing the door behind him.

Henry drummed his fingers on his desktop.

He would soon have details of the deal Upstage and his team at Top Capital were working on. He was not looking for the information that had been sent to investors; despite the confidentiality agreement, James had been able to get his hands on it. Henry was looking for the things that no one ever wanted to discuss with investors, the things that people should never put in writing but that people inevitably did, if only to protect their own precious backsides.

Rhode Island Avenue was quiet at 10am. Tatiana had been jogging around the area for a couple of hours. Her slim body, clad in dark leggings with a white strap on the side that flattered her long legs, and the black-and-white sports jacket that hugged her shapely bust, had attracted quite a few looks. In her business, the name of the game was not always to be discreet or forgettable.

She jogged past number 1308A, crossed the road that was almost empty of cars and stopped on Logan Circle. She found a bench and flopped onto it. Tatiana surveyed the area, taking her time; acting like a jogger recouping from a strenuous run. She slid her rucksack down from her shoulders and peeked into it.

The small yet powerful camera was there, as well as a couple of items of clothing she'd chosen and packed before leaving her apartment.

She dropped the bag to her feet, unzipped her jacket and reversed it. It became a soft pink design with large black-and-white flowers. She loosened her hair from the severe braid. She glanced at the pink cap she'd also brought with her. Was it too much? She put it on, choosing to wear it back to front.

The final touch to her transformation. She put on some subtle makeup that enhanced the green of her eyes.

Tatiana retraced her steps and walked to the rear of 1308A. The alley that turned from Rhode Island Avenue led directly to the back of the houses. Cars and large rubbish bins were parked alongside one another. The alley could have looked squalid, but it wasn't.

She took out the camera she had brought with her and started taking pictures. Her being there looked pretty innocent; an attractive young woman, perhaps an artist or photographer, trying to capture an unusual shot. Henry Newborn's flat was on the top floor and she needed to know how easy it would be to pay it a visit.

She spotted a cat on top of a car bonnet grooming itself. She smiled at the little animal.

How convenient. It was parked just behind the house she was interested in. She made a big fuss of the moggie who pulled the most unimaginable poses for her attention. Cats, her favourite pets, were such enigmatic creatures. She took shots of the cat up close and from afar, able to capture all the angles of 1308A she required.

A woman walked out two doors away and stopped for a moment. Tatiana waved amiably. The woman waved back, got into her car and left. The cat stretched its front legs, then back legs, and hopped off the car, as though Tatiana had never existed.

She walked up to the back door for 1308A, and sat down on the steps from door to street. She took a few more shots. There was a simple alarm protecting the back door. Nothing to worry about. Getting to the top floor would be another matter altogether.

She checked her watch. It was time to go home and take stock of the information she had collected.

Chapter Ten

Jack Shield had come through remarkably fast in finding Henry additional help. Mandy Jackson was in, and Jack had done a good job at convincing Henry she was one of the best analysts he could ever wish for.

Now was the time to test how true Jack's pitch was. Henry scrolled down the list of contacts in his BlackBerry and dialled Mandy's number. She picked up after the first ring.

"Give me a minute." Her voice didn't sound anxious. Something needed doing before she could talk, and she was getting on with it.

Henry heard what he thought were footsteps and the creaking of a door.

"Henry, apologies... needed to leave my desk before we could talk." A brief silence followed. Then she said, "What can I do for you?"

"Thanks for stepping in. Much appreciated."

"Thank me after I've delivered, but good to be part of the team. I rather like the idea of working off grid and in the field for a change."

Henry nodded, not that she could see the gesture. Having someone on his team be upfront about their motivation was refreshing.

"I need to send you a CCTV footage extract," he said. "There is a man on it, as well as some distinct tattoos on his wrist. A name would be good, and address even better."

"You realise that I can only find this guy if he has been of interest to the agency, right? Otherwise, you'll need the Feds."

"I've got good reason to believe he is Russian, or at least entertains Russian sympathies."

"Now, we're talking... Are the tats the reason you say that?"

"They are."

"Interesting. The Russian mafia tats are so distinctive it's rare to see them on display in the US. Most people here would have had them removed."

"A good point..."

Both Henry and Mandy fell silent.

Mandy spoke. "I suppose we'll know why he hasn't bothered when I track him down."

"I was worried for a moment that you might say *if*." Henry was almost sold on his new team member.

"He's Russian. I'll find a way."

Mandy gave Henry a new email address she'd created specifically for Operation RUSSKY BEAR. Henry hung up and sent the CCTV footage to it.

Time to check on Nick's progress and test how good Top Capital Partners' cyber defences truly were.

* * *

His burner phone was ringing already. Harris gave it a surprised look. Natasha had already found something to report?

Harris left the office and headed for the roof terrace. It was time for another much-deserved cigarette. "Talk to me, Tasha."

"This guy Allner-Smith, how much do you know about him?"

The question stopped Harris in his track. "What do you mean? He is one of my assets. I've been handling him for almost seven years."

"You spoke to me about his wheeling and dealing in looted artefacts, but how much do you know about his love life?"

Harris laughed nervously. "I know he does like his birds young. Although, he will make an effort to pursue the right woman, if she's wealthy enough."

"And more recently?"

Harris walked on and boarded the lift to the 4th floor. A couple of colleagues were in it. "I don't know. He doesn't keep me updated on all his various conquests. I'm not exactly his best pal."

"But you must have read him the riot act when it comes to women who are off limits?"

The doors opened. He pushed past his colleagues and made his way to the roof terrace.

"The suspense is killing me, Tasha. Why this long preamble?"

Harris squeezed his phone between his ear and his shoulder and grabbed a cigarette from his packet. The lighter came out next and he managed to get his first drag before Natasha answered.

"Dating the young enough daughter of one of the richest and best-connected Russian oligarchs is what I call off limits."

Harris coughed a few times, and for once, the cigarette was not the cause of it.

"How sure are you?"

"He was caught by an MI5 surveillance team. He's not of interest to them but the Russian guy and his family are."

Harris didn't ask how Natasha had managed to get the information. The fact was that Brett had once more been a very silly boy.

"How much does daddy know about this then?"

"Not sure. I got the feeling he doesn't know anything, but my contact was not very specific. They thought I was more interested in the Russian chap."

"The fact that Brett is still alive probably confirms what you say."

"A very good point. I'm sure daddy would not appreciate his little blue-eyed girl dating a guy who is almost the same age as he is."

"On the other hand, Brett has a title... old aristocracy. Is that of any value?"

Natasha fell silent for a moment. "Now that changes things quite a bit. I presume a title but no money?"

"Spot on."

"That's something a rich chap like daddy might be interested in."

"You mean, get his daughter married off to Brett, and then what?"

"Get a kid or two and make sure the title passes to her and her brood."

Harris almost choked on his laughter. "Playing happy couple is not Brett's style."

"Even if daddy hands over millions of pounds?"

"And what happens if Brett doesn't prove to be the perfect husband?"

"As soon she gets a kid, he gets a bullet."

90

"A bit radical..."

"But effective. Divorce is not an option here. It's all about keeping the title, as I said."

Harris thanked Natasha and hung up. He pulled his packet of cigarettes out of his pocket, hesitated, and took another one out.

"Bloody idiot..." He mumbled.

Harris wasn't surprised Brett was being so uncooperative. He must have felt his peerage gave him an edge over many things. For a toff he was no idiot, and he had proven more than adept at manipulating people.

He popped his second cigarette into his mouth. He used the butt of his first cigarette to light it and inhaled deeply. Harris walked to the edge of the terrace that overlooked the Thames. The river was flowing in slow convoluted swirls, looking grey and cold. The wind had stopped blowing from the north and the temperature felt almost pleasant, despite the low skies.

How calm the scene looked, in comparison to what was happening in the building he occupied – a fortress-like headquarters for UK spies.

He took another drag and returned his thoughts to Brett. A new idea formulated in his mind. Another drink at Brett's club was most certainly warranted.

* * *

The fake email address was ready to use. In his office, Henry sat in front of a newly acquired laptop. Nick perched on his desk.

"OK... here we go." Henry's finger lingered over the return button. He read the email he was about to send one more time.

From: rush.huckerby@topcapiitalpartners.com
To: ron.hernendez@topcapitalpartners.com
Subject: DAVID UPSTAGE

Hello Ron,
I'm about to meet my Davos contact again. I fear there is little progress in terms of introduction to David Upstage. I can't impress

the fact enough that my contact is a well-connected financier who
can open doors for complex financing around the world.
I urge you to check out his website www.exclusivefinance.com
Let's discuss this afternoon.
Rush

"And you're sure it will be impossible to track down the IP address?" Henry asked.

"I'm sure. I use a series of VPNs and other encryption methods that mask the ultimate address. And even if they manage it, the laptop is as anonymous as it can be."

Henry nodded and pressed the return key. The email disappeared.

He sat back and inhaled a slow, deep breath. "And now we wait."

"I'll monitor activities and let you know as soon as this guy Ron opens the email."

"Sounds good."

Nick's gaze rested on the laptop for a moment.

"It's not going to happen just yet," Henry said. "And you have your next assignment."

Nick reluctantly jumped off Henry's desk and moved back to reception. Coming up with a CV that looked truthful enough without disclosing his various illicit interests was proving to be complicated.

Henry sat back in his chair, assessing once more the likelihood that Ron Hernandez would fall into his trap.

The date of sending would be odd, but receiving an email from a man who had died two days previously would not fail to attract Hernandez's attention. Henry did not believe in an afterlife, or at least not one in which the dead looked upon the living from up high, but he almost wished he did. The thought of Huckerby watching as Henry was starting to ensnare Top Capital was comforting.

Rush might laugh at the stir his name was certain to create at Top Capital.

Henry refreshed the inbox for Huckerby's pseudonym. He shook his head at his silliness. He should heed his own advice and move on to something else.

He pushed the laptop to one side and opened up the drive he shared with James. The list of questionable investments made by Upstage Ultra Lux was growing by the minute.

92

Henry raked over the names and stopped on one investment that looked out of place to the usual luxury companies UUL purchased.

What was a mining company doing amongst these other holdings?

Henry shifted to his Bloomberg screen and typed in the company's ISIN, its International Securities Identification Number. The company was Russian and it was involved in gold extraction – perhaps something to meet Upstage's appetite for luxury goods or high-end investments.

The number of shares acquired in the mining company was small. Henry mused over the reasons for such token investing.

A small taster before going big? Possible. A thank you gift for services rendered, whatever these may be? Another possibility, but perhaps more far-fetched. What about –

The squawk box on his desk burst into action, and Nick's voice resounded around his office.

"He opened the email."

Henry checked his watch; it had taken only 20 minutes. Ron Hernandez must be on the edge of his seat. Henry jumped from his and rushed out to Nick's side.

The young man had logged into the domain monitor and was surveying progress. The backroom for the website link Nick had created was open on another screen and the malware ready to download.

"How long ago did he open the email?"

"30 seconds ago." Nick leaned into the screen, as though the move might encourage Hernandez to click on the fake website at the bottom of the email. "He's surely read the email by now."

Henry checked his watch again. Nick's eyes were glued to the clock on the side of his screen that was displaying the time, right down to every elapsing second.

"50 seconds..." Nick's foot beat out a quick rhythm on the floor. "Come on..."

They both fell silent, mesmerised by the slipping away of each second, each one diminishing the chance of Hernandez ever opening the malware link.

90 seconds had elapsed.

"Bugger... Maybe this guy is less of a nerd than I thought." Henry pulled back.

Nick shook his head. "We can try somebody else with a different name and email –" He didn't finish his sentence. The download sequence had started. The algorithm dump was progressing in rapid bursts ready to give Nick access to the IT systems for Top Capital Partners.

* * *

The dozens of photos Tatiana had taken of the man she'd been tasked to follow were organised by locations and dates. She made sure the most relevant ones, not always the best ones, were at the front of the photo gallery.

Henry Newborn was an interesting character; secretive, controlled… and trained. She hadn't gathered enough evidence about this latter quality, but she was working on it.

The background checks had yielded very little information other than to confirm what she'd been given about Henry. This didn't mean anything of course.

Tatiana stretched, rolled her head around a few times. She was starting to feel the impact of the hours of surveillance she'd put in since being asked to trail the man.

She moved to the small kitchen of the apartment she was renting and made herself a cup of tea. She'd found the place a couple of months ago, thinking it an ideal spot to establish herself in the Washington DC community, as well as trail the men she'd been asked to follow. This less upmarket DC neighbourhood afforded a good range of accommodation and Kalorama Park had proven the perfect spot, not in trendy DC, but just on the doorstep of the most affluent neighbourhoods.

She added tea leaves to an old teapot she'd purchased from a local flea market she'd spotted after arriving from Eastern Europe, switched on the kettle and waited.

The smell of the tea leaves reminded her of home. She read the label on the packet and smiled.

Russian Caravan is a blend of oolong, keemun, and lapsang souchong teas. Its distinct taste, aromatic and full-bodied, also carries a sweet, malty, and smoky twist. Traditionally, the smoky character was considered to have been imparted to the tea through the close proximity

94

of the camel caravans to their countless campfires, en route from the Mongolian Steppes to Russia.

Tatiana's mind wandered to the grassland steppes the label described. She wished she was free to travel and, like her parents, report on the people she encountered and the nomadic life some Mongolians still led.

Tatiana shook her head. This was only fantasy. She returned to the tea she was preparing with a small pang of nostalgia.

Her grandmother could never afford such a delicacy, and yet the tea her Babushka brewed had always been the best in the world.

She poured the boiling water into the teapot, closed the lid, and covered the pot with a tea towel. She was about to reach for the top cupboard when her mobile rang. She checked the caller ID and sighed. There was no point delaying this call.

"Hello."

She waited for her interlocutor to state the reason for his call, although she was certain she already knew why he was calling.

"Have you made any progress yet?" McNamara said.

"I can't get into his apartment in broad daylight without preparing a little first." Tatiana switched over to loudspeaker, turned to the cupboards and effortlessly pulled the pot of honey down from the top shelf.

"This is taking forever. I need an answer today or tomorrow."

"Today's out of the question." She removed the tea towel from around the teapot, swirled the pot a few times and poured a little tea out, to check it was ready to drink. "Tomorrow is more promising. He goes to the gym late on Thursdays."

"That's not good enough."

"As opposed to what? Getting some second-rate goon to pickaxe the glass door of his office?" Tatiana opened one of the kitchen drawers; the cutlery rattled a little as she did. She took out a spoon.

"How do you –?"

"Know? That's what I'm employed for – surveillance. By the way, the idiot you used stopped me from doing the reconnaissance I had been planning to do, so next time you have a bright idea like that one, Art, discuss it with me first."

"I don't have to discuss anything with you. That's not the way this works."

"I'd be surprised if *he* sees it that way." She had agreed never to name her Russian minder on any call, no matter how secure the line. "But suit yourself and call him. I've worked with him much longer than you have."

"I will." Art's voice trembled a little; anger was no friend to him, something he might soon learn.

Tatiana spooned a large dollop of honey into her tea and started stirring. "Fine by me. Anyway, no need to call again. I'll reach out to you when I have something new to report."

She killed the call before McNamara could answer back.

The lump of honey dissolved into the tea. She brought the mug close to her face and blew on the liquid. She advanced her lips with caution and sipped... perfect. She took another small mouthful and smiled; not as good as Babu's but still very enjoyable.

Her gaze drifted to a small diptych on the kitchen table, opened out like a book. On one side there was a small icon painting of the Virgin Mary nursing baby Jesus, on the other an old picture of Tatiana holding her brother Anatolie in her arms.

She could still remember the day the picture had been taken. It had been around Easter. Her brother had just turned four and she nineteen. She'd just returned from her first year in the US, where she'd been taking an undergraduate degree in art.

A lump lodged in her throat. Tatiana straightened the picture, pushing away the painful memories that surfaced whenever she returned to this much happier day.

She moved back to the lounge and the laptop on the main table in the open-plan room that also served as a dining area.

An enlarged picture of Henry filled the entire screen. She sat down, drank a little more tea and cocked her head, pouting at the attractive face on screen.

"Mr Newborn... you are giving me trouble."

Chapter Eleven

Nick sat in Henry's chair, his fingers running fast over the keyboard, navigating the IT system for Top Capital Partners. It was only a matter of time before his intrusion would be detected, and if Henry's guess that Top Capital was strong on risk detection and protection, then their cyber defences should already be aware that someone was in.

Henry stood at the back of Nick's chair. "Have you found McNamara's folders yet?" He tried not to sound impatient.

"Almost there... give me... a few... seconds." Nick's staccato speech matched his typing style. He pulled back suddenly. "I'm in. What are we looking for?"

"Search for files containing the name, David Upstage."

Nick's fingers glided over the keys. A long list of documents appeared on screen.

"There are hundreds of them."

"Let's prioritise those that are the most recent, say last year, and dump these onto a USB key." Henry handed over the device to Nick.

He nodded, inserted it into the key port of Henry's new laptop and started the process. The data was migrating at speed with the time bar, changing to completion as soon as the file was captured.

For a couple of minutes the files kept passing across one after the other. But then the rhythm was abruptly interrupted, and Nick moved closer to the screen again.

"Shit, the IT guys are onto us."

"Any way you can speed up the process?"

Nick was no longer listening to Henry. He had focused on the screen again. He was mumbling to himself, following a trail of thoughts. Henry stood back.

Nick brought up a map of the seven VPN nodes he had set up across the world. Each node would show up as soon as it had been breached, giving him time to close the data dumping process before Top Capital's IT team found Henry's laptop.

The files started moving across again, but the VPN nodes' warning signal started sounding as soon as the process resumed.

"We have a few more minutes but they're catching up."

Henry leaned in, hands on his desk, face close to the screen on which the VPN nodes' breaches were displaying.

"We should pull out as soon as there are only two nodes left," said Nick.

"Why?"

"Because once these guys have gotten that far, it will be difficult to predict how quickly they'll locate the other two."

Henry said nothing. Arms crossed over his chest. He surveyed the progress of the opposition and it appeared they were doing well. Nodes 7 and 6 had fallen quickly but it seemed that node 5 was giving them trouble.

"How many files left?" Henry focused on the map.

"A dozen..."

"Total size?"

"A bit more than one Gigabit?"

"Our broadband speed is 35Mb... How long?"

"Around 4 minutes."

Henry started one of the chronographers on his specialist watch. He resumed his position in front of the map, arm out, so that he could see the elapsing time.

Node 5 had just fallen.

Nick shifted on his chair. "We should get ready."

He placed his fingers on the key that would kill the connection.

Henry gripped his shoulder. "Only when I tell you."

Nick's tension released a little. Node 4 fell and the tension returned immediately to his shoulders. "It's getting close."

"How many files?"

"Only three to... Node 3's down.' He looked up at Henry. "We have to close now."

"I heard you the first time. Not yet."

Nick glanced up at Henry. Henry was still only focused on the map. Nick's fingers trembled on the keys.

He squeezed his shoulder. "I said, not yet."

Node 2 fell, and Henry squeezed Nick's shoulder one more time. Nick shot a worried look at him. The man was insane.

The last file was downloading. The time bar was running towards the finishing line.

"Now!" Henry shouted. Node one fell at the same time Nick closed the link.

"Shit... You're crazy." Nick blurted out. He looked up at Henry and burst into laughter. "Wow... How did you know we'd make it?"

"Some might say it was more luck than judgement." Henry smiled. "Let's just say I have lots of experience taking risks."

Nick shook his head.

Henry took the USB key out of the port and handed it to him.

"Prep the data. I need to send that to someone."

* * *

"Seriously, two days in a row? This is starting to sound like harassment." Brett was sitting in the exact same comfortable seat as the night before, drinking the exact same excellent whisky. Brett did not invite Harris to sit but Harris did anyway, joining Brett and ordering a drink.

"You know me, Brett," said Harris. "When the safety of my assets is in play, I'll move heaven and earth for them."

Brett raised a quizzical eyebrow. "And who is it you need to protect me from?"

"How's your love life going?"

Brett's face darkened, and for the first time since Harris sat down, a hint of concern flashed in his asset's eyes.

"None of your damn concern..." Brett reached for the elegant tumbler and took a long sip of the amber liquid.

"Very much my business if this is going to cost you your life."

Harris's whisky arrived, providing him with the perfect moment of suspense.

Brett said nothing. A small nerve at the corner of his mouth started to twitch. He had forgotten about his drink.

"Dating the very young – and I can't emphasise enough the very and young – daughter of a Russian oligarch is a life shortening exercise." Brett went to say something but Harris raised his hand. "Spare me the 'we are in love' or 'she fully consents' crap. I'm sure daddy will almost certainly not see it that way – that is if you live long enough to even have that argument with him."

"And what if daddy, as you call him, is fully aware?"

"Do you know for sure or is it what she's telling you? Have you been invited for dinner at his London mansion or his datcha on Lake Baikal?"

"Surprisingly, I have." Brett smiled weakly.

"To do what? Deliver one of the looted pieces daddy bought from you?"

Brett sighed. "They are not pieces... they are artefacts of great value. How many times do I have to tell you?"

"Don't change the subject. You don't know if daddy is going to welcome you with open arms or send his ex-FSB mob to finish you off."

"The problem with that expected outcome, Steve, is that you are forgetting about a very big asset that I hold." Brett resumed his drinking.

"You mean your title? What are you again, Earl of...?" Harris took a sip.

Brett did not answer. His lips started twitching again.

Harris continued. "This is clever of you. You know a bargain when you see one. I've said it to you often enough, for a toff, you're a bright guy. But do you see yourself playing good husband to this very demanding young lady forever? And what if she gets bored with you once she's got a kid?"

Harris had Brett's attention. "What do you mean?"

"It could happen at any moment. A stray bullet meant for someone else, a robbery gone wrong..."

"We're not there yet." Brett finished his glass and didn't order another.

"Wrong answer. In fact, that is going to end with you swimming with the fish in the River Thames."

Brett's nostrils flared, but he held back. "So, what does clever Steve have to offer as a solution to my perceived predicament?"

"How about this?" Harris drained his glass and lifted a hand to order another one. The waiter came along. "Times two. My friend needs one as well."

"I'm not your friend," Brett said through gritted teeth.

Harris ignored him. "This is my idea. Since you suspect that daddy and his blue-eyed girl are in agreement over your little love story, why don't you carry on for a while? And then have a moment of deep realisation... something along the lines of she's too good, too beautiful, intelligent... young for you. At which point you then introduce her to another eligible young man, with a suitable title, and the need to prop up his family's estate."

"What's the deal for me then?"

"I'm sure daddy will appreciate the offer and he may even be very generous about the introduction. Hell, he may even have a million or two to spare."

The drinks arrived. Both men fell silent. Brett didn't touch his whisky, clearly measuring the impact of Steve's proposition.

"And what do you get out of all this?"

"I make sure my employer and I have your back. And we make sure that if there is a stray bullet, it hits the wall and not your head."

"And if I don't?" Harris was surprised by Brett's question.

"I make sure your long-and-protracted love life history hits daddy's email box."

"I doubt he hasn't got that already." Brett sounded almost calm.

"I doubt he's got as much as MI6 has."

Brett sighed. "You know what this is?"

"Blackmail. Needs must." Harris finished his drink and stood up. "You've got until midnight tomorrow to decide."

* * *

James's email had arrived into Henry's mailbox 10 minutes ago. Henry was still reading through it, flipping between the text and the charts James had created.

His efficacy at extracting the information Henry needed from a large bank of data reminded him why he had chosen James as his number two in the old days of investment banking. A few images of GL Investments' trading floor flashed in his mind.

Henry's deal with MI6 had propelled him into a new environment he relished. His deep understanding of finance and the secrecy that came with it was making all the difference now.

Henry picked up one of his burner phones and dialled James's mobile.

James answered straight away. "You got my message I take it."

"I've just finished reading it and want to discuss options. We only have one crack at this."

"I get that..." James sounded like he was not yet settled wherever he was. "Are you at home?"

"Got in half an hour ago. Nothing from Harris by the way."

"He's sulking. I got the team I needed around me, no thanks to him."

James chuckled. "You mean you spoke to whoever you needed and told him what the score was after."

Henry laughed. "That's the sum of it."

"Tut tut, H. You do realise this is no longer GL."

"Bad habits die hard."

"At least you're getting results. And there is plenty to scupper Upstage's deals in the latest batch of data you sent me."

"Huckerby, my DC contact, had identified one deal he felt might be perfect to create an introduction to Upstage. He'd mentioned the purchase of a luxury hotel, complete with spa, golf course and casino."

"That's by far the most obvious one to me." James agreed. "And the one that will be the most difficult to finance."

"Upstage is suing the US arm of a Swiss bank as well. But I guess you know that."

"I found that out, but surprisingly, this has not been broadcasted widely in London, or even Zurich."

"Any reason why?" Henry rolled his chair closer to his desk.

"No idea, but I intend to find out."

"Back to the deal with Upstage Ultra Lux," Henry said. "What is the deal and who is advising on it?"

"As I said, a luxury hotel complex in the Bahamas, Nassau. This deal has a lot of potential but the resort needs a major revamp."

"So, we're talking about purchase money plus refurb money – not cheap." Henry nodded.

"You can say that again. Over $1 billion."

Henry grinned. "And how much has Upstage got in cash? No, let me guess... less than 10% of the purchase price?"

"Impressive, almost 8%."

"What?" Henry shook his head. "And who the hell is going to lend him the rest?"

"That's where it gets interesting."

Henry breezed in. "Let me guess, smaller banks, micro banks... private equity firms who think they can benefit from his reputation as an inspired businessman." Nothing ever changed in the finance world.

"As well as get their company tagged on his blog or his FB account," James added.

"I'm a bit unclear as to how popular Upstage is on social media." Henry hadn't checked yet, but perhaps he should have done sooner to get a feel for Upstage's popularity.

"He has around 10 million people following him on his FB account. Which sounds impressive, but it's nowhere near as many as some Hollywood stars or singers. Will Smith or Rihanna, for example."

"Seriously, is this guy trying to compete with them?"

"From what I gather almost certainly. His ambition has no boundaries as far as I can tell."

"And what is it that Upstage thinks he's so good at?"

"He's got his own YouTube channel talking about business, but also good fashion for men in the know, and what it takes to be a success. I never thought it would work but the channel is very well done, and for blokes who desperately want to manage their image it's proving popular."

"Got it. Upstage is self-centred and narcissistic." Henry took mental notes.

"But he is entertaining too. Upstage has a sense of humour that verges on abusive. Still, people seem to love it."

"As long as it's not them in the firing line... His followers don't mind him trashing other people of course." Henry started browsing the internet to find Upstage's FB page.

"Or perhaps they'd like to do the same to others but don't know how," James suggested.

Henry found a video on YouTube in which Upstage was pontificating about how to clinch a deal. It was tough-man bullshit that made Henry smile.

"James, I've just found a video... You've got to watch it."

He sent the link to James.

James started watching and sniggered. "This is so basic."

"But the video is very professional, well presented, and Upstage's delivery appeals to the emotions of his followers. It's got nothing to do with being rational. He's not teaching a bunch of MBA students but people who are aiming higher and want to be told how to get there."

James watched more of the video before he answered. "That's a good point. He knows how to be engaging. He hosts one of his followers on his show once a month and makes a big deal out of them."

"As I say it's all about emotions and zip about reason, let alone technical ability."

"Nothing wrong with emotions I suppose," said James.

"Unless what you're saying has not been verified..."

"And you basically talk through your arse." James laughed.

Henry pondered that for a moment.

When he spoke again, he measured the impact of each word. "Upstage will do everything to preserve his image and his future as the leader he thinks he is."

"Without a doubt."

"You've spent more time than me reviewing the Nassau hotel deal. How sound is it? Could it be viable for an honest investor?"

"If you disregard the fact that his cash contribution is low? The figures he's presenting show his ability to repay his debt is very stretched. Why do you ask?"

"As much as I already dislike the man and yet need to be introduced to him, I don't want to scupper a sound deal."

"You won't. I doubt the banks are being told the whole story. My suspicion, of course unfounded, is that dirty money is the reason why this deal will eventually become viable, as you say." James spoke with feeling.

104

"Dig around more, James, and the idea of dirty money being moved around in Nassau. In the meantime, why don't you prepare one of your well-turned-out analytical press releases? It's about time the potential investors learnt a bit more about what they are getting themselves into."

Chapter Twelve

"Are you sure it's him?" Jack had grabbed two coffees from the staff restaurant and was handing one to Mandy in the Memorial Garden.

She took it from him. "Positive."

They found a bench and sat down. Mandy squeezed the collar of her coat around her neck. The sun was out, but it was not warm enough to compensate for the breeze blowing from the east. Still, the large, white pine trees and blue spruce that had been planted around the Memorial Garden were providing some wind shelter.

"It took you no time at all to ID this guy. Whoever's employing him is either stupid or he doesn't care."

"I agree that using a Russian heavy who is linked to organised crime and has a very large question mark hanging over his head regarding spying activity is not smart. But we have more intel perhaps than his current employer has."

"That's true enough about having links to Russian spooks. This type of info is not available unless you're close to one of these spies' circles, but OC? That's got to cross the man or woman's mind... Anyone looking for a heavy who employs a Russian goon must have suspicions."

Mandy took a sip of coffee and closed her eyes for a moment. "I know this is not what you want to hear, but perhaps the whole Huckerby story involves OC connections, not anything deeper. Maybe Rush found out about some illicit activity and this is what got him killed. You and I know there is enough crossover between the FSB, the GRU, and Russian gangs on activity."

Jack sat his cup down on the bench and rested his elbows on his knees.

"I hear you, Mandy, but I'm not ready to go down that route yet. I buy the fact that there is a possible, or even probable, OC element, but not that it is the only element."

"I'm just putting it out there." Mandy paused a moment. "I'll have to tell Crowne."

"I presume he has sent the CCTV footage to the Metro Police in Washington?"

"He has but with a bit of an omission..."

Jack frowned. "You mean he altered the tape?"

"Uhuh. The guy's face and his tats are missing from the images."

"Good one. He and I are on the same page." Jack smiled.

"And which page is that then?"

"Huckerby's death is for the spook community to sort." Jack picked up his cup and took a long sip of coffee. The spook community meant him and Harris, and the sort out part would depend on who was responsible and how easy it would be to get to them.

"You run agents, Jack. You're not a vigilante." Mandy gave him an odd look he couldn't quite figure out. Her tone, though, told him it was not a rebuke.

Jack didn't reply. The death of his asset would not go unpunished.

"Back to Crowne," Mandy said. "This new piece of intel is the perfect opportunity for me to pay a visit to Henry's office and meet the man himself."

"This assumes you have the time to do this?"

"Sure, I do. Remember I work from home for some of the time. I'll just change my pattern of work slightly."

"But no unnecessary risk taking, right?" Jack scrutinised her face.

"None whatsoever." Mandy finished her coffee and stood up. "Come on then, we've got some nasty bastards to catch."

* * *

Henry was giving the press release James had prepared a second read. It was a short two-pager that was to the point – no need for the flowery language of marketing. The only item missing was some of the data Henry knew Top Capital Partners was hiding.

"I've got something for you." Nick stuck his head through the door of Henry's office. "Straight out of McNamara's transaction folder named UPSTAGE."

Henry stood up and moved to his new receptionist-cum-hacker's desk. "Show me."

Nick pulled up a couple of documents on screen. One of them was the last unaudited accounts of the company that owned the hotel complex in Nassau. It did not make good reading. The second was a rework of the same figures, massaged and improved to give the accounts a much healthier look.

"Creative accounting?" Nick wondered aloud.

Henry shook his head. "Simple fraud, nothing creative about it. A good old-fashioned way to make accounts look better. What do the accounts look like for the years prior to this?"

"Much better, but I'm not the expert."

Nick pulled up the audited accounts for the three years prior. They did indeed look healthy, followed by a sudden dip in the last audited year.

"What changed here?" Henry leaned in closer to the screen and scrolled through the pages of numbers, until he came to the performance of the casino. The hotel, spa, and golf course were just about breaking even, but the casino was the saviour of the entire property complex. Suddenly, though, its profits had evaporated.

Nick pursed his lips. "That's odd."

"Was there a change in management?"

"I spotted something to that effect in the accounts summary." Nick took over and scrolled back to the place where he had seen the announcement. He showed it to him.

Henry stood up and smiled. "James was spot on. These guys were laundering money through their casino, right up until management changed."

"James... is that your guy in London?"

"That's right. And he has prepared a neat little document called an analyst's press release that we are going to use shortly. Send me what you've found, and I'll finish the paper on the Nassau deal. I've sent you a list of names and financial institutions. Next, I want you to find a way of plopping the press release into their mailboxes, and it has to come from a credible source."

"How about we use the same domain as last time?"

Henry frowned and then burst into a laugh. "How wicked... I love it. Use the same Top Capital Partners fake email address we used to rumble Hernandez to send a negative press release trashing Top Capital's own transaction... absolutely brilliant."

Nick looked pleased his idea had scored a point. "And that puts Top Capital even more on the back foot with Upstage."

"Stabbed in the back by his own team." Henry's voice became lighter, and a hint of his Northern Irish accent crept in. "This is not going to go down well. Get ready. I'll be sending you the research paper in less than five minutes."

Henry returned to his office and sent the paper to Nick as promised. The chain of events he had started gave him the rush he'd once loved. Although this time the stakes were of a different nature. A deal going wrong could get him killed.

Nick shouted from his desk that he was done, meaning the email had been sent, and added a yee-haw, which made Henry smile.

Henry messaged James, attaching the research paper, with three words as instructions: *Spread it around.*

The clock on the wall of his office indicated 6.30pm East, 11.30pm in London. It was too late for the investors in Europe to take note of the press release but not the case in DC.

By lunchtime tomorrow, Top Capital Partners would be licking its wounds and McNamara would feel the full force of David Upstage's ire.

"Couldn't happen to a nicer guy," Henry murmured, satisfied.

He entered Upstage's name in the Bloomberg search bar and hit return. Articles about Upstage rolled in until one piece of news caught Henry's attention.

Upstage was here in DC for an opening, one of his high-profile ventures: an Ultra Lux Club. The target was on his doorstep.

Henry clicked on the link and read on. Upstage was opening a multi-level complex combining a luxury spa, sports centre with private coaching, and nouvelle cuisine restaurants, the membership of which started at $10,000.

Nick knocked on the open door. "If you don't mind, I'd like to shoot off now."

Henry was still reading from his screen when an idea came to him. "How do you fancy a night out with champagne and caviar?"

"Are we celebrating?" Nick sounded unsure.

"Not yet." Henry looked at him. "And I'm not making a pass at you, either. David Upstage is in town, opening one of his clubs."

"You got an invitation?" Nick ignored Henry's jest.

"No, but if I give you the website details, I'm sure you can get us in."

"Champagne and caviar you said." Nick sounded almost undecided.

Henry grinned. "And lots of stunning women."

"Send me the website." Nick ran back to his desk.

"We shall go to the ball," Henry murmured with a smile.

* * *

The building of Upstage's newest club was only two streets away from the White House. Henry had to give it to Upstage – he knew how to get into the news.

A limo had been booked for 8pm to take Henry and Nick to the event from the office. They had ten minutes to spare. Henry had helped Nick to find a tuxedo that looked perfect on him. Nick had combed his dark hair back.

If he was nervous or excited, he was hiding it well.

"Don't get caught lifting some guy's wallet." Henry spoke to Nick from the open bathroom door. He was fastening his bow tie with expertise. "In fact, don't lift anything unless it has some HUMIT value."

"HUMIT?" Nick asked.

"Human Intelligence. Keep your eyes and ears open. No risk taking tonight. The main focus is Upstage."

"How about this guy McNamara? Won't he recognise me?"

"He might, and if he asks why you're there, you tell him you're networking on my behalf."

"And if he asks about my background?"

"Good point."

Henry checked his reflection one more time. His cream jacket tux and black tie hit the right notes – elegant without being ostentatious, attractive without being overbearing, and more importantly, professional.

"It would have helped if you'd finished the CV I asked you for. I've got no idea what upper education looks like," Henry said as he entered the lounge. Nick nodded sheepishly. "Even if you've not done as well as you thought you should it doesn't matter. It's just a formality."

"So you said, but that doesn't resolve tonight's cover story."

"How comfortable are you faking an Ivy League background?"

Nick cracked a smile. "It wouldn't be the first time."

Henry shot up one eyebrow. "Explain."

Concern replaced the smile on Nick's face.

While he waited for him to speak, Henry checked mentally that he had all the equipment he needed: a small smart card that could decode electronic door pads; a minute microphone lodged in the lining of his tux that would not trigger a metal detector; his special MI6-issued smartphone.

"Come on, don't be shy. You're about to enter the spy community, anything goes."

"I, er, used to take exams for some of these guys." Nick's voice was barely audible.

"Which exams and which guys?" Henry paid attention.

"I've got a good photographic memory and I learn fast, so you know... any exam on tech or mathematics. I'm not bad."

"Right, and which universities are we talking about?"

"MIT, Caltech..."

"Woah, hang on. Are you telling me that you got away with sitting exams for some of these kids?"

Nick nodded. He couldn't quite bring himself to meet Henry's eyes.

Henry roared with laughter and Nick looked up.

"I love it, this is tops." Henry slapped him on the shoulder. "I guess you did it for the cash?"

"$1,000 per exam."

"That's all? You undersold yourself."

Nick flushed. "Really?"

"How about pretending to be a Caltech alumnus for tonight?" Henry checked his watch.

"I know their programme pretty well so I think I can fob that."

"Sounds good. We'll work on your legend a bit more tomorrow but that should do for tonight."

Henry's smartphone rang. The limo had arrived.

"We're in business. Why don't you get the lift?"

Nick left first and Henry placed the devices he used to check on intruders in their usual places. Nick did not need to know about those.

* * *

The spacious pavement was not wide enough to accommodate the red carpet that was spread out in front of Upstage's new exclusive club. A lane of traffic had been closed off to ensure limos and other showy vehicles could access the site's entrance without guests having to walk more than a few steps.

Henry asked the driver to drop them two hundred metres away from the buzz. He and Nick strolled towards their destination. The building had been recently redecorated and the fresh paint made the masonry work stand out, even at night. The neo-classical style inspired by Greek architecture gave the construction an imposing look.

The stream of vehicles hadn't stopped, struggling to drop their guests off at the door. The Hollywood press was there, crushed against the barriers that had been erected, moving like a shoal of fish as soon as a new car door was opened. Who would be getting the best shot of the most famous face this evening?

Henry stopped across the road, observing the activity. He did not want his face caught on camera. The paparazzi seemed to know which car to go for. On instinct or from bribed information Henry didn't know, but this provided an opportunity.

"Get ready to cross the road when I tell you."

Nick nodded.

A US army Humvee pulled out from a side street and parked front of the entrance, ignoring the lane devoted to guests' limos and blocking yet another lane of traffic.

The clamour that came from the photographers gave Henry their cue to move.

"Now." Henry stretched an arm out to slow incoming traffic. The drivers of the lanes closest to the building had already slowed down to a crawl to try and glimpse the star who had arrived.

Henry and Nick arrived at the entrance, managing to avoid the press. Two men in black tuxes, armed with iPads, stopped them. By the looks of their bulging chests, iPads weren't the only items they were carrying.

The tallest of the pair took Henry's and Nick's name. Nick coughed whilst the other started running a handheld metal detector over their bodies. Henry looked back to check on the progress of the new red-carpet arrival.

Arnold Schwarzenegger was making a big entrance, whilst a few screaming fans vied for an autograph. He was moving towards them at a slow enough pace, but soon both Henry and Nick would be on camera.

"Thank you, sirs," said the bouncer. "Have a good evening."

Henry pulled Nick up a short flight of stairs just in time, before the clicking and flashing of the glamour press began.

As soon as they arrived in the large atrium that served as the reception area for tonight, a waiter offered them the requisite glass of champagne. The décor was dazzling. Marbles of various shades gave the room solidity, and yet made it feel spacious. Leather furniture had been scattered around the vast area in small intimate pockets. The choice of neutral tones might have made the space feel cold, but the gold gilding of the preserved classical features on the ceiling and walls brought warmth to the room.

Henry sipped his drink as he took in his surroundings and lifted an appreciative eyebrow at the taste. These were good quality bubbles. Henry gave a side glance to his companion.

He could see it on his face; Nick had never been in the presence of such luxury before. The young man clung to his glass of champagne, ignored the canapés that were starting to circulate and did his best not to gawp.

"How're you doing?" Henry asked after accepting an avocado-and-salmon-mousse-on-rye canapé.

"You said champagne and caviar... I thought you were having me on."

"We need to circulate. Can you do that?" There was no hesitation or disdain in Henry's voice. Nick didn't yet understand wealth, nothing wrong with that. The young man simply needed a little nudge and a reminder that they were here to do business.

Nick nodded and moved. Henry saw him walk up to a young man who looked a little out of his depth. This was a good start.

Henry made his way slowly towards the centre of the room where a tall man was speaking exuberantly to a crowd of gathered admirers. David Upstage was holding court and enjoying the sound of his own voice.

It was too early to engage with the main player. David Upstage was not going anywhere. He had taken root in one spot. Clusters of new people were gathering at the periphery of the inner circle, waiting for a chance to catch a moment with the great man. Even the presence of A-list Hollywood celebs didn't seem to interest Upstage. They'd been invited for show, an expression of his status and power.

Henry scanned the room again and spotted the other man he would have been surprised not to find there. McNamara was hidden behind the imposing figure of his client.

Arthur McNamara Jr was talking to a tall woman. Their tense body language said unhappy, even hostile, but under control. Henry could only see her from behind, but he guessed from her shape that she was attractive. Her light blonde hair was arranged in a fashionably messy bun and her off-the-shoulder black dress showed off her smooth, slender back. She could be one of the models Upstage was known to date whilst still married.

Henry was not the only one watching the scene. Another older gentleman had stopped talking to the group of men he had joined. Henry moved closer, and was offered a fresh glass of champagne at the same time as the man.

"Who's the woman?" Henry asked him.

"I'm not sure. She's not one of the regulars Upstage turns up with."

"Perhaps a new talent?"

The man laughed softly and shook his head. "An understated way of putting it."

Henry smiled. "In these days of *me too* one can never be too careful."

The man nodded and extended his hand. "Matt Dacey, Senator." It appeared the man had found a fellow misogynist in Henry.

"Henry Newborn, financial adviser." Henry returned an assured handshake.

"British?"

"That's right." He shrugged. "No one's perfect."

The faded-grey eyes of Matt Dacey assessed Henry, amused. "You're new in DC?"

"I opened a new office recently. Operating from Switzerland was no longer servicing my US clients adequately."

As they spoke, a shift happened in the cluster of people that surrounded Upstage. Space had suddenly been created and a microphone was being tested a few paces away.

"Here we go..." Dacey turned around. He spotted a waiter and raised his empty glass. Glasses were exchanged in a swift professional move, before the booming voice of David Upstage reminded everyone that he was expecting them to pay attention to his oration.

The microphone sound did not satisfy Upstage. He gave a young man to his right a murderous look. The young man took the device from him gingerly and started making a couple of adjustments.

Henry took leave of Dacey with a suggestion of lunch and swapped business cards with him. He moved closer as people retreated. Perhaps being too close to a combative Upstage in full flight was not a good idea. But there was only one way to find out.

Henry found himself only a yard away from his target. He simply had to endure whatever crap Upstage was about to throw at his audience before making his move.

Someone moved closer to him and brushed against the sleeve of his tuxedo.

"Good to see you here, Mr Newborn." McNamara stood next to Henry. "I don't recall seeing your name on the list."

Henry didn't bother to face the man. "By the looks of it, it's a very long list." He swept his glass around the room, to make his point. "My name must have slipped your attention."

McNamara's voice was drowned out by the booming voice of David Upstage.

"Good evening beautiful people..." Upstage had his left hand stuck in his trouser pocket. He held the mic firmly but without a trace of anxiety. A large enough space had been created for him to leisurely move around.

Henry moved away from McNamara to observe his target in action. Upstage carried his name well – he was on show. The hand gestures Henry had witnessed on the videos were now conveying focus, harshness, and the ability to strike whenever he fancied.

Today's speech was more than a simple confirmation of Upstage's own greatness.

He talked about the economy.

"This government is shit, tremendous discontent in the American people. We need a remedy... defund, cut... they don't perform, more cuts... tax cuts... be dynamic..."

Henry got the gist.

But a cold shiver ran down his spine at the next topic.

"Free trade needs to be fair... the American people are losing jobs to China..."

This was not a private launch speech, or at least not the launch he'd been expecting. The political aspirations of Upstage had just been revealed; Henry knew where they would lead. The spectre of a new-world order had just been revealed to him, but it was not an order Henry would ever support.

Upstage kept going for almost half an hour. The same arguments were rehashed in different forms, with more examples given of how Upstage would resolve the issues. The words were designed to stir the listeners' emotions.

"Our wonderful country, bad people, unfair, unjust... and everybody loses."

And at the end the crowd roared in applause. Henry spotted Dacey. The old man was clapping and nodding.

A convert.

People were pressing the flesh, surrounding Upstage to shake his hand. He was smiling broadly, knowing he had done very well. Henry moved forward. McNamara grabbed his arm. In response, Henry grabbed McNamara's hand, crushing the knuckles of the ring and small fingers. The man winced and pulled away, just enough for Henry to almost reach Upstage.

But Upstage had turned around. The tall woman who had been having an argument with McNamara earlier was talking to him again. Her head was close to his face. She said a few words and moved away. This time Henry captured more of her. Her black dress clung to a perfect body; she did not have the thinness of a model but was someone who trained regularly. Her movements were supple, almost stealthy.

Henry abandoned his study of her when Upstage moved forward, just as McNamara was coming back to the charge.

Upstage stopped in front of Henry, one hand in his left pocket. "Why don't you introduce us, Art?"

Only a few people were tall enough to look Henry in the eye, but Upstage was one of them. His tall, bulky, tuxedo-clad body felt imposing this close. Their eyes briefly met, but it was long enough for Henry. Upstage knew who he was.

"Henry Newborn, financial consultant," McNamara uttered through clenched teeth.

"Rush Huckerby spoke enthusiastically about you," Upstage said without bothering to shake hands. "Terrible thing, suicide... Such a talent."

Upstage shook his head, lips arching up, expressing a sadness that did not reach his eyes.

Chapter Thirteen

The last file Henry Crowne had sent him was open on Harris's computer screen. He brewed yet another cup of coffee for the review. Despite the setback due to Huckerby's assassination, Crowne had come up with an excellent alternative. Harris had to give it to him; he knew how to think on his feet and improvise.

One of his burner phones buzzed in his jacket pocket. He fished out the pay-as-you-go allocated to Crowne, but the screen was black. The noise persisted. Harris dug into his other pocket and pulled out the phone in a leather casing.

Brett was calling back.

"Good evening... actually, good morning," Harris said, casting an eye at the clock on his kitchen wall. It was way past midnight.

"I've thought about your offer." Brett sounded alert. "I need some clarification."

"OK, shoot. What was unclear in my proposition to help?"

"What am I supposed to do in return? And don't tell me that you only need a bit of intel on a couple of Russian oligarchs because you should have that already."

"The service is very stretched at the moment."

"Bullshit... Or is it that Russia is not a priority?"

Harris frowned. Sometimes Brett was too smart for his own good. "It's *my* priority and that's all you need to know."

"Am I pressing on a raw nerve? If I am please tell me, and I'll press harder."

"Then before you do that, let me ask a question of my own. What prompted you to call me an entire 24 hours before the deadline to tell me you're on?" Harris continued before Brett could answer. "Don't give me this crap about needing more information, not at 12.37 in the morning. What's spooked you? Excuse the pun."

"I'm disappointed, Steve. I don't spook that easily, as you well know." Brett allowed a moment's pause.

Harris knew when not to interrupt his asset. And also, Brett had a point. His last assignment in London had been more than hair-raising.

Brett continued. "Granted, tonight's conversation with my blue-eyed-girl took an unexpected turn, but it has also perhaps created an opportunity."

"You've been invited to meet the great and the good in daddy's circle?"

"I've been invited to meet daddy's close friends and offer them the chance to purchase certain artefacts of historical value."

"And you've accepted I hope."

"As long as we have a deal. And as long as I know what intel you want me to collect."

"Simple. For the time being, I want the names of those friends you're going to meet."

"And after the for-the-time-being, what then?" Brett asked.

"If you were to see fit to engage some of these friends further, that would be hugely helpful. And I'm not talking about selling them looted pieces from war-torn Syria – sorry, valuable Middle Eastern antiquities."

"What are you looking for, exactly?" Brett ignored Harris's jibe.

"How many of these British, or American friends for that matter, are in the Kremlin's pocket?"

"If I said to you most of them would that shock you?"

"Nope, but I need proof."

"Now, about our deal..."

"I'll get you registered under the operation I'm running, and you'll get the usual paraphernalia," Harris said. "When are you meeting these people?"

"Day after tomorrow. I'll call again when I have the guest list."

* * *

Upstage barely waved his hand and a tray with fresh champagne glasses materialised in front of him. He picked up one, unconcerned whether Henry might like one too.

"Rush Huckerby met you at Davos. How was it?" Upstage moved away from the centre of the room to a cluster of seats that had been kept free by a couple of dark-suited bodyguards.

"Davos? Informative, although one needs to know how to sieve through some of the crap."

Upstage reached one of the large armchairs and dropped into it, indicating to Henry that he should sit.

"Thought so... tremendously overrated." Upstage had clearly never been invited to Davos. Its exclusivity taunted him and it showed.

"Very insightful." Henry nodded. "Nevertheless, Davos is useful to pick up the trends of what's happening in the market."

"And what might that be?"

"Banks are still very tight when it comes to lending to projects that are more visionary and, perhaps, off the beaten track."

"Hardly something new." Upstage relaxed into his seat, draping one arm over the comfortable back.

"But this reluctance to lend can be circumvented," Henry said.

"How?"

"The right contacts at the right level in the right bank... as ever."

Henry relaxed into his seat too. This was rehearsed bull Upstage was delivering. Unlike Upstage, Henry's name had been added to the enviable list of Davos's most exclusive club.

"And of course, the question of world political dominance is forever present." Henry added.

"What, America still pretending it is the number one power? Ridiculous... look at China. Look at Russia..."

Upstage launched into a rehash of what he'd said less than an hour ago. Henry listened with intent. The conversation was no longer a dialogue between two people but Upstage testing Henry's ability to fit in. Could he become part of the Upstage court? And would some of the more radical views of the man at its centre offend Henry?

120

"Russia's Putin has done very well – a proud people the Russians. And with huge resources of oil, gas, gold, precious minerals. A successful space programme that NASA should seek to replicate... Incredible people." Upstage locked eyes with Henry, daring him to contradict him.

"Couldn't agree more," Henry replied. "Talent is rewarded properly there, no loser tolerated."

Upstage grinned for the first time that evening. Henry had said the magic words.

"Rush Huckerby – God bless his soul – told me you arrange financing... in size?"

"He was right. I never get involved unless the ticket is at least $500 million. I intermediate. There are no places in the world I won't go, bar perhaps North Korea and Iran."

Upstage nodded. "Russia obviously on your list?"

"Very much so, like most finance people in the UK for that matter. London is a very welcoming place for Russian money and Russian ultra-high-net-worth individuals."

"But how about Russian mainland? St Petersburg, Moscow?"

Henry placed his empty glass on the coffee table that was separating them. It was his turn to lock eyes with Upstage. "As I said, nowhere is out of bounds."

"I have a deal on the go... excellent project, but I think we are nearly there. Top Capital Partners have been organising it for me."

"Are you certain it's almost there?" Henry settled into his seat again. "I have received market intel that seems to indicate otherwise."

Upstage's face froze. "What do you mean?"

"I presume you're referring to the Nassau Luxury Hotel complex? A document landed in my inbox this evening, shortly before I came here. I'm not sure how your current investors are going to react... Although as you said Top Capital Partners must have prepared them."

Upstage's fist closed tight and then relaxed. "Are you free for lunch tomorrow?"

"I'm not but I will be."

"Let's meet here again. 12pm."

Henry was about to stand up to take his leave when McNamara appeared at Upstage's side.

"Your receptionist has been waiting for you," McNamara said to Henry, amused.

He had Nick in toe, looking as dignified as he could muster.

Henry hardly raised his head to acknowledge both men. "My assistant, who has kindly agreed to man reception until I find a suitable person, knows when not to interrupt. Which is why he's been waiting."

Upstage's face was like thunder. He glared at McNamara. He, too, did not like to be interrupted.

Henry stood up. "But you probably have a few important matters to discuss with Mr Upstage."

McNamara frowned, to which Upstage nodded. "We do."

"I'll see you as agreed," Henry said to Upstage.

"As agreed." He didn't bother to stand up.

Nick joined Henry without a word, walking alongside him towards the exit. It was only when they turned the corner of the street outside Upstage's club that Nick lost his composure.

"Did I blow it?"

"On the contrary... perfect timing."

"What do you mean?"

"McNamara has not yet been told about the press release we posted to investors and on various sites this afternoon. It's not surprising though. US investors won't see it until tomorrow morning and European investors won't contact him tonight."

"But you told Upstage about it?"

"Yup. Managed to squeeze that into the conversation."

Nick smiled. "That's gonna be tough to explain."

"No doubt. I think Arthur McNamara Jr is, as we speak, enduring a serious dressing down. Upstage is not a forgiving man."

* * *

It was 6.30am, and the security guard at Henry's office block greeted him with bleary eyes. It was the end of his night shift, and he was ready for home and a warm bed.

Henry arrived on the 8th floor with a coffee cup and brown paper bag, and stopped in front of his office door. The glass had not yet been

122

replaced, although the office manager had assured him it would be within the next couple of days.

The only noise Henry could hear were the faint groans of an office block waking up. The cleaning crew he had spotted whilst exiting the lift was likely finishing up the other offices on his floor before the start of the day. Henry had rejected the offer of their services, through the office manager, and hired his own cleaning team, courtesy of the Head of Station at the British Embassy.

Henry opened the door and proceeded with a sweep of each room. Everything was clean. He moved to his office, set down his large coffee cup, took the brown toast out of the paper bag and got to work.

He had received a few emails last night and had replied briefly to them after his late return from the Upstage event.

Harris had made progress on obtaining HUMIT on Russian contacts in London. Jack was sending Mandy Jackson with information about the thug who'd tried to break into his office. Nick had also done well in finding intel last night whilst speaking to the Upstage guests, or through other means – the latter to be discussed in the privacy of this office only.

Henry logged in to his encrypted computer and started on his breakfast. Henry unscrewed the lid off the marmalade jar he kept in his drawer. Thick cut – the only way to have it.

Using a knife from the kitchen, he went to dip it into the jar. But he paused the knife in the air as a memory of Northern Ireland hit Henry most unexpectedly. They always did.

His mother is at the kitchen table. She is peeling a couple of oranges and has bought a tin from the local supermarket that will be part of the preparation. Henry sits on a chair and watches every gesture she makes with interest. He is not trying to learn how to cook. He is waiting for the pan to be cool enough so that he can scrape the remnants of the marmalade and spread it on a piece of warm toast. They make idle conversation about his friends and school until Henry spoils it by asking the one question that never receives a satisfactory reply.

"Where is Dad?"

The sound of the front office door opening dragged Henry out of his reverie. He checked his watch. It was 8am. Nick walked in, his hair again damp from the shower. Henry resisted the urge to tell him he should dry his hair before going out in the winter. He risked sounding like his mother.

"You couldn't sleep?" Henry teased.

"No, I couldn't." Nick was serious. "I have loads to tell you about last night."

"Well then, join me in my office. Close the door and let's get a bit of white noise going, just in case."

Henry switched on the large TV screen on the wall, opposite the sofas and chairs that sat in the corner of his office. He selected the Bloomberg channel and invited Nick to sit with him.

The young man laid his own breakfast down on Henry's desk – cup of coffee and a peanut butter sandwich.

"For a start, people last night were virtually all sympathisers or members of the same political party." Nick took a bite of his sandwich.

"Republican?"

"Yep, and they're all supporting Upstage in his views. Not one person disagreed with him."

"A lot of different origins or same profession?"

"Politicians and lobbyists... but then again we are in DC."

Henry nodded. Politics was the only game in DC.

"Social media influencers," Nick continued. "Lots of TV people from some of the most conservative channels. And, wait for it, a couple of guys from London."

"You were busy networking last night. Good stuff..."

Nick took a large gulp of coffee.

"What?" Henry removed the lid of his coffee cup and stirred in some sugar. "Don't go shy on me now. I told you to get some intel."

"I lifted a few wallets." Nick looked sheepish. "But I didn't take anything, and I made sure they found them again."

"And you're aware the event will have been heavily monitored through CCTV?"

"Course." Nick shrugged. "It's part and parcel of the fun."

Henry understood. "You were able to find the blind spots and use them?"

"Yeah. It's not always obvious where they are, but there are enough of them to allow me to lift a few wallets or mobile phones."

"I can tell this isn't the first time you've done this."

124

Nick shrugged again.

"Ah... well, practice makes perfect. And I'm sure you would have been pinned to the ground by one of Upstage's bodyguards had they suspected anything."

"I noticed they were low-key when it came to the rest of the crowd. They were there to look after Upstage himself."

"Upstage must have felt pretty confident about the clientele." Henry took a bite of toast.

"It felt that way, perhaps, because he knew the type of people he had invited."

"Except you and I, of course," said Henry. "Excessively confident of him... Other intruders could have done the same thing."

"Not *that* easy to gain access to their systems, actually. These people would have needed to hack their way through the invitation portal." Nick looked almost offended.

"OK, smart arse." Henry nodded. "Let's speak about what you discovered rather than how good you are. Who are these people from the UK you mentioned?"

"One's a businessman who does cross-border deals. He was not very forward about which deals, but I got the feeling he wasn't too fussy about what he was dealing with as long as it made him money. The other guy was his friend, a politician. Edward Bound and Nevil Ferguson were their names."

"Why were they there, or didn't you get that far?"

"I think they know Upstage very well. I'm not sure it was all about business though."

"What makes you say that?"

"It's the political jargon they used – snappy slogans like Made In America Not China, and Make the UK Sovereign Again. It's as though they were testing these out on people to see what worked best."

"You think Upstage has some political ambition?" Henry asked Nick, wanting to hear more of the young man's view before he gave his own.

"I don't know but the two Brits I met certainly do. Bound was talking about raising funds for Ferguson's party and supporting him in his campaign."

"I'm surprised they were that forthcoming about their plan."

Nick smiled. "They'd had quite a bit to drink, and I made the right arguments, you know, China's taking all our jobs – that helped."

"Where does Bound think he's going to get the funding from? Upstage?"

"Or one of his contacts. They were pretty buoyant the cash was coming their way."

"But Upstage doesn't have enough to fund his Nassau hotel purchase."

"Perhaps the sum is not that large."

"Unlikely..." Henry was almost finished his toast. "These people are not after a few thousand dollars; they are after a few hundred thousand dollars. Upstage won't part with that sort of money, not now. Perhaps not ever, but that's another conversation."

"So, who are they getting the money from?"

"I'm having lunch with Upstage today. I'll find out."

* * *

Henry and Nick started their day's work. Henry focused on the extra information James had sent overnight and Nick returned to writing his CV.

"We have a visitor... downstairs." Nick appeared at the door of Henry's office, one hand on the frame, half leaning in.

Henry frowned. "Friend or foe?"

"No idea. It's a lady. First name Mandy, that's all she gave to reception."

Henry relaxed. He had enjoyed his first conversation with Mandy when she'd called the day before. "Friend. Tell reception to send her up."

Henry looked around his untidy desk. He gathered up a few documents he would later shred and organised them into a neat pile. He stood up and walked to the main door of the Platinum Suite.

A shadow moved outside the frosted glass that was still bearing the marks of yesterday's assault. The person rang the doorbell. Henry crossed the space between his office and the entrance in a few steps, just as Nick released the door.

Mandy Jackson stepped in. Petite and professional in the well-cut trouser suit she was wearing. The small, colourful scarf she had knotted sideways around her throat was just enough to liven up the dark colour of her jacket without being too loud.

126

With a smile, Mandy presented a slender hand to Henry.

He hesitated for only an instant, but already he'd made a statement. Henry saw the brief flash of understanding in Mandy's eyes. Could he explain the reservation he had to get her involved?

"Very nice to speak to you in person." He shook her hand. "Let me introduce you to the other member of the team... Nick Fox."

"Hello, Nick." Mandy shook hands with him. He smiled broadly at the newcomer. Henry showed her to his office. He closed the door behind him.

"Thanks for coming my way." Henry indicated the seats in the corner. "Drink?"

"No, thank you. And don't thank me yet. Jack wants to make sure the set-up is working well for what comes next."

They sat down, Henry in the armchair he had occupied when McNamara had visited the day before, Mandy in McNamara's seat on the large, leather sofa.

Henry's discomfort grew at her involvement, but he did his best to hide it from her. It had nothing to do with Mandy but rather with the characters he increasingly believed he was dealing with.

"What have you got for me? Or would you like a tour of the premises first so that you can report to Jack that Her Majesty's Secret Service is doing the CIA proud?"

"Don't be cheesed off with Jack. The loss of Rush is still fresh for him."

"I'm sorry... I didn't mean to be insensitive." Henry pulled back his sarcasm. He also felt sad for Huckerby's terrible end.

"I'm not saying you are, but Jack is going to be a bit more nosy than usual, and so is his boss."

"Hunter III must be at least supportive if you are here."

Mandy grinned. "That's probably not the correct set of assumptions."

Henry slumped back in mock despair. "Are we the only people to see the wood for the trees? I know the Cold War sounds a bit old-fashioned and outdated, but Putin is of that era. Or have the people who run the CIA and MI6 forgotten that?"

"I quite like joining this small band of renegades. I'm sold on the idea that something is afoot."

"If that's the case, then what have you got for me?"

Mandy told Henry what she said she'd told Jack.

Yes, the man that had tried to break into Henry's office was a Russian criminal, linked to organised crime. Yes, he also was listed as a man with links to the Russian intelligence community, but Mandy's latest research placed him low in the pecking order.

Mandy continued. "More a go-between, someone who is on hand perhaps more for counterintelligence than direct intel gathering."

"You mean doing some of the wet work?"

"No, that would be left to senior people. Assassination on foreign soil is one of Moscow's specialties and it's got to be done right. No, I rather think logistics, getting the weapon, the poison – whatever they are using."

"But no inkling about who employed him?"

"Unfortunately not yet. I'm working on it."

Henry fell silent for a moment. Then he asked, "How much OC involvement do you think there is? I mean enough to involve the Feds?"

"If it's an indirect way of asking me whether Jack is considering involving these guys, the answer is no."

"Glad to hear we are on the same page."

"His words exactly."

Henry paused and it caught Mandy's attention.

She smiled. "If we are going to work together, Mr Crowne, you need to be frank with me."

She must have overcome plenty of reservations in her time and Henry guessed he would be no exception.

"I'm sorry, Mandy, I will. But let me firm up on what it is that's concerning me. I have a lunch today that should tell me a lot more about it."

Chapter Fourteen

The CIA file Henry had just read had warned him that Upstage was always fashionably late for his meetings. He toyed with the idea of arriving late too, but it would look unprofessional and perhaps overdone. His legend persona placed Henry's business in Geneva and London; late was not part of his half-Swiss DNA.

Henry arrived on the doorsteps of Upstage's luxury club at 12pm precisely. Instructions had been left at reception. A couple of bodyguards put him through a metal detector routine that felt professional yet nonintrusive, as well as a light frisking and a mobile phone check. Immediately afterwards, they whisked Henry up to the top floor, into a room that looked straight out onto the White House.

Impressive.

The Greek temple portico and four iconic columns of the most famous building in DC could not be mistaken for anything else. The sun was shining despite the cold weather, and the building shimmered beneath its glow. The shimmer reminded Henry that the White House had been at the centre of some of the most memorable moments in the history of western democracy.

He was still absorbed in his thoughts when a small woman suddenly materialised at his side.

"Mr Upstage is on his way. Perhaps I could offer you a drink?"

She held out a tray of drinks. Henry selected a tomato juice and checked his watch. It was already 15 minutes past the hour. Had he still been in banking he would have given his guest another five minutes and then left.

But this was not the trading floor at GL Investment Bank, and he didn't care about the posturing from those days. The game he had to play now was much more subtle. Henry finished his drink, moved over to the lunch table that had been set for two and sat down.

He took his smartphone out and began scrolling through Bloomberg news in search of some juicy morsel he could feed his host.

A loud voice coming from the corridor interrupted his search. David Upstage was announcing himself. The voice grew in volume as it got closer to the room. The door opened. The hostess withdrew deferentially and Upstage entered.

He paused, like a showman preparing himself, and gave Henry a perfect white smile.

"I am very glad you made yourself comfortable, Mr Newborn."

The woman re-entered the room carrying a tray with a Diet Coke, unopened, and a tall glass turned upside down. She laid the glass on the table near the plate that would be Upstage's. She opened the can and poured. Was Upstage being overly cautious about what went into his glass?

Henry took his time to stand up and greet Upstage. Upstage held out his hand in greeting, unlike at the event when he hadn't bothered. It was set at an odd angle for a handshake, more of a papal kissing a ring gesture, but Henry played along. At over 6 feet tall Henry could look Upstage in the eye and this gave Henry an advantage.

Both men sat at the table. A menu was folded next to each setting. Upstage didn't bother to look at it.

"I recommend the steak, a 20-ounce bone-in ribeye, medium rare, green salad."

Henry nodded. "Excellent, I'll follow you."

"I never drink alcohol during the day." Upstage didn't need to add that he was expecting his guest to also refrain.

The hostess came in to take their order. Upstage took a long pull of his Diet Coke. He assessed Henry several times, making no attempt to hide it. He was measuring the man seated in front of him.

Henry waited. His legend was in no hurry to make an offer. He was here to listen and perhaps assist.

"How did you know about the Nassau hotel press release?" Upstage said.

"I could tell you it's my job to know, but in this case I don't mind telling you that my team here in DC, and in London, are tracking a number of activists' websites that like to release hacked material."

Upstage's eyes widened.

His bombshell had had the required effect.

Whatever excuse McNamara had given as an explanation for the leak, Top Capital Partners being hacked had not been one of them.

Henry now had Upstage's undivided attention.

"You mean?"

"That's right. Someone hacked your advisers' systems, ferreted around and found the information they were looking for."

The man's jaw clenched. He looked at his mobile with fury, but decided now was not the time to call anyone.

He shifted on his chair. "Do you know who these people are?"

"The hackers? No idea. I simply know they are pretty good at this, and I'm sure that they have been inspired by the likes of WikiLeaks."

"Can you find out?"

"I could." Henry gave Upstage a calm smile. "But it wouldn't repair the damage done. What matters now is you reassure the investors and convince them to still participate, otherwise move on to a fresh lot and manage them better this time."

"Or I could sue the little hacker fuckers…" Upstage's voice wobbled.

"You could, but even if you wrung them dry of every single asset they own, these people are worth peanuts to you."

Upstage took another long pull of Diet Coke. "What do you suggest I do next?"

"It depends on what you want *me* to do. And I would completely understand if you needed to take your time to do your due diligence over me and my business."

"Not necessary, I already have plenty on you. Rush was insistent we should meet. I did my homework."

Henry nodded, a little surprised. Upstage had sent someone to investigate his legend's background and no alarms had sounded at MI6 or the CIA? Worrying.

"In that case, the more you can tell me about the deal, the likely investors, and what you intend to get out of it yourself, the better."

Upstage was precise in the information he offered. He knew in minute detail everything about the intended purchase of the Nassau hotel complex. He was no longer here to impress but to make the deal he so badly wanted to work happen.

"Thank you for being forthcoming with the information." Henry poured himself a glass of water from a bottle on the table. He took a sip. "However, I need to *completely understand* the way this transaction will make money. I say this to you: when it comes to the countries I do business with, I am happy to go almost anywhere, and I'll say this of the transactions I support, *nothing* is off limits."

"Such as?" Upstage swirled his glass, sending ice clanging against its side.

"A lot of money can be moved through a casino." Henry took his mobile out of his jacket pocket and set it on the table, to show he was not recording the conversation. "Do you mind if I take my jacket off?"

Henry stood up, not waiting for Upstage's reply. He removed it and hung it on the back of his chair – to let Upstage know he was not wearing a wire.

There was a knock at the door, and a short pause before it opened. The hostess entered followed by two waiters. They arranged the food in front of both men, making sure the steaks were presented at the bottom of the plate and the salad at the top.

The woman looked at Upstage for a few seconds, and when he didn't acknowledge her, she retreated promptly.

Upstage pursed his lips, grabbed his knife and fork, and started cutting his meat.

"A lot of money can be moved in that way." He put a piece into his mouth and started chewing.

"Origin?" Henry copied Upstage and cut his own steak. "Latin American? Eastern European... Russian?"

Upstage looked up from his plate. "Why mention these places?" He ate more of the meat, ignoring the salad.

"Because these are the countries in which their wealthy citizens are more likely to use a good money laundering infrastructure." Henry ate and nodded. "Excellent steak."

The forbidden word had been spoken: Money laundering. Henry stayed calm, pretending to be preoccupied with the food he was eating.

132

Upstage stopped carving and put his knife and fork down. "That's very direct of you."

"This is no time for subtlety if you want to salvage your Nassau hotel project. I need to know exactly what I'm dealing with." Henry worked through his food methodically – steak-salad-steak-salad.

"Let's assume your assumption is right, how do you propose to go about financing the project?"

"The money will no longer be lent to the project but to you directly."

Upstage shook his head. "That may prove difficult."

"Because you are suing DSB, the bank that originally funded some of your early business ventures?"

"A bunch of crooks," Upstage shot back, then resumed his eating.

"No doubt," Henry ignored him. "But I presume you are a client of their private bank and wealth management business?"

"And so is my family."

"Excellent. Then may I suggest we explore this avenue more?"

Upstage had finished his steak. He pressed a button on the small silver box that was on the table.

"I'm still unclear how a private bank is going to lend me over $810 million."

"The answer to that very relevant question resides in another question I asked earlier on but is yet unanswered."

Upstage sat back in his chair. The moment to commit had arrived.

Henry had also finished his plate. He wiped his mouth, took a sip of water and sat back. He kept his expression neutral. It was just another deal for Henry Newborn.

Upstage's jaw tightened, then relaxed. He looked Henry in the eyes. "Russian."

Henry nodded. "Very good. Senior enough contacts, I presume?"

"We don't meet. We agree percentage through intermediaries."

"Top Capital Partners are facilitating?"

"That's right."

"Then they should be able to create an introduction."

Concern flashed in Upstage's eyes. "And then what?"

Henry's heart raced. Had he been too forward? He tried to pull back.

"We create a deal between DSB Private Bank Moscow and another Russian organisation."

The concern in Upstage's eyes was replaced by an idea. "Perhaps a Russian bank?"

"Yes, as an example. Or another company that deals with highly lucrative businesses, such as gold mining." Henry recalled the small equity stake Upstage was holding in one of the most productive Siberian mining companies.

"I like the way you think, Mr Newborn."

Henry agreed with a brief smile. "There is a lot of work, and I would not expect my team to carry the heavy lifting alone on this transaction."

"Top Capital will help."

"McNamara?"

Upstage's face turned red with anger. "Not him. I'll vet the team."

"Very well. Then I think a more in-depth meeting is in order."

Upstage stood up. "My PA will contact yours to fix a time."

Henry stood up too.

"Before you go, I'd like to introduce you to a member of my team who I trust with sensitive communication." Upstage picked up his iPhone from the table and dialled a number.

"Tatiana, my dear. Are you free for a quick introduction?"

* * *

Upstage's office at his luxury club was as ostentatious as everything else he owned. Tatiana checked out the gold and marble everywhere and very few good pieces of art, as well as some rather well-executed replicas of Greek antiquities.

She moved to the large floor-to-ceiling window that overlooked New York Avenue and, in the distance, the White House. Upstage had wanted an update on her findings. After last night's revelations and disaster regarding the Nassau deal, he was ready to hear anything she had to say about McNamara's handling of his project.

The use of thuggery would not have moved Upstage otherwise but learning of McNamara's instruction to fake a robbery to enter Henry Newborn's offices had triggered another one of Upstage's trouncings for which he was famous. McNamara was on a slippery slope and Tatiana wondered how low he would have to sink before Upstage got rid of him.

134

Top Capital Partners might also cut the cord with McNamara if their client threatened to walk out. Although, Tatiana believed it would be more bluster than reality. Upstage needed Top Capital at least for a while longer.

She returned to the large sofa where she and Upstage had also chatted about Henry Newborn and the latest information she had gleaned. Upstage had sat at one end whilst Tatiana was at the other, well out of his reach.

The plate of food she'd ordered had half-eaten slices of beef brisket on rye bread. The coffee here was good.

Upstage's PA popped her head through the door to check she had everything she needed.

Tatiana nodded with a smile. "Yes, thank you."

People often forgot her true origins whenever they spoke to her. Her American English was perfect. She'd settled on a New York accent, as it was the best one to hide her Russian accent.

Of course, it helped that she was attractive. The Americans would have called her a bombshell; the thought made her laugh. If only they knew how appropriate the word was. Her large, green eyes gave her face an unusual softness. People trusted soft features. She had inherited them from her mother. Her chest tightened to think about her beautiful mum.

Tatiana finished the last piece of sandwich and moved over to Upstage's computer. She doubted there would be anything new to see, but she'd received instructions from Moscow to investigate the man. The recent arrival of Henry Newborn and the determination of Huckerby to introduce him to Upstage had rattled her Russian minder.

She entered Upstage's usual password, getting into his computer without trouble. He hadn't changed the password yet – very good.

She took a USB key from the back pocket of her tight, leather trousers. She smiled at the thought of how her tight clothing affected Upstage. He was such an easy target when it came to women. Not that he respected them or even loved them. They were commodities to him – enjoy and discard.

The download started. It would take a few minutes. She checked his browsing history. A few things there were interesting... Upstage was becoming obsessed with Hillary Clinton. A large chunk of his time in the past week had been devoted to searches on her. Even more telling were the words he had associated with her name: scandal, fraud, dishonesty.

Tatiana made a mental note. The plan was taking hold.

She opened his diary. The time bar on Upstage's computer showed her the download was almost complete. She cast an eye over the week ahead – nothing there she was not aware of. She was about to close it when she spotted something in today's date. Upstage had disappeared for lunch, but it had not been entered in his diary. Something organised at the last minute. There was only one person who had impressed Upstage last night to warrant an impromptu lunch. Newborn must be his undisclosed guest.

Her phone rang. Upstage's name appeared on screen. She removed the USB promptly. Perhaps he was on his way back wanting to finish their conversation about McNamara.

She logged off whilst answering. "David?"

"Tatiana, my dear, are you free for a quick introduction?"

"Of course."

Tatiana bit her lip. This was not the right answer. Meeting Henry Newborn would make it so much more difficult to follow him. She cursed Upstage and his use of her. She was not his trophy girl.

She stood up. Looked at her reflection in the window of Upstage's office. The trousers looked good on her, and so did the black V-neck soft cashmere she was wearing, just enough to show a bit of breast, not enough to be too obvious. She put on her light leather coat, rearranged her long blonde hair.

Perhaps she could get close to the attractive Brit in some other way.

* * *

"This is complete crap," Mandy said to Jack on the phone.

Jack had caught her at home after her visit to Henry's office. Today would be one of her working-from-home days.

"I know," he said. "The worst is that I don't think getting hold of the Metro Police in DC will change anything."

"What have they got to substantiate their decision to class Rush's death as suicide?"

136

"Some emails that indicated he was under a lot of stress at work. And some strange FB posts to the same effect."

"Addressed to whom?"

"To a friend."

"And what did the friend say when you talked to him?"

"He didn't think Rush would have gone that far, but he had been concerned. And then the cops also found a lot of meds for anxiety, depression, and a few illicit pills. "

"Like what... ecstasy and meth?"

"So they say." Jack gritted his teeth.

"Rush Huckerby on drugs? Never." Mandy's outrage matched his.

"Agreed. I've run enough agents to know when one of my guys is on stuff. Huckerby might have been stressed but he was not a druggie. And before you ask, I'm not going to tell the police anything."

"Are you worried there'll be a leak from them?"

"I'm not worried there will be one. I *know* there will be one. It's impossible not to think that given the speed with which they've classified his death as suicide."

"I suppose it would be difficult, although not impossible, to fake emails for a good hacker. Getting into his FB account won't be easy, either."

Jack heard Mandy tapping on her computer.

"I've been thinking about that all morning," he said. "I agree that faking an email exchange might be easier than accessing his FB account, so we need to find out whether this is what happened."

"As long as he sent the emails the police say he did from his personal email account..." Mandy had stopped typing. "I can get someone on the case."

Jack was thinking the same thing. "How about the guy that works with Crowne?"

"Nick Fox?"

"That's the man. Recruited under our noses. Harris owes me on that one... recruiting a US national under the CIA's nose? Really!"

"I'll get in touch with Crowne again," Mandy said, "to check he's happy for me to carry on."

Jack felt bad. The news about Huckerby had superseded his intention to ask Mandy about her first meeting with Henry.

"What do you mean?"

"I could tell he was uncomfortable to meet but I'm not sure why... yet."

"That surprises me as much as it does you," Jack replied.

"I'll get to the bottom of it. My read on him is that he's worried rather than disappointed."

"He crashed one of Upstage's parties last night." Jack grabbed a pad and jotted down a note on it. "I'll find out whether there is something in that."

"Looks like Rush's FB page has not been closed down yet." Mandy had resumed her typing.

"How do you know that?"

"I've just found it and sent a friend request."

"But unless you're accepted as a friend you won't be able to see who else is a friend too," Jack suggested.

"Of course... stupid. Hang on..." Jack heard her typing furiously on her keyboard again. "I'm not sure this is even Rush's FB account."

"What do you mean?"

"I think his account has been duplicated, or copied. Jack, I'll check it out and call you back." Mandy hung up.

* * *

"Tatiana Borodin..." Henry murmured the name as he sat in the cab that was taking him back to his office.

He could still feel her soft hand in his, the smile that was inviting and yet distant. She had all the hallmarks of the perfect honey trap. Upstage was without a doubt smitten by her. But she hadn't seemed pleased to be introduced, or looked ready to pander to his every demand.

Henry searched her name on the internet. She had a website that confirmed what Upstage had said to him. She was a professional photographer and an artist. Some of the photos on display were of good quality and even exhibited talent. Henry had, in his previous life, garnered a collection of contemporary art that had put him in touch with artists of considerable ability. Tatiana had an eye for the unexpected.

She had also travelled a lot for a woman who he pegged to be in her early thirties at most. Henry returned to his search and found more about her.

138

Her parents were Piotr and Yulia Borodin, activists renowned for their fight against corruption in Russia. They'd started in the late '90s when the Soviet Union was being disbanded and wealth in Russia had fallen into the hands of a first wave of oligarchs. Their activism had not stopped under Putin, but it came to an abrupt end ten years ago.

They had been interviewing Chechen rebels when their car was ambushed. The Chechens denied the attack. The Russians blamed a case of mistaken identity and said they had been targeted in error by the rebels. The activists' community didn't believe the explanation, but the investigation into their deaths was closed before it had even started. The true culprits would never be caught.

The cab stopped. Henry clutched his phone loosely in his hand, heart pounding. Memories of Northern Ireland and of his own father's murder assailed him, making him queasy. The cab driver, turned towards him now, repeated the cost of the ride. Henry shook himself out the feelings that had seized him a moment ago.

He paid and left the cab, walking in the direction of his building. He entered the Platinum Suite. Nick said something to him concerning Mandy and Huckerby.

"Later," Henry replied. He entered his office and closed the door.

He went to his computer, logged in and resumed his search into the death of Tatiana Borodin's parents. The newspapers had speculated on the true cause, but no journalist had come up with conclusive proof of the Russian state's involvement. Apparently, the situation in Chechnya had been volatile enough to make the official explanation sound credible.

He looked at the date of the incident, July 2006. Henry typed two names that came to mind whilst reading the article relating to the Borodins' death.

Anna Politkovskaya and Alexander Litvinenko.

Politkovskaya had been the first one to meet her death in October 2006. She had been found murdered in the lift of the block of flats where she lived. Shot at point-blank range. A number of men had been convicted of her murder. Some were eventually acquitted, others received a life sentence, but to this day it was still unclear who had ordered and paid for the contract killing.

Henry knew her because of her reporting of the Chechnyan crisis and her refusal to stop reporting about the war, despite intimidation and being subjected to a mock execution by the Russian military forces. He kept reading the details relating to the kiboshed prosecution and retrial, until a note at the end of the article caught his attention.

A document had been published on the internet after its release by Edward Snowden. A screenshot of the said document showed it had been shared among the US Intelligence Community, and indicated that the Russian FSB had installed malicious software on Politkovskaya's webmail, in December 2005. There was no conclusion drawn, however, from this piece of information.

When it came to Litvinenko, his poisoning with Polonium-210 in a restaurant in the heart of London had made international news. The date had been November 2006. He'd sought refuge in the UK and had been granted political asylum, after accusing his superiors of ordering the assassination of the Russian oligarch, Boris Berezovsky. Litvinenko had subsequently accused the FSB of organising acts of terrorism in order to get Putin re-elected.

Litvinenko had published a couple of books, denouncing what he called the mafia-state in Russia.

Henry sat back in his chair, stunned by the string of events that had unfolded in 2006. The Borodins, Politkovskaya then Litvinenko... Someone at the FSB or above had been doing a serious clearing out of the opposition.

Henry exhaled loudly, and stuck one hand in his hair. What was he trying to find?

The death of Tatiana's parents reminded him too much of his own experience.

Henry stood up abruptly and walked to the bay window of his office, trying to fend off the images that were scrambling for his attention.

The alleyway at the back of the house in Belfast he lived in.

The shadowy figure of his father walking out of the car park at the back of their house and disappearing into the distance.

The terrifying sound of gunshots that came after an argument.

A body on the ground, no longer breathing – his father.

And the blood, so much of it.

Henry rested his head against the pane of glass. The cold soothed his throbbing head.

Whoever Tatiana Borodin really was and whoever she was working for, she was not hiding it. Or perhaps this was the perfect cover? The thought irked Henry. Could she truly use her parents' death in that way?

He returned to his computer and sent an encoded message to James in London.

Tatiana Borodin, daughter of Piotr and Yulia. Need as much intel as possible. URGENT.

Chapter Fifteen

When Henry emerged from his office, Nick had a puzzled look on his face.

"What was that all about?"

"Something very urgent came up." Henry said. "I'm sorry, I didn't mean to be rude."

"That's all right." Nick's frown disappeared, replaced by his dedicated expression. "What's next then?"

Two days in the position had done wonders for the young man's attitude. He no longer looked awkward and out of place but as keen as mustard.

"You've got your interview with the onboarding team today, remember?"

Nick's happiness dropped away. "Shit… I'd completely forgotten."

"Nothing to worry about. You're a priority."

"Who says?"

"I do."

Nick looked impressed. "Does that mean you've got the ear of the top guy at MI6?"

Henry shook his head. Nick could sometimes be disarmingly credulous. The top guy at MI6, as Nick called him, did not speak to an asset on the ground.

"I haven't said that, but the man in London who runs Operation RUSSKY BEAR is a determined pain in the butt."

Nick's frown returned. "And how does that make it easy for me? I'm in DC and he's in London. And then what about the CIA? Are they gonna get pissed off with me if –"

Henry raised a hand. "Stop. Deep breath. No one is going to get pissed off with you if you're helping stop some Russian bastards from trying to interfere with your country. Right?"

"I s'ppose."

"Anyway, London is a great place. Worst that will happen is I relocate you there."

Nick's worried look returned.

"Just kidding." Henry looked at his watch. "Believe you me, with your hacking talents, the likes of MI6 and the CIA would much rather you work for them than the opposition, or simply do it for a laugh."

"I'd never work for the opposition."

"Perhaps not, but you'd happily hack into MI6 or the CIA's systems for fun, and that might cheese them off just as much."

Nick stood up from the reception desk and picked up his sheepskin flying jacket. Another of Nick's acquisitions that he almost certainly did not have the money to buy.

"And where did you lift this jacket from?" Henry asked.

"That's unfair... I bought it from a friend."

"So where did your friend lift it from then?"

Nick smirked. "Don't know... never asked."

"Very wise. What you don't know can't hurt you."

Henry grabbed his coat, a light one he had not bothered with when visiting Upstage. They both made their way down to the first floor and then the street.

Henry hailed a cab.

"Massachusetts Avenue, British Embassy," he told the driver as they got in.

"Doris Remington is expecting us," Henry told Nick as they stood in front of the square building. He paused a moment.

"Who is she?" Nick asked, zipping up his jacket against the cold.

"She is the Chief of Station in Washington DC. That means she supervises all matters that have anything to do with espionage and MI6 in the US."

"That sounds really senior."

Henry nodded. "It *is* really senior." Doubt crept into his mind. He wasn't so sure it had been a good idea to play things by the book and get Nick enrolled officially.

Henry walked towards the entrance of the rather ugly building.

"What's going to happen now?" Nick didn't move.

Henry stopped and turned around; the young man seemed glued to the ground.

"You'll be asked to take a couple of tests and then a quick interview with her."

"Will you be around?"

"You bet. I'm all the way there with you." He jerked his head towards the entrance door. "Better not be late to meet the lady."

"Right..."

Nick followed Henry and they presented themselves to the security guards inside. There was no great surprise there. The usual metal detector procedure followed; metal detector wands over clothing, final light frisking. Henry moved on to reception where he gave his name. The receptionist did not ask who he was visiting. She simply made a call to her interlocutor.

"Your guests have arrived."

Henry was directed to the basement, Level 2, and told to take the last lift at the far end of the bank of lifts.

A man was already waiting for them. Glancing at his lanyard, Henry realised they had not been given a visitor's pass.

"Follow me," their guide said. He led the way through a meander of corridors, and they finally arrived at the door of a small room. He knocked and opened the door without waiting for an answer.

A small woman stood up from the table and her laptop, a little round in shape and full of vigour. Doris Remington moved towards her guests in a few quick steps.

"Hello, Henry." She shook his hand with a firm, yet welcoming grip. "And you must be Nick."

Nick extended a shaky hand and mumbled a low, "Yes, Mrs Remington."

Henry felt like this was the first day of school, except that he was the parent, proud of his child and anxious for him to do well.

144

"First, a couple of tests," Doris said. "Nothing to worry about. And then we'll have a little chat."

She returned to her seat at the table and her laptop. She logged in and invited Nick to sit.

"You have one hour. And please... I'll need your mobile phone for the duration of the exercise."

Nick sat down and handed his mobile absentmindedly over, casting an eye at the questions on screen.

"Jon is outside," Doris said to Nick. "If you need anything, shout." Holding his mobile, she gave a quick smile to the young man. "Let's leave Nick to his test."

She cast a dark look at Henry on her way out. "You and I need to have a word," she said between gritted teeth.

The walk to her office on the second floor of the Embassy was a silent one. Doris retraced her steps towards the lifts, ignored them, opened with her pass a door that led to a staircase and climbed the two floors without stopping.

She presented her pass one final time and walked straight into her office. Henry followed her and closed the door.

He turned around.

"Sit," she commanded. He might as well be her dog, although Henry doubted she would look at her pet with as much anger.

Henry did as he was told.

"Steve Harris is certain you absolutely need this young man to work with you on the operation you're running. I want to hear it from you. Why on God's earth is it that you need to recruit an American on America soil?" Doris sat down but didn't give Henry time to answer. "And I don't want any fluff or some crap like 'he's the best for the job' or 'I couldn't find anybody in the UK'."

Henry leaned back in his chair, taking some time to consider his reply.

"Well, he *is* the best for the job, *and* I couldn't find *anybody* in the UK."

Doris pressed the tips of her fingers together and considered Henry's answer.

"I've already gathered that you make a habit of being a pain in the arse, but I do not need to get into a barney with the CIA this year, especially whilst the US is going through an election."

"I'm trying my best not to rock your special relationship."

"In that case, you will understand why I need a bit more justification for that recruit rather than the lame answer you've just given me."

"I understand why you think it's lame but wait until you see the results of his tests. I have never seen a hacker as good as him. When it comes to doling out resources, the new chief in London is still very focused on the Middle East."

"Understandably," Doris shot back.

"Maybe, but that means that we are stretched in London. Anyway, it's not like we're poaching someone the CIA has identified, or even worse, who is already working for them. Finders keepers I say."

"Your attitude is not helpful."

The phone rang and Doris glared at it. She swiped it up.

"What is it?" She looked surprised. "Already? Are you sure?"

She nodded to her caller. "Very well, go through the results and send them to me."

"Nick?" Henry asked, with as little excitement as he could manage.

"Apparently he has finished." Doris checked her computer, likely her inbox. The results of the test would be almost instantaneous, and she should get the outcome very quickly.

Henry waited, relieved it was almost over. As he predicted, Nick hadn't needed the time usually imparted to an average candidate.

Doris cleared her throat, clicking on what Henry assumed was Nick's results. She cast an eye in Henry's direction, returned to the email.

"Doris, the suspense is killing me." Henry faked anxiety.

"Henry, being calm under duress is a good quality for a spook, unless you're talking to your Chief of Station... Your chap is good."

Henry raised an eyebrow.

"OK... he's outstanding." Doris tapped her fingers a few times on the desk. "Harris told me he's reached some form of agreement with the CIA guy who runs RUSSKY BEAR alongside him."

"Jack Shield. They know each other very well... Middle East, I think."

Doris rolled her chair away from the desk, deep in thought. "Would Nick want to move to London?"

"Are you kidding me? Where has your special relationship concern gone then?"

"Just exploring the possibilities." Doris gave Henry a wry smile. "He is good."

"Can we please get a move on? I've got an impatient target to handle."

"Fine... I'll ask Jon to send him up. If you smell a rat on this op – and after reading your file I have a feeling you will very soon – I want to know first." Her hand was resting on the phone. She was waiting for an answer.

"As soon as." Henry nodded.

Doris still didn't move.

Henry exhaled loudly. "All right. If I suspect something big is going to come out, I'll call you."

"Not entirely convinced, but much better." Doris made the call.

Nick arrived a couple of minutes later, escorted by the same man who had welcomed them at the lift.

"Well done, Nick." Doris stood up and invited him to sit.

Henry got up and gently slapped Nick's shoulder. He left them to talk alone. Outside, he turned to Jon.

"Any chance of a coffee or tea around here?"

"Certainly, follow me."

They walked down the corridor, then turned into a minuscule room that had a couple of vending machines and a large recycling bin. Jon stepped outside and waited for him.

Henry groaned. It was clear his chaperone wouldn't let him loose on the premises.

He chose a regular black coffee with sugar. With Jon in tow he returned to Doris's office, and stood at the window outside her door. The view was of leafy trees, grass, and tidy alleyways that criss-crossed the green open spaces separating the embassies of Embassy Row.

Doris's door opened. Nick stepped out looking surprised. Henry's jaw clenched. Nick had blown it in some way.

But then he noticed the piece of paper Nick was holding in his hand. "What's that?"

He handed it over to Henry. "An invitation to the next event at the Embassy. Doris said I could turn up, as long as it doesn't interfere with work."

"And did Doris also signal when she'd be sending you your contract by any chance?"

"All done. Just signed it."

Henry smiled. He looked at his watch. 11 minutes and a few insignificant seconds – the fastest interview on record.

*　*　*

Harris read through the list once more. It was impressive. The Russian billionaire father of Brett's girlfriend had an address book that certainly included the great and the good, or perhaps not-so-good.

A few Russian oligarchs, including the two names Harris was seeking information about, Rostov and Gurdiev; politicians – some more senior than others – including MPs and members of the House of Lords; and finally, businessmen from various walks of life – oil industry, tech industry, property. All of this topped up with the inevitable bankers and asset managers.

Harris looked at the clock on his computer screen. It was past 11pm. Brett should still be awake, almost certainly waiting for him to call.

Harris picked up the leather-clad burner phone and pressed the redial button.

Brett answered within seconds. "What do you think?"

"That guest list was produced awfully fast for an impromptu event."

"As much as it pains me to admit it, I've got to agree with you."

"The gathering is about collecting antiquities, you said?" Harris moved around his kitchen as noiselessly as possible, to give his wife Sarah the sleep she deserved.

"Correct. And as much as it satisfies my ego to be treated as the best expert in the field, I don't quite buy the idea."

"What makes you say that? By the way, I'm thrown by your sudden surge of humility."

"Be as thrown as you want to be... I've survived in this game by knowing when I'm being conned. Very few of these people are genuine collectors. Those who are would never mingle with such an eclectic crowd."

"Because of the way these pieces are collected?" Harris asked.

"Exactly. The most exciting pieces are coming straight from sites that are not accessible to the public."

"You are amongst friends, Brett. You can use the word looted. I won't hold it against you."

148

Brett ignored Harris's usual dig. "And you also need to know what you're talking about to recognise what is the genuine article."

"Is this not where you come in – to certify stuff is the real deal and genuine, as you say?"

"Of course, but I'm not going to offer a certificate of provenance for some of the pieces coming from, say, Syria, Iraq, or other places further afield, am I?"

"I see your point... But surely these billionaires who buy from you have other experts?"

"The fewer the better. You don't shout about owning such a collection from the rooftop."

"I get that point too." Harris pressed Brett. "So you think the idea of introducing you to these people is what, a cover up?"

"Perhaps, or at least a good way of introducing people who may not otherwise have come to the Russian Embassy, and seeing whether there is a connection."

"Are you telling me you think it's a recruitment exercise by the Russian Intelligence Services like the FSB or the GRU?" Harris could see the potential – and it was rather clever.

"You're the intelligence officer not me, but if I had to organise a get together that allowed me to lure people to the Russian Embassy without attracting too much attention, I'd use the subject of art and collecting as a pretext for it."

"Have you been sent a list of the Embassy staff who will attend?" Harris asked.

"They're not stupid. I've only been given the list of the external guests. If my assumption is right, all the cultural attachés will turn up."

"You mean the Embassy spying community is going to descend *en masse* to your event." Harris wondered whether he could be invited.

"Are you thinking the unthinkable?" Brett's voice tensed.

"I was, if you mean me joining you there, but it might defeat the purpose. I'd be surprised if these people didn't know me as an agent handler. But..."

"You've got someone else in mind," Brett said.

"Have you become a mind reader, Brett?"

"No, I just have to think about what the most compromising request for my position would be. Then I know what you're going to ask."

"Unfair… I always have your back."

"Sure, after you've drawn a bullseye on it."

"She's a pro. You'll be more than fine."

"If you say so –" Brett paused.

His change caught Harris's attention.

"What's up?"

"Someone's just been added to the guest list. David Upstage."

* * *

A couple of missed calls were showing on Henry's phone. They were not from Upstage's mobile – Henry had not yet been given his number – but from his PA, attempting to confirm a meeting for the following day.

Henry called back in the cab from the British Embassy and agreed on an 8am meeting. He asked whether there were any documents he was meant to read. She replied she hadn't been made aware of any.

Nick was still in a state of semi-shock at the idea of having joined the British Intelligence Service. He sat in the cab staring out the window.

They arrived at their offices. The walk to the Platinum Suite appeared to wake Nick up.

"What's next?" he asked Henry as soon as he was back at his reception desk.

"Patience, my young apprentice…" Henry smiled. "I've just been told I have a meeting with Upstage tomorrow."

"Do you need anything else from me?"

"I've got plenty already. We've downloaded the entire file relating to Upstage's Nassau hotel purchase. James in London has broadly circulated the hackers' press release we prepared. We now need to wait until tomorrow. There is always the danger in trying to do too much too soon."

"Less is more – that sort of thing?"

Henry nodded. "Exactly right."

He was still hoping James might come up with some intel on the beautiful, yet enigmatic Tatiana Borodin, but knew better than to chase him on it. Henry needed to exercise patience too. Nick was about to speak when Henry raised a hand to silence him. He took out a search device from his bag and screened reception methodically. The device returned no warning. Henry looked at his watch. They had been away for less than two hours, not enough time to install something in the wall sockets. Any device would be cruder, a magnet underneath a desk or an additional cushion no one would notice.

Henry ran his hand underneath the reception's desk. He checked the other pieces of furniture... still clear.

He handed Nick a $20 note.

"Why don't you get us a couple of proper coffees and whatever else takes your fancy from your favourite coffee shop? Then we'll work on your legend."

Nick frowned.

"Your legend is the story you'll give to people when they ask who you are."

"Like the idea of being a Caltech alumnus... like last night?"

"Good idea. We need to beef the story up and make sure whoever is looking finds only what we want them to and nothing else."

"Sounds fun... Back in no time." Nick grabbed his sheepskin jacket and disappeared down the corridor to the lifts.

Alone in the office, Henry looked around. He hadn't gone through the other rooms. He gave a short exhale and returned to his debugging detection device.

It was all very boring but essential.

Henry finished his sweep of meeting rooms 1 and 2. Nothing to report. He moved to the small kitchen where the device remained inactive. Nick would be back any minute with a good coffee, and perhaps a tasty muffin.

Henry finally moved to his office. He walked the perimeter carefully, looking for any sign of activity – scratches, small debris left in a hurry. The office was clean. He felt along the cushions of the sofa and armchairs in the lounge corner. Nothing.

He walked over to the bay window that overlooked the roof terrace. The view was as impressive as ever. His gaze moved to the bottom part of the doors where they both met. The small piece of translucent string he'd stuck there was gone.

Henry froze. He bent down to check it hadn't slid down. He found nothing.

He stood up slowly and tested the latch. It was closed but loose.

151

"Fuck…"

He took the device out of his pocket again, and ran it methodically through the room a second time. The light started showing as he neared his desk and flashed in the red zone when he stood beside it. Henry deposited the device carefully on his desk chair and ran his hand underneath the desk. He found a small groove in the wood that enabled cables to be run up and through, to reach a series of ground sockets.

Henry felt around some more, and met something that he guessed was a small, round box. He crawled underneath the desk, using the torch of his phone to check what it was. He spotted the small device, and he was in no doubt.

His office had been bugged.

Henry yanked the transmitter from its place of hiding. His detection device was going crazy and flashing. He laid both devices on the desk, pinched the transmitter between thumb and forefinger and examined it up close. It was smooth, and a little on the large size. Something used by criminals, perhaps, but almost certainly not an intelligence agency.

His thoughts returned to the moment he and Nick had walked into the reception area. His office door had been shut. Henry shook his head. At least that was something because they had started to speak freely after that.

It was a close call.

He grabbed the device and moved it into one of the meeting rooms. He would decide what to do with it a little later.

Henry texted Nick. *Change of plan. We're having coffee in the lobby area.*

He arrived in the large reception area of their building just as Nick was walking through the revolving doors. Henry waved at him and walked to the far end of the space.

"What's the matter?" Nick looked around. There were a couple of people waiting at reception.

Henry invited Nick to sit. "What have you got for us?"

He took his cue and changed the subject. "Two coffees, milk on the side, just in case, and two extra-large blueberry muffins – from the best bakery in DC."

"Exactly what we need." Henry picked up one of the muffins and a couple of napkins. He removed the top of the coffee cup, dropped a little milk into it and stirred.

152

Nick copied him.

The people waiting in the reception area left for their meeting.

Henry leaned in a little. "The office has been bugged."

Nick put his muffin down. "Where? Not in reception I hope?"

"I think I would have found it had it been put there... In my office."

Nick shook his head and resumed his eating. "Dirty bastards," he mumbled between bites of muffin.

"Couldn't agree more. The good news, if there is any, is that it's a commercial device. Not something an agency would use."

"A spyware from whom – a criminal gang?"

"Possibly... Or a dubious private eye."

Nick took a couple of sips of coffee, eyes half-closed, thinking. "Do you want me to check where it came from?"

"We can ask Mandy to do that. I'm sure she has access to the right pros. I propose we use the device to feed back the information we want to whoever is listening."

"But how do you know who it is?"

"Two people are the most likely candidates. David Upstage – although this is little early in our relationship – or McNamara."

"He wasn't happy about introducing you to his mega-client last night."

"Possibly. The bugging device used is not quite up to scratch."

"You mean, done on the sly?" Nick finished his muffin.

"And whoever ordered the device plant hasn't got access to top people. So, my take is McNamara."

"What do you want to do?"

"I want McNamara out for good. Upstage is going to have another conversation, or rather give him another dressing down, now that he knows the press release came out after Top Capital was hacked. But McNamara is well connected in the firm. And I bet he is the go-between for Upstage and Russia."

"Russia... wow. It's like a proper spy story."

"It's not a story. It's for real and it's dangerous, OK?"

Nick smiled at Henry. "Yeah, don't worry, I get it. I've done quite a bit of Russian work."

Henry stopped crushing his napkin into a ball, raising a thunder-struck look. "What do you mean?"

"I mean, the friends I spoke to you about... I helped them stop a couple of Russian hacks. They use me whenever a big malware attack comes up. I help them to reverse the hack and sometimes we get our own back on the sender."

"Hang on..." Henry frowned. "Are you telling me you hacked the Russians back?"

Nick shrugged. "Yeah, sometimes."

"Do you know who these people are – the hackers?"

Nick's mouth turned down and he shook his head. "I know their pseudonym but not who they are."

"What's their pseudo?"

"COSY BEAR. Not very original but that's what they call themselves."

Henry finished his coffee, considering his new recruit.

"All right. Let's see what GCHQ knows about them."

Nick hesitated, then picked up the empty cups and dumped them in the recycling bin.

"You hesitated. Why?" Henry asked when he returned.

"I know someone who might be able to find out a lot more about them."

"And where is that someone?"

"I don't know, but I know how to get hold of him. At least I think it's a *he*."

"And does that involve doing anything madly illegal?" Henry asked with a grin.

"Don't think so. It's just that he's picky about the deals he likes and not. If he does go for it, he is pretty good at uncovering the people behind a hack."

"Get in touch and see whether he/she is busy. I might have a deal for them."

154

Chapter Sixteen

After they re-entered the Platinum Suite, Henry and Nick went through another round of checks. Satisfied there was no other device he hadn't found the first time, Henry moved to the meeting room in which he had left the transmitter. Henry placed it on a chair, then rolled it under the table, to give it the same muffled sound it would have transmitted had it still been underneath his desk.

The phone in the room rang. Nick was calling. The only thing the young man had to do was to put the receiver on its side and wait for Henry to finish his monologue before hanging it up.

Henry picked up. "Glad you called back."

Henry imagined McNamara listening to the conversation, and smiled inwardly.

"I have spoken to David Upstage. Productive conversation."

Henry allowed for a pause, pretending there was someone on the line.

"Top Capital Partners can't organise the funding for the Nassau deal. No matter what they pretend."

Another pause.

"Of course I have a plan. Very similar to our last deal... That's right."

Henry stretched. He placed a hand behind his head. The diminishing bump behind his head reminding him of the fight he had a couple of nights ago. And yet there he was, upping the game.

"Next step? I sign an exclusivity deal with Upstage. Maybe I'll keep Top Capital on. I'll need someone to carry my suitcase." Henry gave a nasty laugh and terminated the fake call.

He left the room and went back to Nick's desk.

"Short but sweet. That should rattle whoever was listening."

Henry opened the door to his office. "And now, let's work on your legend. Are you clear on the storyline?"

Nick nodded and repeated what they had just agreed.

"I keep my name and real-life story before I turn 18. Then I win a scholarship to go to Caltech in California. I study computer science and mathematics there. I get an MA in the same field. Then I get a job at Google…" Nick hesitated.

"I know, it's a big and impressive company." Henry picked up on the issue. "But the bigger the better. It's harder to keep track of people there, and much easier to fake than if you were claiming to have worked in a small tech boutique of less than 20 people."

"OK… so I worked at Google in their development department, coming up with new ways of improving the algorithm they use in their search engine."

"I presume you can talk about the maths around that if need be?"

"I know enough to make it look like I know what I'm talking about." Nick agreed in the understated way that Henry had learnt to mean he would beat the crap out of anyone who thought they were an expert in the field.

"And finally, you spent a couple of years on the trading floor of a large Swiss bank, in their quant team." Henry continued.

"Looks OK… I may need to beef that area up a bit."

Henry smiled. "Don't worry. On that front I have plenty of information you can gobble up."

"And I started working for your company… last year?"

"Yup. That way it doesn't look completely absurd that you're helping me at reception until I get someone more suitable."

"Got it. And I keep everything else the same?"

"That's easier, although just be vague on the real details. You don't want friends or family members to give you away."

"I'm not that keen to remember the poor suburbs of Washington, so don't worry." Nick sounded upset. "I was told enough times I was a weirdo."

"Don't let it worry you. Some people get scared and aggressive when dealing with someone they can't figure out."

"You can say that again."

"And since we're talking people... I presume there is no girlfriend, or boyfriend for that matter?"

"Nope, no one." Nick did not elaborate; perhaps it was a sensitive subject.

Henry waited for more questions but when none materialised, he finished composing the email to Harris, read the text again and pressed the send button. Harris would make sure Nick's legend was credible in Europe.

His mobile rang. He nodded at Nick, who took the hint and left. Henry picked up, but it wasn't James with news on Tatiana Borodin. It was Harris.

"You're back from your meeting with Doris?" Harris asked.

"All clear."

"I know. She sent me a note to confirm. I'm not calling about that." Harris's voice was without its usual gruffness.

"Problem?"

"Upstage has been invited to London for a meeting at the Russian Embassy. I'll be surprised if he doesn't turn up. The guest list is impressive and there are a few oligarchs that I'm sure he'd love to meet."

Henry stayed silent for a moment trying, and yet failing, to find a reason why Upstage wouldn't request him there.

"If you're invited, you need to get to London." Harris didn't sound enthusiastic.

"You know this is the best way to blow my legend, right?"

"I'm not a complete moron. I've been in this job long enough to know when I'm stretching one of my agents."

"And?"

"It is one of those instances where we've got zero choice."

"Harris, I have an Interpol international arrest warrant hanging over my head. It's bad enough here in the US, but back in the UK..."

"I know, mate. There are ways we can work around this."

"I frigging hope so." Henry's words stuck in his throat. He recalled Belmarsh prison and within it the High Security Unit, where high-profile criminals were detained and where he had spent almost five years. Going back there to finish out his 30-year sentence did not appeal.

"I need to think about it." Henry hung up. Harris did not ring back. His minder knew better than to insist, at least not yet.

157

A knock on his door irritated Henry. He inhaled deeply, released his breath slowly and answered. "Come in…"

Nick did the usual when Henry's responses didn't sound forthcoming enough. He stuck his head in and checked the mood. He then pushed the door open, remaining in the opening.

"I took a call from Mandy earlier on… I forgot to tell you something when you came in last time." Nick took a step inside the room. "Actually, I didn't forget but you didn't want to talk and –"

Henry waved him in. "I know, I was in a crappy mood. I am in a worse mood now, but I'll try not to take it out on you."

"She talked about someone called Rush Huckerby. Said the Metro thought it was suicide. Who is this guy?"

Henry stood up. "Close the door. Let's have a chat."

Henry told Nick as much as he thought the young man should know. But he didn't shy away from telling him that Huckerby had been murdered. Nick had grown very quiet. He was listening to every detail. Henry seldom saw him this focused unless he was in hacking mode.

A long silence followed Henry's explanation.

"How old was he?" Nick asked.

"A couple of years older than you."

He nodded. "Do you think one of these guys… I mean people in Upstage's team did it?"

"Very probable, although I have no proof."

"Are you going to find out?"

"Yes, Mandy, Jack, and I are working on it. Jack is the CIA agent runner here in DC."

Nick's face had grown paler since Henry told him Huckerby's story, but he was still in the room, sitting bolt upright, determined not to flinch.

"OK, I'm in."

"Thanks, Nick. That's very laudable, and I appreciate that you want to help, but the priority for you is to keep safe. You just started and I'm not losing someone else in the team."

"I can do some research for you – you know get into places. I want to help. That's what I signed up for."

Henry relented. "Fine, but you do not take the initiative and you stick only to what I'm asking you to research. Otherwise, you're off helping duty."

Nick nodded.

Henry gave him a hard look that meant business. "I want to hear it from you."

"I will only work on what you give me."

"Glad we understand each other." Henry stood up and headed for the door. Nick followed him.

"I could try looking at the CCTV of the building where the murder happened."

Henry shook his head; the young man didn't listen. His good intentions had lasted less than ten seconds. But then again, it was a good idea.

"Get on with it then, but remember –"

"Yeah, yeah... I'm not doing anything you haven't told me to do." Nick was already out of Henry's office.

* * *

Nick had reluctantly left the office at the same time as Henry. He claimed he was onto something, but Henry had other ideas. A crash course in countersurveillance was what this newest MI6 recruit needed. He could follow up his new lead when he was back at home.

It took double the time to reach 1308A Rhode Island Avenue, but by the time they did, Nick had learnt a few moves that might enable him to spot a trail.

"The secret to beat the opposition and stay alive –" Henry paused inadvertently on the word alive "– is to be paranoid without becoming obsessed, and to never completely relax."

Nick hadn't commented during the lesson. Nor had he said anything when Henry had asked him not to talk about work or do anything work related in his apartment until he had learnt to check for snooping devices.

When Henry finished his lecture, Nick politely informed him that his apartment was equipped with state-of-the-art detection systems, courtesy of the same friends he helped with hacking issues on a regular basis. Nick very much doubted any intelligence agency could get into his computer devices, but they were welcome to try.

To which Henry had grumbled *fine* and retreated into his own apartment. Thankfully, his own detection routine reported nil and he was able to enjoy a much-needed shower and a glass of red wine before he pulled the MI6 encrypted laptop out of its hiding place.

Henry logged in and accessed the email he'd been waiting for. James had been as busy as ever. He'd sent Henry a comprehensive amount of information about Tatiana Borodin. Although more details had emerged regarding the death of her parents, there was nothing new that Henry had not already gathered from his own search.

A few bits of information looked more interesting though. Tatiana was born in the US and had claimed her US citizenship. She also had a younger brother, Anatolie. There was very little information about him, but he was still young according to James's document – 13 or 14 years old. James had trawled through the agency's records. He'd placed a call with GCHQ; so far nothing on the brother.

Henry went to the kitchen, took a good piece of gorgonzola he'd found in an Italian deli and some ciabatta out of the fridge, put a plate and knife on a tray and returned to the lounge. He poured another glass of wine, cut a slice of bread, spread the gorgonzola on it and took a large bite. He sank into the sofa, wine glass in hand.

Henry went through all the details he had gleaned on Tatiana so far – there was nothing tangible on her. And yet it was almost inconceivable that a young Russian woman was able to get close to Upstage without having any link to the type of business Upstage was involved with in Russia.

Still, Henry should remain without prejudice for now.

Henry's mind drifted to the meeting with Upstage that he would be attending the next morning. The bold attitude he would be adopting for it made him smile.

McNamara would be desperate to stay involved, and Top Capital Partners would be desperate to avoid the exclusivity deal Henry was about to offer Upstage. Henry was almost certain Upstage would sign the contract, not bothered by the exclusivity. Upstage would do what he did with all his providers: ignore the contract if it suited him to, and go to court to shake himself out of it.

The next step would be to determine whether Upstage's contacts with the Russians were established enough to bypass McNamara and Top Capital. This was perhaps where the delightful Tatiana came in. Henry's mind lingered again over their meeting. She had been pleasant, yet distant, without trying to be overly so.

He should be feeling a treat, but he wasn't. Or perhaps she was already working her magic on him.

Henry smiled. Perhaps soon he would be working his magic on her.

* * *

At 7.55am the next morning, Henry entered Upstage's club and underwent the same checks as the day before: metal detector, light frisking, mobile phone check. The hostess who had tended to Henry and Upstage during their lunch appointment was at reception to welcome him. She pleasantly enquired about Henry's morning and rushed him into another room.

Upstage's office had a view as staggering as their lunch room – full view of the White House and the gardens surrounding it.

The man had not arrived yet. No doubt he was preparing his entrance, making sure it was noticed.

Henry was offered a cup of tea or coffee, but he declined. He wanted to be left alone for a few minutes to observe his surroundings. The décor was loud, ostentatious; gold everywhere, some passable pieces of art on the wall that were neither modern nor classical. But also, perhaps to salvage this disaster, a couple of well-executed Greek statue replicas had been arranged around the place for maximum effect.

Upstage's large office was split into two sections. The first section had a large desk, a comfortable chair and a couple of computer screens that had not yet been switched on; bookshelves alongside one wall that were littered with books Upstage was meant to have written; trophies showing his sporting successes at baseball; pictures of Upstage with various celebs – mostly men and a couple of women that looked like models, but Henry didn't recognise any of them.

The other section was organised around expensive, leather sofas, chairs and a coffee table, close to the large bay window overlooking the power centre of the US. A long meeting table was stuck at the back, almost as an afterthought. Upstage likely didn't care about long-and-protracted negotiations.

The coffee table between the sofas and chairs had been laid out for breakfast. Matters were already looking up. There were only two plates on the table, meaning the expected third person would not be present.

Henry moved to the window and glanced at his watch. It was 8.05am. Henry didn't have much longer to wonder about Upstage's punctuality.

The door opened and the man appeared, pausing again before walking into the room and flashing his set of overly bleached teeth at him. But there was something more welcoming today about Upstage's demeanour, more relaxed.

Henry reciprocated with an amiable smile and a warm handshake. He was here as Upstage's new fixer, ready to help with the all-consuming issue he had raised the previous day: the financing of the Nassau deal.

As soon as Upstage entered, the hostess followed with a waiter, who was pushing a trolley laden with food. He promptly started arranging the food on the coffee table. She laid a glass on a small tray, took out a Diet Coke that had been placed on ice, cracked the can open and poured the liquid into the glass.

She then turned to Henry. He decided on a coffee, little milk, no sugar. She and the waiter retreated, and Upstage moved to the sofas and chairs, letting his heavy, yet trained body fall into one of the armchairs. He invited Henry to follow, took a pull of Diet Coke and started helping himself to some food.

"I thought about your idea." Upstage grabbed a salmon-and-cream-cheese bagel and placed it on his plate. "I agree that the private banking arm of DSB owe me a deal."

Henry had never suggested they did, but it was a good sign that Upstage had started thinking about ways to tackle the bank. Henry was more confident he would follow through.

"I'm glad you felt the suggestion was valuable." Henry helped himself to the same food.

"Now –" Upstage sliced the bagel into two and took a bite of one of the halves "– I also see your point in offering a sweetener. A bank can't make an $810 million loan without a bit of an incentive."

Henry nodded. "Over and above the interest rate they'll be charging, you mean?"

"I'll be asking for low interest. Rates are low at the moment. The private bank is gonna have to be commercial."

Henry stayed silent for a short moment, savouring the excellent bagel and the audacity of his guest. Upstage had been declared bankrupt 10 years ago, losing three quarters of a billion... What was the issue with landing him money at a low rate? Obviously none in his mind.

"Everything is possible as long as the incentive, as you call it, is right," he finally replied.

"Any suggestions?" Upstage shifted his gaze up to look at him. He finished the other half of his bagel.

"Plenty, but going down that route does not allow for mistakes."

"That's clear." Upstage frowned. "What do you propose?"

"The team that is going to support that deal must be discreet, trustworthy, and highly skilled."

"I'm sure Top Capital Partners can make the right people available."

"Are you? I have reservations."

Upstage hovered his hand over the display of food, then plunged forward to grab a breakfast parfait.

"If you are referring to the press release debacle, I've had a conversation with their Managing Director," said Upstage. "It won't happen again."

"My concern runs much deeper than that."

Henry took a plastic bag out of his inner jacket pocket. In it was a small, round device. He laid the transmitter on the table.

"If anyone is going to install surveillance in my office, it should at least be done professionally. My premises are swept daily. Equally, if anyone is trying to dissuade me from doing business with their client, they should employ their wits first and not resort to grossly obvious methods, such as taking a pickaxe to my office door." Henry paused to select his next item of breakfast. "Don't get me wrong. I have nothing against using some of the tactics I listed, but there is a time and a place."

Upstage stopped eating. His eyes flicked between Henry and the device he had placed on the coffee table. No one, it seemed, had ever been so blunt about the methods used by Top Capital, or so quick to point the finger either.

"This is not the way I do business," Henry continued. "All these unsubtle measures will only ensure one thing... attract attention – and not the attention we want." He selected a small pastry and sat back.

Upstage had still not responded. Perhaps he had been aware that Top Capital were keeping an eye on Henry, but Henry doubted the botched break-in or the intimidation were part of what had been discussed with him.

"This is not the way I do business either."

Upstage had not contradicted Henry. He was deciding. He was not being impulsive, as he was renowned for doing often. He was taking his time to make his next statement. Upstage was reaching a more fundamental conclusion. Henry waited.

"You said it yesterday, though, some of the heavy lifting for the Nassau deal can't be done by your team," Upstage said.

"And for that we do need Top Capital. But when it comes to the more senior negotiations, I won't want them to be involved. Too risky."

Upstage pulled an angry face. "Why not? After all, I'm the reason why they have gained in credibility in Russia. It's high time I exploited their Russian contacts directly. I still need a proper introduction to some of them."

"Without question. And I'm sure your Russian partners will be more than happy to listen with an open mind to what I think we can suggest."

Upstage nodded. "Now that we have established Top Capital is taking the back seat, I'd like very much to hear your idea."

"I'm sure you won't mind if we first go through a few formalities, such as signing a contract?" Henry hadn't smiled or tried to ingratiate himself. He didn't need to play to Upstage's ego.

Upstage nodded again. "Of course, send it to me and I'll get my lawyers to review it."

"Very well. Let's talk about my plan in broad brush terms."

Chapter Seventeen

"It is an emergency… *Eto srochno.*" Tatiana swapped over to her native Russian, something she rarely did when she was not in the motherland, and only when her minder was angry at her for calling outside the agreed contact dates. Thankfully she had returned to her apartment to make the call.

The man on the line calmed down.

"The Brit's office has been bugged. This was not done very cleverly because he found out."

The man let her carry on. It was the third time that the Brit, as Tatiana liked to call Henry Newborn, had been targeted without prior authorisation, or even proper consideration given to the consequences.

"But worst of all… he told Upstage. Upstage had an almighty blow-up and now he is starting to get paranoid."

The man chuckled. "Upstage should have been a damn sight more cautious before he let you into his business, dear Tatiana." Her minder grew serious again. "But it's a blow, and I'm losing patience with McNamara and his inability to follow orders. Are you fine though?"

"I am, but I can tell you that Upstage won't let me loose in his office for a while. I'm going to have to install spying software now, which I was hoping not to have to do."

"You couldn't expect to keep downloading content all the time. It's time consuming, plus you're more likely to get caught," her minder said.

"True, but it leaves no trace once done."

"What did Upstage say about the Brit's reaction?"

"Very cool about it. The Brit knew exactly what the spying device was and he sussed out who was using it. He only mentioned Top Capital, but of course if he were to name someone, I'm pretty sure he would point to McNamara." Tatiana moved around her lounge like a caged tigress.

"And would he be right, *Printsessa*?"

Tatiana picked up a cushion and threw it across the room. She was not his little princess.

"That's right... that and the failed break-in, as well as the attempted mugging." McNamara was such an idiot, ignoring her warnings.

"The Brit is very lucky that McNamara hasn't got access to the right people."

Tatiana didn't reply. She was certain now it was more than luck. There was skill involved on the Brit's part, but why mention her suspicions to her handler if she had not been asked?

"Have you found anything new on the Brit? I'm a little surprised we haven't heard from him before."

"The background checks haven't thrown up anything, but I'll keep looking. He has been very active in Africa, and the deals he does there wouldn't be advertised on the front page of the *Wall Street Journal*, I can assure you."

"Ah Africa... The Chinese have done very well there but the Russian Federation is playing catch up. Still, a little incursion into the Brit's apartment would be a good idea."

"I know, I'm working on it, but I also have to babysit Upstage at the moment. It's a consuming task."

"Of which you are acquitting yourself admirably. He is like putty in your hands, and why shouldn't he be?" The man laughed and Tatiana knew what it meant. She was not going down that route.

"Upstage has been invited to London. I presume you know that?" Tatiana asked.

"Of course, I initiated the invitation. It's about time we evaluate the strength of his ambitions outside of the business world."

"He can get people to believe anything. It's the way he delivers it – zero rationale, all emotional hit-in-the-guts stuff. Incredibly successful."

"Yes, I've read his tweets and his blog... He'll get on superbly well with the people he will meet in London." Her minder sounded eager.

"Do you want me there?"

166

"No... I think Upstage is about to invite the Brit into his team, from what you've relayed to me. And if he hasn't done so yet, perhaps you should suggest it. It'll be a very good way for you to get close to the Brit in the few days leading up to the trip. It'll also be my pleasure to extend a London invitation to Mr Newborn myself. That will give you plenty of time to pay a visit to his apartment whilst he's gone."

Tatiana nodded. "I'll follow up with Upstage."

"Anything else? I really must go... a dinner to attend at the Kremlin with you-know-who, and I can't be late, even though he certainly will be."

"Do I speak to McNamara?"

"No, get rid of him."

* * *

"Nick confirmed it – it's very possible to fake a string of emails." Jack met Mandy sat in the Memorial Garden. She'd brought with her the coffees they both craved, and had started on hers before Jack arrived.

"Rush's personal account was an old Yahoo account. He only used it for friend chats, and for mundane stuff like online food shopping, etcetera. A good enough hacker can get into it and start creating an email trail."

"What about the FB page?" Jack picked up the coffee cup waiting for him on the bench. "Thanks, by the way."

"Very tricky, but not impossible to replicate and confuse recipients. If you're a good hacker, you'll find a way to befriend the person you want to impersonate, using a friend request that looks very credible. It could be an alumnus from your university or college. Then when you've familiarised yourself with the account, you start the process of replication. FB has almost 1.5 billion users. There are many people who share the same name and the same birth date."

"Are we talking seriously good hackers who have been instructed to construct a fake profile and send fake emails to fool the Metro Police?"

"Yes. We are talking professional hackers, people whose job it is to hack, clone and use social media. After that, it wouldn't be too difficult to break into Rush's apartment and leave some illegal medications."

"Just the right combination of evidence to treat the death as a suicide. And if the Metro Police officer is not entirely clean or too busy

167

to look closer..." Jack did not finish his sentence. They both knew the conclusion that had been drawn.

"Who are these people? Did you manage to find something apart from the fact that we suspect a Russian hack?" Mandy asked, drinking a little more coffee.

"Nothing. And if you want to get our tech analysts to investigate the hack it'll need Hunter's say-so."

Jack groaned. "I have another meeting with him this afternoon. I goddamn hope he hasn't somehow heard about Nick Fox's recruitment."

"He's too busy working on the Middle East problem. And if it were about Nick, he would have summoned you the minute he found out." Mandy grinned. "Hunter's interpretation of the special relationship is a bit one-sided. I bet you he would be happy to recruit a Brit on British soil but the reverse? No way."

"Speaking of Nick, did he have any idea about how to reach the hackers he knows?"

Mandy took another sip of coffee. "He got a little cagey when I asked him about his contacts."

"Worth a second call?" Jack stood up and checked for anyone in the vicinity. The bare trees on this side of the Memorial Garden gave him a clear view. On the other side, the row of pines and ferns were too tall to be providing cover for their secret meeting..

Mandy took her mobile out and dialled Nick's number.

She put the call on speaker.

"This is Nick." The young man's voice sounded tinny in the open.

"Nick, it's Mandy, and I have Jack with me."

Nick made a small gulping sound, taken aback by the call.

"Hey, Nick..." Jack jumped in. Welcome to the spook community. It'll be good to work with you."

When Nick sighed, Mandy gave Jack one thumb up. The CIA was not out to punish Nick for joining MI6.

"I've been talking to Jack about the hack on Rush Huckerby's email and FB account."

Jack took over. "You told Mandy the hacking could be organised all right, but it would have to be very good hackers. Any ideas about how we

168

could find out who these people are? Henry told me you were a hotshot when it comes to breaking into systems."

"On my own I can try, but if the people at the other end are that good, and I think they are, we need help."

Jack frowned. "You mean what? Calling on the hackers' community to help? I won't get approval to involve anyone from within the CIA without the say-so from above and that's not going to happen."

"Understood, but not all people who can track data and identify an anon's ID are hackers," Nick said.

"You mean some people do that because they are good citizens?"

"That's right, and because the data they need is open source... I mean, available freely on the net. They're not breaching any rules by taking it. They are simply being clever at using the mass of information available on social media: FB, Twitter, Google Earth, Google Street View, YouTube. People post a lot of pictures and videos. And then they get to publish their findings in a high-profile newspaper like the *New York Times*."

"Would you know some of these people?"

Nick hesitated. "I'd have to think about it..."

Mandy replied before Jack could. "We need to find out what happened to Rush. It was certainly not suicide and we need to prove it."

"I want to help, but I promised..."

"Henry that you wouldn't get involved without his say-so?" Jack asked. "Just tell him that we won't get the resources here to go through Rush's email and fake FB page. I don't care whether you need to use hackers or not. I want the names of the bastards who killed my asset."

* * *

"And you think they are going to accept?" Harris didn't sound dubious on the phone, just questioning.

Henry sat in the far end of the coffee shop that was almost empty. He continued his call.

"I didn't quite say that, but this is the best way to test the strength of Upstage's Russian connections."

"If I understand your idea right, you're saying DS Bank's private banking arm will lend Upstage the money he needs to close the Nassau deal?"

"Yes, the entire $810 million."

"And through one of his Russian contacts Upstage organises a deal between DS Bank's Moscow branch and RNB, the largest bank in Russia, and the deal says what?"

"The deal allows DS Bank to enter into risky but profitable transactions, and offload that risk onto RNB at minimal cost."

"Is that legal?"

"Which part?"

"The loan to Upstage?" Harris asked.

"Are you fucking kidding me?"

"Yeah, OK, I get it. And the Russian part?"

"Bearing in mind that the cost of the risk cover is kept artificially small because of Upstage's loan, I'm going to say the same thing... Are you fucking kidding me?"

Henry heard the smile in Harris's voice. "I hope Upstage appreciated the ballsiness of the idea."

"He was perhaps a tad jealous he hadn't come up with it, but he liked the idea all right."

"So, Upstage is impressed."

"Without wanting to flatter myself, he is."

"So much so that he has invited you to London then. Things are hotting up for you, mate."

"Don't be an arse, Harris. If I get picked up by Interpol or the NSA you can kiss goodbye to that RUSSKY BEAR op of yours."

"Which is the reason why I'm going to make sure they don't pick you up. I look after my agents, remember?"

"If you are talking about Aleppo..." Henry grumbled.

"I'm talking about that exact mission."

Harris had pulled out all the stops to ensure Henry's safe exfiltration out of Syria's war zone, even though the plan was in danger of falling through. Harris had even been on the ground to make sure Henry made it out alive.

"What's the plan to keep me out of jail for good this time?"

"A good old-fashioned deletion of your arrival into the UK from the database. Henry Crowne will just vanish into thin air." Harris sounded almost upbeat.

170

"Is this legal?"

"Are you fucking kidding me?"

Henry smiled as Harris picked up his earlier comment. "All good for the UK but what about the rest of the world?"

"What do you take me for? The database means all databases. You no longer exist, as far as Interpol, Europol and the NSA are concerned."

"I'm almost impressed."

"But..."

"I still know a lot of people in London."

"Are you in a whiny mood today? London's your best chance to get into the Russian crowd."

"I'm weighing the odds, Harris, and I know they're not in my favour. I spent too much time on the trading floor warding off bad transactions not to know one when I see one."

"What's the alternative?" Harris must have moved outside halfway through their call. Henry heard shrieking seagulls.

"None," Henry conceded. "I want to choose where I stay and how I fly into the country."

"Whatever you say, mate. As long as you make this meeting at the Russian Embassy."

"I'll call you later with my plan."

"Okey dokey..."

"And Harris? I want GCHQ on standby in case I need a fresh information download on the comms exchange between Upstage and the Russians we meet."

"And I'd like to run MI6 one day..." Harris grunted. "I'll see what I can do."

* * *

Henry returned to the office. Nick caught him as he headed for his desk.

"I got something on CCTV and also Jack and Mandy have called."

Henry nodded Nick inside his office and sat him at his computer.

"Show me the footage first?" he asked, standing next to Nick.

Nick opened a file he had stored on a common drive and images appeared. Henry couldn't make out the exact location in the Top

Capital Partners building. Huckerby's appearance in the footage jogged his memory. It was the walkway that ran around the entire atrium.

Nick slowed down the images and the young man's fall started to unfold frame by frame. Nick had gone very quiet. Henry's throat tightened at the sight of Huckerby walking away from his office. He didn't look distressed but in a hurry. The time stamp read 17.50, a mere 10 minutes before he and Henry had been due to meet.

Huckerby was carrying a file, Henry noticed. That file had not been on his body after he fell.

The office door of the Top Capital Partners opened and stayed open. Someone was calling Huckerby back. The young man turned around and replied to an unseen person. He turned away and Arthur McNamara walked out. He didn't look in a hurry to catch up with Huckerby. McNamara picked up his mobile phone and put it to his ear.

Anger grabbed Henry the way it so seldom did anymore. He squeezed the top of his office chair.

"Go back a couple of frames... freeze and zoom."

Nick did.

"There!" Henry pointed at McNamara's gesture. "He picks up the phone but he doesn't dial."

"That's true." Nick replayed the scene. Back a few images, slow-mo, freeze... McNamara was not making a call.

"He knows where the CCTV cameras are," Henry said. "He gives himself an excuse to be walking out, or tries to look as though he is busy doing something else rather than following Huckerby."

Nick started the footage again. Huckerby disappeared from the view followed by McNamara. The time stamp indicated 17.56.

Nick pulled his hands back and rested them in his lap. Henry gathered his thoughts, doing his best to tame the fury that had been unleashed... justice for Huckerby perhaps, but certainly revenge. And yet Henry was flying to London in less than 48 hours.

"Have you spoken to Jack and Mandy about the footage?"

Nick shook his head. "You said you wanted to know first."

Henry managed a quick smile. "Good man. What did they want?"

"Help with Huckerby's private email trail and a FB replica page?"

"Jack can't get someone to help without an OK from his boss, I presume."

"So, he said," Nick thought for a moment. "The person I spoke to you about would be interested in the case, I believe."

"But how much will he want to know?"

"It's not about how much. He'll know everything in the end because he'll find out, one way or the other."

Henry dragged one of the extra chairs over and sat next to Nick.

"Contact him – tell him Huckerby had been suspicious about Russian activity on American soil. Tell him he had contacted the CIA. Your man or woman doesn't need to know Huckerby was run by the agency. If your contact finds out, you can claim you didn't know."

"How do I explain I know about the story?"

"Tell him the agency contacted you to find out about the hack – which is near enough the truth."

Nick nodded. "I'll tell him I don't feel I can do it on my own."

"Which is also near enough the truth – no offence meant to your splendid hacking capabilities."

"None taken... I agree I need some backup."

"We have a plan." Henry stood up, expecting Nick to get out of his chair. But he didn't move, his hands twitching a little on Henry's desk.

"What are you going to do with this guy, McNamara?" Nick asked.

"I don't know yet. I need to think it through."

"If you need me...?"

"I know, and it's very much appreciated."

Nick stood up slowly and walked back to his reception desk, closing the door behind him.

Henry waited for a short moment, turmoil still raging within over Rush's fate. He picked up the burner phone, hidden in his desk, and dialled the only emergency number that was stored on it.

"I have a pretty good idea of who pushed Huckerby," Henry said.

Jack Shield drew in a breath.

Chapter Eighteen

The limo driver closed the door and Henry made himself comfortable for the short ride to Upstage's club.

The man himself had spoken to Henry. It had been a quick phone call initiated by his PA, but he had been put through once Henry had confirmed he was free for early evening drinks.

"Absolutely great you can make it... And by the way, your advisory contract is with my lawyers. I've told them to be gentle." Upstage had roared with laughter.

"And I'll do the same with mine," Henry had replied playfully.

"I've gathered a few friends around. Most of them were at the party last night. I think you already met Senator Dacey, and of course you know Tatiana."

"I'll be delighted to meet like-minded people."

In the limo, Henry checked his watch. It was only 5.30pm, and he had made more progress today than he'd thought he might.

Nick had contacted the hacker he was so impressed by – code name The Rats' Piper or The Pieper to friends. Henry thought Nick was making a joke but no. Nick entered into a long explanation about why this individual saw it as his duty to rid the world of all human rats, just like in the fairy tale.

"Well, he has his work cut out for himself," was Henry's only comment.

Henry had called Harris after about his trip to London to check all was on track. It hadn't gone so smoothly, but then again Harris liked a bit of fisticuffs.

174

"This is my list of must-haves before I agree to come to London."

"We're tight on budget."

Henry had ignored Harris's comment. "I'll be flying in on a private jet, Gulfstream preferably, but a TBM700 will do."

"You'll be lucky if it's not a Cessna."

Still ignoring Harris, Henry carried on. "I need a limo service to pick me up, and if it could be a friendly driving me, all the better. I will stay in an apart-hotel near Regent's Park in London. Hotels are too risky, too many bankers or staff that might recognise me."

"You've been gone almost seven years!"

"You'd be surprised. Some of the staff in five-star hotels have incredible memories, even more so if you tip well."

"OK, fine. Let me get on with it." Harris was about to hang up.

"Not so fast, Steve. I want the woman you use on RUSSKY BEAR at GCHQ as translator. She's fluent and she knows these people pretty well."

"You're raving mad, Crowne! I don't have the authority to involve her operationally, and she's not trained as a translator." Henry imagined Harris fidgeting with his cigarette packet, knowing he would likely need a fag to recover after the call.

"I'm utterly serious, and I bet you she'll be game for it."

"I'm not even going to ask –"

"Course you are. Anyway, got to dash, Upstage is calling me."

The memory of their call faded and Henry looked out at the passing streets. The sun was going down, and the stone building they were driving past was shrouded in a soft cream hue. There was something comfortable about Washington, a more easy-going vibe that Henry had never experienced in fast-paced New York.

The car stopped at a set of traffic lights and Henry went back to his review of the day so far.

The final conversation he'd had with Jack Shield had been the tensest but also the most gratifying. They were making tangible progress on one front – closing in on Huckerby's killer. Henry and Jack had exchanged a few calls and come up with one conclusion. It was time to pay McNamara a visit.

It surprised Henry that the idea had not come from him but from Jack, although he might have done exactly what had been suggested before his departure to London. The mild-mannered CIA man was prepared to be a damn sight more brutal than Henry thought he would ever be. Or perhaps Henry had not spent enough time with Jack to truly assess what he was capable of.

Jack had easily located McNamara's home address.

"Unsurprisingly, one of the richest neighbourhoods in DC," Jack had said, sounding resentful. "He lives in the Bethesda area, near the Chevy Chase Golf Club. He owns a house there, Quincy Street."

"You mean dad has been generous with Junior?"

"He must have been. It's a privileged district, 80% white, average house price in excess of $1 million..."

"I presume his house is detached, looking splendid in the middle of a well-tended lawn?" Henry quipped.

"On Quincy Street..." Jack confirmed. "It's a lovely open street."

"At least we don't have to climb the wall and face rabid guard dogs."

"The surveillance will be electronic but nothing we can't deal with," Jack had said.

Henry had hesitated. "Are you sure you want to do this?"

"I'm sure."

The limo driver's voice snapped Henry out of his thoughts.

"We have arrived, sir."

The driver parked in front of the club's entrance, got out of the car, and opened Henry's door.

Henry stepped out, taking a moment to button up his wool and cashmere suit jacket. He took his mobile out of his inner pocket and put it on mute. It was time to give Upstage and his friends all his attention.

He climbed the three steps to the main door briskly, where he was greeted by a fresh team of security guards. The checks were quick, and Henry didn't have to go through frisking this time. His credentials were on the up.

Inside the club the atmosphere was buzzing; lots of beautiful people talking to more beautiful people. One of the guards escorted Henry to the lift, making sure he moved through the crowd quickly. The lift was already open. Henry rode it alone to the top floor.

The atmosphere changed as soon as he stepped out and into the reception area of the floor Upstage used for meetings. A light buzz of voices caught Henry's attention. It sounded like a meeting of minds, people exchanging ideas, forming plans on how to forward a similar agenda.

Henry entered the room where the informal gathering was taking place. He saw the same breathtaking view of the White House, even more impressive now that the light had almost completely faded and the building was illuminated.

The room was only a door down from the one in which he and Upstage had had their first lunch meeting yesterday. This larger room had been arranged like the lounge area of a welcoming hotel; clusters of comfortable armchairs and sofas allowed people to sit and chat. A more open-plan area near the large bay windows led to a terrace enabling people to mingle. Drinks and canapés were being circulated.

Henry grabbed a glass of champagne, taking in the scene and in no hurry to meet Upstage yet. Someone moved alongside him without a word. Tatiana, glass in hand, was observing the crowd too.

She had changed into a slick cocktail dress – black, sober and rather short. Her hair was up in a messy yet elegant bun. Henry tried not to linger his gaze too much, although he couldn't help noticing she was wearing thigh-high boots in soft leather that perfectly hugged her long legs.

"You also like observing the crowd before stepping in." Tatiana leaned in close; a strand of hair came loose and brushed against her cheek.

"Always good to know who you're dealing with," Henry replied.

"Do you recognise anyone from the party couple of nights ago?"

"I can see Senator Casey speaking to someone I recognise from TV..."

"That's Mort Palmer, Wolf News. A keen supporter of David's."

Henry registered the name but didn't ask what he was a supporter of.

"You know most of these people I assume?" he asked her.

"A majority, although David is rather good at making new friends. I can't always keep up."

"Is he good at keeping them though?"

Tatiana gave him a side look. Henry caught the beginning of a smile.

"A bit of a loaded question, don't you think?"

Henry took a sip of champagne. "You think so?"

He waited for her answer. When none came, he decided on another tack.

"Talking, or not, of friends, I can't see Art McNamara anywhere."

He caught Tatiana tensing a little. She relaxed almost immediately. "Perhaps David is still upset about the press release debacle."

"It was a stupid mistake and not the only one, unfortunately."

"Art is a bright kid, but he sometimes doesn't know when to call it quits."

Henry chuckled. "I'm not sure he'd like you calling him a kid."

"But that's what he is. He plays tough but he doesn't know what it truly means. Anyway, I have been sent over to fetch you. David is in his office with a couple of people from London."

Henry gulped down some champagne, hoping it hid his surprise.

But Tatiana was already moving away. She stopped and looked back. "Come on... we'd better not make David wait."

"Punctuality is a one-way street with him, then?" Henry managed a little humour.

"Everything is a one-way street with him," she replied when Henry caught up to walk alongside her.

Her elegant boots made her look even taller than she was, and there was something soft and feline in the way she moved. She cast an eye over Henry, looking away as soon as he noticed.

"You might have met the two gentlemen from London – Edward Bound and Nevil Ferguson."

"Unfortunately, our paths have never crossed." Henry hoped it sounded convincingly chagrin.

They stopped outside Upstage's office door. Tatiana knocked but didn't wait for an answer before opening the door.

Upstage was sitting in the same armchair he'd sat in that morning. Three other men were seated in the lounge area of the office. Henry recognised the two Brits immediately, both in their pinstripe suits and their public school ties. The third man sat opposite Upstage on one of the sofas.

He looked foreign. Hair bleached by too much sun rather than from a hair dye, and a tan that looked real and gave his skin a parchment-like appearance. He wore no jacket and had rolled up the sleeves of his white shirt. In front of a suited Upstage and the two Londoners this informality gave the foreigner serious sway. He was here not for show, but for business of the sort that would only be discussed in front of a few.

178

Upstage stopped talking when Henry entered. He looked keen rather than angered by the interruption.

"The very man... We've been talking about the trip to London and the latest addition to our party." Upstage stood up with a small jump.

The two Londoners turned around with smiles. Whoever could provide finance was going to be of interest to them. The foreigner took his time, observing Henry with a hint of scepticism.

Henry nodded at the men. The Brits stood and each extended one hand at the same time, eager to welcome a countryman into the group. Upstage waved Henry towards the lounge area. Henry shook hands with the pair, offering a hand to the man he did not yet know.

"Bast Botha... our South Afrikan contact." Henry noticed the way Upstage pronounced the word Afrikan with a heavy k and a roll of the r. A slight chill coursed through him. The gathering was very male, very white and, he now suspected, politically very extreme.

* * *

Jack parked the SUV along Quincy Street almost opposite McNamara's house. It was 6pm, and he moved his car a few times to arrive at the almost perfect place for surveillance. He was anchoring down for the long haul and until Henry arrived.

Jack opened the flask of coffee he'd brought with him and poured a full cup. The smell filled the car, and it unexpectedly threw him back to darker days, and to the time he had met Harris on their first mission together.

A burst of red and orange lights brightens the dark Baghdad skyline. Harris and Jack have been sitting for hours at the window of a flat, near the city centre.

The coalition forces are making their final assault and they have infiltrated Baghdad with more CIA agents. As soon as they can, the forces need to lay their hands on the intelligence inside in Saddam Hussein's palace. Where are the weapons of mass destruction? Harris is smoking a cigarette, his last one, and one he shares with his new CIA contact, Jack.

The flat they've occupied has been vacant for days, abandoned by a fleeing family. April in Baghdad can be cold and dreary. Jack pours out another cup of coffee from the flask Harris brought with him. He is following the progress of a US infantry brigade. They are close to one of Saddam's palaces and the fighting is fierce. US Marines are being hit by heavy shelling from Iraqi artillery. The palace needs to be taken at all costs, even if it means casualties.

Harris brings the binoculars up to his eyes. They are not far from the bridge the coalition forces must cross to reach the palace. Jack knows the city well. Despite his fair skin and light-brown hair, he has managed to move around Baghdad without attracting much attention, sometimes pretending to be a journalist or businessman.

The building rocks with the force of shelling again. The fighting has intensified for the final push. Jack and Harris discuss their concerns but shake them off, nevertheless. The Iraqi forces are too engaged in the battle with the US Marines to divert their attention to the palace. Jack comments on progress. Another large explosion hits; some plaster dislodges from the ceiling and falls next to Harris. Jack turns around towards the inside of the flat to assess the damage. He stops talking and puts down his binoculars in slow motion. Harris slowly reaches for the gun in its holder. Jack can see it on Harris's face. Harris is the one with the gun unsheathed. He's the one who needs to shoot the intruder down.

Jack shuddered and the memory drifted away. He could still hear the discharge of the gun that night.

He checked his watch, 8.52pm. McNamara had arrived home shortly after 7pm. He had parked his car in the driveway and hadn't come out again. He must have been opting for a night in. Jack could only but approve. He and Henry wouldn't have to wait for his return from a late night outing to carry out their plan.

The lights in the large, detached house had been switched on and off in what Jack imagined to be the bedroom and bathroom on the second floor, then McNamara appeared to return to the first floor. The lights had also stayed on at the side of the house and at the back. Jack saw the glow it cast on the lawn that extended all the way around McNamara's property.

Jack finished his cup of coffee, and opened the bag of food he had brought with him. He had bought a simple ham sandwich from the coffee shop at Langley. He didn't want anything fancy, just fuel for the job at hand.

180

Jack's mind drifted to Henry Crowne's evening meeting with Upstage. He'd never worked with the man before, but Harris had praised his resourcefulness under pressure, and his focus. From what Jack had seen of Crowne so far, Harris was right. And he trusted Harris too – with his life. Harris had more than proven his worth in Baghdad.

Movement on the top floor of McNamara's house drew Jack's attention. He concentrated on the area where he thought he'd seen a shadow. Jack hesitated; checking a false alarm could compromise the evening. He took a pair of night vision binoculars out and slowly scanned the area.

There was nothing there.

A light was switched on and off briefly in what Jack assumed was McNamara's bedroom. Everything went back to being quiet.

Jack finished his sandwich, poured himself another cup of coffee and sat back into the seat of his car. The cold was starting to creep in. Jack lifted the collar of his thick winter jacket and hugged his cup.

A light flashed again at the side of the house. Jack frowned. It was odd that a light be switched on and off so quickly. Then it dawned on him, it was not a light being switched on and off. It was a torch beam being flicked around a room.

"Shit." Jack shoved his cup into the cup holder between the front seats, picked up the Sig Sauer he'd hidden underneath his seat, stuffed it in the small of his back and left his car quickly.

There was no one around and Jack crossed the road without being seen, arriving to the right of the property. The light had moved. It was now headed towards the back of the house.

Upon arrival, Jack had checked McNamara's property entrance for surveillance equipment. There was a camera above the front door. But the garden had no trigger alarms. For someone involved in money laundering at a minimum, this was a little careless.

Or perhaps McNamara felt he was too clever, or too well protected by his father's connections.

Jack crept along the boundary of the garden where a tall wooden edge had been erected. He approached the side of the house from where he'd seen the torch beam. It was all dark again. Jack stayed low as he ran towards the house.

He dived behind a shrub underneath one of the windows. After placing his hands on the high window ledge, he pulled himself up slowly to take a look inside the room. The dining room was plunged into darkness, but the open-plan design meant that Jack could see part of the lounge.

His muscles complained at the strain of holding the uncomfortable position. He gritted his teeth and kept scanning the inside of McNamara's house. A shadow walked briefly into the soft light of the lounge, tall, slim – hooded. Someone was inside, moving around freely; Jack doubted McNamara would be wearing a hood inside his own home.

His hands, moist with the effort, slipped off the ledge. He landed with a loud thud on the ground. Jack cursed softly. Had he been heard?

He progressed towards the back of the house quickly. A deck ran along the entire length of it. Low shrubs had been planted to provide a side edge to the deck. The earth was fresh, and it had not been trampled. Whoever was inside had not come that way.

Jack crouched. He could not gain a proper view into the house without walking onto the deck. There was a sudden movement of the sliding doors. They opened and the hooded intruder rushed out, rucksack on their back.

Jack stood up, jumped onto the deck and ran at the intruder. The man swiftly turned left as soon as he was out, running. He had mapped his exit route, aiming for a place in the hedge that he no doubt had used when he'd come in.

Jack was gaining on him, but when the man arrived at the fence, he took hold of a rope that he must have used to enter and left hanging to ensure a swift exit. The man lifted himself along the wood and swung over the top, taking the rope with him before Jack could grab his legs. Jack crashed against the solid wood with a thump. The noise was absorbed by the density of the planks. Jack went flat on the ground and waited.

He stayed there for a couple of minutes. Nothing happened.

Jack stood up and ran back to the house. The place was a mess – a couple of lamps had been toppled. A lounge chair was on its side. In the middle of the floor, McNamara's body lay motionless. Blood was seeping into the light-coloured rug on which he lay. There was too much of it for McNamara to still be alive.

Jack stepped back, torn between frustration and grief – he had lost his chance to get the information he needed from McNamara.

The sound of a distant siren told him it was time to move. He retreated the way he'd come, crossed the street without rushing and climbed into his car.

As he was turning into Connecticut Avenue, a couple of police cars rushed past him. Someone had alerted them fast, and that someone did not want anybody else to check the crime scene.

Chapter Nineteen

Botha's handshake was brief and noncommittal. Henry didn't react to the clear show of disapproval. He settled on one of the sofas next to Upstage's chair.

Upstage sat down again and turned towards Henry. "We were talking about what we hope to achieve in London."

"I presume it is finance we are talking about," Henry said.

The two Londoners nodded. Upstage copied them. "Of course, but not only that."

Botha's eyes flicked to Upstage. Anger flashed in them. He reached for his glass and returned to his circumspect attitude.

"Why don't we talk finance first," Henry suggested. "At least I know I can contribute meaningfully there."

Upstage nodded, giving his consent for the other men to interrogate Henry.

The Londoners launched into a rant about taxes that were savaging the rich in Europe, including the UK.

"Taxed at 45%. This is an absolute disgrace... We are practically living in a socialist country," Bound was whining.

They swiftly moved on to the cumbersome legislation and regulation requirements that made business impossible.

"Goddamn EU!" Ferguson was incensed. "Too many stupid rules that suffocate businesses. Brussels technocrats are fucking incompetent."

Henry waited until the storm of outrage and righteousness had passed.

"Are you asking me how to arrange your business so that you avoid paying taxes?" Henry asked.

The Brits looked at each other. Could they be so blunt? Henry took their silence to mean a yes. He cast an eye at Botha. The man was clearly interested in the debate but Henry doubted it was the technicalities of tax avoidance he was most interested in. He suspected it was more to do with how far greed could drive people.

Henry waited for a verbal response; nothing else mattered. But to show too much eagerness would associate him with the two Brits. The divide was apparent in the small group – the leaders and the followers. Henry had never been a follower.

The two Brits were still hesitating. Henry looked around the room for something, and stood up when he spotted it. He grabbed the notepad, tore a piece of paper and wrote a few words on it. He handed it over to Ferguson, the closest of the pair to where he stood.

"Mossack Fonseca, lawyers in Panama. Speak to this man, mention my name."

Henry returned to his seat, casting a sorry eye over his now empty champagne glass. "Any other questions about wealth preservation?"

Botha almost smiled.

Upstage looked around. Tatiana had disappeared. He picked up his mobile and speed dialled a number. "Drinks and food," was all he said.

"Have you ever done business in South Africa?" Botha's strong SAF accent kicked in, with the letter a sounding more like eh... *South Efrica.*

"No, I'm afraid. I deal more with Central and West African countries – precious metals, oil, some armament deals." Henry's voice was even. No boasting, just facts.

"Do you know Dom Carter? He's very involved in the same sort of trahde, I believe." Botha made eye contact. The coldness of his gaze struck Henry.

Henry's mouth turned down. "I'm afraid I don't know the man."

"Perhaps he goes arouhnd by another name," Botha insisted. "Short man, receding hairline, dahrk hair, a scar over his left eye. You cahn't miss the scar."

"Still can't place the gentleman –" Henry was interrupted by the door opening. The woman who had played hostess twice appeared, followed by a couple of waiters. One carried a tray laden with food; the other pushed a trolley on which drinks, crockery, and glasses had been stacked.

The men said nothing until they disappeared.

Botha came back to the charge. "A big name in the field." He got up and made his way over to the trolley. The others watched his every move, waiting for the verdict on Dom Carter.

"Still can't place him, I'm afraid."

Henry stood up and moved to the trolley too. He was quite a bit taller than the South African, but it made little difference to his advantage. At close range, Botha's disturbing presence had a mix of intensity and coldness Henry had seldom seen in others.

As Henry approached, Botha nodded. "It's fine, the world is a big plehce."

Everybody relaxed, including Upstage. They all congregated around the food.

Upstage stood slightly behind the others. Henry moved to his side with a glass of sparkling water in hand.

"Not drinking?" Upstage asked.

"Another meeting after this one." Henry took a sip.

Upstage nodded. "You did well."

Botha was helping himself to some red wine, his back to them both.

"Because Dom Carter does not exist," Henry said in a low voice.

Upstage simply grinned.

Botha returned to his seat. He picked up a small sandwich of beef and mustard and wolfed it down. Everyone resumed their position.

"We need to tahlk about our next move." Botha had relaxed his posture, but his focus remained sharp.

Upstage took over. "London is an essential step. I will be meeting senior people there, from France, Italy, and perhaps Spain."

"What abouht your Russian contacts?"

"They'll be there, of course. And I'm relying on Henry to close the deal we discussed. This will ensure a steady flow of income into the new Nassau property complex my company plans to purchase."

"A very handy plehce for many other reasons." Botha agreed.

Ferguson piped up. "What happens if the Russians don't play ball?"

"If I have read the situation correctly –" Henry set his glass down on the coffee table "– they will come through. This is a unique opportunity to achieve their aim."

186

"And what aim is thaht?" Botha asked, challenging him.

"Financing the political campaigns of the populist right wing parties in Europe." Henry kept his expression neutral. He was simply stating facts as he saw them.

Everybody went quiet. Botha smiled for the first time. "Not only Europe but Ehmerica as well."

It took Henry a second to understand what Botha was talking about. The strong accent had thrown him, and perhaps the enormity of the statement too... he meant America.

Upstage inhaled deeply and sat up straighter, like a man suddenly called by destiny. "It's about time someone clears up the mess on Capitol Hill."

The two Brits nodded and agreed with a flurry of yeahs. Botha's smile widened. Henry found himself caught short. Was it a joke of the worst kind?

All eyes turned on him. Henry dug deep to maintain his calm. His next response would be make or break. His stomach churned.

"I'm greatly honoured to be part of the campaign team for the future President of the United States of America."

* * *

Jack sent a text to Henry's mobile.

Abort plan. Meet at the agreed address.

Jack had already communicated the address of a small bar in Arlington where he and Henry could meet, in case of emergency.

He was on his way there. He would cross Scott Key Memorial Bridge over the Potomac in 10 minutes. Traffic was light. Another 15 and he would arrive at the bar.

Jack's anger crept in as soon as he knew he was in the clear and that no police car was chasing him. He'd even had to exercise all self control to avoid savaging some idiot driver who had slammed on the brakes in front of him.

He and Crowne had planned to meet after 11pm at McNamara's property. Crowne had expected the gathering at Upstage's club would not last far beyond 9pm. It was now 8.30.

Jack saw the neon sign of the bar in the distance. He parked his car two streets away and applied what he'd taught his agents to do – a good

187

set of counter surveillance measures. He returned to his car and hit the road again, changing directions.

Jack parked the car in a new spot and stayed put. There was no rush. Crowne would not be with him for a while, even if he came straight after his meeting. Jack looked around his car, the half-drunk cup of coffee still ensconced in the cup holder, the bag of food still there containing his ham sandwich.

He slammed his hand on the steering wheel a couple of times. This was not the way the evening had meant to go. He couldn't pretend McNamara's death hadn't touched him. Even if it had been a crude and cruel form of justice, McNamara's punishment was not enough – Jack wanted the people who had ordered Huckerby's murder. He doubted McNamara would have carried out the kill of his own accord.

He took the burner phone out and checked it mechanically. It was too late to get hold of Harris and almost too late to speak to Mandy.

Jack took the work mobile out of his other pocket to call Mandy. He was about to press the redial button, but stopped. He threw the phone onto the passenger seat. "Fuck."

Jack's mobile pinged.

Eta 30 minutes.

Crowne was on his way.

Jack had found a quiet table at the back of the bar. He had already ordered a pint of lager. He liked the Arlington Roof Top bar for its draft beers.

Crowne arrived early. His face was drawn, and Jack knew he'd also had a rough evening. Crowne ordered a pint of New Belgium from the bar and joined Jack. He also sat at an angle so he could see the room.

Both men said nothing for a short while.

"McNamara is dead," Jack volunteered first.

Crowne turned his head to look at Jack. "I'm only half surprised."

"Why?"

"He'd become too careless." Crowne took a long pull of beer. "And from what I've just learnt this evening, these people will tolerate no interference whatsoever with their plan."

"Which is?"

"Sorry, Jack, but why don't you tell me what you know? I'm still processing my own information."

Jack went through the details of what he'd seen from the moment he arrived at McNamara's house.

"Do you think the intruder was there already when you arrived?" Crowne asked.

"That's a good question. I don't know for sure, but I'd say probably. He'd even organised his escape route. He came in the same way he left. The rope was ready for his escape. If he'd arrived after me, I'm almost certain I would have seen him then."

"So what was it? Burglary gone wrong...? I don't buy it." Crowne shook his head.

"Neither do I, but it's a damn good way of staging one."

"Do you know how he died?"

"I could only see the body. He was face down, a lot of blood – far too much for him to be still alive."

"Then someone called the cops?"

"Within seconds of the assailant disappearing on his motorbike. I heard him firing the engine as soon as he'd jumped the wall." Jack gazed into his half-empty pint. "And yet there was no one around that could have witnessed the break-in."

"Someone might have seen *you*."

Jack gave Crowne a look. "I'm not completely incompetent when it comes to entering premises, unnoticed."

"I didn't mean to question your skills as an agent... I'm just pointing out a possibility." Crowne sat back in his chair.

"I think whoever was contracted to terminate McNamara didn't want me getting in after them and rummaging through McNamara's stuff."

Crowne grimaced. "That's pretty ballsy of them to call the cops..."

"It's a pro that's confident enough to make that call."

"That's still ballsy."

"Not unless there was some information in McNamara's house that might still be of value."

"You think the hit man didn't have time to finish what he'd started?"

"I disturbed him when I fell off the window ledge."

"But if he was in McNamara's place staging the burglary, he would have allowed enough time to do all he needed to do then wait for the guy to come home."

189

"That's true." Jack conceded.

Crowne finished his beer. "Unless... he didn't cater for enough time, or couldn't arrive early enough before you disturbed him."

"Yet, I still think it was a pro."

"Someone with an unavoidable commitment beforehand?"

Jack finished his pint. He could do with another one.

Crowne nodded towards the bar. "Let me get the next one. You can decide in the meantime if you've finished with your story."

Jack watched Crowne as he got up and went to the bar. The news about McNamara's murder seemed to have no effect on him. McNamara was the one person they could have interrogated about Huckerby's death.

Crowne returned with two pints. He put both on the table. He sat down again, took a sip of beer, and set the glass down cautiously on the tabletop.

"My turn I guess..."

Jack nodded.

Crowne hadn't omitted any details, Jack could tell. His well-trained mind noticed information others might well have overlooked.

"The London meeting is more than just a financial exercise to get the far-right of Europe enough money to keep going." Crowne's hand was on his thigh. He was squeezing it without noticing.

"What else can it be? Far-right is bad enough." Jack couldn't quite imagine what could be worse than funding fanatics.

Crowne faced Jack. "I know it's going to be difficult to hear, but Upstage..." He trailed off.

Jack noticed the new effort to phrase it correctly.

"Upstage has political aspirations, big ones, and he is well supported by this group of people. I don't know their names yet."

"What, you mean... the Congress, the Senate? This is ridiculous."

"No, he's gunning for much higher than that." Crowne looked Jack in the eyes.

Jack shook his head, as he realised. "You mean... the Oval Office?"

"That's right, POTUS – President of the United States."

Jack was about to argue it was more than ridiculous, but he stopped himself. Crowne was not an idiot.

"And that's why I'm going to London against my better judgement. I've got to find out whether the Russians are truly going to dig deep into their pocket to facilitate his election campaign."

"There is more than money to an election." Jack couldn't hide his outrage at the thought.

"I somehow think this has not escaped the Russians, either." Crowne sounded bleak.

"I'm sorry." Jack pressed the heels of his palms into his eyes. "I just can't take this in."

"Don't apologise, neither could I. And I almost lost it during the meeting when they told me."

"At least we know about McNamara and his involvement with Huckerby." Jack straightened up again.

"Although we don't have a name yet. I would also discard Upstage – not that he is incapable, but he's been sheltered. My inclination would be to go with the South African guy, Botha, or the Russians."

"You know what's pissing me off the most?" Jack didn't wait for Crowne's reply. "If I go to Hunter III about this, he is going to look at me with his usual scepticism and say 'bring me more proof'."

"MI6 will do the same. I haven't spoken to Harris yet, but it's going to be a similar story. I need cast-iron proof of what it is we are suggesting."

They both fell silent again, nursing their pints and measuring what they needed to do next.

"What do you need from me?" Jack asked after a moment.

"Remove Mandy from the RUSSKY BEAR op. If we are dealing with that level of racism, this is not safe for her."

Jack gave a bitterlaugh. "I'll be very surprised if she accepts that excuse. She'll likely want to stay if we are dealing with some of these bastards."

"It's not a contest. In the space of 5 days we already have two bodies in the morgue."

"You don't need to remind me."

"I'll tell Nick not to give her any more intel." Crowne was adamant.

"She'll get to him whatever you say. She's good like that, and we still need her to do the research for us." Jack shook his head. "I should never have asked her to get involved."

"No one could have guessed Operation RUSSKY BEAR was going to evolve that way."

Jack changed the subject. "When are you off to London?"

"Day after tomorrow. Nick is installing state-of-the-art surveillance at the office and upgrading the systems in my apartment. I'll clear the safe of whatever is compromising and get Nick to deliver it to you for safe keeping."

"And I'll get more intel on this guy Bast Botha. The CIA has a strong pool of data on South Africa."

"And get me as much as you can on his links with the far-right in Europe. I need to know who these people are."

"You've got it."

Crowne got up slowly. He put on his coat. "I won't risk being in touch again. I'll only keep Harris in the loop."

"Agreed." It was the only way to keep his people safe.

* * *

The light was on in the office when Henry arrived at 7am the next morning. He slowed down, deciding whether to call security. The entrance to the Platinum Suite opened, and Nick appeared.

Henry relaxed.

"Suffering from insomnia?" He smiled.

"Very unfair... I've been in conversation all night with The Rats' Piper. He's asking a lot of questions, but I think he's hooked."

Henry walked into the office with his breakfast, and put an extra cup of coffee on Nick's desk.

"Cheers... I was running low on caffeine."

"Tell me more about The Rats' Piper then. What does he want to know?"

"I told him what we agreed – that the Russians are behind the assassination of someone who was trying to debunk their spying operation."

"But that conversation can't have lasted all night?" Henry walked into his office. Everything looked exactly the same, despite Nick having installed new spyware and surveillance equipment the day before. Nick followed him in.

"We talked tech stuff – what encryption I thought the company used. What I detected when I got into Top Capital, the crappy device you found in your office."

"I'm not sure it was a good idea to mention Top Capital." Henry dumped his light coat on his office chair and grabbed his own coffee.

"Well, I didn't say the name and he doesn't care, but I spoke about what systems they used. It's pretty complex, so that tells him a lot about who might be designing their stuff."

"Has he got a view on it?"

"I think he does."

"But he hasn't told you?"

"Not until he is in."

"OK, so what is it going to take?"

Nick hesitated but then pressed on. "He wants to speak to you."

Henry laughed. "What, in person?"

"Course not." Nick shrugged. "I don't even know where he lives. He could be next door. He could be in Antarctica..."

"Unlikely. I think all the tech stuff he needs doesn't like the minus 40C they get down there."

"I'm simply saying he won't meet face to face but will connect with you through a special chat room."

"If he won't show his face, then neither will I." Henry was adamant. He was taking enough risks of blowing up his legend as it was.

"He doesn't care about the face, but he cares about the voice."

Henry frowned.

"That's the way he will recognise you in the future." Nick returned to his keyboard. Henry followed him. He typed away to show Henry the instructions he had received from The Rats' Piper.

Henry moved behind Nick and started reading over his shoulder.

No voice synthesiser, no voice alteration device of any form... I'll know if one is used.

"This guy knows people can change their face enough so that a facial recognition system will not ID them. Voice is much more difficult to disguise unless you use one of the devices he mentioned in his last message." Nick said.

"Facial recognition is good, but yeah, it can be fooled well enough."

Henry ran his hand through his hair, thinking about how much his own appearance had changed. Nick was looking at him, waiting for instructions.

"Tell him I agree," Henry said. "But it has to be today, before 6pm."

Nick nodded and started composing a reply.

Henry took his cup of coffee back to his office and closed the door. He had a few hours to reacquaint himself with an accent he'd made every effort to lose after moving to London – his very own Northern Irish accent.

Chapter Twenty

The image of McNamara's pleading face woke Tatiana up with a jolt.

She hadn't liked the man, but the tears running down his face when she'd pointed the gun at him made him look so much younger than he was. A boy about to meet his sorry end.

She sat up in bed, gathered her knees to her chest and rocked slowly. She thought about her parents, about her Babushka and her brother, Anatolie. Anger flared in her belly; she kicked the blanket off with her feet.

"No choice," she said aloud.

Tatiana walked barefoot to the small kitchen, wearing an old T-shirt as a nightie. She filled the kettle, switched it on and started making some tea. She folded her arms around her body and ran her hands over her shoulders, feeling stiff from the night before.

The kettle started humming. Tatiana took the teapot and the tea caddy out of the cupboard. She laid both on the counter and stopped. Her anger returned, stronger than before. The shot to the head had been merciful. McNamara had died instantly. But was it what she now called mercy, to shoot a man without making him suffer? Her parents would be ashamed.

Tatiana rubbed her hands vigorously along her arms to dispel last evening's memories once more. She resumed her tea making, comforted by its routine. She spooned a couple of tea measures into the pot, then poured the boiling water in afterwards. She placed a mug, the teapot and a jar of honey on a tray and entered the lounge.

She wrapped an old woollen shawl around her, one her Babushka had knitted for her when she'd still been living in Russia. She moved to the dining table she was using as an office desk and logged in to her computer. Her Russian handler was expecting a call. He had given her a one-hour slot during which to make it. She would be a little on the early side, but so be it.

Tatiana poured some tea into the mug, opened the jar of honey, tilted it and let a large dollop of the thick amber liquid fall into her drink. She'd forgotten a spoon in her distraction over McNamara's killing. It wasn't the first time her handler had asked her to terminate a target, but last night had jarred her more than usual. Art had looked so young, and she couldn't help but think about her brother.

Tatiana forced herself to return to her cup of tea. She looked around, took a pencil she'd been using for sketching and stirred her tea with it.

The log in took a few minutes. and as soon as her laptop was prepped, she dialled a number in Russia she knew by heart.

"*Kak dela*?" Her handler's face was covered by a mask overlay.

"Fine... It's done." Tatiana took a large mouthful of burning tea, to stop her emotions from tightening her throat.

"Anything of interest as you went through his personal effects?" her handler asked.

"Apart from a bit of soft porn... nothing. If he kept anything compromising it was not at his place."

"Do you think he may have?"

"I can't be sure. His office is another place I need to investigate, but that will require a bit more preparation."

"Good... do it. I'll make sure that my team disables the surveillance equipment we installed before you get in."

Tatiana nodded.

"Anything else to report?"

"Nothing." She drank more tea. There was no need to mention the man at McNamara's property. Although his presence was setting off new alarm bells, she was not ready to talk to her handler about her suspicions.

"How about the Brit?"

"He has been invited to London."

"Did you speak to Upstage about it?"

"I made some comments about how well connected the Brit was. Upstage knows I made some inquiries about Henry Newborn. My advice seems to have done the trick."

196

"What about the others?"

"Botha was a bit harder to convince but he came around."

"Botha is a sharp man. If he has doubts about the Brit, follow through."

"Botha doesn't trust anyone." Tatiana was not complaining; it was just an observation.

"That's advisable in our profession, and that's what's kept Botha alive and free to spread views that are now branded extreme, even more so in today's South Africa."

"He hasn't mentioned anything specific about Newborn, but I'll keep an eye open."

"Will you meet with Newborn before he goes?"

"I'm about to invite myself for a cup of coffee. I would have preferred a drink, but Upstage wants me around to prepare for the London trip tonight. He can get jealous of the time I spend with other men."

"And does he have cause to be jealous at all?"

The question surprised Tatiana, perhaps more because she was no longer sure about the answer.

"Why would he be? It's my job to find information." Her tone was a little defensive. She took a final sip of tea.

"It is, but Upstage remains your priority." Her masked handler shifted a little on Tatiana's screen. He was moving around whatever room he was in.

"That's understood and Upstage knows that."

They both fell silent; Tatiana waited for her handler to terminate the call.

"When was the last time you spoke to Anatolie? Must be a little while...?"

Tatiana bit the inside of her cheek. She nodded. "It's been three months."

"You should call. They grow so fast at that age. 13 years old. A few years and he will be a man."

This was spoken without warmth or interest. It was just a cold reminder of what and who was at stake.

"I will call him." Tatiana knew the rules. She called only when she was allowed to.

"Good. I won't be reachable for a couple of days, unless absolutely necessary."

Her handler disappeared off screen. Tatiana logged off. She closed her laptop, and only when she was sure the connection was dead did she bring a cushion to her face and screamed her heart out.

* * *

"You're on." Nick rolled the chair away from Henry's desk and stood up. "You're on. The chat is open and Pieper controls the visuals... Just follow the flow."

A strange landscape had appeared on screen. The fluorescent colours had turned conventional colour attribution on its head – red trees, blue lawn, orange skies... there was something weirdly geometric about the composition. Henry wondered for a moment whether there was some sinister motive at play, some subliminal message hidden in this striking picture.

But Henry recalled seeing art pieces similar to the image displayed before him.

He sat down, moved the chair close to his desk and waited.

A small figure in a hoodie appeared in the distance on screen and started walking towards him. The effect was playful. The closer the figure got the more vibrant the colours became.

The figure stopped in the middle of the screen and a synthesised voice came on.

"Good afternoon, Henry. You don't mind if we skip formalities, do you?"

"I'm not sure I have the choice, Pieper." Henry made sure to clip the pronunciation of his words with his soft, Northern Irish accent.

The voice chuckled. "So, you're not English then?"

"I'm glad you can tell." Henry glanced at Nick who was transfixed by the sudden change in intonation.

"Where from in Northern Ireland?"

"It was a long time ago, so not relevant to this conversation." Had it been a mistake to invoke a past that had started haunting him again?

But Pieper seemed to accept Henry's pushback. "And how do you like my surroundings?"

"Very good. Olafur Eliasson inspired, I believe."

The voice stayed silent for a short time. Then a long whistle and a nod. "I don't mind saying it, but I'm surprised. No one knows this guy."

"But I'm not no one, am I?"

"No... You're a man on a mission."

"I am, and so are you."

"The question, Henry-who-knows-Olafur-Eliasson, is as follows: Are our missions compatible?"

"Let's find out, Pieper, the rat catcher."

"Nick told me about the Russian connection to Rush Huckerby's death."

"That's what I am trying to establish with certainty."

"The company has military-grade encryption. Nick was good enough to lay a trap and gain access, but it was lucky that the document you were looking for had not yet been moved to the cache."

"We got chased out pretty fast too."

The Pieper continued. "I think whoever is looking after their IT is also from the same background. It's a package, installation of the software, maintenance and 24/7 monitoring. The company outsources its IT, or a large part of it, to the military-grade software provider I've seen before."

"What else do you need from me to help us chase and identify these guys?" said Henry.

"What's in it for you, Henry?"

"Same as you I presume – justice."

There was a raucous laugh. "Justice is a big word. And you don't know me well enough to know what I want."

Henry pushed back. "I thought we were trying to establish whether our missions were aligned."

"That doesn't mean you get to *know* what I want. Our missions might be the same at least for now, but your end game and my end game is a different matter."

Henry stopped himself from responding. He could try to convincingly bullshit The Pieper, but he would not be doing himself any favours.

The Pieper continued. "I can see why you want justice for the man who died, but in my view justice can only be rendered by a law court. You don't trust the police to do their job and bring the case in front of one of courts? Fine. But you want more."

"I need the names of the people who are taking these decisions – who lives, who dies. I want to know who the decision makers are because I doubt they live in the US."

"Or because that's what you're paid for? Finding out who they are and perhaps eliminate them?" The use of the synthesiser made it hard to read the inflection in Pieper's voice.

"That's a question I can't answer."

"Good answer. I'd rather you be straight with me."

Henry thought about what he had witnessed so far; the two murders, the meetings with Upstage and his lot, and the trip to London.

"Western democracies are not without reproach," Henry said, "but when I consider the alternative, I'd like to make sure they stay what they are – democracies." Henry wondered whether this might just be another fluffy statement.

"That's more like it, Henry-who-knows-Olafur-Eliasson. I'll be in touch soon."

The screen collapsed into a myriad of dots and then turned black.

Henry stared at it for a minute or so.

"That's it?" He resumed his English pronunciation, careful to add a diphthong to the letters that needed it. It had taken years of training for him to lose his Belfast accent.

Nick nodded encouragingly. "Yeah, I think it went well."

He seemed to have a question; Henry assumed it had to do with Northern Ireland. But then he asked something else. "Who's Olafur Eliasson?"

"An Icelandic contemporary artist. Works a lot with colour diffraction, installations and photographs. He's just starting to become known."

"How do you know this guy?"

Henry smiled. "*That* story belongs to another life."

He pushed away from his desk and got up. "Close the chat room and make sure The Pieper hasn't left us with some unwelcomed spyware."

Nick sighed "That's the problem with The Pieper, you can never tell."

* * *

200

The taxi dropped Tatiana off in front of Henry's office building. She'd just had a long meeting with Upstage, making sure he was fully prepared for his London meeting. Botha had spent a lot of the afternoon with Upstage as well. She knew Botha did not hold women in high esteem, but she was different. He tolerated her, knowing what she was capable of.

Tatiana had returned to her apartment first and changed. The sexy dress and high heels felt too obvious a play for a man like Henry Newborn. Instead, she had opted for a pair of jeans, a light-blue roll neck jumper that hugged her figure just enough, and a fake-fur coat that looked fun, yet elegant.

She ignored reception, walked straight to the turnstile doors and flashed a smile at the security guard.

"I've left my badge in the Platinum Suite. I'm really sorry?"

The man hesitated, but her smile did not falter. He scanned his own badge to let her in.

Tatiana walked into the lift, joined by a couple of businessmen, who then missed their stop just to check on which floor she was alighting. She left them behind, waving a small goodbye at them without turning back.

She stopped in front of the entrance door. The broken glass had been replaced. She smiled at the camera she knew was above the door, and rang the bell.

A slim figure moved behind the frosted glass. She imagined Nick at reception, checking the camera and wondering what to do.

She smiled again, gave a little wave and mouthed *Henry* with the assurance of someone who was expected.

Nick released the catch. He pulled it open and stood in front of Tatiana.

She extended an elegant hand. "I'm Tatiana Borodin. We haven't had the pleasure of being introduced."

Nick took her hand and a little colour rose to his cheeks. "I'm Nick Fox. Lovely to meet you."

"I need to speak to Henry about his London trip."

"Oh... OK." Nick stood back to let Tatiana in. "He's been very busy organising. I'll get him for you."

Tatiana took her coat off and the figure-hugging pullover had the desired effect. She handed her coat to a blushing Nick.

"Sorry." He put the coat in the cloakroom.

Tatiana walked towards the closed door of Henry's office. "I'll just let him know I've arrived."

Before Nick could ask her to wait, she had knocked at the door.

"Come in," Henry answered.

Tatiana pushed the door open and took a step inside.

"I hope I'm not interrupting...?"

Henry was standing in front of his desk, the sleeves of his shirt rolled up to his elbows. His jacket and tie were hanging over the back of his desk chair, and his shirt collar was open in a gesture she imagined might have been deliberate, rather than out of exasperation.

It took a few seconds for him to register it was not Nick. The surprised look on his face made her want to smile, but she kept her composure. She stood very still, giving him time to do away with any document he didn't want her to see. She was not here to get that sort of intel. That would come later.

"Upstage asked me to check you have everything you need for tomorrow's trip." She should have said David. Too late now.

Henry gave a quick glance around the room. Irritation flashed in his eyes. Then he broke into a smile.

"I believe I'm getting there, but perhaps you can tell me what you think I need to pay attention to?"

Tatiana smiled at the speed with which he'd turned awkwardness to his advantage. She looked around the room. Henry watched her, and extended his hand towards the lounge area.

"Would you like something to drink?"

"Coffee would be nice, milk no sugar, please."

She turned to face the sofas and chairs and heard him place an order with Nick for both of them, making sure Nick got something for himself too.

"Won't be a minute. There's a rather good coffee shop around the corner."

Tatiana nodded and sat in the middle of one of the sofas. Her position was deliberate, to show there was no invitation for Henry to come and sit next to her.

Amusement showed in his eyes. He sat opposite her in one of the armchairs.

202

"So, tell me. Who are all these people in London?"

"The Russian Embassy likes to invite a broad range of people, from entrepreneurs to politicians – the occasional artist. It's a way to drum up business." Tatiana kicked off her low boots and gathered her legs underneath her.

"Is there a political agenda?"

"Really?" Tatiana frowned. "There is always a political agenda when Russia is involved."

She would play a straight bat with him and see how far it would get her.

Henry pouted. "Putin doesn't shy away from controversy, I suppose."

Tatiana nodded. "It is his trademark."

Nick knocked at the door and entered with two coffees. He set them down on the coffee table and disappeared.

Henry bent forward to grab his cup, showing off the muscles of his shoulder and back. She glanced at his figure – trained body, alert. Tatiana registered this as she grabbed her coffee. There was something precise in the way he moved that showed a focus she couldn't quite yet figure out.

"Do you think David is going to win?" Henry asked as he sat back in his seat.

The directness of his question stopped her in her tracks. She gave a small laugh and shook her head. "The billion-dollar question."

Tatiana sipped some coffee and grew serious. "I do, and so do you, despite all that your rational brain may be telling you. This is the reason why you are going to London."

"I'm very intrigued."

"No, you're not... You've made up your mind."

Tatiana met Henry's eyes for a brief moment, both wishing to read the other. They pulled away at the same time, and she became certain that they were cut from the same cloth.

"David is a charismatic leader. I can't deny that."

"He also is incredibly good at zeroing in on what people want to hear – and he knows how to use social media to convey his thoughts."

"What's in it for *you*?" Henry's voice had moved its register a little. Was there a little emotion? Tatiana wondered.

"I'm an artist. I like to capture images of events and people that could change the world."

Henry nodded, and yet he looked unconvinced.

"But you haven't said much about what's in it for you," Tatiana said. "Apart from the money side."

"I'm a fixer. I help people do deals and it would be the most incredible deal if I helped the next President of the United States to get elected." Henry's gaze remained steady. He didn't blink, nor did his gaze shift away, as it usually did with liars.

Why was it then that she did not believe him?

Perhaps his eerie stillness showed he was controlling his emotions perfectly well.

Tatiana balanced her cup in one hand and pushed a strand of hair back off her face. It was a simple gesture that she didn't need to make more seductive than it already was.

Henry's eyes sparkled with interest. She could tell he appreciated all he saw, but he wasn't the sort of man she could entrap the way she had Upstage, and so many others. Or perhaps, it wouldn't need to be entrapment at all.

"It's strange," she said. "I'm offering to give you as much information as you want on the London meeting, and you've hardly asked a question. Are you that confident you've obtained all the details you need already?"

"It's my job to be successful at finding information no one else can." Henry replied, moving his arm to the side of the armchair. Her question had elicited a disturbed response.

"I understand you may not trust me yet – we've only just met – but *intelligence* is always worth having, even if it means sifting through it later on to decide what you believe and what you don't."

Tatiana emphasised the word intelligence and she felt it again, this slight stillness from Henry she'd detected before.

"You're right, I don't trust easily." Henry agreed. "Nothing personal of course, but it goes with the territory."

"Finance is a cut-throat business. Art can be too, you know." Tatiana drank some more coffee.

"I understand a bit about it. At the high end of contemporary art the competition is fierce."

"You don't need to reach that level to encounter that sort of competition. It's present at almost all levels. It's hard to make a sale, even more so in photography."

"But surely you can sell to the papers? With your name?" Henry faltered. Tatiana could see he regretted mentioning the Borodin name and reference to her parents.

"Don't worry, people say this to me all the time, and it's true. Being the daughter of journalists who have been assassinated is a sad, yet unique calling card."

Henry moved his hand forward, as though he wanted to lay it on hers, but he pulled back. "I'm very sorry. I never meant the remark to be cruel."

Tatiana shrugged and she felt her throat tighten. But she could read it on his face; he was sorry, not so much because he had spoken in haste and with little consideration, but because he understood the pain.

"I believe you."

She unfolded her legs and put the cup of coffee on the table. The bottom of it caught on the edge and hot liquid splashed across the table. Henry moved out of its trajectory with a swift and effective move.

Tatiana brought her hand to her mouth.

"I'm sorry." She stood up with a small jump. "I'll get some napkins."

As she entered the reception area in search of paper towels, she recalled Henry's move. She was now certain of one thing: Henry had received hand-to-hand combat training, just the way she had.

Chapter Twenty-One

The early departure from Andrews Air Force Base near Washington had been uneventful. Jack had made a few calls and ensured Henry could leave as early as 5am. Henry would have a seven-hour flight on a private jet that was secure enough to make all the calls needed to prepare for his upcoming meeting at the Russian Embassy.

Even Harris had managed to surprise Henry by delivering a Gulfstream G550 aircraft that looked exactly like what Henry's legend might take to cross the Atlantic.

Henry got to work as soon as the aircraft had taken off. Harris had assured him that the personnel on board had been vetted by MI6 and that *he would be looked after*. Henry was served a good old-fashioned English breakfast that he wolfed down, even at the early hour.

Nick had loaded his laptop with the latest information about the people Henry was about to meet. Jack had sent some information about Botha but promised a much more in-depth CV before touchdown.

Henry had not heard from The Pieper, but Nick assured him it was a good sign.

"He would have told you straight away if he didn't want to work with us," Nick had said. "He's got a reputation for being very vocal and doesn't care who he annoys. If he doesn't like it, he's not going to pretend."

Henry was leaving it up to Nick to sort this one out. His orders to Nick had been short:

"Don't get involved in anything above your pay grade. No snooping, no investigating, no nothing, unless you speak to me first or Jack Shield only in an extreme emergency. Agreed?"

Nick had shrugged. "Yeah, all right."

"I want a resounding 'I agree, Henry'."

Nick had then smiled. "I agree, Henry." It was the first time Nick had dropped the "sir" and used his first name.

"Good man."

Henry hoped he'd moved enough of the action to London to deflect interest away from his DC office. His meeting with Tatiana had been less of a success and it lingered in his mind.

She had hardly pried into his background, offering up information instead – a clever way of getting close. But there had also been something unguarded about her views that made it difficult for Henry to decide what to make of her.

Then there had been his insensitive remark about her parents, which he still felt terrible about. How could he not relate to the dread and the pain surrounding such an event? His own father had been murdered by people who had never been caught.

Henry stood up and moved to the galley, to chase the memories away. The steward was preparing a cup of tea for the captain and his co-pilot.

"I wouldn't mind a refill, please?" Henry asked him.

"Sure, give me a moment and I'll come your way with a fresh pot."

Henry returned to his seat. He looked at his watch. He was over three hours into the flight. Tailwinds were pushing the plane, making it go faster. Landing would be almost one hour ahead of schedule.

He relaxed on the comfortable, cream-leather armchair and looked at the document he had called up on his laptop. But his mind drifted once more to Northern Ireland and Belfast. In two hours' time the plane would be grazing the most southern tip of Ireland before making its slow descent into RAF Northolt, where they would land.

Henry rested his head against the cool window pane.

He remembered the fighting on the streets and the sounds of bombs detonating in the distance.

He recalled his friendship with the O'Connor brothers and their betrayal that he believed he would never recover from.

He thought of the day he'd left Northern Ireland never to return – or at least that had been his cover story.

Someone was hovering near his seat. Henry jerked out of his reverie. The steward had arrived with a tray carrying a fresh mug, a pot of tea, and some milk.

"Here you are. Shall I pour?"

"No, thank you. Just leave it on the table."

The young man nodded and left Henry alone.

Henry exhaled out the past and poured tea followed by a dash of milk. Just the way his English mother had taught him. He allowed himself a moment to drink it before returning to the document.

The list of guests for the gathering was impressive. Politicians – some high-ranking parliamentarians and some coming from Europe; businessmen including the expected Russian oligarchs; bankers of large investments banks, including the two banks he and Upstage were targeting – DS Bank, and RNB, the largest bank in Russia. Henry wondered whether the presence of these two banks was a coincidence, but he very much doubted it. Perhaps McNamara had made the call before his untimely end, or perhaps this was Tatiana's doing at the behest of Upstage.

Henry had almost finished going through the various CVs, grateful that the international bakers present were not people he'd known in a previous life. A message flashed on his screen. Jack had sent the file he had promised about Botha. Henry went to his inbox and opened the document. He read it quickly and it took his breath away.

According to the CIA research papers, Botha was a South African journalist who had established contacts with Afrikaner Nationalists. In some of his tweets, he had started to reinvigorate *deep state* conspiracy theories, with echoes of Apartheid-era *swart gewaar* (black danger) and *rooi gewaar* (red danger) fake stories.

Botha and his followers, of which he seemed to have many, were adapting old conspiracy theories. Theories spreading ideas that the South African government was encouraging the murder of white farmers and the deposition of their land, or that the country's president was plotting a new-world order with wealthy US Americans such as Bill Gates.

Henry remembered the gleeful look on Botha's face at the idea of adding America to the list of countries in which he had senior contacts.

208

If Upstage managed to fulfil his goal of presidency, his position would transcend above senior. Botha would have the ear of the most powerful man in the world, with a finger on the nuclear button.

The idea made Henry sick to his stomach.

He switched back to the list of guests. Someone was attending from the French far-right. The niece of its leader was attending the event, and so were a couple of Italians from the Salvini party.

The steward returned and took the tray away.

"Do you fancy anything else? We're landing in under two hours. Coffee and a sandwich selection?"

"Perfect."

Henry finished reading the rest of the data Harris had sent about the guests, and decided it was time to call his minder from his laptop. He connected the call easily.

"How's the plane? And don't tell me you're not impressed." Harris was his usual boisterous self.

"What else would Henry Newborn fly?"

Harris shook his head. "You're such an ungrateful brat."

"No, I'm trying to keep alive."

"And such a drama queen... Although, I might concede that point. The body count is growing at an alarming rate on this op."

"I read the docs you sent to me. They confirm Botha's statement that the far-right would be represented at the meeting. I don't see any Brits on the list though."

"I think it might have been a bit too much to invite the British National Party as well, but believe you me, the two London businessmen you met have got the right connections, if I can put it that way."

"How about the rest of Europe?"

"The French and Italians are the conduit. They'll relay back to their contacts what they've learnt and what the plan is next." Harris sounded confident.

"Brexit is stirring up UK politics. Anti-EU movements are spreading across the continent. It's the right time to jump on the bandwagon."

Henry's plate of sandwiches and coffee had just been delivered. He gave the steward a thumbs up.

"Exactly right," said Harris. "I'm waiting to see how the Russians use all this."

"Have you had time to read what Jack sent to us about Botha?"

"I read it as soon as it hit my screen. I nearly fell off my chair, but then again these are typical extremist tactics – engage people emotionally, tap into their greatest fears, such as fake theories about white genocides, then off you go."

"But Botha is a journalist, and he is very good at using social media to propagate his views."

"I've noticed. Just the way Upstage is very good at doing this too."

"How far do you think these people will go?" Henry had a firm view on the matter, but he wanted to hear Harris's own take on the issue.

"They'll be merciless. Anything goes, including manipulation on a grand scale."

"I'm glad we agree on that. And what can MI6 do about it?"

"Unless we have very solid proof, we'll do sweet FA."

"What does solid mean?" Henry asked.

"Follow the money I say... That's what got Nixon fired as president. The US Congress didn't even need to impeach him."

"Harris, you're aware that London is the laundromat for Eastern Europe, right?"

"Not only Eastern Europe, unfortunately, but what is your point?"

"There might be a great deal of reluctance within the political spheres running the country to rock the boat of what is a lucrative property business for them."

"I'm still not getting it?" Harris sounded genuinely at sea.

"Money laundering brings in a lot of cash that then needs to be cleaned through the property market in the UK. And property companies have a strong connection to the political elites."

"MI6 doesn't give a shit about political elites..." Harris paused. "Unless what you are saying is that some of MI6's management might be compromised?"

"Could they be?" Henry asked.

"Anything is possible in this job – we've had moles in the past. But the service has moved on from the seventies when everyone was coming from the same gentlemen's club or the same university. For God's sake, they even recruited me."

"Valid point. Who would have thought an East End boy like you could run a successful team at MI6?"

Harris laughed. "Not the first guy who interviewed me, that's for sure."

"What happened then?"

"That's classified, mate."

Henry pictured Harris at his interview wearing the best suit he could afford from M&S, and a tie borrowed from his dad. Not the tailored suit type like most of MI6, and good on him for being different.

A short silence followed and Henry moved on to the list of documents he had gathered so far.

"Has GCHQ been monitoring the social media accounts of any of these people?" he asked.

"They do intercept traffic, but there is still an overwhelming priority given to the Middle East."

"What does Natasha say?"

"About what – joining you for the Russian Embassy knees-up? Or intel gathering?"

"Her views on both counts would be good."

"She can't wait to meet an oligarch face to face." Harris grumbled. He clearly was not happy asking for assistance from someone outside his team, albeit help that was coming from a sister service.

"And...?"

"She can't wait to collect more details for RUSSKY BEAR."

Henry grinned. "We're going to get on like a house on fire then."

"Steady on, matey, she's government property and a no-go area."

"I'll be a perfect gentleman. I have enough on my plate not to get entangled with some government property, even if that property turns out to be very hot."

"Just as well, Crowne. She's half Russian and the Slavs have a slightly different take on death."

"Is that so?"

"Worth remembering."

Henry didn't ask how Harris had come to know this. His mind turned to another Russian woman who was getting closer to him than was perhaps advisable.

"Anything else I need to know before I go to this meeting?"

"No, just be prepared for the unexpected." Harris killed the call, leaving Henry with a frown.

Natasha arrived dead on time at the flat Harris had rented for Henry in Marylebone, soon to be ferried by the limo that would be taking Henry and her to the Russian Embassy in Kensington Place Gardens.

She wore a light-blue chiffon dress that made her round features attractive. She had her red hair up in an elegant bun and was all smiles.

"I can't believe I'm going to be so close to all these bastards." Natasha was positively jubilant.

Henry smiled as he was adjusting his bow tie in the mirror of the lounge. "Don't take the Kalashnikov out just yet."

"I'd rather go for something more painful – a bit of rat poisoning, maybe." Natasha smiled and two small dimples appeared.

"I've been told the Russians have a different view about death." Henry stepped back to look at the overall effect. The tuxedo fitted perfectly. The bow tie was nicely tight. He was ready to do business. "Did Harris tell you that?"

Henry nodded, unsure whether Natasha was about to give him a lecture on tolerance for other cultures. But she laughed instead.

"I once told him that my grandmother was very superstitious, and that she used to regale me with all these folk stories where people die and get resurrected. It always involves the devil in some way. And she used to have strange rituals when she learnt about someone's death."

"Did you get into the nitty gritty details with Harris?"

"You bet I did."

Henry laughed. "Let's go and cast a spell on the Russian mafia, shall we?" Henry gallantly helped Natasha into her fur coat.

"If Harris needs to contact you during the evening, he'll call me on my MI6 mobile. We've agreed on a coded conversation." Natasha checked her reflection in the full-length mirror of the entrance hall and nodded. "I'll give you the codes in the car."

"What could ever go wrong?" Henry smiled, uncertain he believed his sudden burst of confidence.

212

"You're right... it's only Russia we are talking about, a country with a most ruthless regime and one of the best spying agencies in the world." Natasha grabbed Henry's arm and they walked out of the flat.

The queue of limos, taxis, and other luxury cars in front of the Russian Embassy waiting to deliver their passengers was staggering. Upstage was inevitably going to be late, and Henry had no intention of showing up early. Like all these meetings, the timing of arrival was an art that needed to be exercised with care.

He looked out to check what was happening. The limo driver put on the brakes and got out of the car.

"Half a dozen cars in front of us," he reported.

Natasha didn't look anxious, or if she was, she was hiding it well.

"Any news from GCHQ whilst we are waiting?" he asked her.

"Nothing yet, but I've only recently spoken to the team tracking the chatter that comes out of Europe. We won't have much until a couple of days' time, when they've analysed what they've got based on our request."

"Have you heard about people called COSY BEAR?"

Natasha turned towards Henry with surprise.

"The hackers... yes, of course. A bloody difficult lot to stop and even more so to ID. MI6 have been trying for years to find out who they are. GCHQ tries to track their hacks, but they are really good."

Henry nodded. He hadn't heard from Nick yet, and would call as soon as he was back at the flat. He hoped The Pieper was on board.

"Why, do you have new intel on these guys?" Natasha sounded excited at the thought.

"I'm afraid not. I just suspect they are involved somewhere along the line."

"The operation you and Harris are running is high-profile enough for them to be involved, so you're right to be vigilant."

"Last question before we leave the limo and go into the lion's den... Any idea about their background? Mafia, ex-KGB?"

"Certainly not direct mafia, although in my view, the distinction between mafia and intelligence services in Russia is fluid. KGB has been disbanded and replaced by a couple of organisations – so I'd say either FSB, or more likely GRU."

The limo stopped in Kensington Palace Gardens, in front of the gates of the Russian Federation's Embassy.

A couple of armed security guards moved alongside the car. The driver opened his window and gave the names of the guests. One of the men with an old-fashioned paper list checked the names. The other ran a small mirror mounted on wheels beneath the car to inspect the chassis. He then shone a torch through the windows of the car, temporarily blinding Natasha. As she recoiled beneath the glare, Henry moved forward to protest. She stopped him with an iron grip.

"Stay quiet," she ordered.

The guard nodded and the limo moved forward.

The driver got out and opened Natasha's door. Henry stepped out and took a moment to collect himself. He hadn't been to a formal gathering of the sort happening at the Embassy since his arrest, seven years ago.

Henry closed the door and thanked the driver, who would be waiting for the return journey, and was on hand, should they both need assistance of a less conventional nature.

Natasha was taking in the scene and as Henry approached, she leaned into him.

"That is Mikhail Rostov, one of the more powerful oligarchs living in London with a direct line to Putin." She was nodding at a man who was walking through the door of the Embassy.

"We are in good company, then?"

Natasha chuckled. "How good is your Russian?"

"Nonexistent." Henry moved closer to the gate where visitors were presenting their invitation.

Natasha took two cards out of her bag, embossed with Russia's coat of arms. The security guard checked their names again on his list of guests, nodded. He radioed in their names to the guards inside who would be carrying out the final security checks.

Henry released a short exhale. Time to test how good his legend was and the change in appearance he had made to fit with it.

The old-fashioned opulence of the Embassy's ground floor reminded Henry more of the Russian Tzars than a former communist country. People had already arrived, and champagne and vodka were being offered to the guests by waiters and waitresses in white uniforms.

Henry spotted the two English businessmen he had now met a few times at Upstage's club. Edward Bound and Nevil Ferguson were in deep conversation with a young woman who was elegantly dressed. He recognised the French envoy from the far-right party, Le Front National.

Botha didn't appear to have arrived yet, and neither had Upstage.

Mikhail Rostov was also in conversation with a tall and gangly man Henry thought he recognised. The man had his back to him. Henry shook the thought away. He scanned the audience for a moment, deciding who he would be approaching first to strike up a conversation. But there was no need.

A man with a shock of white hair, a pleasant smile, and an alertness that meant experience moved towards him with an open hand. "Hans Mueller, DS Bank in Washington. David Upstage told me you would be attending."

Henry shook hands with Mueller, surprised at how quickly the news of his arrival had already made the rounds.

"May I introduce you to Natasha Kelly, my interpreter?" Henry said.

Mueller shook hands with Natasha with equal enthusiasm.

"David has not arrived yet." Mueller scanned the room to make sure he was not speaking too hastily.

"This shouldn't prevent us from having a conversation, though." Henry sipped a little champagne. To his surprise, it was of excellent quality.

Mueller's smile dropped a little. "Should we not wait for him to arrive?"

"I don't think it is necessary." Henry moved a little closer to Mueller. "You know David. If we could iron out the broad lines of the deal he and I have discussed, it would save him time and would be appreciated."

"Perhaps you're right." Mueller thought about it in the same time it took to have a sip of champagne. "David can be..." He was looking for the right word.

Henry smiled an understanding smile.

"A little impatient sometimes?" Henry gestured to a corner of the room that looked less busy. Both men made their way there.

Natasha had moved away and was engaged in a Russian conversation with a young man. She checked on Henry and shifted position a little, to make sure she could still see him. Henry nodded discreetly to say he was fine.

"David told me you're now handling one of his most promising new transactions?" Mueller was keen.

"The Nassau hotel complex. Luxury hotel, spa, golf course – and more importantly, a casino. There is work to be done, of course, to bring the property up to its full potential, but it is a unique opportunity."

"And David doesn't think he needs to call on investors?"

Henry nodded, silently congratulating himself. Upstage must have called Mueller after the conversation they'd had at his club. Henry's idea must have convinced Upstage to present the deal as his own.

"That's right. David wants tight control of the redevelopment process without being hampered by investors who do not understand the market as well as he does."

"Very wise, of course." Mueller's glass was empty. Not for long though. A smiling young man arrived with a bottle and replenished the glass.

"This is what we think would be fair for your bank." Henry shook his head at the offer of a glass refill. He carried on when the waiter left. "The cost of the transaction is shy of $1bn."

Mueller didn't balk at the number. Henry suspected he'd already been told what the price tag was.

"The loan would be made directly to David Upstage in a personal capacity, not to Upstage Ultra Lux. The company would purchase the Nassau hotel complex outright. I'd propose for the company to keep you informed of the development schedule."

"Who guarantees the loan?" Mueller asked without concern.

"I will come to that." Henry scanned the room. Upstage hadn't arrived yet. Or perhaps he was in another part of the building having a different private meeting.

"When it comes to the terms of the loan, I expect David to be granted the same favourable terms as his company, Upstage Ultra Lux."

Mueller was still following, although a little doubt had now crept into his eyes.

"You spoke about a guarantee earlier. I propose David and I facilitate a transaction whereby RNB, the largest bank in Russia, takes away the risk inherent to the $1bn loan to David Upstage." Henry briefly met Mueller's gaze. He knew it sounded extraordinary, but he was being serious.

"And you know they will agree?" Mueller was still listening.

Henry spoke about the existing links between the Upstage luxury empire and Russia, observing Mueller as he did so. It was not the first

216

time Mueller had dealt with difficult clients, and perhaps transactions that banks should have shied away from altogether.

"As soon as David arrives, we'll have a conversation with one of RNB's senior management representatives," Henry said. He refused yet another offer for a refill of his glass. Mueller didn't even notice his glass was being topped up.

Natasha had found another victim, making sure Henry could still spot her and call if needed. Henry had started questioning Mueller about other more mundane issues when a flurry of activity erupted at the far end of the room.

The Russian Ambassador to the UK and Upstage appeared, accompanied by two pretty women who seemed to be there for show rather than any other reason. People started greeting the pair as though they were long-lost friends.

Upstage and the Ambassador stopped to shake hands, making their way as quickly as they could without offending the guests, to the corner where Mikhail Rostov was standing. Upstage glanced at Henry, acknowledging his presence but indicating he couldn't yet join him.

Henry was still surprised at how effective Upstage was at handling messages – the ability to convey meaning with one look, hand gesture or through body language. Upstage was without a doubt a born communicator.

Mueller was still at Henry's side, content to wait until the great man was free. Henry accepted a fresh glass of champagne. Canapés were circulating and he chose caviar on a small blini. Upstage reached Rostov. The Ambassador shook hands warmly with the oligarch and the man he was speaking to. He then introduced Upstage to Rostov with eagerness.

Upstage was out to make his mark, calmer and more controlled than Henry had ever seen him. His demeanour was relaxed, just one billionaire talking to another – although the billions in Upstage's bank account were in low single digits. Rostov was worth almost $15bn.

The man who had been speaking to Rostov turned around to pick up one of the canapés. Henry's blood ran cold. Mueller was speaking to Henry, but Henry didn't notice.

Brett Allner-Smith was standing a few feet away from them. Henry felt a few beads of perspiration form on his forehead. He glanced at the exit door, but it was at the far end of the room, and if he moved, he was sure to be noticed by the man he needed to avoid.

Why hadn't Harris known Henry's former art dealer would be at the Embassy?

Mueller stopped talking and Henry turned to him. "I'm sorry. What was your question again?"

"I was wondering whether you were into antiquities. Tonight's guest speaker is a well-known expert."

"What do you mean?" Henry's reply must have sounded curt because Mueller looked startled.

"He's a consultant at Christie's. But perhaps you don't rate them so much."

"I have nothing against them, but the fees they charge can be a bit on the heavy side."

"You're a collector then?" Mueller seemed reassured. "You should enjoy the talk that Mr Allner-Smith will give this evening – antiquities in the early Sumerian period, how to recognise a fake."

Henry clenched his fist and drank more of his champagne. It was all he could do to keep control of his rising anger. Harris had known all along Allner-Smith would be here, but he had decided not to tell Henry. The reason was obvious. Henry would never have accepted to be in the same room with a man he despised and who had played him in the past – or was it the reverse? Had it not been Henry who had played Brett?

Natasha joined them. She asked Mueller a question but Henry was not listening to the conversation.

Allner-Smith had walked away to speak to another guest and moved closer to where Henry stood. His eyes drifted towards the small group. He briefly glanced at Henry, then Mueller and Natasha. His eyes lingered on her but his attention soon returned to the man he was talking to.

There was no inkling that Brett recognised Henry, or that he was at all familiar to him. Whatever it was that MI6 had taught Henry in the past few years, it had transformed him in both looks and personality, more than he could have expected.

Still, there was no room for complacency.

Natasha was having a conversation with Mueller about the construction of the Nord Stream Two pipelines bringing gas to Europe through Germany. She thought it would be completed by now, despite the opposition of certain European countries.

218

Henry joined the conversation, until one of the women who accompanied Upstage came to him and murmured softly. "The Ambassador and Mr Upstage would like you to join them."

Chapter Twenty-Two

Someone was in Henry's apartment.

Tatiana had parked her bike at the top of the alleyway that led to the back of his house. From there, she'd walked slowly to the far end of the small street. The lights were on when she had arrived and they had been switching on and off from one room to another. The shift pattern was such that she doubted it was coming from some electronic device.

There was only one way to find out.

She moved to the front of the house and pressed the bell a few times. No answer. She insisted again. Still no reply.

Tatiana retraced her steps. It was almost 7pm, and the old lady who lived on the ground floor was due to feed the stray cats she looked after every day.

True to form, Mrs Bartlett opened the back door of her house, and came down the steps with a little wobble that made Tatiana want to help the old woman. Instead, she pulled back to the corner of the alleyway and waited. Mrs Bartlett laid a large tray down on the ground and started to pour some dry food into it. She called the cats at the same time.

"Fluffy, Suety...!"

Tatiana could not help smiling at the scene.

Mrs Bartlett kept calling other names, and as she did, a few cats emerged from various corners of the street. Some ran towards her, some were more cautious. She was soon surrounded by a dozen cats, and she made sure each had been stroked and fed.

Tatiana pulled her hoodie up and moved swiftly towards the back door that had been left ajar. She slid through the opening and crossed the apartment without stopping to survey her surroundings. She came to the main door and stopped. Two of the bolts could be undone from inside, but the third required a key.

She looked around to check if the key she needed was close by. Nothing.

She moved back to the lounge looking for a handbag. She spotted the item, neatly placed next to an old armchair that must be Mrs Bartlett's usual seat. Tatiana opened the bag and found a set of keys. She was about to return to the hallway when she heard the door close. Mrs Bartlett had finished her feeding round and was back inside.

Tatiana put the bag down without noise, clenching the keys in her hand. She returned to the main door. Mrs Bartlett was in the kitchen, opening and shutting cupboards, and running water in the kitchen sink. If she came out of the kitchen through the second entrance, she would spot Tatiana immediately.

Tatiana started to fiddle with the bunch of keys; some looked well used and didn't fit the main door locks. Mrs Bartlett started humming and Tatiana could tell she had moved into her lounge. Tatiana tried the first Amsec key that looked as though it might match the lock. It didn't work.

She gritted her teeth. Mrs Bartlett's humming was just across from the open lounge door. Tatiana tried the second Amsec key. The lock opened with a small click. She unbolted the two other locks, left the Amsec key in the third lock and opened the door as quietly as she could.

Tatiana slid through the opening, and closed the door behind her with as much care as she could muster. She moved quickly towards the lift, exhaling in relief. She could never have hurt the old woman, but what would have happened if she'd been caught?

She shook her head. Everything was fine. She needed to concentrate on getting into Henry's apartment.

She bypassed the lift and climbed the stairs to the top of the building. She stopped for a moment, surveying the landing area outside Henry's apartment. She took out a jamming device from her small rucksack and switched it on. She calibrated it to overpower the frequency she knew surveillance cameras and systems would operate on.

The device had picked up a signal. She boosted the strength of it. The device in her hand indicated the system had been disabled. Tatiana smiled, but as she was about to put it back in her rucksack, the device beeped again. Whatever system Henry was using had rebooted itself and found another frequency.

This was serious tech. Tatiana recalibrated her own device to match the new frequency.

She increased the strength of its output. Dropping onto her belly, she crawled to the wall socket at the bottom of the wall in the small hallway on the right, and plugged the device in. She waited for a few seconds. A small bang followed and the entire building went dark.

She waited for a moment and stood up. It wouldn't be long until someone realised that they simply needed to reboot the fuse box. She walked to Henry's door and took out a flap pouch, in which she'd stored a few tools. She selected a couple of lock-picking wrenches in the dark.

Through her gloves, Tatiana felt the hole she had to pick. Within a few seconds the door had unlocked. She pushed it opened cautiously.

From inside the apartment she could hear someone swearing quietly, bumping into the furniture. The man's voice sounded familiar, but it didn't matter. Tatiana pressed against the wall, hoping the man would take a little more time to find the fuse box.

She had the floor plan of Henry's apartment, obtained from the planning office in DC. Tatiana moved without hesitation along the small entrance area, heading to the left and away from where the footsteps were coming from. She flattened herself against the wall. Someone walked past her without noticing her. She slid along the wall, farther into the flat and towards the kitchen.

The light flicked on a few seconds later and she dived for cover under the kitchen counter.

The person returned to the large open-plan room that combined a lounge and dining area. Tatiana heard the footsteps stop in the middle of the room and the furniture being pushed around. The person disappeared into what she knew was the bathroom. Tatiana stood up, moved back to the corner of the kitchen and corridor. She took out a small blowpipe, inserted a tiny dart into it from the small case she carried and waited. The man walked past her towards the sofa, away from the bathroom. She blew the dart and it hit him in the neck.

He yelped in surprise more than pain. By the time his hand reached his neck he was already sliding to the ground. Tatiana ran a couple of steps and caught him before he hit the ground.

To her surprise, she was holding the sleeping Nick Fox in her arms. She removed the dart after setting him on the ground and massaged the spot where the dart had hit. The analgesic would work faster through the body and the pinprick would become invisible. She dragged him to one of the settees and heaved him onto it. Many people who had been darted believed they'd simply fallen asleep, not remembering how.

Tatiana stopped for a moment, to catch her breath from the effort of dealing with the dead weight of Nick. Henry obviously trusted Nick to look after his apartment whilst away, but she wondered why the need for extra security. Then again, Henry was into the sort of business where it paid to be extra cautious. From what she had seen in her research on him, his clients would not forgive any indiscretion.

Tatiana took time to look around, moving to the bedroom first. She opened the wardrobe and went methodically through the drawers. There was nothing of interest there. She returned to the wardrobe to give it another check. Her face brushed against one of the jackets hanging in it. The scent of discreet aftershave made her linger, and she recollected the evening at Upstage's club where she'd first met Henry. She ran her hand over the jacket, wishing he was in it.

Tatiana pulled back a few steps. What was she thinking?

She looked at her watch, to remind herself she was under time pressure. The room looked very orderly, almost staged. Someone – she presumed Henry – had cleaned anything that may attract attention, it seemed.

She moved back to the lounge. Nick was still fast asleep, his eyes moving rapidly underneath his eyelids. She surveyed the lounge and dining area. The same staged, neat scene awaited, and nothing on show that might betray Henry. She walked around to make sure she was not missing anything, but returned empty handed after 10 minutes.

Nick groaned softly. She had another 10 minutes at most before the sedative wore off. Tatiana recalled Nick moving furniture around. The rug looked askew and the coffee table at an odd angle. She pushed it back and lifted the rug.

At first she couldn't see anything, but then she noticed a small groove in the floorboards. She pressed a few times on separate sections of the floor, until one of the slats shifted. She pressed one more time and four slats gave way to reveal a small opening. She took her phone out and used the torch to shine inside the hole. There was a small vault secured with a security pad – fingerprint recognition and password protected.

This was also high-grade quality.

Tatiana thought about the type of surveillance Top Capital Partners had installed at their offices. Theirs was coming straight from the toolkit of the GRU. What was the origin of Henry's top-end installation, she wondered? The surveillance equipment she'd seen in the hallway could be bought on the market, if you knew where to go.

But the quality of the vault, and that of its protection mechanism, spoke of something much more sophisticated. Another intelligence service? She took a few pictures of the set-up and closed the vault. Nick mumbled something and Tatiana replaced the wooden panel back in a hurry. She unfolded the rug back over the floorboards, pushed the coffee table back to where it belonged.

Nick's eyes had started to flutter. Within seconds they would open. She crossed the lounge without a sound, walked along the corridor, making sure her hoodie was obscuring her face. She left the apartment, closing the door softly behind her.

Of one thing Tatiana was now sure: Henry Newborn was not his real name.

* * *

The pretty woman who led Henry to where the Ambassador, Rostov, and Upstage stood had attracted Allner-Smith's attention. Allner-Smith's eyes followed her until they reached their destination. Henry kept his head turned away slightly, making it difficult for Allner-Smith to catch a good view of Henry's profile.

The Ambassador was the first to extend a welcoming hand. Upstage made the presentations. Rostov extended a hand as well, expressing his interest in learning more about Africa.

"The Russian Federation is late coming to the table there," he said, "and it wants to make quick progress."

Henry nodded. "China has been very quick to offer infrastructure deals and other forms of support against the purchase of raw materials. No questions asked about methods of extractions or human rights."

There were conspicuous smiles all round.

The Ambassador glanced at his watch and cast an eye in the direction of Allner-Smith. Henry felt his throat tighten. Was the Ambassador about to offer an introduction to the star speaker of the evening? To Henry's relief, he turned instead to Upstage.

"The presentation is about to start. I am going to welcome our speaker and ask people to move next door where the room has been set up. Just hang back. We'll move to my office as soon as Brett takes the floor."

Everyone nodded. Henry wondered how the Ambassador was so familiar with Allner-Smith. But he recalled that Eastern European tycoons were very fond of the types of antiquities Allner-Smith was able to procure – exceptional artefacts of museum quality that came from war-torn Middle Eastern countries.

Once upon a time, Henry had also been tempted to acquire such a piece, but he had chickened out at the last minute, leaving Allner-Smith with the artefact and a demanding bunch of jihadists to pay. No wonder Henry had become Allner-Smith's least favourite person. That had not been one of Henry's finer moments.

The Ambassador moved to the centre of the room, calling people's attention. He welcomed Allner-Smith with wit and much praise. Allner-Smith smiled but to Henry's surprise he was restrained, only displaying enough pleasure so as not to displease his host.

People started moving towards the room next door. Doors had been opened during the Ambassador's introduction. Natasha started to move forward, still chatting with Mueller. She cast an eye at Henry, but he shook his head almost imperceptibly. He had to do this meeting alone.

Rostov went back to talking about Africa and Upstage was listening intently. The doors of the conference room were closed. The Ambassador emerged a few minutes later.

Upstage and Rostov moved to where he stood. Everyone was silent. The Ambassador led the way, out into the reception area, across the large hallway, down a corridor, and into an office that smelt of cigar and spices.

Two men were already there. They were standing next to the large French doors that overlooked the garden, drink in hand – most likely whisky. They were speaking Russian when the small group had entered. The conversation died away without haste. They were not hiding, but simply finishing a conversation that had run its course.

Henry was introduced to the men, this time by the Ambassador. There was deference in the way the Ambassador spoke one of the men's names: Alexei Pietrovich Andropov. Henry reasoned he must be close to the Kremlin. Rostov shook his hand warmly. Rostov was the man of the moment as far as the Kremlin was concerned.

The other man, Ivan Petrov, was representing RN Bank, the largest bank in Russia. He was senior enough, but Henry guessed he wouldn't go against any of what was decided by the key men in the room. Henry had worked with many of these senior managers before – good enough at executing the deals, never courageous enough to take the initiative themselves.

The Ambassador pointed to the seats around the large boardroom table occupying the far end of his office. Upstage sat next to Henry. The Ambassador chose the head of the table, with Andropov deciding not to sit but stand at the window closest to the Ambassador.

Rostov chose the seat that was the closest to Andropov, and Petrov sat next to him.

"Gentlemen." The Ambassador grabbed a small bottle of water and poured its content into a crystal tumbler. "We all know why we are here this evening. Our friend David Upstage has presented us with a unique opportunity to restore a working relationship with his great country, and at the same time take part in a lucrative deal." The Ambassador gestured to Upstage. "Please, David."

Upstage nodded and turned to Henry. "And I'm in turn indebted to Mr Newborn here for designing the plan that will enable us to move forward together."

Classic buck-passing exercise if Henry had ever seen one. He'd half expected it from Upstage, but perhaps not so soon.

Henry gave a nod, a smile. He stood up, about to do what he'd always been good at, persuading people to do what they thought could never be done. But this time he could also see the catch. It was not Upstage who

226

was making the proposition but him, and if matters went sour, Upstage would be quick to point the finger.

"Thank you, David. The first leg of the proposition is a rather classic purchase of a property complex offshore in the Bahamas. The Nassau hotel is held by a typical multilayer structure of trusts and offshore companies. It's well protected from taxation. It is tax avoidance not tax evasion."

Rostov raised an eyebrow.

Henry clarified. "Evasion is fraud, avoidance is within the law."

"What is so spectacular about the Nassau hotel complex?" Petrov, the Russian banker, spread his hands on the table, waiting for the answer he must have guessed already.

"The casino of course. The perfect way to deal with money that needs recycling." Henry did not use the word laundering but everybody around the table nodded. Andropov was the only one who didn't.

Henry kept going. "To maximise the effectiveness of the deal, the money needed for the purchase will be lent directly to David, not his main holding company."

"That must be a private bank deal." Rostov nodded. He was looking around for something else to drink. The bottled water on the table did not seem to appeal.

"Which is the reason why Hans Mueller of DSB, head of the International Swiss bank David has been doing business with, is here tonight."

Petrov took over. "Have you spoken to him yet?"

"I have. The bank is willing to lend the necessary $810m but would like to edge its risk."

Petrov glanced at Andropov. The other man didn't budge. Henry assumed it was an indication Petrov could speak.

"If the price is right," said Petrov. "I'm sure Russia's Narodni Brevick will be prepared to offer a cover for the risk."

"I am glad we came to pricing quickly." All eyes were on him, including Upstage's. "There are many ways of calculating a price. The conventional way dictates we look at the credit score of the borrower, but in this case, I suggest we consider the additional contributions David is offering."

Henry opened a small bottle of water and poured the content into a glass. He took a few sips. No one spoke. Upstage was still silent. Andropov, although still standing next to a window, had straightened up.

"What do you have in mind?" Andropov's Russian accent was harsher than Petrov's. The rhythm with which he spoke sounded very different too.

"A presence in the presidential campaign team for David Upstage." Henry stopped from clenching his fist. He could not quite believe what he was offering the Kremlin.

"That's an interesting idea..." Andropov had moved closer to the table. The Ambassador stood up and gave Andropov his seat at the top of the boardroom table. "And then?"

"A partnership with Russia, once David is elected." This time Henry turned towards Upstage and sat down.

Upstage leaned forward, forearms on the edge of the large table. He gave a satisfied smile. "That is indeed the deal on offer. Access to the White House and collaboration between our two countries at the highest level."

Andropov's light-blue eyes flicked to Henry, then to Upstage. He had understood the deal, but its boldness had managed to surprise him. Upstage made it sound easy to sell one's country.

Henry stopped himself from taking another sip of water. He feared that any move he made would betray his disgust and release the bile that was rising in his throat.

Opposite to him, Upstage was relaxed. He knew the value of the offer on the table.

Andropov broke the silence by addressing Petrov.

"Ivan, speak to Mueller and agree a price for the cost of the risk cover that suits the Swiss bank. Whatever that is."

Petrov nodded. "Of course, I'll make a competitive offer."

Andropov shook his head. "Not competitive, cheap."

Petrov's face blanched a little. "This is what I meant." He spoke in Russian to confirm, and Andropov nodded.

Henry made an effort to stay in character. "Mueller and I have had a good conversation. I'll make the introduction."

The Ambassador had disappeared. He came back with a tray laden with small shot glasses and a bottle of Beluga Noble Russian vodka. He poured six shots and placed them in the centre of the table.

The four Russians smiled. This was a proper drink. Henry picked up a vodka too; Upstage was the last one to take a glass.

"*Na Zdorovie...* To your health." Henry joined the Russians in their toast. A few hours ago, Natasha had given him a crash course in a few Russians dos and don'ts. He tilted his head back and let the liquid fire flow down his gullet in one swoop.

Henry shook his head. "That was strong..."

His comment made Petrov and the Ambassador smile.

Rostov rolled his eyes. "You Brits can be so tame."

Upstage put his glass in the centre of the table. "Let's have another one, then."

The idea was greeted with acclamation. Rostov took the bottle and poured vodka into each glass.

"Cheers... to a beautiful association." The six men downed their vodka again. Andropov was the last one to return his glass to the centre of the table.

"Let's continue this fruitful conversation in a few days' time." Andropov grinned. "Moscow is a wonderful city you will love."

Chapter Twenty-Three

"Nick… I can hardly hear you." Jack parked his car after the traffic lights. Nick's voice sounded far away, and yet the line was clear.

"Something strange has happened." Nick managed to articulate despite his breathing sounding erratic.

"Where are you?"

"In Henry's apartment."

Jack looked at his watch. He was on his way to Arlington, but could cross the Potomac at Chain Bridge instead and make his way to Massachusetts Avenue along the north side of the river.

"I'll be with you in less than 20 minutes."

Jack rejoined the flow of cars moving along the river and did a U-turn. He ignored the flurry of horns that sounded following his manoeuvre. He was in the mood to tell the complaining drivers to get lost but thought better of it. A spell of road rage was not what he needed right now.

He ignored the speed limit, quite a few red lights, and accepted the possible threat of being chased down by police who might take him as a rogue driver.

Jack parked in front of Henry's apartment within the time.

The lights were on inside. He hesitated, then opened his rucksack and took his Sig Sauer out of it. He pushed it into the small of his back, took the spare key he always kept on his key ring in case of emergencies, left his car, and entered the building. At Henry's door he knocked, and opened the door slowly without waiting for a reply.

The apartment was quiet, and he could hear sounds coming from what he recollected was the kitchen from the plans he'd seen before.

Jack followed the small entrance hall to the end, waited again, hand on the butt of his gun. Nick's reflection in the tall windows of the lounge was showing him making something in the kitchen.

Jack stepped into view, prompting Nick to grab a knife from the sideboard.

"I did knock." Jack relaxed at the sight of the wobbly knife. "That's not the way to hold a weapon if you're looking to defend yourself."

Nick looked at the long blade and dropped it on the worktop. "Yeah, well, it's not as if I've been part of the agency for long."

"The service," Jack corrected, pursing his lips. "You joined the Brits, remember?"

Nick was about to speak, but he grew unsteady on his feet. He grabbed the kitchen top. Jack grabbed his arm and slowly led him over to one of the armchairs in the lounge.

Jack sat on the coffee table in front of him. "Tell me what happened."

After a short moment Nick started his story.

"I was told to check the apartment regularly. So when I came home, I went straight upstairs... I mean, to here. Everything was fine." Nick hesitated. "Then everything went dark, like a massive power surge. I went to the electric board to check the fuses. They'd tripped."

"All of them?"

"Yes. I switched the electricity on again. Went back to the lounge and then –" Nick stopped, clearly struggling with how to describe what occurred next. "I don't know whether I passed out or what, but I woke up on the sofa, feeling really odd."

Jack eyebrows shot up. "Do you mind if I take a look at your neck?"

Nick looked surprised, but he nodded. Jack moved closer and checked the skin on both sides. It looked intact, apart from a small, red area on the left side. Jack pressed on the red spot. Nick flinched but said nothing.

"You've been drugged."

"What? How? I didn't drink anything from anywhere."

Jack lifted a hand to calm Nick down. "I don't quite believe it myself, but someone got into this apartment and administered drugs to you through a small needle or dart. I haven't seen that done in a very long time."

Nick's eyes opened wider. "Someone was here?"

"Yes, created a power surge, got into the apartment without you noticing, and darted you."

"Motherfucker…"

Nick looked indignant, much to Jack's surprise. He'd expected scared, but the young man was, simply very… very annoyed he'd been played.

"I presume the power surge also tripped the surveillance systems you've installed?" Jack asked.

"What do you take me for…? Of course not. I have a backup. Special battery operation. It can't support the entire network of cameras and audio, but it functions in a few key places."

"Impressive." Jack smiled. "Where are these key places then?"

"Above the entrance door, and in the lounge overlooking the vault."

"Can you access it now?"

"Sure." Nick turned towards the kitchen. "I could do with a coffee first though."

"You get your equipment and I'll make the coffee."

Nick stood up, still a bit unsteady on his legs. Jack reached for him. "I'll be fine."

He disappeared, and Jack rummaged through Henry's cupboards, to find the ingredients for a decent cup of coffee.

Nick returned a few minutes later with a laptop that looked as though it had been fished out of a recycling bin. "I use it a lot on the go."

Jack didn't ask what the *on the go* meant.

Nick logged in and called up the screen with the surveillance backup. Nick sat on the sofa. Jack joined him. He turned the laptop so Jack could see the screen.

By the time the backup had started the intruder was already in the lounge, moving the rug back to inspect the floorboards.

"Shit…" Nick blurted.

They saw the intruder prod the floor, find the catch, and discover the vault underneath. The intruder was taking pictures of the safe.

"Shit is definitely the word." Jack ran his hand over his neck. "Whoever that person is he's a pro, and has access to drugs not easily found in the private sector."

"Another agency?" Nick frowned. "Or is it service?"

Jack grumbled that it didn't matter which word he used.

Nick nodded and enlarged the picture of the man on screen. Nick stopped to check a detail.

"Anything useful?"

Nick hesitated, then shook his head. He locked eyes with Nick for a moment, but the young man didn't offer anything new.

Jack pulled a worried face. "The fact is Henry's cover is starting to look very thin if another agency is investigating his apartment and has discovered the safe."

"He is at the Russian Embassy."

"I know. Let me make a call. I want to be sure he gets out of there in one piece and alive."

* * *

The two bankers were chatting away about how best to move forward with the new deal they had coined: an $810m loan to Upstage from Mueller's Swiss bank against the risk cover from Petrov's Russian bank.

The group of men from the meeting rejoined the guests shortly before the end of the conference. As people were pouring back into the reception room for more drinks, Henry had got hold of Mueller and made the introduction to Petrov.

Henry slowly disengaged from the conversation when he felt no longer needed. Rostov and Upstage were now talking about the trip to Russia. Andropov was engaged in a lively conversation with the two representatives from the far-right in France and Italy. It was rather bold, but perhaps there was a message Russia wanted to give the West as a whole – we're supporting these racist, fascist bastards and we don't care what the pro-democracy wimps say. Fuck you!

Henry was pondering what it all meant for Europe and America, when the English businessman and politician he'd met in Washington interrupted his thoughts.

Nevil Ferguson was standing too close to him, eyes shiny with too much drink. "You no longer seem busy with your contacts."

"I'm almost done for the evening. It's been a long day. I flew in this morning from DC." Henry looked around for someone to save him from a conversation with Ferguson.

Edward Bound joined his mate. "You can't go before meeting with our friends from France and Italy."

"David might need me..." Henry checked on Upstage, but he was still busy with Rostov.

"Won't take a moment." Ferguson insisted in a way that put Henry on alert.

It didn't help that Botha had still not turned up for the party. Perhaps he'd stayed in DC to oversee Upstage's affairs and start shaping his presidency campaign. Wherever he was, his absence was casting a long shadow over Henry's evening. Botha was clearly not convinced about Henry's allegiance to the cause and was happily hunting for ways to prove it.

Henry managed a smile. "Looks like David is still engaged with Mikhail... Sure, it's an excellent opportunity to meet like-minded people."

The two men looked suitably impressed with Henry's casual use of the billionaires' first names.

Henry stilled himself in preparation to meet them. The two far-right Europeans were surrounded by a small gathering of *friends* who were exchanging views on immigration policies and the evils of Europe.

The French woman was the first to notice Henry. She had short blonde hair, brown eyes, an attractive smile, and spoke English with a strong American accent. Her Italian co-conspirator was less interested in the introduction, annoyed he'd been interrupted. Henry nevertheless extended a hand. The man's attitude changed miraculously as soon as he was told about Henry's connection to Upstage.

"A great-ah man with a great-ah future." The Italian accent was strong whilst he gave his short eulogy of Upstage.

The group gathered around Henry to ask him about the US elections. Was Hillary Clinton going to win? Yet another Democrat – a disgrace and a threat to America's greatness.

Henry answered with the confidence of a man who had learnt to identify BS but also deliver it if needs be. The City of London had been an excellent training ground. Everyone was nodding at his delivery. Someone squeezed next to him whilst he was in full flow. Then he noticed Natasha. The look of urgency on her face almost stopped him in his tracks.

"I apologise for this interruption," Natasha said with smooth confidence.

The group almost moved as one, giving her an understanding nod. Anyone close to Upstage unavoidably had urgent matters to attend to.

Henry's first fear was that Allner-Smith had finally recognised him.

"Harris needs a word. It's urgent," Natasha whispered.

His jaw clenched. Was Harris finally aware of Allner-Smith's presence?

"Tell him I'll call on my way back to the flat in Marylebone."

Natasha frowned. "But –"

"I know why he's calling. I'm fine." Upstage was looking in his direction. "I've got to go."

Henry made his way to the corner where Upstage was standing on his own. Rostov had disappeared for the evening, and so had the two bankers.

"Beautiful outcome." Upstage nodded. "We've been invited to Moscow for further conversation."

Henry didn't bother to thank Upstage for his compliment. By not doing so, Henry was telling him that he knew what he could deliver. But it was a gamble to ignore a man with such an ego.

"How quickly do they want us there?"

"Day after tomorrow. The Ambassador and Rostov are flying to Moscow. We've been invited to join them on Mikhail's private jet." Henry was right in his assumption. Upstage hadn't taken offence. He needed Henry now more than ever.

"That gives us one day to prepare. Let's meet tomorrow afternoon," Henry suggested. "I'll cancel my other appointments."

"I'll get my PA to organise the meeting."

Henry nodded. "Who else is accompanying us to Moscow?"

"Botha is already there." Upstage took his mobile out of his pocket. "And Tatiana will join us. She just called."

Henry looked for Natasha, but she was no longer around. Instead, Brett Allner-Smith walked straight to him, extending a hand.

"I don't believe we've met," he said almost grabbing Henry's hand from his side. "Brett Allner-Smith..." He shook Henry's hand, then proceeded to shake Upstage's hand too.

He said to Henry, "Your translator, Natasha, was looking for you a minute ago. I believe it was urgent."

* * *

The picture was enlarged on the biggest screen Nick owned. There was something odd about the hoodie that he couldn't quite figure out. The closest he could get to defining what troubled him was that the clothes hung weirdly on the intruder.

Nick ruffled his hair with both hands and entered his kitchen. He and Jack had left Henry's apartment secure. Well, as secure as it could be, with a promise from Nick to call Jack as soon as he found something new.

Nick made another cup of coffee. His head was still a little light from the drug he had been given. He rubbed his neck in a slow gingerly move, and winced.

"Bastard..."

Having been played was much worse than the small wound. He took his coffee back to his desk. The four screens he'd had installed there were active with data streaming and footage of the backup surveillance system. Nick took a mouthful of coffee and fished his battered laptop from the floor, where he'd dropped it after returning home from Henry's flat.

It took him almost an hour to find what he was looking for. He placed a request for entry into the chat room and waited. The Pieper didn't like to be intruded upon, but Nick was in crisis mode. He needed help.

The image on Nick's computer screen morphed into a brilliant sunrise, and a small dot in its centre transformed into a hooded figure.

"Hello, Nick." The same synthesised voice greeted him.

"Hello, Pieper. I don't mean to chase but I need your help, big time."

"Everybody says that."

"Not fair. I never do." Nick was offended, and quite rightly too, in his opinion.

"My friend, that is true." The small figure nodded. "New developments, I guess?"

"You can say that, yeah." Nick told The Pieper what had happened; the man didn't interrupt.

"And now you want me to help ID this intruder?" The Pieper's voice had become serious. "Send me all you have right away."

Nick moved to his computer, shifting the laptop to one side, so that he could still see The Pieper. He created a zip file and sent the lot to him.

"Got it... Stay online."

236

The small figure started moving around, and Nick wondered whether The Pieper was using augmented reality goggles to move around the landscapes he created.

Nick drank his coffee slowly. When the cup was empty, he stayed put.

"One thing's for sure," The Pieper's voice announced after a little while, "this ain't a man you're looking for, my friend, but a woman."

"Are you sure?"

The synthesised voice spluttered and guffawed into laughter. "A zillion percent. You've been tranquilised by a little lady."

"She was not little and I'm not sure she qualifies as a lady."

"Just kidding. I could be one of these little ladies."

"Is there anything else I've missed on the footage?" Nick asked.

"Not sure. I'll need to give it a more in-depth look. I can also try CCTV cameras of your area."

"I can do that too."

"Then why don't you get access to one of those and call me again if you run into trouble. Tell this boss of yours Henry that I'm in. I've made some progress, but I need a little more time." The Pieper was moving around the screen again.

"Anything you can share?"

"Not until I'm sure." The rising sun brightened the horizon of Nick's laptop screen, until it exploded into hundreds of fragments, announcing it was the end of the chat.

Nick shut down his laptop and returned to his computer screen. He closed the surveillance camera file. Called up another piece of software he'd used before to follow McNamara on his trip to the Russian Embassy in DC.

Nick was still working on gaining access when his mobile rang. Henry's name was flashing on screen. Nick froze.

Had Henry been told about the early evening disaster? Was he going to be mad that he'd called Jack first? But it had been an emergency. Henry would never have been caught out the way Nick had.

The call went to voice mail.

"Shit..." Nick grabbed his phone, about to ring back, but he paused. Perhaps he should do a little more research and have something to show for his bad night.

237

Nick went back to the task at hand, to gain access to the CCTV cameras around the building's perimeter.

* * *

Brett had struck up a conversation with Upstage about antiquities and Upstage looked genuinely impressed by what Brett had to tell him.

Natasha walked straight up to Henry and pushed her mobile into his hand, with one set of instructions: "Call him." She'd just had had a coded conversation with Harris. Henry had overheard her having a blazing row with her boyfriend – for the purpose of the Russian eavesdropping team.

It had all been about being out with a single and very eligible man named Henry Newborn.

Henry grabbed her phone in annoyance. He walked out of the room, found a spot that looked reasonably secluded and made the call.

Harris picked up instantly.

"Why are you still at the Embassy with *her*?" He spoke in code.

"Because it's my job and hers as well." Henry's return salvo of anger had been scripted, so no surprise there.

"You need to bugger off, or I'll be the one coming to the goddamn Embassy to pull you out." Harris was telling Henry he needed to leave now.

"You shouldn't be worried about me. Your girlfriend is very happy to be chatting up other blokes. She seems to rather like this guy, Brett, who was the guest speaker tonight." Henry was still pissed off about not being told about Allner-Smith – even more so now that Brett had been used to approach him.

Harris didn't falter at Henry's angry remark. "He'll get it in the neck too if he does anything stupid, but right now it's you I'm talking to."

"You're being ridiculously jealous and rather pathetic. Unless you have another good reason, I'm staying put." Henry was not playing ball. He would not compromise a successful evening. If Harris wanted him out, he would have to...

Henry taunted, "Come and get me."

He killed the call and returned to find Natasha in deep conversation with Upstage and Brett. Henry had to give it to her. She had a knack with people.

Henry handed the mobile to her. "All sorted," he said with a smile and joined the group.

He hadn't seen Brett in over eight years, and he was only half surprised to discover the man was clearly one of MI6's assets. Brett had hardly made eye contact with Henry all night, and Henry wondered what Harris had on him that could compel Brett to work for him.

Brett kept talking a good story to Upstage about salvaging antiquities of great value from the mayhem that was the Middle East. Upstage was in his element, stressing the superiority of the West when it came to conservation.

"All these countries wanting their pieces back, and for what? They should be honoured our museums agreed to display them at all." Upstage loved the controversy.

"I couldn't agree more," said Brett. "And at least if they are in museums, they are not being blown to bits by the jihadists... But taking them out of the country, not everybody can do that. Some people don't like to take the risk." Brett's dig at Henry made him wonder how far he would go if matters turned tough tonight.

Upstage's mobile phone rang again. He took it out of his pocket and checked it, but didn't answer. He put it back.

"Tatiana?" Henry ventured.

"That's right." Upstage turned back to Brett and the slagging off of countries in the Middle East continued, as well as Obama's "Dis-as-trous" policy and intervention over there, according to Brett.

Brett seemed content to fuel the conversation with even more controversial arguments. He was in no hurry to leave, despite the late hour. There were very few people left now. Henry stifled a yawn, looked at his watch. Upstage caught the move.

"It's been good to meet so many beautiful people." Upstage made a move that indicated he was about to leave. His phone rang again.

He walked away from the small gathering without apologising.

"I'll be on my way too." Henry nodded to Natasha and Brett.

"If I were you, I would leave now." Brett pursed his lips. "He is talking to the woman you mentioned, Tatiana. He may not notice you've left.."

Natasha was yet on another call to her fake boyfriend. She hung up abruptly and Henry didn't have time to ask why Brett thought he should leave right away.. Natasha had said her goodbyes to Brett. She turned to Henry. "I need a lift... now. The boyfriend is getting very agitated."

Henry was about to protest when he saw Upstage looking over his shoulder at him. Perhaps Tatiana had other things to talk about than simply the trip to Moscow.

Natasha led the way towards the exit. A couple of security personnel were waiting near the cloakroom.

Henry hesitated when he saw them. He considered leaving their coats, but it would look odd if they both walked out without them in the middle of winter. The two businessmen Henry had spoken at length were also leaving.

"Superb evening," Ferguson commented. His friend tried to engage in more conversation as they were being handed their coats and bags.

Henry shook hands with them. To shut them up, he promised they *must have lunch or dinner.*

The security team radioed to their colleagues at the door that people were about to leave.

Henry and Natasha walked down the long corridor. One of the guards was unlocking the front door. His walkie-talkie crackled with a voice and the door stayed shut.

The man at the door stopped Henry with a hand to his chest.

"You're wanted back in the main room," he said in his heavy Russian accent.

Chapter Twenty-Four

"Harris, it's one o'clock in the morning," Henry protested.

"So bloody what? You told me to come and get you and I have." Harris's slight East End accent got stronger with anger.

Henry walked to the window in the Marylebone flat and looked outside. A black cab had parked opposite the entrance to his building. The hiring light was off, and it looked as though the driver was waiting for its passenger to get in.

"Are you serious?"

"Completely. You and I are going for a cab ride. And before you ask, I have re-checked the Marylebone flat is not under surveillance. You have 5 minutes before I break your door down."

Harris hung up and Henry threw the towel he had put in haste around his waist as he walked out of the shower to answer Harris's call. He donned a pair of dark jeans, a T-shirt and a thick jumper, chose a pair of running shoes, and left his flat a few minutes later.

Harris was in the driver's seat. As soon as Henry got in the back, he drove off.

Henry looked around. "This is a novelty. Since when do you drive a black cab?"

"Since I have to meet some pigheaded agent who can't follow the course of action we agreed."

"This is goddamn rich, Harris, coming from you. Why didn't you tell me I was about to meet Allner-Smith?"

"The RUSSKY BEAR op has many moving parts you don't need to know the details of. Brett was – is under control, as you've seen."

Henry leaned forward, left hand tightly squeezing the handle above the door. "But did I know that when he turned up? No." He could thump Harris.

"So says the man who was worried about blowing his cover, and now you're going all gung-ho on me when there is a real issue?"

"The Russians let me out of the Embassy, so where's the big problem you're talking about?"

"You were lucky that it was only Upstage exercising a bit of authority by calling you back into the room and nothing else."

"Stop complaining, Harris. One moment you want me to deliver Upstage and his clique of far-right nutters, as well as their Russian contacts, and the next you want me to pull out at the worst time."

Harris stopped at a set of traffic lights and turned around to Henry. "Your apartment in DC has been compromised. Someone got in, tranquilised Nick with a dart and went through your things thoroughly. They also found the vault. Do I have your attention now?" His gruff expression underneath his cap gave him the look of a bad boy looking for trouble.

Henry sank into the back seat of the cab. "Fuck... How did that happen? I thought Nick had installed a new surveillance system."

"He did, but I rather think whoever got in is a well-seasoned pro."

Henry's jaw tightened. "Is Nick all right?"

"Apart from a bruised ego, he is fine."

Henry shook his head. "He's still very green."

"From what Jack told me he took it pretty well. He is a resourceful lad."

"I'm not sure he'd like to be called a lad, but at least there was nothing of value left in the apartment."

"You told him not to play James Bond, I hope?" Harris drove on as soon as the lights had turned green.

"Of course, that part is reserved for me." Henry managed a smile.

"Someone is now on your tail," Harris grumbled. "And may I remind you of the body count?"

"We can't give up. What I've unearthed is far too big." Henry's mind drifted back to Nick.

"Who says we're giving up? But extending your stay at the Russian Embassy was careless. What if that person had reported their findings to the Russians or Upstage?"

Henry was about to shoot a quick reply, but thought it through instead. "That's a really good point, you know."

Harris shot a murderous look at him in the rear-view mirror. "I am serious, Crowne. You should have done as agreed. The coded message was clear. I had new, actionable intel that meant you needed to leave."

"And I'm bloody serious too." Henry leaned forward again. "Perhaps I'll concede that I should have been more careful, but why haven't we seen a fallout yet?"

"I don't follow you?" A frowning Harris glanced over his shoulder.

"Think about it. Any diligent agent or hired pro would have reported on what they'd found, right? If we assume that the level of sophistication of the intruder means intelligence services, then yes, I agree, I would have had a very unpleasant end to my evening at the Russian Embassy. Or an army of spooks would be trying to take me out in London... but instead nothing."

Harris gave a slow nod, keeping his eyes on the road. "I'm listening."

"I think whoever has the information is holding back."

"Why would that be?" Harris was not discarding the idea outright.

"A bargaining chip maybe or leverage? I'm not sure."

"While we don't know what that person wants, you need to be careful when dealing with Upstage."

"Careful yes, but the risk has gone up a lot, Steve." Henry shook his head. "I'm going to Russia with him tomorrow onboard Rostov's private jet."

Harris parked the cab in the first free space he found.

"Shit, this guy's timing really sucks."

"But it's what we've been waiting for. If I don't go the RUSSKY BEAR op is dead. The Russians will know they've been outed and they'll go to ground."

Harris took out a packet of cigarettes from his jacket pocket, fidgeted with one of the cigarettes. He took a lighter out of the same pocket and lit his smoke.

He turned around partially.

"You are convinced Upstage has a chance to win the presidency?" Harris wry face was suddenly serious.

"I would not be putting myself in danger if I didn't think that. The guy is a psycho with zero moral compass. The only thing that matters to David Upstage is David Upstage."

"I hear you." Harris dragged on his cigarette; the tip grew bright red in the darkness.

"Backup would be good." Henry placed his elbows on his knees, hands loosely folded together.

"That goes without saying. I'll get James appointed as your new business attaché this morning. There may be a day's lag, but he'll be in Moscow one day after you."

"What about Natasha? She's made a big impact already. Upstage and the Russians have met her."

"She shouldn't have been there in the first place. Even if I crawl on my knees in front of the chief, cap in hand, he won't let her go."

"How about she takes a few days' holiday?"

"She's not trained." Harris half protested, but Henry could see his heart was not in it.

"You could have fooled me." Natasha had played her part beautifully tonight.

"You'll be going straight into the beast's lair."

"I've got a feeling she knows that lair pretty well."

Harris shook his head. "She does, been listening to them at GCHQ, using an inside knowledge few have."

"You're not convinced it's a bad idea?" Henry turned his head to see Harris better.

"I'm completely convinced it's a bad idea, but we would be bringing GCHQ capability to the trip, and you're going to need that."

"Is it a yes?"

"It's a maybe. I'll let you know this afternoon."

Henry sat back into his seat again. Harris opened the window and flicked the butt of his cigarette onto the street. He started the cab and moved out onto the road. They both fell silent for the rest of the journey.

Harris parked the cab in front of Henry's block of flats. Henry pretended as though he were paying the driver.

He was about to leave the cab when Harris turned partially to face him.

"If you're having second thoughts, I'll understand."

Henry nodded, opened the door and stepped out. He caught some movement in his peripheral vision. Looked like the Russian surveillance machinery had caught up with him.

244

The initial images Nick had found of the intruder disappointed him. She was walking along the street, her face still hidden by the hoodie, but there was nothing concerning about her pace. She could have been walking back from a friend's house or heading home after work.

Nick muttered a string of insults and the idea of following this self-assured little madam gave him a kick. But his enthusiasm did not last long. A few blocks away from Logan Circle, the set of cameras he was following returned only blank images.

"No, no..." Nick kept repeating the same word, trying to regain access to the signal, but there was nothing.

"Shit, fuck, God damn it!" Nick shouted, no longer caring about keeping his voice down. The tall figure had vanished around the corner of a street. He fell back into his chair. The Pieper had said to call him if there was an issue.

Nick shook his head. He could do this by himself.

He called up a map of the area where he'd lost the signal, and checked for all possible routes the woman could have taken. He could try to systematically review all the cameras in the immediate vicinity of the small area near where the other cameras were showing no footage, and he had therefore lost her.

Nick went into his kitchen, didn't bother with a cup but this time made of pot of coffee and returned to his desk. A couple of hours later he still had nothing to show for his efforts. It was as though the woman had vanished into thin air.

He discarded the idea of her living within the area. It was too obvious. The alternative was that she'd changed her appearance so much she would be difficult to spot.

Nick leaned back in his chair, heels of his hands pressed against his temples. He straightened up again and returned to his keyboard. He discarded any change of clothes that was so dramatic he wouldn't be able to find her. She might also still be trying to hide her face.

"Two ways – first, she parks her car in the area where the cameras don't work. In that case no way to spot her. Bummer..." Nick called up the CCTV footage he had been reviewing earlier.

"Or, second – she used a bike and a helmet..." Nick trawled through the camera footage. A few bikes appeared but they were being driven by men.

245

His eyes grew heavy, and he'd almost fallen asleep twice already. Then he noticed a tall, slim biker on his computer screen. The body was a little bulkier with the leather jacket, but the long legs looked identical to the intruder's. More importantly, the person was wearing the same dark jeans as the intruder.

Nick stood up in one jump and pointed at the screen.

"Got you...!"

With a grin, he returned to the kitchen to brew another pot of coffee, deliberating whether he should call The Pieper or Henry.

"Nope, too early."

Nick returned to his desk, armed with the right amount of caffeine to carry him until he found where she lived.

The bike had been much easier to follow than he had anticipated. It had turned into a small street where Nick had then lost sight of her, but he'd checked the possible other exit route and he was now certain she'd stopped in Allen Pl.

Nick jotted down an address. Kalorama district, Allen Pl NW.

He looked at his watch, almost 2am here in DC, 7am in London. Nick shook his head once more. He needed some sleep first, then he would call Henry.

* * *

The mobile phone went to voice mail. Why was Nick not answering? Henry switched off the burner phone, logged out of his laptop, and readied himself for his planned meeting with Upstage.

His morning had been spent on a secure line speaking with James about the impending trip to Russia. Henry had been to Moscow many years ago, before he'd worked for GL Investments, the bank that had made him famous.

James, on the other hand, had been there recently, and from what he described, the city was very different to what Henry remembered.

Henry's visit to Moscow was shortly after the Berlin Wall had come down. It was the early '90s and everything was in short supply. The Soviet Union had collapsed, and the future looked full of new possibilities. He had visited the small outpost of the UK bank he was working for then, and had brought some shortbread biscuits and Marmite for the colleagues he was meeting there.

Henry shook his head at the memory.

James had described a very different city to his, with ultra-luxurious suburbs that housed the rich and famous, who had benefitted from an open market economy. It was not supposed to have gone that way, but the allocation of national resources to a small number of men close to the Kremlin had created a class of citizens removed from the rest of the Russian people. The political sweetener had been a somewhat improved standard of living, but was it enough?

Henry placed the burner phone into his rucksack, then followed with the laptop. He was not leaving anything in this flat. He was almost certain someone from the Russian surveillance team he had spotted last night would pay a visit.

The black cab he'd ordered had already arrived. Henry looked around once more. Paranoia was about to become his greatest friend. Someone now suspected he was a CIA agent or an MI6 intelligence officer. He hoped that his analysis of why that person had not come forward was right, otherwise his trip to Moscow would prove very uncomfortable.

The taxi ride took him to the Corinthia Hotel on Whitehall, a stone's throw from Buckingham Palace. Upstage had booked a suite there, and at £24,000 a night Henry expected it to be spectacular.

He was not disappointed. After the usual security checks and only cursory frisking, Henry was introduced to the Royal Penthouse on the top floor of the hotel. Upstage was on the roof terrace in his coat, nursing a cup of coffee and taking in the view.

The penthouse suite took advantage of the situation and shape of the hotel... at the end of a leafy street, overlooking the River Thames, the London Eye and in the far distance Big Ben and the Houses of Parliament. Upstage waved Henry onto the terrace.

"Just amazing, absolutely great," Upstage gushed. "The Russian Ambassador told me this was the best place in London. The man is such a star."

"It's impressive." Henry had to agree. The view was spectacular, and the weather, clear and sunny despite being cold, made it even more so.

Upstage finished his coffee and dragged himself from the spectacle he'd been mesmerised by.

"Yesterday went well," he said. "I think our Russian friends are starting to get the message."

"Agreed. Andropov is the man to convince. Even Rostov will defer to him when it comes to involving RNB."

"Andropov is the man who will also make political decisions. No one else can, and no one else is as close to the Kremlin as he is."

"I fail to see why the Kremlin would refuse your offer."

Upstage gave Henry an indulgent smile. "It's more than accepting my offer. I want other things from them."

He sat on a chair on the terrace. Henry sat at an angle to Upstage.

"You want some social media help with your campaign." Henry looked at him when he made the statement. He felt an instant change in attitude from Upstage.

Upstage perked up. "What makes you say that?"

"Because this is where opinions can be formed and –" Henry thought about the word he wanted to use "– reshaped or affirmed."

He checked if Upstage was annoyed by his perceptive remarks. But Upstage was grinning.

"You pick up things pretty quickly... I'm glad you're on the team."

"These are exciting times. Reshaping the political landscape of America is a once-in-a-lifetime opportunity."

Upstage nodded vigorously. "And we are just getting started."

Henry couldn't stop the chill that ran along his spine.

"I met some interesting people from France and Italy last night," said Henry. "They are getting very organised."

"They are, and the exchange of information between like-minded people is so much easier with the internet. Botha's website has links to other European countries, Germany and Austria of course, but also Spain, Portugal, and Eastern European countries like Hungary and Ukraine."

"Is Botha using the dark web?"

Upstage was taken aback by the question.

Henry quickly added, "Only I haven't found Botha's website, not for want of searching."

"I'm afraid the world is not yet ready for what we have to say, but the time is coming when we will soon be able to speak openly about the impending white genocide." Upstage was being dramatic. Henry

248

couldn't figure out whether he was putting on an act or believed what he was saying.

"When did Botha start his movement?" Henry asked.

"As soon as he realised there was a systematic elimination of white farmers being carried out in South Africa, or that their land was being unlawfully confiscated."

Henry nodded. He had never heard about such nonsense and he struggled to believe Upstage.

"That must have been very bad."

"Very bad people... very bad people." Upstage pulled a face and stood up. "Let's get in and prepare for the trip to Moscow."

Upstage moved inside, rang the butler's bell and asked for more coffee. He started talking to Henry about the excellent antiques dealer they had met last night. Brett had made an impression.

"I'll invite him to Washington. I need to improve the décor in my office there."

"I'm sure he can find the perfect pieces that will give the place the right authority."

"Authority... good word."

Coffee was served and Upstage focused on the terms he was prepared to accept from the banks. He had thought it through in detail, and the capacity Upstage had for deep-thinking when he applied his mind surprised Henry.

They went through the deal with the Swiss bank, DSB. Upstage omitted only minor points. When it came to the transaction between the Russian bank RNB and DSB, Henry pointed out that Upstage would not be privy to the deal.

"On paper this is true," Upstage said. "But these two lovely banks are going to price my offer in a way that will get Russia involved at the highest level for when I am in place. I want to have a say in the deal."

"I see your point, but I don't think Petrov from RNB will do anything without the Kremlin's approval. You need to engage with Andropov."

"And *I* don't want only one transaction to be underwritten by RNB." Upstage poured himself some more coffee, added some sugar, and stirred, scraping his spoon against the bottom of the cup.

Henry sat back. "That's an interesting idea. A permanent undertaking to support your credit score against a direct line into the White House."

"That's only fair..." Upstage added. "A direct line into the most powerful office in the world is worth a lot of money."

"I couldn't agree more." Henry was almost impressed by the boldness of the man.

Upstage locked his gaze on Henry. "And since it is your job, I'd like you to suggest an amount."

"It will be my pleasure. It's a complicated task that I'm looking forward to meeting." Henry both grinned and chastised himself at the same time. Yes, he was going to enjoy the challenge. He just needed to make sure he didn't enjoy it too much.

The conversation focused on the methods Henry might use to come up with a number, and what that number might be. After arguing on the number of billions he had in mind, Upstage stood up and walked to the sliding doors leading out to the terrace. His mobile rang and he opened the door to step outside.

Henry saw playfulness on Upstage's face as he took the call. He was having a conversation with a woman; Henry wondered whether this was Tatiana.

Upstage returned and threw the mobile on the sofa.

"Good news?" Henry asked.

"It's all looking good. Tatiana is on her way, and Botha has been having positive conversations with like-minded people in Russia." Upstage looked more relaxed, less guarded than he had been so far.

Henry looked at his watch. "Has Tatiana arrived? Most commercial flights land at this hour in London."

"No, she's on a private jet with one of her friends on her way to Moscow..." Upstage trailed off. His mind was already on something that drove him as much as success – beautiful women.

Chapter Twenty-Five

The Boeing 787-8 BBJ glided over the runway for less than a minute, before landing with a small thud on the tarmac of Kubinka military airbase in Moscow Oblast. Rostov's private jet had been one of the most opulent Henry had ever been on. His days of hitching a ride aboard the jet of the CEO of GL Investments Bank had shown him corporate luxury, but this was wealth on a different scale.

The inside of the plane had been fitted with a dining room, a couple of lounges – which were used also for landing and takeoff – an office kitted out with the latest tech, and a spacious bedroom. Rostov had bragged about how comfortable the bed was and Upstage had laughed heartily. Henry had joined in, of course. He had to pretend to be one of the boys. He'd also heard far worse bragging on the trading floor.

The Boeing rolled towards a hangar, whilst a couple of MIG fighter jets took off in a clap of thunder. The plane eventually parked alongside a Sukhoi Su-57, the most recent attack aircraft designed for the Russian military. Harris had sent Henry a guide for what he could expect to encounter on Russian soil. Henry looked outside to check how many aircraft were parked at the base. He counted at least 20 jets.

The two pretty stewardesses who had looked after them during the 4-hour flight stood up, to make sure the three men didn't need anything before they disembarked.

Rostov shook his head and spoke a few words in Russian to one of them. She responded and he seemed relieved she had given Rostov the information he as expecting. Rostov had the right connections; not many could land at one of the military bases, the closest to Moscow, and have a couple of limos with security personnel waiting for them. Rostov's own bodyguards were already at the door of the aircraft, ready to disembark and check the credentials of the people working at the airbase.

Rostov stood up as soon as the aircraft stopped. Henry did the same. Upstage took his time, waiting for one of the stewardesses to come and help him. Henry was curious to see if there would be some luggage checks, but the hold was already open. The luggage was being transferred to the boot of the limos on the ground.

The checks at London City Airport had been extensive for Upstage, Henry and their suitcases, before they'd boarded Rostov's private jet. Henry had left behind any items that might prove controversial. His new laptop had been equipped with encrypted technology that was impossible to detect upon simple inspection; his mobile phone was in the same category. He would get the rest of the equipment he needed from a connection at the British Embassy in Moscow.

The main door of the aircraft opened, and a blast of freezing air rushed through the plane. Henry grabbed the thick, waterproof down coat he had been told was essential, and his hat. Upstage was still chatting up the blonde stewardess and didn't seem to notice the arctic air invading the space.

Rostov stood on the top of the steps that had been brought in and checked by his security team. He breathed in deep and laughed. "Welcome to Russia. This cold will freeze you stiff, my friends. Beware."

As Rostov's heavy steps resounded on the metallic stairs, the door of one of the limos opened, and a tall figure emerged from the vehicle. Tatiana was wearing a fur coat, tailored to her figure. Her blonde hair was loose and the hat she was wearing almost covered her eyes.

Rostov spoke to her as soon as he reached the tarmac, then he disappeared into one of the limos. Henry stood at the top of the aircraft. Tatiana looked in his direction for an instant and smiled. She moved closer to the bottom of the stairs.

"He is going to his house directly," Upstage said as he joined Henry, ready to disembark as well.

Tatiana nodded.

"Let's go." Henry walked down the stairs, smiling and yet shivering at the same time.

Tatiana asked, "Not too cold for you?"

252

"Freezing," Henry admitted.

He stopped next to her, turning around to check on Upstage's progress. The man had disappeared back inside the plane, preparing himself no doubt for his grand entrance to Moscow.

Henry removed his glove and extended a hand to Tatiana. "Good to see you again."

Tatiana removed her own fur-lined leather glove and placed her hand in Henry's.

"I'm very happy you made it on this trip," she said, squeezing Henry's hand for a little longer than might be expected. Henry returned her grip with a warm clasp that he was the first to break.

Upstage appeared at the top of the stairs again, dressed in a long fur coat and a trendy fur toque. He could have risked looking ridiculous, but he had chosen a good combination that made him appear more local than foreign.

Tatiana grinned and clapped a few times as he walked down the stairs.

"Hello, David. You look splendid in your winter outfit."

Upstage grinned back and bent forward to kiss her cheek. They all got into the limo.

Less than an hour after they'd left Kubinka military airbase, the limo pulled into the arches outside The Ritz-Carlton on Tverskaya street. The presence of security detail and cars had helped make it a smooth and speedy ride.

A couple was getting out of another black limo and the doorman greeted them when they walked in. Henry surveyed the front of the hotel in the time it took for the driver to stop the car at the main entrance and for three porters to open the car doors and start unloading luggage.

The building was a superb expression of 18th century Imperial Russian architecture, large cream stones, some of them rendered and painted red, with tall windows and fancy garland detail. It could have been too heavy but instead it was elegantly opulent.

At reception, Tatiana gave the two men's names. She had arrived yesterday and was already set up in one of the large superior rooms, at the end of the corridor and on the same floor as the Carlton Suite Upstage had reserved at the top of the hotel. Henry was not on the same floor, he noticed, when Tatiana handed the electronic key to him.

She gave him a curious look, to which Henry smiled. It didn't matter. He had already sprayed a special combination of chemicals on Upstage's shoes yesterday that would enable him and James to trace Upstage wherever he went in Moscow. Henry wasn't sure James had arrived yet at the Embassy, but he hoped he had.

The porter opened Henry's room for him, giving him a quick overview of all its features. It was a typical five-star luxury room, with an additional remarkable view of Red Square on the left and the Kremlin on the right. Henry tipped the porter and asked to be called by reception at 4pm. The man nodded and disappeared.

Henry looked around the room. There were plenty of ornaments where surveillance equipment could be placed, including small cameras similar to the ones implanted in the buttons of his suit jacket – 1 millimetre in size and as small as a grain of salt.

Henry had been allocated a room with two double beds. One of the beds was slightly off centre, closer to the corridor than where it had been placed previously. The indentations made by the legs were visible in the thick carpet. One side of the bed was shielded from the large TV screen that hung on the opposite wall. The ornaments had been displaced and skewed heavily towards the other bed.

Someone had recently rearranged the room.

He called room service and was put through to a man whose accent didn't sound Russian, but Slavic.

"I'm not sure you'll have it, but I'd very much like a pot of Irish breakfast tea." Henry said.

"I'll enquire, sir." The tone was polished and helpful. Henry was put on hold and the same person picked up after a couple of minutes.

"We do have Irish breakfast tea, sir."

"Excellent... Low-fat milk, please, and biscuits if you have them?"

"I have been told there will be some Kimberley biscuits sent up with your tea."

Henry smiled. Harris had told Henry he would action MI6's contacts at The Ritz, and he clearly had. How Harris had managed to get Irish biscuits to Moscow was a mystery. Although Henry suspected there might be more to these biscuits than met the eye.

Henry had just finished unpacking when the bell for his bedroom rang.

A young man stood there with a smile

"Good afternoon, sir. Your tea and biscuits," he said with a mixed American and Russian accent.

"Perfect. Why don't you set the tray on the main table?"

"May I suggest the side table, sir?"

The young man walked in, not waiting for Henry's answer. He poured Henry a cup of tea.

"I hope the bed is in the right position?" the young man asked.

"It's all very good."

"I understand that you needed help with the music port in this room?"

"If you could show me that would be excellent."

The young man moved to the side of the TV and showed Henry the port that could house his phone device and play his music – the perfect way for the FSB to connect to his phone.

"Or if you prefer, you can select a music channel from the TV?"

The young man gave Henry a quick look that indicated it was best to play enough music to cover a call. He chose a classical music channel and left it on.

He showed Henry the remote. "Choose radio channels on the TV and select channel 5."

The young man opened a couple of the wrapped biscuits. A small device slid out of one. Henry recognised a set of small tools, useful for opening a variety of locked spaces. The second packet had four pills encapsulated in foil.

"Rohypnol," he murmured. "Acts very fast. No smell, taste or colour."

The third packet had a small key in it.

"Private locker in the hotel club gym. Glock 26, 5 rounds of ammo."

Henry looked at the fourth wrapper on the plate.

The young man smiled. "Enjoy your Kimberley."

He left the room with a nod.

Henry pocketed two of the items and put the small toolkit to immediate use. He unscrewed the plug of the lamp between the bed and the wall, in the room's blind spot. He pushed the key into the plug's casing. He closed it up again and plugged it back in.

He lay down flat on the floor and cut a small nick in the mattress, then pushed the pills and the small kit inside it.

Henry sat up on the bed and grabbed the cup of tea and the last biscuit. The tea was too cold now for his liking, so he emptied the contents out into the sink and poured a second cup. Much better. He moved to the window and watched for movement in the street below. Snow had fallen heavily in the past few days, according to the weather forecast on his phone, but the pavement had been cleared and people hurried around the street, unimpeded.

Henry finished the Kimberley biscuit in two mouthfuls and drank his tea. He had a couple of hours before the planned meeting with Andropov. Time for a quick reconnaissance of the area.

* * *

Henry zipped up his thick coat. He secured his woollen hat and scarf in place and walked out of The Ritz. The sun was low on the horizon and in less than an hour it would be dark. Henry turned right and crossed a busy main road, headed in Red Square's direction. His heavy boots crushed the grit that had been spread on the pavement.

Red Square's main entrance was surrounded by movable metal barriers that funnelled pedestrians into a small area with heavy surveillance. Henry flipped up the hood of his coat and walked through the opening. The snow had accumulated around a few features of the square. Henry stopped to get his bearings.

Someone came alongside him, hood over their head.

"You need a guide?" Tatiana's voice was muffled by the scarf she'd wrapped over her mouth. She slid her arm through Henry's and moved him along.

Henry kept his composure. "Shouldn't you be with David?"

"He has a few business calls to make, and I said I needed a walk. It's too cold for him out here."

"Despite the fur coat and hat?" Henry couldn't resist the jibe.

Tatiana chuckled.

"Let's walk to Red Square. It's a grand attraction, despite the security."

Henry nodded and allowed himself to be led by his guide.

"To the right you will note a couple of small, round Russian Empire buildings," Tatiana said, pointing. "Perfectly preserved, but invaded by some of the best capitalist's endeavours."

Henry stopped to look and burst into laughter. The neon light of a McDonalds sign and a KFC were overshadowing the buildings.

"Lenin would be sad indeed."

Tatiana nodded. "Lenin would be sad about many things he didn't foresee."

She pressed closer to him, and Henry felt the movement of her body as they walked together.

"Is this wise?" Henry asked. "You being alone with me?"

"David doesn't own me."

"I would have thought very few people did."

"But freedom is not for me."

"Why?"

Tatiana slowed down. "It's the fate of all Russians, bar a few."

"Do you want to be free?"

Tatiana smiled. "You don't understand."

"I do, more than you think."

"No, Henry – or whatever your real name is – you don't."

Henry's chest tightened at her confession. "Why are you speaking to me?"

"Call it a hunch. Although you don't understand it now, perhaps you will soon."

Henry fell silent as they approached the main wall of the Kremlin. The pavement had turned to smooth and neat cobblestones. Another set of metal barriers were preventing people from getting within a foot of the wall.

"Are you wired?" Henry asked.

Tatiana shook her head. "I can't prove it to you, but you'll have to believe me."

"What is it that you want?"

Tatiana stopped and faced Henry. He could almost make out her eyes beneath the fur hood.

"You never asked me once about my parents," she said. "Most people can't help it. They do it to either commiserate with the pain of their own loss or to satisfy a rather disgusting obsession with death. But not you."

It was not the answer he was expecting. "I don't like to prey on others' misfortunes."

"Is that all?"

"What else should there be?"

He clenched his fist, not ready to trust her yet.

Tatiana came closer. Her gaze locked onto his. She was searching for an answer.

"Do you know that pain, Henry? Not the loss, but the not knowing?"

He couldn't answer, not in words, but the torment he'd felt was real. It must have flashed in his eyes because Tatiana pulled her scarf down and quickly pressed her lips to his.

"Let's go back to the hotel. The meeting with Andropov is in less than an hour."

* * *

The car taking Henry, Upstage, and Tatiana to the meeting stopped inside the Kremlin complex, near the Armoury Chamber.

They walked into a grand building that was adjacent to the main Kremlin Palace. All three of them, together with Upstage's security detail, were ushered by more guards into a large hallway, then escorted up a broad stone staircase. They walked past displays of old swords and antique guns that looked pristine in their casings.

The room on the first floor did not disappoint, containing old furniture that must have belonged to the last Tsar of Russia – ornate yet elegant. Andropov's meeting was not taking place at his office nor at his private residence, but in a place that felt more like an Imperial Russian enclave.

Upstage's own bodyguards were told to wait outside. He reluctantly agreed to it after Tatiana's intervention. If the FSB wanted Upstage dead on Russian soil, she'd told him, he would be dead – with or without security. It wasn't a particularly reassuring thing for her to say, but it seemed to do the trick.

Tatiana could control the man. Henry took note. He needed to watch that he wasn't also falling into that camp. He pushed away the memories of their walk an hour ago. It was time to focus on the Andropov meeting.

Andropov was already inside. A log fire was blazing heat into the room. He had chosen the corner sofa, comfortably close to the warmth the fireplace radiated.

258

"*Dobro pozhalovat...* Welcome."

Two young women materialised at their side. They relieved Upstage, Henry, and Tatiana of their coats. The guards that had accompanied them vanished as soon as they entered the room. Upstage was the first to move towards the fire and meet Androprov's stretched hand. Henry hung back a moment.

As soon as Henry had returned to his room after his meeting with Tatiana, his head still buzzing with the implications of what she was trying to do or say to him, he had tested the two microscopic cameras and transmitters hidden in the buttons of his jacket. He'd taken out his laptop and logged in, making sure the screen was sheltered from prying eyes. The recording software was working.

Henry had let it run and logged off. The screensaver was of a seascape, tranquil and uneventful. He'd gone to his wardrobe, selected the jacket for the meeting and moved back to the blind spot between the second bed and the wall.

He'd pressed on the button on his jacket once, walked around the room and returned to the same place, switching it off. He'd picked up the laptop, logged in again and checked – the image looked clear. He'd even heard the sound of his own footsteps.

Now, Henry unfastened his jacket. The recording equipment lodged there could be easily operated by buttoning or unbuttoning his jacket, a move he had rehearsed in his bedroom.

Andropov gave Upstage a warm handshake. Tatiana moved to another sofa opposite the one Andropov had chosen. Henry shook hands with Andropov for the first time. The man had been much more formal and distant at the Embassy in London.

Henry chose a single armchair away from the fire. Upstage took his seat next to Tatiana. Tea was brought in in a tall samovar, served in thick glasses ensconced in delicately elaborate silver holders.

"Won't Mikhail be joining us?" Upstage asked, leaning back into the deep sofa he was sharing with Tatiana.

"Rostov unfortunately has other business to attend to next door." Andropov inclined his head in the direction of the Kremlin main palace.

"When shall I meet him?" Upstage asked.

Andropov smiled. "As soon as the deal is done."

"I thought the deal *was* done." Upstage's voice had an angry edge that Andropov didn't seem to be concerned about.

"Without a doubt it is, although we need to put a little more flesh on the bone." Despite the strong Russian accent, Andropov's English was clear, even subtle. Henry wondered where he had been educated.

"You mean when David walks into the Oval Office?" Henry added.

"A meeting at that stage would be the perfect way to introduce this renewed friendship between both our nations," said Andropov. "After all, we fought in WWII alongside one another."

"A very good point." Upstage's anger fell away. He had been handed a point that could become central to his argument about promoting a link to the Kremlin and Russia.

"I have spoken to the Swiss banker you met in London," said Andropov. "Petrov has called Mueller at the DSB. You should receive confirmation that the loan has gone through, on the strength of the risk cover the Russian Narodni Brevick has given you."

"$810m?" Upstage took a sip of tea.

"As agreed."

Upstage nodded. "It's an excellent start."

"It is." Andropov sat back in the sofa, a man not in any hurry to make an offer, but fully expecting to be asked for more.

"You will agree that what we are offering is exceptional," said Upstage.

Andropov nodded. "I wouldn't put it any other way."

Upstage turned to Henry. The horse trading had started.

"Access to the White House is worth a lot more than $810m. We all know that. No need to be coy about this. It's now a question of how much we agree this is worth." Henry leaned forward to grab his tea.

"Before we speak numbers, I'd like you to consider adding the following proposition in the mix," Andropov replied.

He stood up and refilled his glass mug from the samovar, then continued.

"Hillary Clinton is still doing well in the polls."

Upstage was about to launch into his usual 'Clinton has achieved nothing in office' speech, but Andropov lifted a hand that silenced the man. It had the authority of someone who not only knew what Upstage was about to say but also someone who knew much more.

"The reach you have on social media is remarkable, David. You can harness this to your advantage, as very few people can. You speak to people like no other candidate can, but it's not always enough."

Upstage looked back at the samovar. Tatiana took his mug and refilled both their glasses.

"You need access to a more systematic way of leveraging social media." Andropov sat back, relaxed.

"That would mean acquiring tools that can determine who to reach with success," Henry countered.

Andropov smiled. "Tools which we have."

"You mean you've mapped users on FB and Twitter so that you can predict their preferences?" Henry asked.

"Also what can motivate them to do certain things," said Andropov. "I'm pretty confident voting is one of them. Goddamn, we even have an entire small town in the US."

Henry frowned at what Andropov said. "You mean, you've created a small town in the US – virtually? People who do not exist and spread news on your behalf?"

Andropov straightened up. Perhaps he hadn't meant to divulge the depth of the Russian penetration into American social media so readily. "It's all relative, of course."

"But that's a brilliant idea." Upstage's face lit up. "As long as what is spread on FB or Twitter is the message we are trying to spread, why not?"

Andropov settled back into the sofa. He had found the right person in Upstage. No moral compass and the desire to win, come what may.

"How broad do you think your reach can be?" Henry asked as casually as he could.

"We can start engaging with our FB contacts and tweeters to reach several million in a month, but we need a good piece of information to launch the campaign."

"There is nothing new on Clinton," Henry said.

"Not yet..." Andropov shot back.

Upstage raised an eyebrow, but said nothing.

Henry walked over to the samovar and refilled his glass mug. "Do you have links with large hackers and other organisation that publish classified information, such as WikiLeaks?"

"We keep our sources confidential." Andropov replied. He didn't need to read the man's reaction to know he had guessed right again.

Henry batted straight back. "How can we verify the content?"

"Does it matter?" Andropov's eyes glinted with malice. "As long as we get the gist of it right."

Upstage nodded. "Very good point. As long as we know we are broadly right... that all sounds like a beautiful idea."

"What's the timing of the document release?" Henry sat down again, hoping his camera was recording everything.

"Imminent. We'll give you the heads up so that David can be ready to react on FB and Twitter."

"Any inkling about the content?" Henry ventured.

Andropov grinned. "Now that *would* be telling..."

Henry faked a grin back.

He needed that information more than anything.

Chapter Twenty-Six

The smell of pizza made Nick's mouth water. He had sourced the right Domino's Pizza cap from a reject shop he used sometimes to find funky T-shirts to wear, whilst doing a hacking job. The black winter jacket he wore over it completed a credible delivery man's outfit.

His first excursion earlier that morning had revealed a place in Kalamora with an unusual little garage at the back of the property. He had spent the previous day gathering more information about the area for his planned recon. Or was it that the incident at Henry's apartment had rattled him more than he'd like to admit, and he was glad to find an excuse to delay his trip?

But today, he had pulled himself together and scoped the surrounds of the place, detecting no surveillance cameras. There had been no one around again, and he'd climbed over the garage's wooden fence easily enough. He'd picked the lock of the garage and crept in. There, he'd found the bike he had identified earlier on the CCTV cameras, hidden under a cover.

It was then Nick had had a moment of panic. If the bike was here, so must be the owner. He'd retraced his steps, and sat on a low wall at the top of the small lane that led to the intruder's property. Nick had waited more than 40 minutes, and when nothing had stirred in the lane, he'd gone back to his apartment.

The plan now was to revisit the property, comprised of two apartments. He had a delivery of a hot pizza to make. If the intruder was not there, he hoped to gain access by convincing the other apartment owner to let him in. If no one was around, the solution would be to use his locksmith tools. He would gain entry in no time at all.

What he hadn't catered for was the offer of help from Mandy to further his plan. She'd turned up on his doorstep after he'd returned from his first recce.

"Don't tell me you don't know anything or that there are no new developments." Mandy had marched straight into his apartment. "I'm not going to be shut out of this operation. Jack is intent in not involving me any longer but that's not the way it's gonna be."

"I'm not saying anything, Mandy."

"What do you mean? You've been told to keep quiet?"

"No, sorry... I didn't mean it quite that way."

"I damn well hope not."

"It's just –" Nick scratched the back of his head. "I'm a bit of a newbie and I don't want to screw up."

"So where were you just now? I've just come from your office, and it hasn't been opened today."

Nick blinked a couple of times. *Shit, she knows I'm up to something.*

Mandy had folded her arms. "You've just said it yourself, Nick. You're a newbie and you don't want to screw up. I can help you."

"It will be the second time I don't follow Henry's instructions."

"No, I'd say the third, because I'm pretty sure that you not turning up to the office and doing whatever it is on your own were not part of his instructions, either."

Nick bit his lip. He slumped into the sofa.

Mandy had sat next to him. "I also looked after Rush Huckerby, you know. I'm a data analyst but I know a thing or two about the world of intelligence, OK?"

"OK..." Nick nodded. "OK. I'll tell you what I know so far."

Mandy had parked her car opposite the property and was waiting for Nick to deliver the pizza. Nick pressed the buzzer for the intruder's apartment a few times. There was no answer.

He waited a moment and used the buzzer again. She was not around.

Nick pressed the second button to the other apartment. Still no answer. Nick repeated the process and waited a couple of minutes before he deposited the pizza box on the floor. He inspected the frame and detected the presence of an alarm system.

He returned to Mandy's car. She had a laptop open on her knees, which Nick took from her.

"Got to disable the alarm system."

He searched for the radio frequency the alarm system had been set up on. He found what he was looking for. Nick then enabled the jamming software he'd used before and stepped out of the car. Mandy fired up the engine.

Nick shot her a look.

"Just in case," she said.

Nick shrugged. He returned to the entrance and used his tools on the latch. It caved in after a little effort and Nick stepped inside with his Domino's Pizza box.

He moved around slowly, mindful of any secondary alarm system, but the house didn't look wealthy enough to warrant such an expense. He reached the top floor. Nobody was home.

Nick returned to the front door and cracked it open a little. He gave her a signal. Mandy turned off the engine, came to the door, and rang for good measure.

Nick opened it and let her in.

"Which flat do we start with?" he murmured.

"Top floor." Mandy sounded sure.

"Why?"

"If you're ever gonna be caught, you want time to know if people are after you. If they need to go all the way up the stairs to find you, you can hear them coming. There is also a very close rooftop next to the top floor apartment – a good escape route."

Nick nodded impressed.

He repeated the process of identifying the presence of any alarm that might be inside the top floor apartment. He used the same jamming device to kill the alarm.

The door lock resisted more than the entrance one, but Nick managed to open it. They were in.

"What are we looking for?" Nick murmured.

"Electronic devices, ID, weapons – anything that can help us identify who we are dealing with."

Mandy moved to the bedroom, whilst Nick concentrated on the lounge/dining room. They both took their time to go through the cupboards, shelves, or few personal effects they found. There was nothing telling.

Mandy was the first one to interrupt their search.

"Found anything?"

"Nothing, no mobile, computer, laptop."

"Same in the bedroom. A few items of clothes, bit of makeup, but we knew we were looking for a woman. I've even looked for a secret vault – nothing so far."

"I've done the same thing here. She's taken all the electronic gear with her."

"Let go through the kitchen next, but I'm almost certain it will be the same."

"Shit, we're gonna have nothing to show for."

Mandy shook her head. "Not true. With that level of anonymity, I'm pretty sure the woman is not only a pro but a spook."

"You mean like...?"

"Yep, just like you."

Nick stopped. "It doesn't feel that way."

Mandy was already opening the cupboards and looking at the various packets and tins of food stacked there. She replaced the staple items. Then she came to a tea caddy that looked old and battered. She opened it and took a sniff.

"Russian Caravan," she said.

"What's that?"

"Russian Caravan – it's a brand of tea that the Russians like a lot. Was very expensive back in the days, when camels' caravan used to bring it all the way from the Far East to Russia."

"A Russian spy then?"

"It would tally with all we've learnt so far."

They both went through the kitchen. The search yielded nothing, as Mandy had predicted. Mandy left the apartment first. She sat in the driver seat whilst Nick locked the door and restored the main alarm.

He sat in the car next to Mandy, reopened his laptop and said, "I've got an idea about who this woman might be."

Someone knocked at Mandy's window.

She had prepared an angry look of exasperation that said, *Yes, I am moving.*

266

Nick looked up and froze. A man was pointing a gun at her head. Another in a balaclava was standing in front of their vehicle, with a small machine gun pointed at them both.

* * *

Tatiana flicked the lights off and the bedroom plunged into darkness. She lay on the bed, one arm covering her eyes. The series of events that that led to this evening's unexpected development were replaying in her head. She had been working on her plan for a long while but she no longer had the luxury of time.

The morning had been near perfect. She'd visited her grandmother's comfortable flat in Moscow's Basmanny district. The building was only four floors tall, surrounded by trees and well-kept communal gardens. The old lady was ageing only the way her Babushka could – with resilience and generosity. Tatiana's brother Anatolie had returned from school for lunch; not something he did every day but today was an exception, as she was calling on them.

He was much taller than she remembered. Andropov had been right. Young children changed fast. She always feared that one day she would become a stranger to her brother. But today wasn't that day.

Anatolie had been full of stories, telling her about his school, his friends, his favourite subjects – Russian literature and mathematics. He reminded her so much of her parents, the perfect combination. It was as though both had poured the best of themselves into a crucible and created a child from it.

Babushka had been plying her with plenty of tea. It had been hard to leave the cosy flat and return to The Ritz and Upstage, and a life she had not chosen for herself. At least she had managed to have a conversation she'd long wanted with her Babushka, and was glad they were both in agreement about her choices.

Tatiana removed her arm from her eyes and stared up at the ceiling. After the meeting, when she and Upstage had returned to his suite, he had thrown the biggest tantrum. Lunch had been awful on the plane; Henry was not staying on the same floor as they were; Tatiana was at the far end of the corridor. The meeting with Andropov had been weighing on his mind, but he wouldn't admit it.

Despite his claim of allegiance to the Russian cause, Tatiana wondered what Upstage's ultimate end game was. The White House most certainly, but he didn't like to be bound to or take orders from anyone. She didn't care one way or the other. Her role was to facilitate, until she was told otherwise. But she could see why Upstage had chosen someone like Henry to deal with the negotiations with Andropov. He was a shrewd adviser, and perhaps a scapegoat.

Her thoughts settled on Henry, and she let her arms flop either side of her. Their walk to Red Square had convinced her Henry might understand her choices. She hadn't spoken to Andropov about the vault in Henry's apartment, or Henry's quick reactions, which had persuaded her he was a trained operative. Kissing him so soon might not have been such a good idea. Although the memory brought a smile to her face. It was a lot more than Upstage had ever got from her.

Her mobile rang. She was expecting a call from Upstage, complaining about one thing or another. But instead it was Andropov.

She frowned. *"Privyet...* Hi. What's up?"

"I have disturbing news from Washington," he said.

Tatiana sat up in one swift move.

"What kind of problem?"

"Someone got into your apartment."

That didn't worry her. "They won't find anything."

"I know they won't, but it's more their identity that troubles me."

"What do you mean?"

"You know a Nick Fox?"

Tatiana cursed silently. "He works for Henry Newborn."

"And there is a woman with him who says she's called Jane."

"I haven't found any woman involved with them."

"No one? Even a cleaner or a receptionist?"

"No one."

Andropov fell silent.

He continued a moment later. "I'm having Henry picked up for a conversation about it. Why don't you come along? I'll want to check his story against yours." The phone went dead. Tatiana felt sick. She struggled not to retch.

She had placed so much hope in the Brit. He was the contact she'd been waiting for and now Andropov had him in his clutches. Why had his stupid assistant gotten caught? This was Russian intelligence, not some flouncy little financial company they were dealing with.

Tatiana got up and ran cold water over her wrists in the bathroom. It was a trick her mother had taught her many years ago to calm herself down. She returned to the bedroom, put her sweater on and her winter boots. She slipped her fur coat and hat on, and made her way to where Andropov would be having his so-called chat with Henry.

Tatiana hoped Henry was indeed a very well-trained operative.

* * *

The meeting between Upstage and Andropov had yielded more information than Henry had expected. He had saved the visual and audio recording on his camera. Harris would want to receive the files as soon as they were ready to be transmitted.

Upstage had looked pleased when they'd climbed into the limo taking them back to The Ritz. Henry had not suggested dinner and Upstage, despite his exuberance, hadn't either, preferring a *tête-a-tête* with Tatiana.

When Henry entered his bedroom, he switched on the TV, chose Channel 5, and moved to his laptop. Andropov had no doubt sent someone to try to break the encryption on it and upload spyware. Henry logged in, checked for any alert –nothing. Perhaps they had tried but hadn't succeeded. The laptop's encryption was state of the art and MI6 was constantly monitoring its integrity.

Henry sent the file of the recordings to Harris, resisting the urge to revisit some of the more telling moments of the meeting. He didn't need to have a chat with his handler yet. He checked his emails. Nothing was yet confirming that James had arrived in Moscow as an economic attaché.

A setback.

Henry cast a glance at his watch. It was 4pm in DC. Time to try Nick again, to discuss the intrusion in his apartment, and to talk about Nick's progress with The Pieper.

Nick's phone went to voice mail. Henry left a grumpy message and returned to his mail. He called back a few minutes later, but still nothing. This was not what they had agreed, and Henry's annoyance turned into concern. Nick was enthusiastic, talented but still inexperienced – a bad combination if Henry knew one.

Someone rattling the door handle startled him. He hesitated for a second, pressed the voice control command of his laptop and moved to the door. Three men were outside. He ran back to his bedroom.

"Remind me to finish email tomorrow," he said into the recorder.

The simple sentence put an emergency message into action, signalling London that his position might be compromised. The computer screen went black just as the front door burst open and three men entered. There was no point in resisting, at least not yet.

The punch to the stomach winded him. The taller of the three thugs pushed him against the wall, using an arm lock on him.

"Come now, no resist, otherwise big trouble." The Russian accent was thick, but the message clear.

Henry nodded. The man who had him in an arm lock released his grip a little and turned him around.

The man who hadn't yet touched Henry threw a punch. It landed on his jaw. The taste of blood filled Henry's mouth; his head swam for a moment.

"Move."

Henry felt the bulk of their guns in their holsters. He would have no chance of making it to the end of the long corridor without a bullet in his back.

A fourth man appeared, moved silently into the bedroom. He would almost certainly give it a thorough check and his laptop would be taken away.

One of the men pushed Henry forward. He was only wearing a light jumper – no match for Moscow's minus 10C and its howling winds. The shorter and stockier of the thugs moved him on. They passed the bank of lifts heading in the direction of the emergency exit. The thug opened the door and they all started climbing down.

At the bottom of the eight flights of stairs another man was waiting. He opened the door to the street, blocked any escape route, and opened the door of a black SUV. Henry slowed down, only to be shoved against the body of the car.

A hood came down over his head. A pair of cuffs brought his hands together behind his back. Someone pushed Henry into the back seat, one man on his right, one on his left. The journey started.

Henry tried to keep a sense of where they were going. He had memorised a map of Moscow city's centre. The SUV was moving north in what felt like a straight line. It then turned left and left again. Henry thought they were going round in a circle, but he couldn't be sure.

The car stopped and he was shoved out. The cold gripped him as soon as he stepped into the open air. A door opened and he was pushed into a space that sounded hollow. A lift took them a couple of floors underground. The temperature was not much better there than it had been outside.

"Wait," someone said.

A door opened. The hood was taken off. Henry squinted at the bright strip lighting overhead.

In the room there was one table and two chairs, one with its back to the door. The man who had taken the hood off Henry dragged him to the first chair, and pushed him into it. Two sets of plastic cable ties fastened him to the chair. The man turned and left, locking the door behind him.

The room smelt stale and rancid. The paint was peeling off the walls. There was no opening to the outside. Henry's throat tightened. It was the sort of room that Stalin must have used during the heyday of his reign, before sending hordes of men to the Gulag.

Henry checked the ties. He could get out of them. The cuffs were another matter. They were made of strong metal, and it would be difficult to break out of them.

The door opened again. With his back to it, Henry couldn't see who had come in. He braced for another bashing. Instead, a man he recognised by his voice walked towards him. Someone else settled next to the door, out of his field of vision.

"I'm very sorry I had to bring you out at this late hour." Andropov moved past the table. He dragged the other chair away from it and sat down. "And I can see my men have been a little rough. I had told them there was no need but it's difficult to restrain them at the best of times."

"I'm sure we could have ironed out our differences in a more civilised environment." Henry articulated his words despite the searing pain in his jaw. He must still be in the clear, as far as the incursion into his Washington apartment was concerned, otherwise Andropov's men would have already started questioning him.

"If it was only about the agreement we have with David Upstage, I'm sure we could, but the issue we face – or rather you face – is a little trickier."

Henry gave Andropov a surprised look. "I genuinely don't follow you."

Perhaps it was all about his apartment after all.

Andropov took his time to observe Henry. "You don't seem very alarmed for someone who is two floors below ground, with no means of escaping."

"Who says I'm not alarmed? I have done enough business in Africa to know how to keep my cool."

"I suppose doing deals with some of the rebels in Central Africa must be –" Andropov was searching for the right word "– challenging."

"I'm sure we're not here to discuss the deals I've closed there," Henry cut back. "Why don't you come to the point?"

"Very well." Andropov nodded. "Your assistant, Nick Fox, has been caught breaking into the apartment of one of our citizens."

Henry's eyebrows shot up. "Nick Fox? Are you sure?"

"Positive. He was accompanied by a woman – a little older than him, coloured."

Henry could picture the scene. Nick caught red-handed, giving his assailants his best disarming puppy look. But the men Andropov had hired didn't care for puppies, except perhaps to use them as targets.

"Who is the woman?" Henry was trying to gain a little time. Why would Nick have taken such a stupid risk?

"I was hoping you could tell me."

"I'm sorry I can't be of help here."

"It's a shame."

"Frankly, the only reason Nick would do anything as remotely unlawful as you suggest would be if he were forced into it." Henry's mind pondered his previous wonderings. Nick had found out the identity of the intruder in Henry's apartment, and now so had Henry. There was only one person he knew who would hold back on the information contained there.

Andropov pouted. "Explain?"

It seemed Henry had scored a small point.

"Nick is not only my receptionist, but he also is an excellent tech person in charge of cyber security, amongst other things. Hence the reason why I knew someone had bugged my office."

Andropov's eyes rested on Henry's, cold and measuring. Some movement near the door caught his attention.

"Have you spoken to him since you left DC?" Andropov said.

"No. I have been preparing for our meeting and catching up with other contacts in London. He knows to call me if something urgent arises. I did try to call though. He was not around, which I assumed meant all was fine."

"You're prepared to go very far to protect your business," Andropov mused. He was wavering.

"In my line of work secrecy is a given. The people I deal with do not want their names splattered all over the papers, or be on Interpol's or other agencies' radars."

Andropov leaned into the table and rested his forearms on its top.

"I'm prepared to say that perhaps your assistant Nick had just cause to be inquisitive." Andropov cast a glance at the door and added. "This is what I am proposing. You're free to keep doing business here, but I have your passport, and I'm going to keep it until I'm clear about what Nick was hoping to achieve. And of course, until I know who this woman is."

"Keeping my passport is rather unjustified since I won't be able to leave without you knowing." A vain protest, Henry knew, but he couldn't just accept Andropov's terms.

"A simple precaution." Andropov stood up.

"Do you have a picture of the woman?" Henry asked.

Andropov nodded. "A good idea."

He made a call in Russian and within a minute his mobile pinged. He brought up the picture on screen and slid the phone towards Henry.

Mandy's face, bruised yet defiant, startled him. Henry forced himself to look detached.

"Her face looks familiar, but I can't tell you why."

"Give it some thought. It's in your and Nick's interest."

Andropov pocketed his phone and moved towards the door. He stopped before exiting. Henry heard him turn on his heels.

"Any attempt to contact the British Embassy will be frowned upon. I hope we are clear."

"Very much so." Henry heard the door close behind him.

It was only a matter of time before Andropov and his men realised Mandy worked for the CIA.

Chapter Twenty-Seven

"Your phone's alarm is making a real racket." Harris's wife Sarah shouted through the door. They had just finished dinner and Harris had gone outside to smoke one last cigarette for the evening.

"Shit..." Harris darted back in. "Sorry, I mean thanks for telling me."

The emergency alert had been triggered on Crowne's laptop. Harris killed the alarm, grimaced another sorry to his wife, and disappeared outside again. He called one of his team back at the SIS building.

"The alarm has been triggered on Crowne's laptop," Harris reported.

"We received comms from him a few minutes before," the man said. "Video and audio. The beacon went up after the transmission and the laptop was moved half an hour later, and so was his mobile. I'm in the process of cleaning both devices."

"When will you be done? The Russians can't find that we are shadowing his laptop and phone."

"Just a few more minutes..."

"That gives me a bit of breathing space. I'm on my way."

Harris walked back in to his wife.

"I'm sorry –"

"You've been apologising for the past 15 years, Steve," said Sarah. "And every time I say the same thing. Go get them." She smiled and made herself comfortable in an armchair.

Harris sighed. "You're a saint... even my agents know it."

He kissed the top of her head, grabbed his keys and his winter jacket. The drive to the office would at least be quick at this hour.

As soon as he was in the car he called Natasha.

"Our favourite person is in trouble."

"Do they know the full story?" she replied.

"I don't know yet. He triggered the alarm on his laptop and sent some data across. Video and audio – it's all encrypted. I'll be sending this to you tonight."

"Fine. I'll get back to the office and start working on it as soon as I have it." Harris dialled James's number next.

James picked up immediately. "New developments regarding Henry?"

"Alarm triggered on his laptop. How about your trip to Moscow?"

"Just got the tickets, the British Embassy has made a credible story about one of their attachés having to return to the UK for family reasons. I'm leaving tomorrow on the first flight to Moscow."

"We might be moving from a support mission to a quick exfiltration mission. Get ready for that."

"Understood. I'll load the diplomatic bag with what Henry and I will need. I'll see whether I can get tactical support to prepare some new ID papers for Henry."

"Good thinking. Anything you need from me you call. I'm back at the office."

Harris hung up. He was almost at Vauxhall Cross. The main road leading to the banks of the River Thames were still busy with traffic. Harris overtook a slumbering bus and got an angry response from the driver. The lights were about to turn red at the intersection of the Vauxhall Bridge Road and Albert Embankment. Harris accelerated and swore. If he kept driving like this, he would be threatened with the loss of his driving licence once more.

He moved past the SIS building, indicated left. He stopped at a set of heavily guarded gates. The security guard recognised him and opened the large doors. Harris drove in and parked his car.

The lifts took him as far as the ground floor. He went through the usual security checks and was finally allowed in. Harris arrived in the office and moved to his desk without bothering to greet anyone.

He logged in and called Jack Shield.

"I haven't got any news yet," Jack said.

"I'm not talking about Crowne's apartment, Jack. He has activated the emergency protocol on his laptop."

"What do you need me to do?"

"Have you heard about Nick?"

"I called him early this morning. I left a message and he called back a little later, saying he was feeling better, taking it easy."

"Nothing since then?"

"No and I haven't tried. Why?"

"Something has triggered a reaction," Harris said. "I don't think it was the visit to Crowne's apartment. Henry has a theory about that visit, and I share it. He thinks that whoever got into his apartment is holding back on the intel they gathered there. I agree with him."

"Otherwise, he would have been picked up before he left London," Jack said.

"Or at least as soon he arrived in Moscow. I can't imagine whoever he is meeting out there would let Crowne approach him if he suspected foul play."

"I'll try to get hold of Nick."

"Fine, I don't want to call myself. Let's try to keep things as compartmentalised as we can. That'll make it more difficult for these Russian buggers to find out about RUSSKY BEAR."

"I'll call you straight back." Jack hung up and Harris slumped in his chair. His mobile rang. It was Natasha.

"Shit... too early. That's never good," Harris mumbled.

"The quality of the files Henry sent over has been compromised."

"Why? How?"

"Don't know yet... I'm just giving you the heads up. Maybe I can salvage a lot of it, maybe not. I'll call back as soon as I know more."

Natasha hung up.

His mobile rang again. "What now?" Harris grumbled.

"Crowne's laptop is clean, mobile too," one of the team at SIS said.

"Thanks, mate. Some good news, which I needed."

Harris fished out the packet of cigarettes he'd stuffed in his jacket pocket. He called up a map of Russia on screen and started considering their options. The quickest way out of Russia from Moscow was a 500 km drive to Belarus. But, the Russians would happily follow their target into that country, and square away any fallout with their neighbours afterwards.

Ukraine was 600 km from Moscow and a more reliable country to work with. A long exfiltration over land would only work with help from within Russia, which Harris could summon. He had a couple of safe houses he could activate on the way out, but success meant an early start, and Henry was already marked.

Harris kept playing with his cigarette packet, until a video conference call came through from the US.

"Can't get hold of Nick," Jack said. "I can't get hold of Mandy either."

That surprised Harris. "Did you not ask her to lay low on this one?"

"I did, but of course Mandy never takes no for an answer, although this time I thought she might listen."

"How well does she know Nick?"

"She's met him, and they've been in touch about intel exchange."

Harris said nothing for a moment. Then he asked, "Do you think they could be working together?"

"Nick was told not to engage with her too."

"But when has it stopped her? I warned you she's a frustrated agent, wasted talents. She'd be good in the field."

"That's not helpful in this situation, is it?" said Jack.

"It is. They both disappeared at the same time, but it's unlikely it's not a coincidence."

Jack shook his head. "I'll track them both down."

He hung up and Harris consulted his watch. It was almost 10.30pm. Brett's club closed in an hour. Harris picked up the burner phone with a leather casing and dialled.

"Fancy a nightcap?" he asked his asset.

Brett huffed. "Do I have a choice?"

"Unless you're otherwise engaged with your young girlie, then no."

"I'll meet you at the club in 30 minutes."

"30 minutes." Harris hung up, pocketed his cigarettes, and made a dash for the door.

Brett had arrived before him. Harris, wearing a suit from the Airlock, slumped into the large, leather armchair next to Brett. A glass was waiting for Harris. For once, Brett had been thoughtful and ordered for the two of them.

278

"Had to change into more suitable clothes."

Brett eyed him. "I couldn't tell."

"Very unfair. It's a Savile Row suit." But the anger was not in him tonight.

Brett bent forward to pick up his glass of whisky. "Has Crowne got himself into trouble again? I recall being asked for help last time it happened."

"And you enjoyed every bit of it."

"I wouldn't go that far. Although, the cash payment that came with it was a balm to soothe my still very sore wounds."

"How long are you going to hold a grudge? So, Crowne decided against purchasing a stolen piece of antiquity from you. Who could blame him?"

"From a financial terrorist like Crowne, his crisis of conscience was rich," Brett shot back.

"No, it's called an assessment of risk."

"So now you're going to tell me he was right to recant on the deal and leave me at the mercy of jihadists, which I still had to pay whether I got Crowne's money or not?"

"I'm just saying that in his shoes, you would have done the same thing."

Brett was about to disagree, but Harris shot him a look that for once silenced the man.

Harris switched topics. "Do you have any consignment going to Russia?"

"Not in the immediate future."

"Could you have a consignment going to Russia in the immediate future?" Harris persevered.

Brett hesitated for a fraction too long. "No."

"It's a no that says maybe."

"I told you. I'm not pissing off the Russians."

"The plan will be that they won't know it's you."

"You can't guarantee that, and don't tell me otherwise."

"Who do you use in Russia to transit your looted antiques?"

Brett's face turned from irritated to thunder. "Keep your damn voice down..."

"Oops, sorry." Harris failed to look contrite. "So how do you do it?"

"It's not like the Middle East. There, I have to extract the pieces out of their countries of origin. When I sell, the clients take care of the piece either in London or Europe. Most of the time they pick them up from Italy."

Harris drank some of his whisky in silence. Brett was right. What had worked in the Middle East would not work in Russia.

"Do you know how your buyers transport the stuff they purchase from you to where they want it to go?"

"It's not stuff, it's valuable –" Brett shook his head. "Never mind. Private jets are my best guess."

Harris drank some more whisky. "Where is your young girlfriend at the moment?"

"Spending time with billionaire dad on the Baltic Sea. Not my cup of tea but the Russians love it."

"And how is the plan to replace you with a younger version coming along?"

"Surprisingly well, much to my consternation..."

"I assume you have found a suitable young chap with an equally suitable title and short chin?"

"My chin is not short –" Brett replied stiffly.

"What if this young chap was to try to woo your soon-to-be-ex-girlfriend or her papa with a remarkable piece of antiquity?"

Brett gave the whisky in his glass a slow swirl. "How quickly do you need this little charade to be put in place?"

"Yesterday." Harris kept a straight face.

"Our deal still stands?"

"Yup. You say the word, and I get round-the-clock surveillance looking after you, plus the usual compensation of course."

"Well, I've just received a consignment."

"And this young chap will be willing to drop everything to fly a piece of salvaged antiquity – I do hope you appreciate I have expanded my vocabulary – to fly this *relic* to the Baltic Sea?"

"The young chap, as you say, is not exactly busy at this time, and is rather keen to ingratiate himself to my girlfriend."

"Get this going. At least if it goes tits up, it's not you in the frame but him."

"My thinking exactly. Why take risks when you can get someone else taking these for you?"

Harris raised his glass. "I'll drink to that."

* * *

Henry's room had been thoroughly searched; clothes strewn across the floor; sheets yanked off the bed; and in the bathroom, the contents of his toiletry bag tipped into the bath.

Henry had been gruffly manhandled back to The Ritz. Andropov's men accompanied him back to his room the same way they'd left, through the emergency exit. No one was around to witness his arrival back. Or perhaps Andropov's men had made sure there wouldn't be.

He took the scene in and felt anger rising in his chest, knowing his attempt to put things back in place would almost certainly be filmed by the same people who'd caused the havoc. At least the microscopic devices hidden in the buttons of his jacket had not been detected.

Henry ignored the mess and moved back to the bathroom, where he indulged in a long shower. His jaw ached, and the tension in his body had knotted the muscles around his neck and back. His face would no doubt bruise, but his closely cropped beard should cover most of it.

He got out of the shower, dried himself off and wrapped the towel around his waist. Henry moved back to the bedroom and started to tidy the room, his mind replaying the events of tonight. Andropov was only letting him loose to see what his next move would be. His laptop had been taken, and so had his mobile phone. Henry had already booked an airline ticket to London, but without a passport it was worth nothing.

He pushed the mattress back into place, threw the sheets over, and under the pretence of tucking them in, felt for the small incision he had made the day before. He pushed his fingers into the cavity, relieved to find the contents were still there – Rohypnol pills, locksmith tools, pen knife.

He had just finished making the bed when he heard the door of his bedroom open. Henry dragged the penknife out of its hiding place and moved to the corner of the room. If they were coming back, it was to finish the job.

Someone called his name and closed the door softly. Tatiana. She was in the corridor. Henry hesitated. He was certain she had been the other person in the room when Andropov had questioned him.

"Henry, I know you're here... I just want to check on you."

He didn't reply. Instead, he switched off all the lights from the central switch and lunged forward. The move from light to darkness blinded them both for an instant but he was quicker to find his bearings. He pinned her with a similar arm lock move that had been used on him a few hours ago.

"What do you want?" He growled, not caring if he was hurting her.

Tatiana let her body relax.

"I know you're angry, I understand," she murmured.

"That doesn't answer my question." Henry tightened his grip.

"If you want an answer you need to put some music on."

Tatiana's answer surprised him. She was right of course. If they were to have any meaningful conversation, they needed impenetrable background noise.

"Henry, we haven't got much time."

The sense of urgency in her voice sounded real. He let her go, tucked the penknife in the waistband of his towel and stepped back out of reach.

She switched on the light in the corridor and spoke in a normal volume.

"I've been told to make sure you were fine and that there were no hard feelings."

Tatiana's voice had become playful, the smile on her face seductive. Her eyes didn't tell the same story. She was pleading with Henry to trust her.

She took her time to move closer to him.

She reached for his chest, and he didn't stop her. Her touch was electrifying. He ran his hands down her back drawing her closer. Her lips brushed his, as they'd done on Red Square, but this time there was no urgency, no meeting to go to.

He ran his hand through her blonde hair as he returned her kiss. Henry picked her up in his arms. The bedroom was lit only by the light in the hallway. Henry deposited her gently on the bed. She closed her arms around him, but her embrace had tensed. They stayed in each other's arms for a moment.

"This is what they're expecting," Tatiana murmured in his ear.

Henry nodded and reluctantly let go of her. He moved over to the TV, chose the radio channels and switched on Channel 5. Music filled the room.

"What now?" Henry returned to the bed and sat next to Tatiana. He pushed a strand of hair away that had fallen across her brow.

Tatiana hesitated, then grabbed his hand and squeezed it tight between hers.

"I know it's not easy for us to trust each other but we need to work together."

"At the moment, it feels as though I need you more than you need me," Henry said.

"Appearances can be deceptive." Tatiana gave him a quick smile. "You know about my parents. But do you know about my brother?"

"I read something about him. Quite a bit younger than you."

"Anatolie is only 13 but growing fast. It's only a matter of time before they come for him."

"Who are they?"

"Andropov, or some other bastards who think that they own their people. It's the way the system works here." Tatiana swept her arm around to make her point.

"How long have you been working for Andropov?"

"Too long." Tatiana averted her gaze for a moment, but she returned it to Henry. "I don't want Anatolie to follow the same path as me."

He squeezed her hands and drew them closer. "Do you want to defect?"

"I want my brother to be safe. That's all that matters."

"But what will happen to you when Andropov finds out?"

"I'll deal with it."

In the dim light, Tatiana's gaze searched his face.

Henry pulled her to him gently. "I'm sure I can get both of you out."

She rested her head on his chest. Then she pulled back. Henry let go of her.

"I can get your mobile back. The laptop will be more difficult..."

"That's a good start."

"Tomorrow, there is a meeting between Upstage and Botha. I've convinced Upstage you should attend. It's here, but I've booked lunch at a restaurant not very far from the British Embassy."

"I presume you were there when Andropov questioned me?"

Tatiana nodded. "I had no choice."

"Then you know that the Embassy is a no-go."

"Can't you make contact with someone?"

"I'll think it over."

They both fell silent for a moment.

"Anything else I need to be aware of?" Henry said.

"Upstage is playing an even more dangerous game than you think."

"How so?"

"He has been guarded with me of late, but I believe he sees Andropov as a stepping stone not a partner."

"I'll bear that in mind."

Tatiana hesitated. Henry could tell she wanted to ask a question but wasn't sure she could.

"Tell me."

"You understand how it feels... not knowing for sure who killed them, not having justice?"

Henry shivered at the question. Yes, he knew, and that knowledge would be forever with him. He nodded.

"Was it a long time ago?"

"It was."

Tatiana sighed. "Thank you for telling me."

She curled up in a ball on the bed. Henry moved closer and wrapped an arm around her. They only had a few hours' rest before the next part.

Chapter Twenty-Eight

Tatiana slipped out of Henry's room after what Andropov's eaves-droppers would assume was a night of passion.

Henry got ready. He checked his face in the bathroom mirror. The bruise he'd been expecting was well hidden by his short beard. He returned to the bedroom and sat for a moment. He was putting a lot of trust in a woman he knew so little about.

It was so easy to draw him out on a subject that was still raw, but her request to defect to the West to save her brother had felt genuine. He would have to trust her for the time being until he made contact with London.

A few minutes later, Henry was knocking on David Upstage's suite door for the planned meeting with Bast Botha. Tatiana opened it. She gave him a brief smile and slid something quickly into his hand. His mobile.

"It's switched off. Don't use it until you're out of the hotel," she murmured as she closed the door behind him. "There are tracers that will know a phone has been activated in the hotel, and they'll want to know whose."

Henry smiled back and pocketed his phone.

Upstage was at the window surveying the street below. Botha had already arrived and was chatting to him. He stopped talking the minute he saw Henry.

Upstage welcomed Henry as he would a long-lost friend.

"Fantastic meeting yesterday. Andropov was impressed."

Henry nodded. "The proposition you are putting forward is unprecedented. Andropov knows that."

"The idea he and his team of hackers can help us is even more interesting." Upstage pouted. "What do you think, Bast?"

"I've always been supportive of sharing news thaht people don't want to hear." Botha nodded.

"Perhaps we could discuss what that sharing of unwanted information could look like?" Henry suggested.

Upstage clapped his hands. "Splendid idea." He moved to the long table against one of the walls of the suite and helped himself to coffee. He surveyed the food that had been brought to accompany the beverages and shook his head.

"Not good for my diet..." Yet he indulged in a slice of Russian honey cake. "But very appropriate though." Upstage chuckled.

"I'll grab a slice of Russian honey cake too." Henry said. Both men laughed.

Henry helped himself to the same and moved to the sofa corner where Upstage and Botha had already settled.

"How far have our Russian friends gone with information gathering on the Hillary Clinton campaign?" Upstage addressed Botha before taking a large bite of cake.

Botha sipped some coffee before considering his answer.

"They've gained access to the emails of key campaign stahffers, including Clinton's campaign chairman."

"They've accessed Podesta's email?" Henry couldn't hide his surprise.

Botha simply nodded, but Upstage was more forthcoming. "Serves them right. They should be more careful about what emails their people respond to."

Henry ignored Upstage's comment and turned to Botha. "What is the plan? An attack based on disinformation and fake news? A one-sided attack the US is not aware of?"

"Cyber war is exahctly that." Botha grunted. "It's ferocious, if cahrried out properly."

"And completely deniable too," Henry added.

"That's the point. It's impossible to trahce these people."

"The GRU has a new unit full of young mathematicians and cyber experts that regularly target the West." Henry was not asking a question, simply making a statement that no one contradicted.

"First stage is complete." Upstage had almost finished his cake. He cast a glance at the food table. He pulled himself back. "The

Democrat servers have been compromised. Emails and other data are being downloaded as we speak. We've got an inner track of what's going on."

"I presume they used phishing – sending an email that looks official, like a proper Google email, and requesting a change of password?" Henry asked.

Upstage moved his head in Botha's direction.

"Thaht's correct. Have you used this before yourself?" Botha met Henry's gaze for a short moment.

Henry smiled. "No. My clients are rather forthcoming when it comes to letting me have information."

"What do you do when you need details abouht what the competition has in store for your so-called clients?" Botha shot back.

"Then I use people who can find that information for me. I like to stay one step removed from illicit operations, which is what David is cleverly doing." Henry's calm reply earned him a murderous look from Botha but approbation from Upstage.

"Beautiful summary." Upstage finished his coffee and relaxed in his armchair.

Henry sat back too "Next step?" Upstage was in a talkative mood.

"Bast, enlighten our friend."

"Setting up a fahke email – purportedly from one of Clinton's employees."

"Then send more links to keep phishing, I presume?" said Henry.

"Thaht's right. Then install GRU spyware called X-Agent onto the Democrahtic Party's systems."

"They'll be able to follow Hillary's campaign in real time... I'm impressed," said Henry.

"And interact with Democraht supporters. Some of that dahta is being scooped up."

"Our Russian friends need a way to leak the details they have collected, though." Henry didn't push for an answer.

"They're setting up a website," said Bast. "It will leak information to reporters, candidates, and vohters too."

"But who will be the so-called hackers feeding the leaks? People are going to need to trust the source of the hacks?"

"A very good question, Henry." Upstage nodded at him. "It will come from the small fake American village Andropov mentioned yesterday."

"Most of these fahke identities have been created already and they have opened FB and Twitter accounts."

"So that they can disseminate the news or leaks credibly," said Henry.

"That's right," Upstage said. "It's a technique Bast has used in South Africa with great success."

"Not relevahnt here, though," Botha replied in anger.

"Perhaps –" Upstage ignored his outburst. "But since Henry has met our other friends in London, there is no harm in discussing the techniques we all plan to use to advance our cause."

"As long as you share thaht cause, of course." Botha directed his question at Henry.

"White supremacy sounds like a very good cause to me." Henry gestured convincingly.

"And whaht are you going to do to support it?" Botha hadn't finished with him.

"Make sure Andropov keeps paying the millions of dollars he has committed to pay, and enable you to wash that money clean so that you can use it."

"That's a superb plan." Upstage stretched his legs out and looked at his watch. He looked around him.

"Where is Tatiana? It's almost time for lunch, and she's supposed to be accompanying us to the restaurant."

Upstage picked up his mobile and pressed the recall button.

"Where are you?" he purred into the phone. His voice was both playful and childish.

Upstage listened to the answer. It didn't please him, and he pushed his lower lip into a sulky pout. "OK, we'll see you there."

"Tatiana?" Henry enquired nonchalantly.

"She'll meet us at the restaurant. The Sakhalin. The best in Moscow. Amazing seafood and an incredible 360 degree view of the city." Upstage recited the merits of the place, but his frustration with Tatiana was obvious. Perhaps he was not getting as far as he would like to go with her.

"If we are going now, I'll nip quickly to my bedroom and get my coat," said Henry.

288

Upstage nodded; Botha couldn't care less.

"I'll meet you both downstairs."

Henry walked to the door. When he opened it two men were waiting. He recognised one of them. He had entered his bedroom last night after the others had rounded him up.

"Perhaps I can help you, sir." Unlike the other thugs whose English was only half decent, this man's English was fluent.

"Just going to my bedroom to get my coat." Henry remained calm.

"Allow me to accompany you."

"It's wholly unnecessary. It won't take a moment."

The man started walking with him towards the bank of lifts, ignoring Henry's answer. He called the lift and kept the door open until Henry walked in. They both alighted and walked to Henry's bedroom. The man opened the door for Henry with his pass.

The message from Andropov was clear. There was no place to hide and no place to go where he wouldn't be watched.

Henry entered his bedroom, followed by his unwanted bodyguard.

He picked up his thick coat from the wardrobe, together with his hat. His snowshoes were on the other side of the bed. He switched quickly into them.

"I need to use the bathroom. I can manage on my own... unless you'd like to join?"

The man's face recorded no expression. "Leave the door open."

Henry simply raised an eyebrow and moved to the bathroom. He sat heavily on the toilet – long enough to do his fake business – slid out of one of his snowshoes and retrieved the Rohypnol, the locker key, and the small set of tools he had hidden into them that morning.

He moved the toolkit into the side of the same shoe and the chemicals into the other. Henry flushed the toilet, made a fuss about washing his hands, and came out, faking relief.

The man was still standing in the middle of the room waiting for him.

When they reached The Ritz lobby, Upstage and Botha were there. Andropov had sent a car, and Henry's minder took the front seat.

They arrived at the restaurant. Tatiana was waiting for them in Sakhalin's reception area. She'd changed into a new and elegant fur coat that made her slender figure more attractive.

The second Upstage saw her he perked up. She greeted him first with a kiss on each cheek, but abstained from the third kiss that Russians would customarily deliver on the lips. Tatiana welcomed Botha and Henry more formally. They walked to the lifts that would take them to the top floor of the panoramic restaurant.

When they reached the top, Tatiana stood off to the side of the lift's door. Upstage stepped first into the cosier reception area of the restaurant, where another attractive woman took his coat and Botha's.

Tatiana brushed Henry's hand and placed a small piece of paper in it. Her touch lingered for a little longer. Henry moved his fingers slowly along hers to acknowledge her touch.

The table they were guided to had a spectacular view. It faced the historical Moscow city centre and some of the most imposing Stalin skyscrapers, reminding visitors of Russia's not-so-distant communist past. The frame of the structures was a brutal design – a mass of concrete, with slender windows that didn't allow for enough light. In the distance, the Kremlin Palace looked dwarfed by the modern constructions around it.

The two guards that had accompanied the small party were standing at the door of the restaurant. Other patrons arriving to have lunch ignored them. The presence of security teams seemed to be a well-established routine in upper class Moscow.

"Putin dines here regularly," Tatiana explained to Henry as she sat down opposite him, next to Upstage.

"What do they do – shut the restaurant to other diners and let him have the view for himself?"

"The view *and* the food. He trusts the Chef, Boris Markov, with the food he eats."

Henry nodded. "He is frightened of being poisoned."

"Always." Tatiana smiled at him.

Judging from Upstage's mood, Henry knew it had been a mistake to sit in front of her. Botha had plonked himself in front of Upstage, not giving him much choice of seat, but Upstage would not see it that way. The dynamics around the table had become awkward.

Tatiana must have sensed it. She made a big show of taking Upstage to the seawater tanks where live crustaceans were waiting for their fate.

Botha stood up to inspect the tanks as well and chose his lunch. Henry decided to go for what the *maître d'* would recommend as the best.

Champagne was ordered and consumed with oysters and caviar. The atmosphere improved, with Tatiana speaking about the gossip that surrounded Putin and the Moscow elite. Henry made an excuse to visit the restroom, just before the main course arrived. He dived into a cubicle before his minder could object.

Tatiana's piece of paper gave him the address of the British Embassy and a mobile number he didn't recognise. She'd added it was for the new burner phone she had acquired that morning.

The final message was more sobering.

Need to leave in next 48 hours. Andropov suspicious.

Henry memorised the address and the phone number. He tore up the message and flushed it down the toilet. He took out his mobile, switched it on and composed a text to James.

At Sakhalin for next 2 hours. Need extraction within next 48 hours. Will be accompanied x2. Mobile compromised.

James would relay the message to Harris. Henry had no time to send another text. He switched his mobile off again.

The subject at the table had turned to the US elections again. Apparently, Upstage had thrown his hat in the political ring, just before he'd left for London. The Republican Party had reacted with a mixture of disbelief and scepticism.

Henry enjoyed playing devil's advocate and Upstage enjoyed taking the bait. Upstage could deploy his skills at arguing anything he fancied by wrapping it in a coat of emotions. No one was immune to the effect his arguments had on them. Henry reluctantly admitted it – David Upstage was in good stead to become the next president of the White House.

After they had their main course, Tatiana ordered everyone coffee. It arrived with a selection of petit fours. Henry apologised and stretched over Botha's cup to gain access to the sugar. Botha ignored Henry. The subject around the table had moved to South Africa and the man couldn't care less what Henry did.

"Would it be greedy to ask for another cup?" Henry asked after finishing his coffee.

Everyone agreed and Tatiana ordered more.

Botha had slumped a little in his seat. Everyone around the table assumed it was the result of a good lunch. But Henry felt Botha lean towards him. He waited a few more seconds. The Rohypnol was about to kick in.

Botha slid to one side of his chair. Henry grabbed his arm in time to stop him crashing to the ground. Tatiana stood up fast and helped him. Henry slid his hand into Botha's jacket pocket, picked out Botha's phone and dropped in his mobile instead.

Botha fought a last-ditch attempt to stay awake, and then he was out. The two bodyguards that were waiting for them arrived, and without a word, lifted Botha up. People in the restaurant looked surprised, but they returned to their meals once Botha had disappeared.

Upstage looked pale and shocked.

"Let's go. We don't need to settle the bill." Tatiana was already moving away.

Henry was the last to leave the table. As he did, a familiar face entered the restaurant. James walked towards Henry, bumped into him and apologised.

"Mind where you're going!" Henry managed an angry tone. He felt a small item being dropped into his jacket pocket. He was in possession of a new burner phone.

* * *

"How quickly can you get the jet plane to St Petersburg?" Harris asked his asset.

"Three days, perhaps four." Brett sounded unsure.

"We have 48 hours."

"It's a ridiculous timetable! I need to massage the idea slowly into girlfriend and dad's mind."

"How about her future boyfriend?"

"He'll do anything I tell him to. He can't believe his luck."

"I bet he can't." Harris was driving along the Thames on his way to Cheltenham. It was time he paid a visit to Natasha at GCHQ to see if she could help.

Harris added. "How about I find a new bidder for the exceptional piece of antiquity your replacement will be offering to his soon-to-be father in law?"

Brett paused. "That could work... Nothing pisses off one Russian oligarch more than to know another Russian oligarch is going to get something he wants."

"Leave it with me, but I need that plane in St Petersburg in two days."

"I heard you the first time," Brett shot back. "You deliver the new buyer, I'll get the plane there in time."

"You're the best," Harris teased.

"Glad you finally noticed," Brett huffed and hung up.

Harris changed phones and placed his office mobile into the cradle on the dashboard of his beaten up old car. It had taken all the ingenuity of his technical team to fit the phone device in his antique vehicle, but Harris had insisted it happen. Some of his assets knew the car and were more comfortable with its understated appearance.

"It's not understated, it's just scrap heap material," one of the engineers had complained.

"No one wants to steal it or even notices it. That's fine by me," Harris had replied stubbornly.

He smiled at the memory and pressed the redial button for one of his recent calls.

"I was hoping you'd call." Jack sounded breathless.

"James has landed in Moscow. But no news yet."

"Some progress here. Mandy and Nick met at his apartment yesterday – don't ask me why. I know these two spoke from their phone records. They left together, and the only odd thing was that Nick was wearing a Domino's Pizza cap."

Harris said nothing.

"Are you still here?" Jack asked.

"Yes, sorry... I was thinking. Does this guy Nick usually wear caps?"

"Why do you ask?"

"It's the old pizza delivery trick, mate. You pretend to deliver a pizza to get access to someone's property."

"That's a bit obvious," Jack protested.

"But more to the point it still works. If this is what I think it is, these two have gone on a recce."

"Shit... Mandy, she just has to follow through, no matter what."

"That's why she's good at her job."

"Not when it lands her in hot water."

"We don't know that yet." Harris tried to sound hopeful.

"You know that's crap, Steve. Besides, I've had Mandy's car traced."

"And?"

"We tracked it to a neighbourhood in Kalorama, a less trendy part of DC. Then it vanishes."

Harris had reached the motorway. He spotted a petrol station, changed lanes and turned into it.

"Gone is my optimism then." Harris became sombre.

"I'm having a meeting with my boss Hunter this morning. I need more resources to track them before it's too late."

"I'm sorry I can't be of more help."

"You've got your own agent to look after," Jack said. "Let's agree to touch base as soon as we have news."

Harris agreed and the line went dead. It took a few seconds for him to kill the call on his end.

"Fuck!" Harris started the engine angrily and rejoined the flow of traffic to Cheltenham.

He turned into the entrance for the GCHQ building. His credentials were vetted. Natasha had let security know he was visiting.

Harris parked and called her on his mobile.

"I'll come and collect you," she said. "You need to hear what I've managed to salvage from the audio and images Henry sent."

"Good stuff?" Harris hadn't heard Natasha sound so uptight for a very long time.

"Bloody explosive. I had to listen to it twice to make sure I really got it right."

Harris wore a set of headphones to listen to the audio Natasha had cleaned using a deciphering key, to make the tape audible. The images were of good enough quality, although interference sometimes created blank patches.

Natasha warned him. "The Russians used something electronic to disable the type of recording device Crowne was carrying, but we still got enough to make sense of what has been recorded."

Harris listened to the tapes and viewed the images a few times. He was stunned. He pulled the headphones from his ears slowly. Natasha returned with two cups of tea.

"I've got to speak to the Chief," he said.

"And we need more ears on Andropov's team."

"Crowne has sent an emergency signal. I'm going to try to extract him in the next 48 hours."

Natasha shook her head. "Andropov is going to do anything to protect this deal. It's just too good to be true – access to the White House, and plenty of ammunition to blackmail the president. I wonder whether Upstage has the full measure of who he is dealing with."

"Not my problem. I want my guys out. James has flown in to help with the exfiltration."

"Do you need help?" Natasha asked.

Harris nodded. "I was hoping you'd say that."

"Anything to stuff these bastards..." Natasha took a large gulp of tea.

"I need the name of an oligarch known to collect antiquities on a large scale. I'm hoping to create a bit of a bidding war between two of these guys. I'm targeting the daddy of Brett's girlfriend."

"Very good. Daddy is getting into this big time from the data we've gathered."

"Who's the worthy opponent then?"

"Rostov, of course," Natasha said. "He's invited Brett to the Russian Embassy for a talk, on daddy's recommendation. Daddy is not going to like the fact that Rostov may want to pilfer a piece earmarked for him."

"Sounds like a plan. How quickly can we put the word out there?"

"Tell your team I'm sending them enough details of Rostov's collection to put the word out there. As you say, he is on the antiques acquisition war path. I'll set up a Russian mobile number. You can send a text from it to Brett asking for details of the piece. He can show that to daddy."

"Anything else you get on Andropov and his team..." Harris added.

"I'll let you know." Natasha hesitated. "I don't want to tell you how to do your job, but these guys, Andropov's guys, are good. GRU or FSB, handpicked, smart, and completely ruthless."

"And I'm running RUSSKY BEAR on a shoestring."

Chapter Twenty-Nine

Andropov was not in the suite of rooms they usually met in. Tatiana waited for 20 minutes before she stuck her head out of the door to check for him.

The security guards were dotted in the corridor outside and waiting at the entrance to search and vet newcomers.

If there was one place that had not been fitted with video cameras or audio recording it was Andropov's suite. A couple of mobile phones were scattered on the coffee table between the sofas and chairs. His laptop had been left open, but the screensaver was on. She wouldn't get anywhere on his highly protected device.

There was only one reason Andropov had left in a hurry. The Kremlin had placed a call and he was needed there urgently.

Tatiana picked up one of the phones, unsure as to what it would yield, but perhaps she'd learn something useful. The phone was prepaid and there was only one number on it. She recognised the American mobile number.

She hesitated and pressed the recall button.

"Alexei Pietrovich, oni yeshche nichego ne shazali."

Tatiana killed the call and bit her lip. The man on the call just said that whoever they were interrogating hadn't talked. Nick and the woman who was with him were being handled by some of the mafia connections Andropov had in the US. They could be anywhere by now, and it would only be a matter of time before they spoke.

Tatiana suspected the only reason they hadn't been broken yet was that Andropov did not want to damage his relationship with Upstage through Henry.

297

She memorised the phone number she'd just called, and still had the phone in her hand when the door opened. Tatiana put the phone down quickly and straightened up, hoping Andropov had not noticed.

His expression was smooth, and she couldn't read it. She took a few steps towards him. He stood waiting until she reached him.

"Alexei Pietrovich, you called –" she said.

The punch to her stomach was as violent as it was unexpected. Tatiana opened her mouth to speak, but nothing came out. Andropov grabbed her hair and threw her against an ornate table that stood in the centre of the room. Tatiana crashed into it, falling like a rag doll. An ornament on the table toppled to the floor, smashing, then the table followed with a deafening sound.

Andropov didn't give Tatiana any time to recover and put her training in practice. He, too, had been trained at the same school of spies. He threw himself at her, caught her in an arm lock, pinned her on the floor, one knee on the base of her neck.

"Are you playing a silly game with me?"

Tatiana tried to shake her head, but couldn't. She croaked "No" instead.

"Then why has Henry Newborn's phone disappeared from my care and been switched on again?"

"I don't know," Tatiana managed to articulate.

"And you expect me to believe this?"

Andropov pushed his knee harder into her neck. She slapped the floor the way a boxer asking for mercy did, but there was none coming from Andropov.

"You are the only one to know his phone and laptop have been taken away."

"No..." Tatiana tried to lift her chest a little so that she could breathe, but Andropov's weight was too great. She would soon lose consciousness.

"Then who else?"

"Botha..." she whispered.

Andropov slid his knee further down her shoulder blades, grabbed her hair again and lifted her head a little.

"How do you know?"

"He mentioned to Upstage that Henry had lost his phone."

It was a lie of course, but Tatiana needed to gain time.

"How did he get hold of it?"

"I don't know... ask him." She tried to wriggle under Andropov's weight, but she couldn't shake free.

Andropov stayed there for a couple of minutes. Tatiana's breathing was getting shallower. He finally released her and stood up. Tatiana rolled onto her back, gasping in air. The room was hazy and Andropov's figure kept swimming in front of her eyes.

"Get up..." he demanded.

Andropov moved to the coffee table with the mobiles and his laptop.

"I said, get up."

Tatiana lifted herself up onto one elbow. Her entire body was pleading for rest, but she forced herself to sit up.

"I will have a conversation with Botha and Upstage," Andropov said. "You know what will happen if I learn you've been lying to me?"

Tatiana nodded. She stood slowly. The hatred she felt must have shown on her face because Andropov smiled coldly.

"That feeling will get you nowhere. You won't pay for your mistakes, but your brother will."

"What if Botha and Upstage lie to you?"

"No one lies to me, Tatiana. You of all people should know that."

"If you touch them now you lose everything – the White House, a link to the next president..."

"Do I?" Andropov smiled. "Who says I am relying on only one candidate?"

Tatiana's mind went blank. What was Andropov saying?

"Although I agree with you that Upstage is the best of the lot. Hence the reason why he still is my priority. If he tries to be too smart, then..." Andropov shrugged.

"What about Henry?"

"The two people we picked up in the US are sticking to their story so far. They were trying to find out who got into his apartment and they didn't speak to the police for the reasons Henry has explained. His clients don't like that sort of publicity, which also suits me fine."

Tatiana didn't ask whether she should keep interacting with Henry. Better not give Andropov the opportunity to say no.

"Go back to The Ritz," he said. "I don't want you to leave the hotel unless I say so."

* * *

The knock on his bedroom door surprised Henry. The man Andropov had sent to pick him up in the morning had become a permanent fixture outside his door, but Henry doubted he would be polite enough to knock before entering.

He opened it, preparing for some unpleasant surprise. Instead, the waiter who had brought him tea, with the few additional items he had concealed and already made use of, stood there.

"You've ordered tea, sir."

The waiter was about to enter but Andropov's man stopped him. He lifted the lid of the teapot, then inspected the couple of pastries that had been arranged on a small plate. He nodded the waiter in.

The waiter walked past Henry with a smile. Henry closed the door. The waiter went straight over to the blind spot.

"Where shall I put the tray, sir?"

As he spoke, he pulled out a small piece of paper from his pocket and dropped it on the bed.

Henry moved to the side of the bed and read it quickly.

Hotel club gym, 30 minutes.

Henry nodded. "How about the table next to the window?"

"Certainly, sir."

The waiter put the piece of paper in his mouth. He chewed a couple of times and swallowed. Henry held back a smile – an old-fashioned but effective way of disposing of a note.

The waiter left and he made himself some tea, changed into his gym gear and stepped out of his room 25 minutes later.

"I'm going to the club gym."

Andropov's man nodded and started walking towards the lift. There was no point in complaining. It would be all Andropov needed to ground Henry to his room permanently.

The Ritz's gym was everything one could expect from a hotel of such standing: the latest equipment organised around a spacious room;

300

a couple of gym studios for individual classes. A woman and her yoga coach were having a private lesson.

A few men were using some of the equipment. Henry scanned the room and spotted the broad back of someone he already knew. James was pulling on the oars of one of the rowing machines.

Henry moved to the traction bars that were situated a few steps away from where James was exercising. He unzipped his sports jacket and started loading the weights.

Andropov's man was standing near the door, far enough not to disturb the other club members but to keep his eyes on Henry.

Henry started his routine. After a few minutes he stood up again, adding another plate to the weight load. Henry detected an almost imperceptible movement of James's head. James had seen him.

His former colleague stood up to modify the pull of the rowing machine and sat back down. He wiped his brow with the small towel around his neck.

"Who are the other two people?" James said softly, addressing the wall rather than Henry.

Henry moved his arms up to release the weights. "One defector and her brother."

Henry pulled and let go again. "She spies on Upstage for Andropov. Tatiana Borodin."

James kept going on the rowing machine for five more minutes and stopped again, this time wiping his entire face with the towel.

"The woman I tried to find information on?" James said. He took a swig of water from his water bottle and carried on. "Adds complication. You sure she's trustworthy?"

Henry pulled the weights down. "I am. What's the plan?"

"Train to St Petersburg, plane to Finland."

James stood up, went to the glass fridge, and took a cold bottle of water from inside. He walked over to the running machine and started another routine.

Henry went to the other side of the room stacked with small towels. He used one to wipe his face and took a fresh one. He slung it over his shoulders.

Henry moved to the rowing machines, inspected the one James had sat on and pulled a face, for his minder. He moved to the next one, closest to the running machine James was using.

"Why Petersburg?" Henry asked as he was adjusting the machine's setting.

"Finland's more reliable than other neighbouring countries."

"News of Nick and Mandy?" Henry sat heavily into the seat of the rowing machine.

James remained silent.

"Fuck..." Henry gritted his teeth and started pulling hard.

The two men concentrated on their routine for a while.

Henry slowed down, stopped, and stood up to change the setting of the rower. "Are you coming with us on the train?"

"Yes." James slowed down a little so that he could reply.

"Not a good idea." Henry moved back into his seat.

"Why?"

"If we are caught, better one of us than two."

"That's not the deal."

"Borodin is my responsibility, not yours."

James slowed down to a fast walk. He didn't reply, and Henry knew he was angry that Henry was right. James couldn't take the risk.

* * *

His time at the gym had done Henry a lot of good. Andropov's man had been a little distracted by one of the women who had started exercising there. She had arrived with her personal coach, and her clingy outfit stretched over a perfect body must have given Andropov's man quite a lot to think about.

Henry showered back in his bedroom, grateful that he'd been left alone to do this. He changed into a pair of black jeans and a light-blue roll neck pullover. He would visit Upstage again in an hour's time, feigning concern for Botha's health.

He was about to switch on the TV in the hope of catching the news, even if it was from a government approved broadcaster, when he heard two voices at the door. He moved closer to listen to the conversation.

It was in Russian and one of the voices was Tatiana's. Henry opened the door. Tatiana said something angrily to the minder, walked in and shut the door behind her.

302

"I need a drink." She moved into the bedroom and sat on the bed in the blind spot.

"I'm sure I can find something suitable in the bar." Henry made a show of going to the well-stocked fridge, took out a bottle of champagne and picked up a couple of glasses from the fridge. The Russians certainly knew how to serve their drinks.

He popped the cork open, and with an expert hand, poured two glasses.

"A little music, perhaps?" Henry switched on the TV, selected Radio Channel 5.

He came to sit on the bed next to Tatiana and offered her a glass. Only then did he notice the mark on her neck, peeking out from under her scarf.

"What is this?" Henry murmured, moving his fingers closer to the bruise.

Tatiana recoiled and spilt a few drops of champagne on the bed.

"I'm so clumsy." She stood up to wipe the liquid from the blanket. Henry caught her hand and guided her back down.

He felt her resist and let go. "Won't you talk to me?"

Tatiana took a couple of mouthfuls of champagne and settled against the headrest of the bed. She closed her eyes for a moment, then shook herself up straight. There was no position in which she seemed comfortable.

Henry joined her, back against the headrest, legs stretched out in front of him.

"Andropov knows about your mobile phone," she said.

"I didn't use it inside The Ritz though."

"Well... it seems he's been tracking it across Moscow and hadn't told me."

"You don't need to worry about it. It's no longer in my possession."

Tatiana turned to face him, surprised. She winced, bringing a hand to her stomach.

"Are you hurt?"

Henry quickly left his glass on the bedside table and took her hand.

"It's nothing, not the first time... I'll recover." Tatiana's fist clenched and she gave Henry a sad smile.

"Andropov?" The name almost stuck in Henry's throat.

Tatiana closed her fingers tight over Henry's. "Don't concern yourself about this. What matters now is leaving this place."

Henry went to touch her neck. She made a feeble attempt to stop him. He pulled the scarf off her neck in a slow and gentle motion. The injury was starting to show; the red marks were turning purple.

Anger coursed through Henry. He would enjoy savaging Andropov, even more so now that he had seen the full extent of the man's callousness.

Henry breathed in deeply to quieten his outrage. He managed a smile and brought Tatiana's fingers to his lips.

"I promise you I will get you out of Russia."

Tatiana dropped her head to his shoulder. "I know you will."

They stayed together for a moment. Tatiana pulled back and disappeared into the bathroom. Henry heard the taps running, and when she came back, her face was damp with water.

"I have one important number for you," she said.

Tatiana grabbed a pen from the bedside table. She pulled the sleeve of his pullover up and wrote a number on his forearm.

"It's a US mobile that belongs to one of the men who is holding Nick and the other woman. Your people should be able to geo-localise them."

Henry nodded a thank you. His mind raced. How was he going to get it to Harris?

"My brother is ready to leave..." Tatiana looked as though she wanted to say more but held back.

"Tomorrow evening. I'll tell you where to meet me in the morning."

"Do you know the route?" She shook her head. "That's a silly question, you shouldn't answer."

Henry smiled. "Then I won't answer it."

"Andropov made some odd comments about Upstage that I can't quite figure out."

"Can you tell me more?"

"'Who says I rely on one candidate only?' His exact words to me when I told him he couldn't do without Upstage if he wanted to gain access to the White House."

"Was he pretending?"

304

"No, Andropov never pretends, or at least not in that sort of way. He was strangely confident... He said Upstage was still at the top of his list, but I got the impression he was sliding down it fast."

"But there is a list." Henry couldn't quite believe it either.

"So he says."

They said nothing for a little while.

"One last question." Henry looked at his watch. It was almost time for his last visit to Upstage. "If Andropov disposes of Upstage, how will he do it?"

Tatiana's eyes widened. "Why do you want to know?"

"I'm covering all eventualities..."

"Poison." Tatiana didn't hesitate. "Andropov likes the idea of making his enemy suffer."

"Poison is a pretty dangerous thing to handle."

"He's done it before, although these days, someone else will deliver the fatal dose for him."

They both stood up slowly.

"We'll be ready by tomorrow evening," Tatiana said.

"Keep out of Upstage and Andropov's way."

Tatiana frowned but she didn't reply. She walked past Henry, then stopped to touch his face. "Thank you."

* * *

"The article talking about Rostov wanting to acquire a new piece of antiquity from the Middle East is live on the internet, and a couple of papers have agreed to publish it," Harris said, having just arrived back from GCHQ.

"That sounds promising... and I just had a missed call coming from a Russian mobile phone, which I presume is from your lot rather than someone who's actually in Russia," Brett replied.

"Well spotted... I could ask someone to leave a message telling you that Rostov is looking for a piece similar to the one you're trying to fly to Russia, but why lie when you don't have to? At least not yet." Harris added.

"If daddy is not convinced, then I'll come back to you. For the time being, I'll get on with it."

"That's the spirit."

Brett hung up before Harris could tell him once more what a valuable asset he was.

Harris pocketed the leather-clad burner phone and turned to his computer screen. It was almost 5pm, 8pm in Moscow – the time he had agreed he would be calling James.

Harris opened the FB account his COMMS team had set up for the purpose of communicating – one old friend to another.

Harris started the chat under his alias, Steve Jackson.

Steve: *Hullo old chap, I hear you've landed a new job in Moscow. Well done.*

The reply came after a few minutes; long enough not to look like a rushed communication.

James: *Hullo Steve, news travels fast. I arrived today and was given a tour of the Embassy. It looks good but one of my suitcases hasn't arrived yet.*

There was a change of plan. Harris braced for what was coming next.

Steve: *That's never fun... Can I help at all?*

James: *Since you're asking, perhaps. I'm missing a couple of unusual jumpers I bought from Harrods. Be a chum, purchase the same and send them to me.*

Harris's eyebrows shot up. It was an unusual request to say the least, and one that he needed to double check on the code equivalents. He hadn't used this communication for a while. Perhaps he had picked James up wrong. He checked.

No, he hadn't. Someone was proposing to defect. Harris went back to the FB chat.

Steve: *If you had the name of the jumpers that would be even easier.*

James: *Can't remember just yet. Give me a day and I'm sure it'll come back to me.*

James was suggesting he take this conversation to the secure comms centre from the Moscow Embassy.

Harris wished him a good stay and walked out of his office. He took the lift down to the basement, Level 1, followed a maze of corridors and ended up in COMMS CONTROL. He pressed the intercom and asked permission to enter. A new person appeared on screen at the door and buzzed him in.

"I need to place an urgent call to the British Embassy in Moscow, to the secure comms space there."

306

The young woman nodded. She took his name and disappeared. A few minutes later the head of COMMS for Eastern Europe and Russia appeared.

"Urgent call to Moscow?" he simply said by way of greeting.

"Please. I have a situation hotting up there."

"You're in luck. We've just finished a call that required a lot of bandwidth. I'll get it set up for you. I presume your contact is waiting there?"

"Yes, my contact is waiting."

Harris was shown into a small room. A couple of technicians made the connection. James's voice bounced around the room.

"Steve, we're connected."

Harris switched from loudspeaker to headset. The comms people retreated, leaving Harris on his own.

"What is happening now? Two defectors? Have I got that right?"

"Yes... the woman Tatiana Borodin and her brother."

"Who does she work for, GRU, FSB?"

"Andropov."

"Is she the one who has been assigned to Upstage as well as Crowne?"

"That's what Henry said..." James hesitated a moment. "I'm sure he wouldn't fall for a good old-fashioned honey trap."

"Her background story says that she lost her parents in an assassination?"

"That's right. She and her brother were young when it happened."

Harris breathed in deep. If there was one weakness Henry had, it was for stories similar to the unresolved death of his father.

"We can't exclude anything," said Harris. "Although if we assume it was her who visited his apartment in DC, she didn't report the vault or her suspicions to Andropov."

"And if she turns up with her brother, maybe it's for real," James suggested.

"I need to check if we can find a recent picture of the young lad. She could be bringing any old kid and we wouldn't be the wiser."

"The plan still stands though?"

"It stands, with one modification – you're not going with Crowne. You're now flying to St Petersburg."

"Henry said the same thing to me, but I still believe it's risky for us to be separated."

"Crowne is right," said Harris. "If this woman is playing him, he goes down on his own."

307

"Fine, I'll get the last flight out to St Petersburg. It leaves Moscow at 9.30pm, which gives me time to see them off at the train station."

"Good point. If something happens it will be either there or on their arrival at St Petersburg."

James said, "Henry has a new burner phone, which he won't activate until mid-morning tomorrow. By then I'll have figured out how to get the train tickets to him, as well as the address of our meeting point in St Petersburg."

Harris unfastened his watch and changed the time. "I've moved my watch to Moscow time... GMT plus 3 hrs."

"Understood. Let's fix a call for tomorrow, 10am."

"By the way, which airline are you flying?

"Aeroflot, of course." James sounded annoyed.

Harris couldn't help but chuckle. "Crowne might have the better deal after all."

Harris hung up, returned to his desk and called Natasha straight away.

"You're missing me already?" she said.

"Always, especially as you're about to get me what I really, really need..."

"A complete turn-on. What do you need so very much then?"

"A recent picture of a young lad, who has almost certainly been kept out of the media since he was 3 years old."

"Name, please."

"Anatolie Borodin, son of Piotr and Yulia Borodin."

"The two journalists assassinated for reporting about Chechnya?"

"Exactly right."

"And you needed it yesterday, I presume."

"No, the day before yesterday. I have an exfiltration that depends on this."

Chapter Thirty

Henry took the stairs to Upstage's suite. He needed the short walk to release some of the anger he still felt. The beating Tatiana had endured was incomprehensible to him, and he sensed that Andropov had enjoyed doing it. Rule by fear and deception, and inflict pain whenever he could.

Andropov's man was still following Henry, but he managed to ignore his presence.

One of Upstage's bodyguards let Henry in. Upstage was on his own. Botha was still recovering from the Rohypnol Henry had administered. Tatiana had decided to nurse her wounds in her bedroom. Henry was glad she was not around.

"What a crazy thing... Botha's been drugged." Upstage sounded more annoyed than scared.

"Are you sure?" Henry sat down on the sofa opposite Upstage.

"That's what the doctor said."

"Who would want to do that?"

"No idea, but the Russians can be a bit odd when it comes to drugs and so on." Upstage leaned forward and lowered his voice. "You heard what Tatiana said to us about Putin and poison."

Henry leaned in conspiratorially. "I found that a little unsettling to hear, to tell you the truth."

Upstage nodded. "That's OK. As long as the Russians help us, I can live with their quirky ways. Once I'm installed in the Oval Office, matters will be different."

"The Russians will have to be more cautious dealing with you."

"If I deal with them at all..." Upstage gave Henry a small nod that told him there was more to his statement.

"I see." Henry sat back. "Aren't you worried about the consequences?"

"I'll deny it all. Will say the Russians are trying to discredit me. And when it comes to arranging the credit risk edge for the loan, what can they prove? I received a loan from a Swiss bank, which happens to be a private bank I'm a client of anyway. That Swiss bank is free to find any counterpart, including a Russian one, to edge that risk. There is nothing in writing linking me to the Russian edge. I'm clean."

"Very true." Henry gave the minimum response. Unless the man was on a suicide mission, perhaps it had not occurred to Upstage that his suite was almost certainly bugged, and that even if he'd had it swept by his own security team, nothing was assured.

Tatiana's words kept coming back to Henry. Russia was courting several potential candidates, grooming them, with the plan to select the one they'd find the most eligible. Andropov would then unleash the vast cyber war machine he'd constructed, flooding social media and the internet with news they could manipulate or simply fabricate...

The era of fake news was upon them.

Upstage was talking about his next series of inflammatory tweets. He'd been warming up his fan base for whatever Andropov had promised to release on Hillary Clinton. Henry didn't have much to do except listen, nod and let the man revel in his own bloated ego.

"Is there anything else I can do for you?" Henry eventually asked.

"Keep Andropov off my back." Upstage had returned to the real world. "I need to convince Botha to follow me in the way *I* want to run things."

Henry smiled. He had every intention of getting Andropov off Upstage's back, in a way that would be final.

Henry stood up for a break. He moved to the suite's small corridor and one of Upstage's bodyguards indicated the door to the guest toilet. Henry entered, waited a moment there, and slipped out and into Upstage's private bathroom.

He looked around for the perfect place to plant the spare Rohypnol pill he'd brought with him. Somewhere hidden, but that would be easy to find if trained investigators were to look.

310

He found a pack of paracetamol, slid the pill into it, returned to the door and checked. He snuck out and returned to the lounge. Upstage was on his mobile. Henry pointed to his watch indicating he too had a call to make.

Upstage gave Henry the thumbs up. Henry nodded his goodbye and left. He took the stairs again to reach his room and make his next move.

He thought about the way he had muddied the waters for Upstage and Botha. The Rohypnol in Upstage's personal effects would draw some questions, and so too would the fact that Botha was in possession of Henry's mobile phone.

Andropov's man followed him down to his room, and as soon as Henry opened the door, he turned around to ask a question the man was not expecting.

"I need to speak to Andropov... in person. Make the call."

Henry closed the door, ignoring the question that was forming on the man's lips. He moved to the blind spot, pulled out a small backpack out of his suitcase, and started assembling what he needed for the journey he was about to take that evening.

His bedroom phone rang and Henry picked up.

"Do you have things to say to me that I need to hear?" Andropov sounded amused.

"I've recalled where I've seen the woman you picked up with Nick Fox."

"It's a good start. Anything else?"

"Not over the phone and only in person."

Andropov paused. "I'll see you shortly."

Andropov had sent one of his SUVs to pick Henry up. The trip to Andropov's office only took 10 minutes. Henry went through the same security routine as usual. He surrendered the mobile he had pick-pocketed from Botha at the Sakhalin restaurant.

Andropov was waiting in his office, sitting comfortably in the same armchair as the last time. Henry wondered whether there were some hidden advantages to sitting there. He walked in, thinking the layout looked different.

Andropov signalled Henry to approach him. "What have you got for me?"

Henry sat down where Upstage had sat before – a message to Andropov he was ready to take over.

"The woman you showed me on your phone visited Nick at the office a few days before I left for the UK. I had been looking for a new receptionist. She'd been temping for someone else in the building. She was very insistent she could do the job. There was something odd about her that I couldn't figure out at the time..."

"Apart from the fact that not choosing a coloured woman plays to the white audience you cultivate, why is this of interest?" Andropov tapped his fingers a few times on the armrest of his chair.

"I think she was from an agency." Henry didn't show hesitation. He had to commit now to the course of action he had chosen, otherwise Mandy would be in desperate trouble.

"You mean intelligence agency?" Andropov stared at Henry.

"Nothing else would be worth mentioning."

"Why not mention it when we first spoke?"

"I had to think it through." Henry shook his head. "It's a loaded statement, and I needed to be sure."

Andropov nodded. "Let's have some tea."

He picked up his phone and spoke a few words into it, then put it down.

Andropov sat back. "But why would your assistant, Nick, get involved with her?"

"Perhaps the agency got some intel after surveying my apartment and she convinced him to work with her. Nick can be a little gullible, sometimes."

Tea arrived. The small samovar was put on the table. The mugs were turned upside down. The man serving the tea picked them up, laid them near the samovar and left.

Andropov stood up first and helped himself to some tea. Henry followed hoping his reading of the situation was right.

"No matter." Andropov sipped his tea. "My people have been very restrained so far. I'll get to the bottom of this. No one can resist a Russian mafia interrogation."

"I would be grateful if you could spare Nick."

"Is he *that* good?"

312

"He is. An excellent asset if you know how to use him."

Andropov drank his tea in silence. Henry hesitated, then took a mouthful. A part of him expected to feel woozy after exposure to some drug or another. But he was still feeling fine after a few sips.

"I presume this is not the only thing you want talk about, is it?"

"You're right." Henry finished his tea and set the mug down on the coffee table.

"Upstage?" Andropov smiled, amused.

"You've made some pretty open commitments to supporting David in his campaign. I can't help wondering why. You don't need to be that open with him. You can help quietly."

Andropov's eyes lit up with recognition that the man before him was worth cultivating. There was something else fleeting that appeared in Andropov's eyes – disappointment or regret. Regret that he may have to inflict on Henry now what he'd already decided to inflict on Upstage.

Andropov nodded. "And you're concerned about the implications of my honesty."

"I'd like to at least understand the idea behind it."

"Let me explain." Andropov stood up and refilled his mug. Henry did the same with his.

Andropov casually checked his phone. He returned to his seat.

"There are many ways to play my game of influence. I never bet on only one horse."

Andropov had just exposed his plan to Henry. He was referring to the list of US presidential candidates. Also, how he knew the weakness of each of them, and ways he could use those weaknesses to guarantee they feared him.

Henry had made a few astute comments that had been well received. But he also knew he would not be allowed to leave this room alive.

Andropov had finished his exposé, looking satisfied with the plan he had explained to Henry.

"I'm parched." Andropov picked up his phone again. "Let's have some fresh tea."

He called again and Henry noticed a change in the vocabulary.

"This is incredibly ingenious of you. And I rarely pay anyone compliments." Henry tried to look relaxed, an unsuspecting victim.

Two people arrived with refreshments. The man who had served them the first time picked up the used mugs and samovar, and left. The woman carrying fresh tea walked cautiously forward. She was holding the tray straight; her body looked tense. She laid the tray on the coffee table in a slow, careful motion. She stepped back quickly and left.

Henry noticed the glass mugs were turned up, ready for use. Andropov signalled in a graceful manner that Henry should help himself.

Henry poured some tea into a mug. He picked it up and moved back towards his seat.

And with a flick of his wrist, he flung the scalding contents into Andropov's face.

Andropov jerked and he swore. Rage showed in his eyes, replaced almost instantly by complete and utter dread.

His face muscles started to twitch. He tried to lift a hand, but he couldn't. The poison was already coursing through his body, ripping apart every cell it touched.

Henry raced to a table along one wall. He grabbed a bottle of water, opened it and quickly drenched his hands. He had been careful, but he couldn't be certain he hadn't spilt tea on them.

Andropov was sinking low into his chair, gagging for air. Henry picked up the handset of the phone on the table. The line was live, and he dialled a UK number he knew by heart.

"Crowne... Where are you?" Harris sounded alarmed.

"Take down this number and trace it. It should lead you to Nick and Mandy." Henry gave him the number Tatiana had written on his arm. "We are leaving tonight. There is a night train to St Petersburg. It's a slow train but we need to get out now."

"Shit... Do you have a death wish? We've not prepped your exfil that way."

"No, I very much want to stay alive, and I have no time to explain."

"I'll get James on the case. And before you do anything even more stupid than what I suspect you've just done, check the image I'm about to send to the burner phone James gave you."

"Fine, I'll see you in Finland."

"I bloody well hope so, mate."

314

Henry hung up and turned to Andropov. The man's body was now agitated, as though moved only by the memories of a nightmare. His eyes had rolled back in his head. Drool had begun to leak from his mouth.

Henry started shouting and ran towards the door, crying for help.

The guards outside rushed in, but stopped dead when they saw Andropov. They knew what it meant. Andropov's body had stopped twitching. He was on his side, perfectly still.

The men turned to Henry. They noticed his wet hands and took a step back in fear. Had he been contaminated too?

More people arrived. The man and the woman who had served Henry and Andropov burst into the room. The woman shrieked and started giving orders to the guards. Henry stepped back slowly, and then a little bit more, until he was out the door.

* * *

Andropov's poisoning on his own premises had sent shock waves through the place. Someone had left a coat and hat on the chair outside the room. Henry grabbed both.

He walked away from Andropov's office as confidently as he could, and down the large staircase. Two guards were posted at the main entrance door. They would almost certainly challenge him. He turned left before he reached the hallway, heading towards what were likely more rooms. A couple of people ran past him in the direction of Andropov's office.

Soon the place would go into lockdown.

Henry reached the end of the corridor. He found the door of one of the offices had been left open. He walked in and gave the ground floor office a quick look. He moved to the window. The window was triple glazed and thick set, almost impossible to break. Henry inspected it up close. There was a small lock at the bottom of the frame that meant the window could be opened.

Henry bent down and extracted the lock picking tools from his winter boots. He started working on the lock. Voices could be heard at the far end of the corridor. He inserted the long needle into the hole and started to grapple for the hook to move the catch. He almost got it, but then the tool slipped in his sweaty hand.

Someone was running down the corridor. Henry pressed his fingers harder against the tool. He was almost there. The lock clicked open just as someone went to open the door. Henry hid underneath the desk closest to the window. He listened to the footsteps of a man walking right up to it.

The man grabbed something from the desk. Henry could hear him dial a number. He had a short conversation in Russian and put the phone down. The man hesitated. His mobile rang. He turned on his heels and walked out whilst answering the other call.

Henry stood up and opened the window. The ledge was covered in snow and the ground below looked like it had not been cleared for a while. Henry could not be sure what he would be landing on, but it was his best chance of escape.

He pushed the window open and jumped up, grabbing the frame for support. He closed the window as best as he could behind him and jumped into the darkness below.

He landed with a muffled thud and stayed crouched for a moment. There were a few cars still parked in the nearby yard, but no movement around them. Henry stood up, brushed the snow from his clothes, put on the stolen coat and hat, and walked in the direction of the car park exit.

A couple of guards were walking the perimeter. One stopped to exchange a few words with his colleague. As Henry was approaching, they broke off their conversation and resumed their walk. One of them nodded at him. Henry nodded back.

He kept going straight until he arrived at a place he recognised from before. Red Square's northern entrance. He was less than 10 minutes from The Ritz.

A short while later, Henry walked as calmly as he could through The Ritz reception and took the lift to his bedroom floor. As soon as the doors opened, he jogged to it, entered his room and stripped out of his clothes. He ran to the shower and scrubbed himself clean several times. He let the water course over his back for a few minutes.

It was probably too late to counteract any delayed effects the poison may have, but he had to try to minimise its impact. Henry got out of the shower and dried himself off. He returned to his bedroom, where he knelt next to his bed and ran his hand along the edge of the mattress. He couldn't find the hole at first and cursed a few times.

He found what he was looking for, and pulled the burner phone out that James had given him. Henry ignored the message on screen and called Tatiana's room number.

"*Allo...?*" Tatiana sounded wary.

"I'm in my room," Henry said and hung up.

He started dressing and selected the warmest trousers he had, then slipped on a T-shirt. The doorbell rang and he moved to the door swiftly. He drew Tatiana inside and closed the door behind them. She hesitated, but the pile of clothes on the floor caught her attention.

"What happened?"

Henry took her hand and led her towards the bedroom. He switched on the TV, selecting Channel 5. He drew her against him, resting his lips against her temple.

"Andropov is dead."

Tatiana muffled a cry. She pulled back a little, just enough so Henry could see her face. She touched his cheek and ran her fingers through his hair.

"How?"

"I don't have time to tell you the details... He tried his poison trick, but he's the one now lying on the floor."

Tatiana's face had turned ashen. "You didn't get any on you?"

"I don't think so... I scrubbed myself as soon as I came in."

She wrapped her arms tight around his body. "Novichok is a terrifying nerve agent."

They fell silent for a moment, then Henry reluctantly pulled away.

"We're leaving tonight. You said your brother is ready?"

She nodded. Anguish flashed in her eyes. "He is... I am."

"Leningradsky train station, 11pm."

"Understood." Tatiana squeezed his hand.

She moved to the exit. As she passed by the stolen clothes Henry had dropped in the corridor, she shook her head.

"What is it?"

"It's funny. You stole Andropov's hat and coat."

Chapter Thirty-One

The intel they were acting upon had reached Jack a little over two hours ago. Jack lay flat on his stomach and pressed the binoculars to his eyes. The fishermen's cottage that the abductors had selected was a difficult place to storm.

The small house was at the edge of the water and the shoreline was visible on each side for over a mile. The woods surrounding the cottage on other sides didn't reach the place. There was only a stretch of sandy ground overgrown with brambles leading up to it.

The commander of one of the Special Activities Division teams at the CIA was giving Jack the latest update on progress.

"My men are getting into position," he said. "We've detected movement at the back of the property. One of the hostiles went to check the boat moored at the end of the jetty."

"Copy that." Jack returned to his observation. The string of events that led to this moment played on his mind.

Harris's number flashes on Jack's mobile.

"News?" They don't greet each other any longer. What only matters now is finding intel that will allow Harris and Jack to locate Nick and Mandy.

"Jot down this number." Harris gives Jack a string of figures – a mobile phone registered in the US. "Crowne has been in touch. He thinks it belongs to one of the kidnappers. He's also asked for extraction to be accelerated, so expect some fallout from that on our end."

Harris hangs up and Jack moves immediately to his landline, dialling the number for Hunter III's PA.

"Hello Jack, your meeting is confirmed for 5pm today. Don't tell me –"

Jack interrupted her. "I need a meeting. Now. It's a life or death situation."

The line goes quiet. It's not like Jack to use this sort of excuse to see his boss.

"He is in a long conference call..." She hesitates. "But perhaps you can pop in and he'll speak to you, as he doesn't need to interact with the call all the time."

"I'm coming up. Tell him I need SAD's involvement, asap."

Jack hangs up and jogs to the elevators. One opens. People are coming back from lunch. He squeezes in and a few voices protest at being squashed. Jack barely apologises. He's rehearsing what he's going to say to Hunter.

RUSSKY BEAR has so far got two people killed, Huckerby and McNamara, and two of their own have been kidnapped. This is not a good intro.

Hunter's PA is walking out of his office when Jack arrives. He knows he must look worried because she is taken aback. "The call he's on is a difficult one. I can't let you in just yet –"

Jack ignores her, knocks on Hunter's door, and enters. Hunter raises his head, surprised.

"I need a team of para ops for a hostage situation... here in DC."

The SAD team commander's voice interrupted Jack's recollection. "We've detected infrared monitors around the property."

"Can you disable?"

"We can try, make sure they're not triggered, but my team needs to get close enough."

"Under the cover of darkness would be best," Jack said.

"Agreed."

"We don't have that luxury."

"Copy." The line went silent, but Jack knew the man was consulting with one of his specialists.

The commander returned. "Will come in at the house from the water. The jetty is long enough, and we should be able to launch the assault from underneath it."

"Copy."

Jack waited for what felt like an eternity.

The commander's voice came in one last time. "My men are in position."

Jack braced himself. The silence that surrounded the place felt artificial, and then it all started. There were shouts and gun discharges at the back of the cottage. Jack couldn't see anything. One of the windows on the second floor opened. One of the kidnappers was trying to escape.

A sniper from the SAD team took him out in one clean shot.

More gunshots rang from inside the house. He heard discharges from different guns that must have belonged to the abductors. He knew the Special Ops team were using suppressors.

The front door of the cottage opened cautiously. Mandy walked out first, a gun to her head.

Bile rose up in Jack's throat. The man was walking her sideways towards a small strip headed for the water. There must have been a boat there no one knew about.

Jack slid backwards on his belly, changing position. He moved forward on his elbows. He heard the man making threats.

"You move, she dies!"

Jack reached the shore. He saw a mass of branches and a net. An inflatable speed boat was hidden below the camouflage. The kidnapper moved towards it, but was too focused on the distant woods, where he must have known snipers were waiting to take their shot. He must have spotted his colleague on the ground with half his head missing.

Jack edged towards the boat. He reached it and stopped, gathered the gun from its holster and waited.

The man was still shouting. He arrived at the boat. He ordered Mandy to take the branches off. There was no shot coming from the snipers, so she must have been shielding him.

Jack crouched and circled the back of the inflatable. He risked a peek. The man's back was to him. Still, any bullet he fired could hurt Mandy, or worse.

Jack pulled back a little and thought about the angle. The camouflage cover had been pulled back from the inflatable.

Jack refocused and stood up in one go.

"Hey!" he shouted.

The man looked around, startled. Jack fired two rounds into the man's head. Mandy dived to the ground, whilst Jack kept the gun pointed at the fallen man. The rest of the elite team arrived.

320

It was over.

Jack helped Mandy to her feet and squeezed her with a bear hug. "You're safe."

Mandy nodded and her lower lip wobbled. Her eyes glistened with tears.

"Nick." she managed to say. "They took him away this morning."

* * *

Henry waited for a moment after Tatiana had left. He pulled a second T-shirt on, then a jacket, and walked out of his room. He took the lift to the top floor and made his way to the gym club.

A smiling young woman welcomed him.

"I'm very sorry, but I left a T-shirt in one of your lockers. Would you mind if I went to check?"

"Not at all, sir. Would you remember the number by any chance?"

Henry cast an eye on the row of keys on the board behind her.

"I think it was locker 25."

The young woman turned around. "You're in luck. It hasn't been assigned again."

Henry took the key and walked into the changing room. Two men were getting ready to leave. Henry passed them by and locker 25, heading for the back of the room. He took a different key out of his trouser pocket and opened the door for the last locker in the last row.

The Glock was still there. He removed his jacket, and his second T-shirt, put the jacket back on, and slid the gun into the back of his waistband. He pocketed the suppressor that came with the gun and wrapped the 5 ammunitions clips in the T-shirt he had just taken off. He left the key in the door of the locker and returned to reception.

"I found it. Thank you."

"Very pleased for you, sir."

Henry returned to his room and the blind spot, drew the backpack out from underneath the bed, and stuffed the gun, suppressor, and clips into it.

In the bathroom, he made the changes he had planned the minute he had decided to kill Andropov.

The man who walked out of Henry Newborn's room looked very different – clean-shaven, silver-grey hair. His dark, fashionable fur coat and hat made him look distinguished. The light backpack he wore over his shoulder added a little youth to an otherwise severe appearance.

Henry took the lift to the ground floor. When he walked out into the large foyer, a group of men were entering the hotel. In similar dark coats and hats, they could only be coming from one of Russia's agencies. Henry guessed FSB. One of the men had already reached reception, and although he spoke Russian, Henry heard the names he was asking about. David Upstage, Bast Botha and Henry Newborn.

The FSB agents fanned out through the hotel lobby, two of them already at the door. Henry slowed down. They were already asking for people to identify themselves and guests obliged without question. The arrest of Upstage and Botha would promise to be a fraught one. Perhaps Henry could wait and seize his chance at escape.

Someone walked through the hotel doors and shouted a name. "Vladimir Vladimirovich!"

Henry did not recognise the name but he did the voice.

James walked purposefully towards him, dressed in a full Russian Air Force uniform. Henry smiled at the sight of him. James rarely mentioned his time in the British Armed Forces, but today he was pushing his background to the fore.

His confident demeanour left no one in doubt that he was the senior officer the stripes on his uniform indicated. He stopped before Henry and gave him a warm embrace only a friend would.

"Car outside," James murmured.

Henry clapped James on the back and they both headed for the exit. The guards hesitated, but James gave them a nod of recognition, and they stood to order. It wouldn't do them any good to upset a high-ranking officer in the Air Force, the favourites of President Putin.

James got into a limo and Henry followed, sagging into the seat in relief.

"Shit, that was close."

"I saw the FSB come in and gathered there was trouble ahead."

"They've come in for Upstage, Botha and –" Henry stopped dead.

"That's OK. We can speak freely."

The driver gave Henry a friendly nod.

"And me."

As the limo moved away from The Ritz access lane to join the main road, more official-looking cars arrived to block the hotel's access. The place would soon be swarming with FSB agents.

James handed him documentation. "These are your new papers, and those for Tatiana and her brother. If you haven't yet, take a look at the picture of Anatolie that Harris has sent you."

"I'll do that when I arrive at the train station. What else have you got for me?"

"Train tickets, meeting point in St Petersburg. We're flying a private jet to Helsinki."

"Has Harris confirmed it's on its way?"

"Not yet."

"When are you flying to St Petersburg?" Henry wondered what the alternative would be if Harris couldn't find a jet.

"Tomorrow morning, first thing. I'll arrive at 9.30am. I'll head straight to our rendezvous point."

"Understood. We'll be arriving at Moskovsky station at 8.30am."

The limo driver slowed down. They had arrived at Leningradsky railway station. Henry glanced at his watch.

"I have 15 minutes before the agreed meeting time."

"The limo will be parked two streets away. Any hesitation..."

"I know, I walk." Henry smiled. "It won't happen though. I've seen what Andropov can do and I understand why Tatiana wants out."

"Paranoia." James didn't need to say more.

"That's what keeps us alive."

Henry slid the papers into his rucksack. "Why did you call me Vladimir Vladimirovich by the way?"

"That's Putin's full name and the correct way to address him. It doesn't fail to impress."

* * *

The railway station was almost deserted. The outside temperature had dropped to minus 10C, and the cold had forced people into the waiting room or the only restaurant that remained open. Henry avoided both. He did not want to have to address anyone in the few Russian

323

expressions he'd learnt since arriving. A foreigner taking the night train to St Petersburg was not unusual, but most people preferred the bullet trains that ran during the day.

Henry walked through the station slowly. Nothing looked out of order. He'd already spotted CCTV cameras at the top of each platform, and some more in the station, over the entrance and exit doors. His change of appearance would provide him with a head start, but he had no illusion that the advantage wouldn't last. Henry wouldn't be safe until he was out of the country.

There were only five minutes before the agreed meeting time with Tatiana. Henry walked past the restaurant and peered briefly inside. A woman and a child were sipping their drink, but the boy looked too young to be Anatolie.

Henry moved to the entrance of the waiting room and leaned against the wall. The cold had started to seep into his shoes. He stamped his feet a few times, to try to warm them up a little. A few people stepped out of the waiting room, and rushed towards the platforms from where their trains were departing.

Henry checked his watch. Tatiana was now a few minutes late. Their train to St Petersburg would be leaving in less than 15 minutes.

A young man and what looked like his girlfriend walked past Henry, in the direction of the train's platform. An older man followed. An entire family was also making its way, kids excited by the adventure ahead, despite the late hour.

Henry started to make his way to the train too. The last people were boarding and it would soon leave. Henry couldn't believe that Tatiana had changed her mind.

But was Tatiana even her real name?

The question he should have asked a few days ago stopped him in his thoughts. He hadn't told her they were going to St Petersburg, but only a few trains departed at this late hour. It wouldn't be difficult to track the five or six trains that had left and have the FSB thoroughly search them.

Henry moved closer to the platform and his train. Only five minutes to go. A few more people were making their way there. One looked like a train attendant; the other, a middle-aged man, tottered towards the first car.

324

The young woman he had seen in the restaurant had disembarked and was walking towards him, looking uncertain. When she got closer, she smiled and removed her beanie hat. Her eyes sparkled in recognition. Her spiky, short blonde hair made Tatiana look so much younger.

"Can I help you at all? You seem lost." She looked into Henry's eyes, likely to reassure herself she had the right man.

"How very kind of you," Henry murmured. "Train to St Petersburg."

There was an announcement over the tannoy. Henry only recognised the name of his destination.

"Hurry." Tatiana grabbed his hand. They ran to the train, boarding it just as the departure whistle was blowing.

With a shudder the train pulled out of the station, and its harsh lights faded slowly.

"I almost didn't recognise you." Tatiana was still staring at Henry.

He smiled. "You walked straight past me, and I certainly didn't recognise you, either."

Tatiana ruffled her short hair. "You and I know the drill... best way to change your appearance is to change your hairstyle."

"Your brother?"

"He's on board. I took a gamble... St Petersburg felt the obvious choice."

Henry took two tickets out of his rucksack and handed them over. "The story is that we are all going to St Petersburg for a short weekend break."

Henry stopped talking when a train attendant walked past them. He nodded at them; both Henry and Tatiana nodded back.

"Let's get into our cabin and then we can talk." Henry murmured. Tatiana nodded, and they moved in silence towards the car with their reservation.

They located the cabin reserved for the three of them.

"Anatolie is waiting in the next car." Tatiana said. Her concern sounded genuine. "I need to get him. He was scared when I left him alone."

Henry remembered Harris's warning about Anatolie and the picture on his phone.

He closed the door, blocking her exit.

"What have you told him?"

"He knows we are leaving Russia and I've told him you are helping us."

"Did he not want to know more?"

"No. He knows not to ask questions that may get people killed. He learnt that lesson early in life."

Tatiana opened the door and left.

Henry pulled out his Glock mounted with a suppressor, and loaded it with the clip. He stepped out of the compartment and checked the corridor both ways. There was no one around. He stepped back inside, slung his backpack onto the lowest of the bunk beds, opened the bag and arranged the gun, so that he could reach it easily.

He returned to the corridor and waited. A young teenager was with Tatiana, walking awkwardly towards Henry. Anatolie was almost as tall as his sister. Henry took out his burner phone and glanced one last time at the picture Harris had sent him.

As the boy got closer, Henry recognised the same features in the picture that belonged to both his parents. The soulful green eyes of his father, like Tatiana's, and the slim face of his mother. He was in no doubt. This was the son of Piotr and Yulia Borodin.

Anatolie hesitated when he reached Henry, but stepped into the car, followed by Tatiana.

"Anatolie, this is Henry." Tatiana made a small movement of the hand.

The young lad bowed a little. "Very nice to meet you, sir." His English was fluent, with a combination of Russian and American undertones.

"Very nice to meet you too." He smiled. "And I'm Henry, not sir."

Anatolie looked at his sister for guidance.

"*Vse v poryadke...* That's OK." She nodded encouragingly at him.

"OK," he replied.

Anatolie slung his small backpack onto the upper bed, then climbed up and lay down, hugging his bag close to his chest.

Tatiana moved to the bunk bed underneath her brother's. The three of them sat in awkward silence. Henry took a flask of tea James had given him for the trip. *This one at least will not have been poisoned.* Henry had commented.

He took three plastic tumblers out and offered a round of tea. Anatolie was still cautious, but Henry could see the prospect of a warm cup of tea with honey pleased him.

Henry offered a cup to Tatiana, filled his own, and suggested they drink it out in the corridor without Anatolie.

326

"The FSB is now officially looking for me," Henry murmured as he sipped the burning liquid.

Tatiana blew on her tea and nodded. "And they'll be looking for me and Anatolie before the end of the night."

"They've picked up Upstage and Botha." Henry leaned against the closed cabin door.

"Why?"

"I left a few clues behind... Botha's mobile phone, not mine, was left at Andropov's office. Botha is unwittingly in possession of my old mobile, and Upstage has inherited a Rohypnol pill I no longer needed. Upstage and I were also the last foreigners to meet with Andropov."

"David has been stupid. He's acting like he's already the President of the United States."

"Andropov didn't seem bothered about Upstage's bluster, though. He spoke about a list of presidential candidates."

"He has a list, but he never disclosed to me who was on that list." Tatiana sipped her tea. "I was assigned to Upstage and that was it. It's possible other female agents were assigned to other men, in the US or in Russia."

They drank in silence for a little while. Outside, the scenery hadn't changed since they'd left the station; rows of massive concrete towers, some lit up, most of them plunged into darkness, whizzed past the train windows.

"What happened to Andropov?" Tatiana's voice quivered.

"He spiked my drink with poison. I threw it in his face."

"He didn't drink it?"

"No, but the results were almost instant. He was no longer moving when I left."

Tatiana nodded. She was resting her forearms on the transversal handlebar of the train window. She dropped her forehead to them.

Henry moved closer to her "What is it?"

"Novichok is a terrifying nerve agent, but it's most efficient if ingested. Then there is no recourse." Her revelation hung in the air between them.

Henry frowned. "Is there an antidote?"

"I don't know."

"Even if there is one, and his people managed to administer it to him, it will take time for Andropov to recover..." Henry squeezed her shoulder.

Tatiana looked up at him. "You're right."

"And by then –"

Tatiana put a finger on Henry's lips to stop him saying more.

"We Russians have a reputation for being superstitious, and tonight, I'll stick to that tradition." She slipped her arms around him and rested her head on his shoulder. "I'm scared, but not for myself."

"I know." Henry rested his cheek on the top of her head, her spiky hair bristling against his skin.

"Thank you for trusting me."

The door at one end of the corridor opened with force. A couple of controllers started their ticket checks.

Tatiana and Henry broke out of their embrace and returned to their compartment.

Chapter Thirty-Two

The Chief was still in a meeting at 9pm. Harris sat in the reception area, waiting for his turn to see the head of MI6. The Chief's PA cast a look in his direction. He hadn't had time to change into something a little more office-like. His old and tattered jeans looked out of place in the grand reception area.

The door to the Chief's office opened and someone Harris didn't know walked out. He barely looked at Harris, moved to the lifts, and promptly disappeared into them.

The Chief walked to the threshold of the antechamber to his office and stretched his back. "Could I trouble you for some coffee please, Emma?"

"Certainly, sir." His PA got up and disappeared into another room.

"Come on, Steve." The Chief signalled for Harris to follow him with a sharp movement of the head. He turned on his heels and walked back inside his office.

Harris followed, closed the door behind him, and stood in the middle of the room.

"Take a seat." The Chief's eyes were suddenly on his computer, but he ignored whatever had come in, sat down, and turned his attention to Harris.

"You said it was urgent."

"Operation RUSSKY BEAR is turning out to be more complex than we thought." Harris opted for *we* rather than *you*. He was still cursing himself for not having insisted on more resources.

"I'm listening."

His PA announced herself with a couple of knocks at the door, waited a few seconds and entered. She left the tray on the Chief's desk and disappeared.

"We have been presented with the opportunity to welcome a Russian defector and one member of her family. She's of interest to us and linked directly to Operation RUSSKY BEAR."

The Chief poured coffee into two cups and nodded. "Who's her Russian minder?"

"Alexei Andropov."

The Chief paused with the jug of milk in the air.

"Are you sure?"

"Without question. Our own operative, Crowne, is running their exfiltration as we speak. And he met with Andropov."

"Are the Russians aware of her defection?"

"Not yet. The Russians *have* raided the hotel in which our operative was staying. They arrested one American and one South African. I must add that I believe Andropov is dead, or at least in very poor health."

The Chief shook his head. "Hang on Steve, backtrack for me... Last time we spoke about RUSSKY BEAR, you and your team were gathering information about a Russian attempt to *recruit*, for want of a better word, western businessmen and politicians."

"That was the premise on which RUSSKY BEAR started, but the op has given us HUMIT we never suspected could run that deep." Harris helped himself to the second cup of coffee, loaded it with milk and sugar and started explaining what Henry, James, and Nick had discovered.

The Chief listened whilst Steve finished with the current exfiltration. The Chief hadn't touched his coffee. He lifted a hand to stop Steve and pinched the bridge of his nose.

"You are telling me that you have uncovered a credible conspiracy that could affect the outcome of the American presidential campaign? That the Russians are using social media on a large scale, together with the release of fake news, to do so? And that they are, at a minimum, manipulating confidential data to discredit the current Democrat candidate, Hillary Clinton?"

"That's what I'm saying, sir."

"The campaign is being run by Andropov and his main candidate – this chap is called David Upstage, you say – but why arrest him, then?"

"We think Upstage got a little ahead of himself and he, not very cleverly, thinks he can play the Russians."

"That is indeed goddamn stupid."

Harris continued. "Crowne had become part of Upstage's inner circle, and the defector Tatiana Borodin was playing Upstage, on Andropov's request. Our intel is solid."

"My question still stands – why arrest Upstage rather than have a discreet chat the way the Russians do, showing him what would happen if he messed around with them?"

"Crowne spoke of a list Andropov has..." Harris trailed off.

The Chief took a sip of coffee and put it down again.

"You mean Upstage is not the only presidential candidate the Russians are courting? That sounds –" The Chief broke off and drank a little more coffee. "Actually, Steve, I'll reserve judgement."

"Perhaps Borodin will tell us more."

"You, therefore, need an immediate authorisation to treat her as a defector with whom we want to engage?"

Harris nodded. "That would be helpful, sir."

The Chief returned the nod. "How are you exfiltrating them from Russia?"

"Train to St Petersburg, then private jet to Helsinki."

The Chief raised an eyebrow. "You're hiring a private jet?"

Harris shifted on his chair. "No, we're borrowing a private jet... from a Russian oligarch."

"I presume this *oligarch* is not aware?"

"Not exactly, no."

"Anything else *I* need to be aware of?"

"We managed to free one of the hostages in the US, but one is still missing."

"One of ours?"

"Unfortunately. Nick Fox."

"When did we recruit him?"

"A few days ago..." Harris hesitated. He could wait until the Chief asked the question, as he assumed he would, or he could volunteer the information now. "Crowne recruited him in DC. Nick is a superhacker."

"We've only breached a couple of rules here, why not add a few more?" The Chief exhaled slowly. "You recruited a yank on American soil, right?"

Harris nodded.

"And how have our friends across the Atlantic taken it? Should I expect the head of the CIA to fire a rocket in my direction, blasting our special relationship into smithereens?"

"I don't think so, sir. My counterpart, Jack Shield, was OK with the recruitment."

"And was Jack Shield's boss also content with the very same recruitment, or did Jack Shield not bother to ask?"

Harris pouted. "I'm not sure."

The Chief mulled over the information.

He continued. "Still, this young chap, Nick, is in trouble. Let's try to get him out alive. We can worry about recruitment once he is safe and sound."

"My thinking, exactly," Harris ventured.

"Any news about his whereabouts?"

"No luck yet. But we are on full alert on both sides of the Atlantic."

"All right, Harris. Since you seem to have thrown the rule book out a long time ago on this op, I want to know what comes next. If we are going to tell our American friends the presidential election has been hijacked, we need some rock-solid evidence."

"I'm flying to Helsinki tomorrow first thing." Harris stood up slowly.

"What – are you borrowing another private jet?" The Chief smiled.

* * *

Tatiana had taken care of the tickets and the controllers. Henry moved to his bunk bed, facing the wall, eyes closed, his hand resting on his Glock.

The noise of voices in the corridor subsided and eventually disappeared, and Henry lay down.

Anatolie had switched on the light above his head and was reading a book. It was in Russian, and Henry couldn't make out the title or the author. The book looked old and well used. Henry wondered whether it had some sentimental value. Perhaps it was the only thing he had decided to take with him before he left his home and his country forever.

332

Jumbled memories of Northern Ireland surfaced unexpectedly. Henry sat up, his head almost hitting the bottom of the bunk bed above him. Tatiana refilled their plastic cups from the tea flask and sat next to him.

"We should rest in turn," she suggested. "I'm sure they know by now that Anatolie and I have disappeared."

"How many stops between Moscow and St Petersburg?"

"Quite a few towards the end of the journey."

"Easy for someone to board?"

Tatiana nodded as she drank.

"You rest first," Henry suggested.

Tatiana squeezed his hand, slid off his bunk and curled up onto hers opposite.

Henry took his burner phone out and set up a string of alarms at 20-minute intervals; the cabin was starting to get very hot, and he didn't want to be caught out by sleep. He moved position, back resting against the wall partition, legs stretched in front of him.

He called up on his phone a map of the Russian area they would be crossing and checked the number of possible stops. The train was due to stop a dozen times, which would give the FSB too many opportunities to intercept them.

Anatolie stopped reading and turned off his light. Henry could hardly make out his profile in the dark. The boy turned to face the wall and Henry thought he heard muffled sobs. Henry leaned his head against the wall. He didn't have the words to relieve a sorrow he knew only too well.

Henry waited until he couldn't hear Anatolie's soft cries. Then he slid out of the compartment and walked to the end of the corridor. The door to the outside was secured with an old-fashioned door lock. It didn't need to be released electronically.

He moved to the next car. As he crossed into it, the intensity of the cold surprised him. This car was not a sleeper. It had open seats, and towards the far end, a bar selling snacks and drinks. The bar was still open and a sleepy attendant was sitting inside the booth, propped up against it.

Henry returned to their cabin and checked his watch. There was another five hours to go before they arrived in St Petersburg. He had no intention of waking up Tatiana. He would simply doze off between alarms.

The voices, male, become more audible... the words sound severe, perhaps even angry. At the bottom of the wall Henry looks around. He's only a small lad but he could heave himself up and peer over the top.

The tone of the conversation changes suddenly. Someone lets out a small cry. Someone is now scared. Henry feels the terror overwhelming one of the men. He scrambles onto an old crate and reaches the top of the wooden fence. Two gun discharges bounce off the walls of the small street.

Henry jerked upright and the memory faded. He ran a weary hand over his damp face and forehead. He checked on Tatiana's bunk. It was empty and so was Anatolie's.

Henry went still for a moment listening for noise outside the cabin. It was quiet. He grabbed his rucksack. The gun was still in there. He stood up slowly and slid the door of the cabin open a fraction. The train was slowing down.

Henry heard hurried footsteps along the corridor. He shut the door again and slipped back into bed. He took the Glock out and waited. The door opened and Henry readied to point the gun at whoever was coming in. Tatiana and Anatolie entered in a hurry and she shut the door quickly.

"You're awake?" she said with surprise.

"Where have you been?" Henry still had his hand on his Glock.

Tatiana noticed it. She shook her head. "Anatolie needed a bit of air, but the train started to slow down so we came back."

"You should have told me." He was in two minds about believing her. But why come back if she was going to betray him?

The train gave an unhealthy jerk and slowed right down.

"Are we coming to another train station?" Henry asked.

He moved to the window of their cabin and lifted the blind. There was nothing around but trees in the distance, and the deep blanket of snow between them and the train.

Henry opened the door of the cabin and walked to the window in the corridor. The same landscape was spread out on that side of the track too.

"The train is stopping in the middle of nowhere." Henry moved back inside the compartment.

"They're coming for us."

Tatiana spoke to Anatolie in hurried Russian.

He grabbed his small bag and coat. Tatiana did the same with her stuff. Henry took his mobile out and tried to use geolocation to pinpoint where they were.

"Fuck... we haven't got any signal here." He looked at his watch. "I looked at our progress 20 minutes ago. We'd passed Tosno."

"That's 40 kilometres from St Petersburg."

The brakes of the train shrieked. The three of them were thrown about and the train came to a sudden halt.

"Put your coats on. We're leaving the train."

Henry slid the Glock into his coat pocket. Tatiana and Anatolie were ready. She grabbed Henry's arm before he could leave the compartment.

"It's minus 15C outside, and even during the day the temperature won't rise much above 5C or 6C."

"If we stay here we're not going to get out alive."

Tatiana looked at her brother, hesitating.

"We go." Anatolie nodded.

Raised voices bounced around the corridor, and cabin doors were being opened with force. People started shrieking.

Henry moved to the window of the cabin and checked it. It was double-glazed and felt solid.

"Stand back."

Henry pointed the Glock at the window and fired two rounds at the glass. It partially shattered, letting in a blast of frigid air that made them all shiver. He gave the glass a strong kick and it collapsed, shattering to the outside.

He crouched on the window base and jumped into the night.

His landing was cushioned by deep snow and he sunk up to his knees. He turned around. Tatiana was already helping her brother to leave the cabin. He landed next to Henry and Tatiana followed. They moved towards the trees, their speed hampered by the thick snow.

The cold air was freezing Henry's breath and burning his lungs. The snow started to thicken as they moved closer to the forest. Henry looked back. Tatiana and Anatolie were keeping up. It hadn't occurred to him that he might be the one to struggle in this cold and hostile environment.

Shouts came from the train. Men had broken into their cabin. Henry and the others accelerated their efforts to reach the trees, only a few yards away.

The cracking noise of gun fires made them dive to the ground. There was no way of hiding. Their tracks were easy to follow, and the shooter had a clear target.

"Come on." Henry stood up and hurried them along.

Tatiana and her brother raced towards the woods. Henry waited for another discharge of the rifle to pinpoint the location of his target. When another shot rang out, Henry lifted his gun and fired two rounds. The shooting stopped. He reached the woods after Tatiana and Anatolie had taken refuge amongst the trees.

"We need to walk northwest," Tatiana murmured.

Henry lifted his head, to get his bearings.

He turned to Anatolie and Tatiana. "You walk on. More will be coming after us soon, and I need to make sure I can fire at them freely without worrying about you being hit."

The sound of their footsteps crushing the snow was interrupted by loud voices. Torch lights swept the area. Henry counted four men. He checked on Tatiana's progress. The distance between them and the four men was not sufficient.

"We're outnumbered." Tatiana shook her head.

Anatolie called to Henry softly and pointed at something on their left. "There is a hut."

"What's it used for?"

"They help people who work in the woods. They have enough to sustain someone, in case of a blizzard. I learnt about them in school."

"Let's go..."

Anatolie was already moving fast towards it, but Tatiana fell back to speak to Henry.

"There is no way we can hold out there. Even if I had a gun, we would likely run out of ammunition."

"I don't intend to stay there for long."

When they reached the hut, they checked the door and discovered it was open.

"I need candles and petrol..." Henry said. "Is there a back door?"

"No back door but a back window." Anatolie pointed to it.

Tatiana opened drawers to find some candles and a couple of glass lights to hold them. Henry grabbed two jerry cans of petrol from a stockpile of supplies.

"Open the back window and get out through there," he ordered the pair. "Wait for me outside."

Henry lit the candles with a lighter from the stock. He placed a couple of candles in two separate glass holders and handed them to Tatiana outside.

He returned to the centre of the room and spilt some petrol on the floor near the door, and near the back window through which Anatolie and Tatiana had disappeared. He climbed out through the same window, placed the candles on the inner window seal and pushed the window closed.

Henry turned to Anatolie. "Jump on my back."

The lad hesitated.

"Come on, we haven't got much time."

Tatiana nodded and he did. Henry started walking backwards.

"If you copy my walk, Tatiana, it will look as though more people have joined us, arriving from the direction of the woods. They'll only see two tracks. It won't fool them for long, but just enough for what I want to do."

They tracked backwards to the woods. It was slow progress and the torch lights in the distance were moving fast towards the hut. Henry dropped Anatolie to the ground after 50 yards or so.

"You keep going... I'll catch up with you."

Anatolie grabbed Henry's hand. "No, we stay."

"I'll be with you in no time."

Anatolie hesitated but Tatiana hurried him along.

"ICE café bar lounge near Pulkovo airport," Henry simply said to her as she was about to follow her brother.

Henry drops to one knee and leans against a tree. The men have reached the hut. In the moonlight Henry can see they have their guns drawn. Two of them circle the cabin, looking at the boot prints. They crouch and approach the window from each side slowly. The two men at the front go in firing a few rounds.

Henry aims for the candles in the window. The muffled sound of his gunshots are hardly audible. But the result is spectacular. The candles drop to the floor and set fire to the petrol, flames immediately surrounding the men inside. It takes a few seconds for the men crouching near the windows to realise where the suppressed gun shots are coming from.

By then it is too late.

Henry groups a series of shots, hitting legs, torso, head, reloading his gun as soon as he has dropped an empty clip. The men collapse one after the other.

Henry turns back, leaving the hut on fire and the two other men rolling in the snow desperately trying to extinguish the flames that have engulfed them.

He starts running in the direction of the footsteps Tatiana and her brother have left in the snow.

He reaches the top of a small hill he didn't suspect was there. Tatiana and Anatolie have slowed down and are looking back in his direction. They stop and wave at him. Henry runs harder towards them. They have reached the outskirts of what looks like a small village.

Chapter Thirty-Three

A few lights were on in some of the houses. Tatiana walked up the main track that led to the house closest to the woods. The path had been used a lot and the lack of fresh snow made it slippery with ice.

She kept going until she spotted what she wanted. Three houses down the lane, a reconditioned Soviet truck was parked along the side of the house it probably belonged to. She hesitated. Stealing that truck would bring harshness upon what she suspected was a poor family. But she had no choice.

She moved around to the driver's side and pulled the handle. It wasn't locked. She opened it slowly. The wires under the dashboard were hanging lose. Whoever was driving the truck simply hotwired it every time they drove it.

She shook her head and smiled. So much for feeling sorry about stealing it.

She walked back to the cluster of fern trees where she'd told Henry and Anatolie to wait.

"I found a truck I can hotwire," she said. "I'll drive it out of the village and onto the motorway."

Henry grinned. "You don't trust my driving on ice then?"

Tatiana returned the grin. "Not one bit."

They moved silently back to the truck. Henry and Anatolie slid into the passenger seat, Tatiana into the driver's seat.

"Ready?"

The pair nodded.

She sparked two wires off each other. The engine spluttered, then after a half-hearted effort cut out. She sparked the wires again and this time the engine's noise sounded more promising. Lights came on in the house. Tatiana pressed on the accelerator gently; she couldn't risk flooding the engine.

Someone opened the door of the house. A man wearing a heavy coat and boots appeared. She switched gear into reverse. The truck slid out of the driveway. She engaged first gear and managed to correct the slide the truck was taking. She accelerated and the truck bounced forward, back wheels still not gripping the icy road.

The man was shouting at them, but it was too late. They were on their way.

The road was treacherous. Ice hidden under packs of hard snow forced the vehicle to slide sideways. Tatiana kept using a combination of the accelerator and the handbrake to manoeuvre the vehicle.

Henry gave her an appreciative smile.

"What? You're not one of these guys who thinks a woman can't drive, are you?"

"Even if I was, I wouldn't dare say it. You might chuck me out of the car."

"I'd never do that."

"Yes, she would." Anatolie piped up unexpectedly.

"You two are ganging up against me now?" Tatiana teased.

"Never," both Henry and Anatolie replied in unison.

They exchanged a gang fist bump and a nod of agreement. Tatiana smiled, eyes fixed on the road. They had a few miles to go before reaching the motorway.

* * *

They entered the motorway as the sun was rising. Henry and Tatiana changed seats. Henry argued it was more likely a man would be driving the truck than a woman, and it was all about keeping a low profile.

"How far are we from St Petersburg?" Henry was getting used to the cranky change of gear, pulling a face when the gear box was reluctant to engage.

"30 kilometres, no more, from the outskirts of the city."

"20 miles..." Henry muttered. "Our rendezvous is scheduled for 10am."

Traffic was gradually building up and Henry slowed down with it. He moved lanes to let more impatient motorists take over. As the truck was slumbering next to the hard shoulder, Henry noticed an old woman with a plastic bag, walking with difficulty along the road in the same direction. She was wrapped in layers of clothing that looked shabby and unclean, but the scarf on her head reminded him of the typical floral shawls he had seen in shops, and on Matryoshka dolls.

"What is she doing out here?" Henry asked.

"She's taking her work to town, probably some local market full of tourists."

"20 miles away?" Henry didn't believe it.

"She'll get a lift if she's lucky, otherwise, yes. There's still a lot of poverty in the countryside, and people will sell whatever craft they can produce to make ends meet."

Henry looked in the rear-view mirror as the small, hunched woman faded away from sight. He regretted not being able to offer her a lift.

Tatiana's attention moved to what was happening on the opposite lane of the motorway. She turned her head to get a better look.

"I think we have a problem..." She detached her words as though she was hoping she was wrong.

The optimism that had slowly crept into the vehicle vanished instantly.

"What do you mean?"

"I spotted a few cars flashing their lights coming from the direction of St Petersburg. I think there's a checkpoint on the motorway ahead of us."

"Is this usual?"

Tatiana shook her head.

"This means the FSB know we are still on our way to St Petersburg." Henry looked into the rear-view mirror.

"More cars flashing their lights," she said.

Henry indicated and stopped the truck. He unbuttoned his coat and slid it down to his waist, hiding the expensive fur coat he was wearing. He removed his hat and ruffled his hair, also glad that designer stubble was settling on his jaw.

"Can you convince the old lady we just drove past I'm not a foreigner?"

"Perhaps... I can tell her you're from another country like Latvia."

"Fine."

341

Henry reversed the truck, following the line of the hard shoulder. A few cars sounded their horn. So much for discretion. In the rear-view mirror Henry saw the old woman still making slow progress on foot towards the city.

"Ask her whether she wants a lift and let's hope she's not too talkative." Henry stopped the truck.

Tatiana climbed out and walked up to the old woman, striking up a short conversation with her. She nodded vigorously and made a gesture that looked like a blessing to Henry.

Anatolie moved to the back of the truck's cabin where a small space enabled a couple of people to squeeze in together.

Tatiana opened the door and helped the old woman to sit in the front seat. Tatiana moved to the back to share Anatolie's small space. The old lady mumbled a few words and gave Henry and Anatolie a toothless smile.

Henry smiled back. He fought the gear box again and resumed the journey towards St Petersburg.

Traffic had slowed down even further after only a couple of miles. The old lady seemed to have fallen asleep, shrouded in a scent of spices and raw onions. Henry couldn't help but admire her resilience.

Tatiana leaned forward and squeezed Henry's shoulder. In the distance two men appeared. One of them was checking inside the vehicles with a torch and the other was carrying a rifle. The three lanes of traffic had been reduced to two and cars were moving at a crawl.

The old lady must have sensed the lack of motion. She mumbled a question and Tatiana answered. The woman nodded and picked up her old plastic bag, full of the goods she was bringing to market.

The truck was only a few cars away from the checkpoint now. Henry braced himself. Their vehicle was trapped, and he could not hope to outrun the FSB men this time.

Someone shone a light in his face. Henry squirmed and recoiled from the glare. Tatiana and Anatolie huddled together at the back pretending to be asleep. The old lady was the only one smiling. She took an exquisitely intricate ornament out of her bag that she showed to the man who was inspecting her side of the truck.

He stopped and looked for a moment at what she was holding. He called his colleague over, and the other man pointed the torch beam on it. There was a debate between the two men. The man with the rifle took some change out of his coat pocket. The old lady opened the window and seemed to think it was not enough. The man dug again in his pocket and threw in another coin. She gave then another toothless smile and handed over her piece of craft.

The man on Henry's side moved them on with a wave of the hand.

Henry drove the truck forward slowly. The lane ahead was much less congested. A few minutes later they were speeding down the motorway in the direction of St Petersburg.

Henry barked a laugh and the other two joined in. The old lady was nodding, putting her money away in the recesses of her layered garments. Henry gave her a smile and she returned one of her own.

The landscape along the edge of the motorway had changed dramatically. Massive tower blocks organised in regular rows framed the lanes in both directions. As they arrived at a large roundabout, the old lady mumbled a few words. Henry understood she had arrived at her destination.

He parked the truck as soon as he could, and helped her out of the truck. Tatiana said a few words to her and the old lady replied, making the same blessing gesture.

She ambled along the pavement.

Henry climbed back into the truck and rejoined the traffic.

"What did she say to you?" he asked Tatiana, who had moved into the old lady's seat.

"She said her late husband was Latvian and he didn't look anything like you."

Henry shook his head and smiled. "Let's find the rendezvous café. We are late."

Henry parked the truck a few blocks away from the shopping centre where the ICE café bar lounge was situated. They agreed to split up. He would go in first and Tatiana and Anatolie would follow.

He entered the building, dressed in his fur coat and hat. He had combed his hair back into a neat, grey hairdo. No one could tell he had spent the night escaping the FSB.

He entered the café and spotted the person he was looking for immediately. James was reading an international aviation magazine. He was also glancing at his watch – something Henry imagined he'd been doing a lot in the past 30 minutes.

The café was half full with a crowd that looked international – a function of its proximity to the airport, but also a testament to St Petersburg's popularity with tourists.

Henry sat down in one of the chairs opposite James. James dropped the magazine and shook his head.

"At last! I thought they'd got you."

"We had a few close encounters but here we are."

James slid a bag towards Henry with his foot.

"When they arrive, get them to change into these. The flight plan has been logged with the airport for 12.30pm departure. We need to get there an hour before to do the routine aircraft checks."

Henry didn't understand. "Routine what?"

"I'm flying the goddamn plane and you're my co-pilot. Hope you don't mind."

"What, you flying, or me being the co-pilot?"

"Being the co-pilot of course." James smiled.

"You know me too well... What about the other two?"

"Mum and kid, as per their new passports, flying to Helsinki for a bit of fun. Talking of which, here they come now."

Tatiana and Anatolie joined them.

"Nice to meet you." Tatiana didn't hold her hand out, but her smile said it all. Another small step towards freedom.

James nodded. "Likewise."

Henry headed for the men's lavatory and chose a cubicle the farthest from the door. He opened the bag and took out the uniform, coat and co-pilot hat. Henry waited until a few people had come and gone. He walked out of the toilets and into the corridor, ready to rejoin his party.

He was about to walk into the café's main room when he spotted three men almost having arrived at the door. Their suits and demeanour put him on high alert. The FSB had caught up with them once more.

Henry retraced his steps and re-entered the toilets. There was no one around. He opened the bag with his clothes and pulled his rucksack out of it. He found the lighter he had taken from the hut that morning. He grabbed a paper towel from the dispenser, bunched it together and set fire to it. He stuffed the burning paper into the bag and walked out without it.

He reached the table where James, Tatiana and Anatolie were sitting. James was looking alert, having already noticed the newcomers. The three men had just walked in and were looking around at the assembled crowd.

Henry slid in next to James. "Don't look over, the FSB is here. Get ready to leave when I tell you to."

The sudden sound of a fire alarm startled everyone. The smell of burning filled the air and there was a collective cry of panic.

"Now." Henry stood up, grabbed Anatolie's hand, and started running to the door. The FSB agents hesitated, but soon they too moved towards the door, joining the crowd of panic-stricken guests. Henry rushed past them, followed by Tatiana and James. The FSB was not looking for two men, a woman and a child, and certainly not two pilots. They climbed down the escalator to the ground floor and dashed out onto the street. More FSB men were waiting outside, but the flow of people escaping the premises confused them for a moment.

The four turned into the first side street they found and kept running until Henry stopped, when he felt it was safe to do so. They'd reached a quieter street that looked residential. Blocks of flats were surrounded a large green.

Henry grabbed Tatiana by the arm and pushed her towards the far side of the green. "We need to talk."

She looked surprised. Anatolie froze but she nodded at him. "It's OK."

When they were far enough away, Henry turned abruptly to face her.

"This is no longer a coincidence. The FSB is tracking our every move. Why?"

It took a few seconds for Tatiana to register what Henry was implying.

"I – I don't know. But I've got nothing to do with this."

"Why not?"

"Are you mad?" Her eyes were wide with anger.

"I am completely serious. We are not boarding that plane until I understand how it is they are tracking us."

"Why should it be me? Perhaps they have marked you."

"Impossible. I changed my clothes before I left The Ritz and every item I had on the train had been well concealed."

"And I did the same when I collected Anatolie." Tatiana's voice wobbled, anger and fear now grabbing her.

"Show me your coat and turn out your pockets."

She removed her coat and flung it at him. She peeled off the two jumpers she was wearing underneath and turned out the pockets of her jeans. Henry dropped his rucksack, then searched the lining of the coat, inspected the jumpers. Tatiana was standing in front of him, shivering in the cold.

When Henry couldn't find anything, he flung the jumpers and coat back at her.

"Satisfied?" Tatiana said, whilst putting her clothes back on.

"No. They are tracing us, and I need to know how."

Tatiana ran a shaky hand through her hair. "I don't know."

They both fell silent. James and Anatolie had moved closer.

"We need to get moving if we're going to make the time slot allocated on the flight manifesto." James sounded breezy and calm.

Henry frowned and turned to Anatolie. Tatiana saw his move and stepped in front of her brother. "Leave him alone. He's got nothing to do with it."

"I'll be the judge of that."

Tatiana was getting ready for a fight.

Henry put a hand out, trying to appease her. "I just want to ask a few questions."

"OK. It'll be fine." Anatolie nodded and stepped away from his sister.

"Have you taken anything with you that you haven't discussed with Tatiana?"

"No."

"And you followed every step she told you to?"

"Yes."

Henry thought for a moment.

"Do you mind turning out your pockets?"

Tatiana was readying to step in, but Anatolie opened his winter coat and pulled the lining of his pocket out – nothing at the front. He reached into his back pocket and his face turned white.

"That's all right." Henry tried to sound friendly. "What is it?"

Anatolie drew out his house keys. His eyes widened and he stumbled over his next words. "I'm sorry. I forgot."

346

Henry stretched out his hand. Anatolie dropped the keys into it. Henry jogged to a nearby dustbin and dropped them in it. He returned and picked up his rucksack.

"Let's go... we have a plane to fly."

* * *

Henry and James made it to the plane. The fake passports and pilot licences had hardly been scrutinised, and neither had their bags. They were in the cockpit, putting the final touch to the pre-takeoff debrief.

"At least I had started flying lessons." Henry checked each instrument after James called them out.

"We're good," James said. "I'll call the lounge, tell them to let Tatiana and Anatolie through."

James had provided the pair with fresh winter coats and hats. Something more suitable for the wife and child of a Russian billionaire.

James made a couple of calls to the ground crew claiming urgency, as the flight window was closing. Two figures emerged from the private jet terminal and walked, whilst escorted by a chatty attendant.

Tatiana and Anatolie boarded the plane. The steps were removed. Henry slid the door closed and secured it. Tatiana and her brother took their seats without a word.

The tension was palpable. So close and yet so far.

Henry returned to the cockpit just as James was contacting Pulkovo airport's control tower. He was asked to wait for final checks to be carried out. Henry was sitting in the right-hand seat, ready to put into practice what he had recently learnt.

The magical words finally came. "Flight AKF 1732 you are clear for takeoff."

Henry used the tannoy to announce takeoff. The plane started to taxi along the tarmac towards the runway.

"Pulkovo international, Flight AKF 1732 ready for takeoff," James announced when they reached the top of the runway.

"AKF 1732, confirmed. Safe flight."

James revved up the engine and pushed the throttle.

Henry started giving the count – 20 knots, 30 knots, 50 knots, and takeoff. The Gulfstream glided up effortlessly.

"How far are we from Helsinki?" Henry was going through the post-takeoff checks with James.

"55 minutes, tops."

"And out of Russian airspace?"

"25 minutes."

Henry nodded. The plane was still climbing to its cruising altitude. As soon as he could he would leave James to do the flying. An apology to Tatiana was necessary. He'd been right to suspect an FSB trace, but Anatolie's mistake had been an honest one.

"We've reached cruising altitude," James announced.

Henry unclipped his seat belt and stood up. "I'll go have a word with our passengers."

"By the way, only 10 minutes left in Russian airspace."

Henry moved into the main cabin. He stalled for a few seconds before walking towards the only occupied seats on the plane. Tatiana was looking out the window. Anatolie was sitting next to her, his head resting on her shoulder and his hands squeezing his sister's hand.

Tatiana must have sensed him there because she turned her head slowly towards him.

"I'm sorry." Henry sat in the seat opposite hers.

She nodded and straightened up a little. "That's all right. If you hadn't been suspicious, they would have caught us at the airport."

"Still, I could have been a little more subtle about it."

"When the FSB is after you I'm not sure subtlety counts."

Anatolie straightened up. "Can I take a look at the cockpit, please?"

"I'm sure James will be fine with it."

Anatolie unbuckled his seat belt and stood up.

"Less than 10 minutes in Russian airspace," Henry said to her.

Tatiana ran her hand slowly over her face. "10 minutes…"

A shape materialised outside, flying alongside the plane.

"You need to come back to the cockpit," James said over the tannoy.

Anatolie sat down again in a hurry and Henry ran to his seat. He noticed two jet fighters were shadowing their plane.

"Who are they?"

"I don't know... I'm trying to make contact." James got on the radio, trying to find a frequency that worked.

Henry put on his headset again. He looked out of the large cockpit window to get a better look at the aircraft.

"James, those are not Sukhoi or Migs. They are F-16s."

"I realised that, but why are they here?"

The roar of two Russian Sukhoi jet fighters passing overhead was the answer to James's question. The F-16s didn't budge.

"That's it," James shouted. "We are out of Russian airspace."

Henry punched the air. James slammed his hand on the yoke. Only 30 minutes to Helsinki.

The voice of one of the F-16's pilots came over their headsets.

"Flight AKF 1732, this is Captain Portman from Amari, Estonian NATO base. Please redirect your flight to the following coordinates 61.0550°N, 28.1897°E."

"This is flight AKF 1732. Please justify new coordinates," James replied.

"Unable to confirm, flight AKF 1732. Acknowledge new coordinates."

"At least this is still in Finland," James told Henry off the air.

Henry took over. "This is flight AKF 1732. Unable to comply with request unless credible confirmation given."

"Stand by, flight AKF 1732."

A garbled voice came over the airwave. An adjustment made the voice audible.

"Just follow the fighters we've scrambled to escort you." Harris's voice echoed into Henry's headset. "I'll explain when you're on the ground."

Chapter Thirty-Four

The landing at the small airport near Lapeenranta in Finland had been smooth. James brought the Gulfstream to a stop near the small building that served as terminal. Three black SUVs were waiting for them.

Harris was already on the tarmac, holding back until one of the ground staff had secured the plane. James switched off the engines and all became calm. He stood up just as Henry was preparing to leave the cockpit.

James nodded. "You go. I'll deal with the door and the steps."

Henry walked into the main cabin. Tatiana and Anatolie were strapped in their seats, looking unsure as to whether they'd reach safety.

Henry grinned at the pair. "We're in Finland."

Tatiana muffled a small cry of joy. She and her brother unfastened their seatbelts and sprang out of their seats. They hugged each other whilst a smiling Henry looked on.

The door opened, letting a draught of cold air in. James lowered the steps and turned towards the small gathering.

"Care to disembark onto Finnish soil?" He too was all smiles.

"Can I go?" Anatolie's eyes were shining with curiosity and excitement.

Tatiana nodded. "Of course... I'm right behind you."

She watched after her brother until he'd disappeared, then stepped out from the seat to join Henry at the front of the cabin.

"Why here, do you know?" she asked.

"I haven't been told. I imagine it's easier to erase the landing of a plane at such a small airport than it would have been at Helsinki."

"That must be right."

They both stepped forward at the same time and closed their arms around each other.

"Thank you for leading us to safety," Tatiana murmured, forehead against his cheek.

Henry hugged her a little tighter. "Where will you want to go?"

"As far as away from Russia as possible. Maybe America."

Henry released her. "We should get going."

"We should."

But instead, Tatiana ran her hand from his shoulder to his neck and brought her lips to his in a slow kiss.

Henry cupped her face with his hand. He brushed a few strands of hair away from her cheek and pulled away gently.

"It's time to step into the free world," he said.

Tatiana sighed but was smiling. She faced the open door and disembarked the plane slowly.

Henry grabbed his rucksack and followed a couple of minutes later. James had made the introduction to Harris. Tatiana and her brother were holding each other by the shoulders. Henry took his time to reach them.

Harris moved away from the small group and walked towards Henry. Henry stopped. For once, Harris looked smart, dressed in a sober, navy winter coat, navy winter scarf tucked into the collar. Even his trousers looked as though they were one half of a quality suit.

Harris's boisterous demeanour was serious.

"You look unhappy for a man who has just bagged a high-profile defector," Henry said.

"Nothing is done until the fat lady sings," Harris replied rather cryptically.

"What do you mean?"

"Until their relocation is complete we mustn't cry victory."

"I suppose that's true."

"James told me about a list." Harris started walking towards the terminal, nodding that Henry should follow.

"The list of potential presidential candidates Andropov claimed he was courting?"

"That's the one."

"Nothing more on this, I'm afraid."

"And nothing either on the identity of the Russian hackers who are manipulating social media?"

"No. I think we'll have a better chance of finding out about them from outside Russia. Their identity is well guarded in their home country. Nick and I spoke to this hacker, The Pieper..." Henry stopped walking. "I should have asked, did you manage to find Nick and Mandy?"

Harris nodded. "We found them."

Henry's throat tightened. "Alive?"

"Yes, alive." Harris slowed down. "Come on. I need to have a chat with Tatiana, and you and James need to keep moving. Finland is a friendly country, but we don't want to overstay our welcome."

Harris walked faster towards the terminal and disappeared into it.

Just as Henry arrived inside the small building, he saw Tatiana follow Harris into a room. He spotted Anatolie with a sandwich and a can of Coke. He was devouring what he'd been given, and James was taking more food out of a large paper bag. When Henry joined them, James automatically handed him a cup of coffee.

Some of the security team that had been dispatched from the British Embassy to help finalise the exfiltration started to move out again. One of them had received a message and was organising transport. James would be leaving with the first car. Henry and Anatolie would be in the second. Harris and Tatiana in the third.

"Why split Anatolie up from his sister?" Henry asked the man. "He's only 13."

The man's lips tightened. "Just a precaution."

James stretched out a hand to Henry.

Henry shook it and clapped his shoulder. "Thanks for everything, as ever, James."

Despite their success, something didn't feel quite right. Henry hesitated, looked around, then back at James. "Do you mind waiting for a moment?"

"Something wrong?"

"I'm not sure."

Tatiana was walking towards them. She was smiling but her steps looked hurried and tight. She called to Anatolie and spoke to him quickly. The boy didn't seem to like what he'd heard, but he nodded. She hugged him tight and turned back to the room in which she and Harris had been talking.

"Everything all right?" he asked the boy.

"I am leaving with you first, and Tatiana will follow," Anatolie replied to Henry.

"Let's go." The man organising the transport clapped his hands and made a move towards the doors.

Henry heard a car engine start outside and drive away.

"How far are we from the Russian border?" Henry turned to James.

"I don't know... 6 miles, maybe less," James replied.

"What happened to Nick and Mandy?"

"Mandy was rescued. I'm not sure about Nick. Why?"

Henry's heart thumped. Harris would have told James if Nick had been in the clear.

James was looking at him, alert.

Henry walked back to him. "Look after the kid."

He strode out of the terminal and to the two remaining SUVs. The drivers were waiting outside their cars, chatting. One of the drivers had moved away a little more than the other, finishing his cigarette. Henry got close to the car.

"Do you mind if I jump in?"

The man nodded. Henry opened the passenger door. The keys were still in the ignition. He got into the passenger seat, slid over to the driver's side, and started the engine.

The two men reacted almost instantly, but Henry locked the doors and reversed the car at speed. He turned the car in a swift, 90-degree angle and dashed off in the direction Harris's car had taken.

* * *

The Russian border is visible in the distance. There is no one else on the road. What the hell is Harris up to? He can't imagine Harris entering Russian soil, even to do business – whatever that business may be.

Henry stops the car and gets out. The landscape changes slightly where the frontier between Finland and Russia lies. Henry takes a few more steps and notices there is a small ravine, curving to the left of the

353

road he is on. He can't quite see its shape and how far it goes but the depression in the land is there.

Henry jumps back in the car. He doubles back, looking for a lane that will bring him closer to the ravine. He finds a track, leading deep into the forest that stretches on both sides of the road. A car has travelled recently, leaving its mark in the damp earth.

He turns the SUV into the track and accelerates, sending mud flying out. In the distance a dark vehicle is parked, and a man is waiting next to it. Henry resists the urge to ram the SUV. He drives at a steady pace and stops a few yards away.

The man has already drawn his gun by the time Henry opens his door and steps out slowly, hands in the air. The man recognises him and lowers the weapon, still on alert.

"I have a new set of instructions for Steve Harris," Henry shouts, proceeding steadily towards the driver.

The man lowers the gun a little more. "They left for the bridge a few minutes ago."

He nods in a direction farther along the path. Henry starts to run. He sees in the distance an overpass and Harris standing stock still, waiting.

Harris moves forward when Henry gets within 10 yards of him. Harris stretches his arm out to grab someone who has just reached him.

And that's when he sees him.

Nick's pale face is turned towards Harris. He is shaking and unable to speak the words of thanks he seems to want to say.

Henry slows down and Nick catches sight of him. The young man collapses to the ground, head in his hands, sobbing. Harris turns to Henry with a look of anger in his eyes.

"It's too late."

Henry ignores Harris.

In the distance, Tatiana has arrived at her destination, the end of the bridge crossing the ravine. A man in a wheelchair is waiting for her. It seems that the Novichok nerve agent Henry threw at Andropov was not lethal enough to finish him off.

"No..." Henry shakes his head in disbelief.

Harris uses his arm to block him. Henry glares at him and pushes Harris aside.

"You can't save –" The sharp clatter of a firearm being discharged cuts Harris off.

One of the FSB men is on the ground with a bloody face and has been disarmed. Another couple of shots fire, and Andropov's wheelchair moves back a few paces from the force of the bullets. The sound travels through the woods, frightening birds that fly up to escape the danger.

Tatiana drops the Glock she wrestled moments ago from the FSB man and turns back. If they are to shoot her, they will have to do so in the back.

The response from Andropov's men is brutal. The volley of gunfire that follows throws Tatiana to the ground. She raises herself up on one elbow, stuck there for a few seconds, until one of the men walks up to her. He places his gun to her head and pulls the trigger.

Henry's cry sticks in his throat. He goes to run in her direction. He doesn't see the butt of Harris's gun come down on the back of his neck until it is too late.

* * *

Henry leaned against the frame of the French doors he'd left open. The view in front of him was spectacular, and yet restful. He ran his hand over the back of his neck. The wound had healed a while ago, but the memory lingered.

"Still sore about it?" Harris materialised behind him.

"It'll be sore for a while." It was all he was prepared to say.

Henry moved away from the doors and joined Harris in the lounge.

"No rush. You've got a bit more time before you go into your next assignment."

"Are you going soft on me, Steve? I only spent a couple of months at the recuperation site." Henry sat down in the armchair closest to the bay window of his new house.

"Don't kid yourself. The debrief for Operation RUSSKY BEAR is still ongoing, and when it comes to the other matter – well, as you say, it will take time."

Henry changed the subject. He understood that Harris couldn't let Nick die, or that Tatiana knew Andropov would not rest until he found her and her brother, and that there would be no escape until Andropov was dead. But the pain of yet another loss would take time to subside.

"I'm glad to hear that Jack found a good family for Anatolie."

"America was the safest place for him. Or at least I presume it's America. Jack took over from us after..." Harris didn't finish.

Henry bit his lip a few times and stood up. He went to the kitchen and returned with coffee for them both.

"I got in touch with The Pieper yesterday. We managed to track the last of the Russian hackers Andropov used to manipulate social media, on behalf of Upstage."

"What about the other list? The presidential candidates Andropov was supposed to cultivate?" Harris took a cup from Henry.

"Nothing on this. If there was one, it wouldn't have been written down anyway. The intelligence agencies in the West have got to be on high alert. I don't believe Andropov was bluffing."

"But now that he is dead, everyone back at HQ seems to have relaxed." Henry shook his head. "That's a big mistake."

"You don't have to tell me. I'm with you on this, and so is Jack."

"I suppose SIS and the CIA are even happier now that Upstage is on trial in Russia. He no longer represents a threat, so, all is good and well."

"That hasn't helped as you say. The Chief gave me a nice pat on the back and returned his focus to the Middle East." Harris stirred in sugar and milk, blew on his cup and drank some.

"The West *is* becoming complacent about Russia."

"Agree again, although I couldn't find an answer to my question. Why lock Upstage up when the Russians could use him and blackmail him?"

Henry sat back in his chair, coffee in hand. He drank a little of it, closed his eyes.

"It's a warning."

Harris frowned.

Henry continued. "A warning to those who try to do what Upstage attempted – take the Russians for granted, and then become too sure of themselves."

"You mean 'you mess with us see what happens'?"

Henry nodded. "Exactly. Which indicates to me that the Russians have someone else in mind for the presidency."

"Andropov was a formidable opponent, but no one is irreplaceable. And someone else will step in to implement his plan."

"No one is irreplaceable as you say. The Kremlin will find someone keen and willing."

"Running a war of influence through social media is a damn sight cheaper than building a nuclear warhead, in any case. So yes, Andropov will be replaced." Harris finished his cup.

The sun beamed in through the open doors. Henry took his time to finish his coffee.

"What's the timetable for the next operation?" Henry asked Harris. "You said I had time but what does that mean?"

"Six months, maybe a little less."

Henry glanced at the pile of documents that were scattered on the coffee table.

"You always choose the most auspicious locations for my ops."

Harris grinned. "Only the best for one of my best."

Acknowledgements

It takes many people to write and publish a book… for their generosity and support I want to say thank you.

Kate Gallagher, my editor and story consultant, for her immense knowledge of good language and of what makes a book great. Ryan O'Hara, for his expertise in design and for producing a super book cover – yet again. Danny Lyle, for his patience and proficiency in typesetting the text! Abbie Headon, for her eagle-eyed proofreading.

To the friends who have patiently read, reread, and advised: Kathy Vanderhook, Alison Thorne, Susan Rosenberg, Helena Halme – author and books marketing coach – and to my very cool ARC team.

Dear Reader,

I hope you have enjoyed IMPOSTOR IN CHIEF as much as I have enjoyed writing it!

So, perhaps you would like to know more about Henry Crowne. What are the ghosts that haunt him? What is it in his past that made him who he is?

Delve into HENRY CROWNE PAYING THE PRICE series with

COLLAPSE:
mybook.to/COLLAPSE

BREAKING POINT:
mybook.to/BREAKINGPOINT

NO TURNING BACK:
mybook.to/NOTURNINGBACK

SPY SHADOWS:
mybook.to/SPYSHADOWS

HENRY CROWNE PAYING THE PRICE, BOOKS 1-3:
mybook.to/HCPTPBKS1-3

Or check out my new series

A NANCY WU CRIME THRILLER:

BLOOD DRAGON:
mybook.to/BLOODDRAGON

It's also time for me to ask you for a small favour...

Please take a few minutes to leave a review either on Amazon.

Reviews are incredibly important to authors like me. They increase the book's visibility and help with promotions. So, if you'd like to spread the word, get writing, or leave a star review.

Thank you so very much.

Finally, don't forget. You can gain FREE access to the backstories that underpin the HENRY CROWNE PAYING THE PRICE series and get to know the author's creative process and how the books are conceived.

Read FREE chapters and the exclusive Prequel to the HENRY CROWNE PAYING THE PRICE series: INSURGENT

Go to https://freddieppeters.com and join Freddie's Book Club now...

Looking forward to connecting with you!

Freddie